The
Seduction of
Phaeton Black

The Seduction of Phaeton Black

Jillian Stone

BRAVA

KENSINGTON PUBLISHING CORP.

www.kensingtonbooks.com

BRAVA BOOKS are published by

Kensington Publishing Corp.
119 West 40th Street
New York, NY 10018

All Kensington titles, imprints, and distributed lines are available at special quantity discounts for bulk purchases for sales promotions, premiums, fund-raising, educational, or institutional use. Special book excerpts or customized printings can also be created to fit specific needs. For details, write or phone the office of the Kensington special sales manager: Kensington Publishing Corp., 119 West 40th Street, New York, NY 10018, attn: Special Sales Department; phone 1-800-221-2647.

ISBN-13: 978-0-7582-6896-9
ISBN-10: 0-7582-6896-3

First Trade Paperback Printing: April 2012

10 9 8 7 6 5 4 3 2 1

Printed in the United States of America

Chapter One

4 FEBRUARY 1889
SCOTLAND YARD, SECRET BRANCH
MEMORANDUM TO: E. CHILCOTT
FROM: Z. FARRELL
RE: AGENT REASSIGNMENT

Believe I have located Phaeton Black. Appears to have let a flat below Madam Parker's brothel. Though the suggestion will undoubtedly cause you pain, I must continue to recommend Phaeton as the best man for this unusual case.

"OH, PLEASE NO, MADAM, HE IS A BEAST," THE HARLOT WAILED. "I beg of you, Mrs. Parker, do not send me down to Mr. Black."

Phaeton Black turned his back on the hubbub, and paced the length of corridor between the foyer and staircase. A sultry sway of hip caught his eye. A luscious copper-colored wench descended the stairs. Her dark eyes lusty, curious, she ventured closer. "Fancy adding another dollymop, sir?"

Slouched against the stair rail, he swept a lazy gaze over her every curve. "Yes, why not? The more the merrier." He ducked his head around the corner and caught a glimpse of the bickering females in the salon. "We are waiting, my timid little sparrow."

The pretty whore beside him tilted an ear toward the clamor and quirked a brow. "Lucy?"

The din from the parlor hardly dampened his grin. "I believe so."

Right on cue, the reluctant whore let loose a shriek that pricked up the ears of every hound in the neighborhood. "I promise I'll work double the number of gents, just don't send me—"

"Hush, Lucy, before you have all the customers in an uproar." Esmeralda Parker stood just inside the parlor, arms crossed under an ample chest.

His stare trailed the baroque details of velvet flock-work wallpaper. "Does my reputation precede me?"

"Oh yes, something the size of an elephant's trunk, sir." The cocotte flashed a flirty smile.

He foraged back in his mind through a blur of absinthe and opium. "How long has it been since I rented the flat below stairs?"

"Near a week, Mr. Black."

He sighed. "I toss up a few petticoats, just to try out the wares, and already I am obliged to face down frightfully depraved and exaggerated rumors."

"Not a bad thing if you ask me, sir. Pay no mind to Lucy. She's a nervous little goose—believes everything she hears. Hasn't yet figured out a girl can pretty much work any size in, as long as she has a bit o' sloppy down there."

He dropped his head back against the wall, angling his gaze at the bronze beauty. He patted his leg. "Come closer."

She pressed against him and rubbed.

"Lovely."

The whining and whimpering from the parlor continued unabated.

"And your name is?"

"Mason, sir."

"What kind of a name is—?"

"Mason." She sucked in a breath and pushed her breasts up and out at him.

Mentally, he undressed her voluptuous curves. Cheeky toffer, this one.

"Named after me da, who was a stone mason by trade—all I know of him." Her deep, coffee-colored eyes brightened. "Mrs. Parker calls me Layla."

"Ah, the ancient Persian tale, Layla and Majnun." The wanton strumpet brushed back and forth across his lower anatomy. "And do you promise to drive me mad, Layla?"

The parlor door rolled open and Madam Parker swept down the hall, dragging the miserable little tart behind her. He noted the vitality in Esmeralda Parker's determined stride, a fine looking middle-aged woman. Truly a shame she had retired early to run one of the more reputable bawdy houses in town.

Things grew wonderfully cozy as two more women crowded onto the stairs. He inhaled the myriad scents of the female flesh surrounding him. "Esmeralda. Care to join?"

"Phaeton, be a dear and assure Lucy you will be reasonable with her."

Blinking back tears, the pretty whore shrank behind Madam's skirts.

He considered her again. Round bosom, tiny waist, lovely hips. Yes, there were very good reasons why he had selected her. "Lucy, might I assure you I am a man of . . . tolerable size, bone-hard." He tucked a finger under her chin and tilted upward. "Though I am not entirely safe to play with, at the moment I am far from dangerous. In fact, it may take the two of you to flog me into a state of excitement."

Esmeralda snorted. "I imagine that will be quick work, ladies."

He held his hand out until Lucy placed a trembling, clammy palm in his. He frowned. "This one has been on the job how long?"

"She has a crippled brother and rummy father. Teach her well, Phaeton—she is their only means of support." Esmeralda stuck him with a fierce look before she turned to climb the stairs.

The sway of Mrs. Parker's bustle captivated him. He had attempted several times to lure her into his bed. So far, to no avail. With each refusal she became more attractive.

He cocked his head. "Any house credits for the instruction?" A faint echo of laughter and the muffled rumble of a door rolling shut answered the question.

Two delectable lovelies stood before him.

"Are you done crying and being afraid, Lucy?" In the darkened stairwell, he could just make out a nervous nod. A terrified doxy just wouldn't do.

"Suppose I make you a bargain. If, at any time during the frolicking and frivolity, you decide things have gotten a bit—"

"Whopping?" The copper-colored vixen offered.

He dipped his chin. "Do try to be helpful Layla." He closed his eyes and inhaled a deep breath. "Now, where was I?" A hooded gaze shifted from one comely wench to the other. "If our interchange gets a bit too impassioned, shall we say? You may call a break in play. Exactly like a game of rugby—not entirely an unlike activity. What do you say, Lucy?"

"Very kind of you, Mr. Black."

"You're sure?"

Her eyes shone with relief. "Yes, sir."

He leaned closer. "Prove it with a kiss." He touched his mouth. "Here."

Tentative, soft lips pressed to his and shyly pulled back. "Charming." He pulled Layla close for a taste. Ah yes, sensuous lips with a bit of tongue. "Delightful."

"I believe this might turn out to be satisfying." Hands pressed to his lower back, he stretched. "Well then, shall we visit my den of iniquity? After you, ladies."

Descending into his flat, he opened the stove and poked at a few coals. The act of love should be something reasonably well-enjoyed by all participants. Even for ladies who made a living on their back. Phaeton bristled at the thought of Lucy's inexperience and terror. Well, he would make it a point to show her some pleasure. Pleasant enough duty.

"Madeira, or perhaps something stronger?" He perused several pantry shelves, upper and lower, and shuffled several packages and bottles about.

He passed through a cold spot and shivered. A low, unearthly vibrating snarl drifted up from below. The ghastly creature's purr was familiar enough. Phaeton took a peak at the girls. Predictably oblivious to his otherworld intruder. A shadow of movement swept past the corner of his eye. The end of a leathery scaled tail slithered around a cabinet opening. Phaeton stomped hard but missed. The fey creature disappeared into the blackness of the cupboard.

"Damned little demon."

"Rats, sir? Mrs. Parker set traps out just last week." Keen-eyed Layla dipped to get a look. He suspected she didn't miss much.

Phaeton kicked the lower door shut. "Harmless as a dormouse. Nothing to fear, ladies."

He decided to pour something stiff. A brief inspection of the young women had him imagining two sweet derrieres. "To a most favored position." He lifted his glass with a wink. "Bottoms up."

At the moment, his informal sitting room featured a single overstuffed club chair and a comfortable old chaise longue. Phaeton flopped onto the divan and reclined against a curvy pillowed end. He opened his arms wide. "I invite you to loose the dragon."

Reluctant Lucy made him grin, for she now eagerly climbed onto his lap. "Ah ah ah." He wagged a finger. "This teasing prelude has a caveat. For every button of mine undone, you must remove one article of clothing apiece."

He studied his evening's leisure through half-closed eyes. A man could be infinitely happy, at least for an hour or two, with a beauty settled on each knee. And the diversion was sorely needed. Purge the jabberwocky from his head and calm the racing thoughts that threatened to drive him round the bend. After a few hours of vigorous love play, he fancied himself dead to the world, thoroughly spent, snoring between two naked lovelies.

An ephemeral breeze bristled the hair on the back of his neck. The subtle shift in air pressure signaled yet another presence. A shadow drifted overhead and the stairs creaked. Just above, in the darkness, something moved. His gaze shifted away from nubile flesh spilling out of unhooked corsets and untied petticoats. "Why, I believe we have a visitor, ladies. Care to join? One for each, I don't mind sharing."

The tall, dark-haired man on the landing frowned and continued his descent.

"Such unfortunate timing." Phaeton nuzzled a supple neck and groaned. "And I so dislike postponing pleasure."

He shifted both doxies off his lap. "I promise you will each have a turn on top of me." An exposed fanny invited a gentle smack. "Off you go."

The pretty trollops gathered a few undergarments and paused for a brazen inspection of the intruder before vanishing upstairs in a clamor of footsteps and twittering.

"Well, well. Scotland Yard's most celebrated agent, Zander Farrell, come calling." Phaeton buttoned his pants and settled back with a grin. "Something desperate has happened to bring you here, below stairs."

"I admit it took a bit of ferreting about." Zander ducked under a sagging floor joist. "You've made quite a comfortable nest for yourself down here." He lifted an aquiline nose and sniffed the air. "A bit moldy in winter, perhaps."

"Due to my recent loss of employment, I have found it necessary, indeed prudent, to conserve resources."

Never one for small talk, which Phaeton greatly appreciated, Zander got straight to it. "We appear to have another monstrous character about on a killing spree. Chilcott wants the case solved before the bloody press clobbers us. He'll not have another debacle like the Ripper."

"I can assure you Jack is gone. I took a stroll through Whitechapel just yesterday. Not a trace of the fiend's miasma."

Zander glared. "Exactly the kind of green fairy talk that got your contract cancelled."

"Chilcott doesn't like me. Never has." Phaeton noted the barely perceptible clench in the man's jaw. Zander seemed strangely unnerved, a rare state of being for him. "Something's got you rattled. What is it?"

"There is some kind of beast or—vampire stalking the Strand."

Phaeton never laughed, a self-imposed rule that had remained unbroken for years. Otherwise, he would have been rolling all over the cold stone floor of his new flat at that very moment.

So he simply grinned. "Perhaps an actor costumed as *Varney the Vampire*? Or an Empusa. Might I look forward to a seduction by a bewitching female bloodsucker?"

Zander's glower gave way to a wide-eyed stare. "I thought you'd be pleased. You claim to believe in fairies and all that undead rubbish."

"My interest in the occult is not a matter of faith, actually." He rose off the couch and signaled Zander to follow. Rummaging through a set of pantry cabinets, he withdrew a bottle of liquor. "Nevertheless, I am honored and amused that Scotland Yard appears ready to consult the fey world."

He sensed darker undercurrents and listened momentarily to a fog of whispers. "The notion of an unearthly murderous evildoer is intriguing." He pulled out a chair. "Why don't you brief me while I *louche* us a glass?"

"Whiskey for me."

He swung back and raised a brow. "Certain about that? A bit of absinthe might help the investigation right about now."

Zander exhaled a bit too loudly. "As you wish, Mr. Black."

Phaeton set up two glasses and poured the dark green distillate. He angled slotted silver spoons etched with the likeness of a naked flying nymph across the rim of each vessel, and placed a lump of sugar on top.

The number two Yard man leaned back in his chair. "Quite an elaborate ritual."

"Hmm, yes. I suppose it falls somewhere between a witches' Sabbath and the Eucharist." He retrieved a pitcher of iced water from a makeshift cold closet. "Just as the water looses the spirit of absinthe, so does the absinthe free the mind."

As the chilled liquid dripped slowly over the sugar cube, Zander's glass changed from deep emerald to a delicate, cloudy swirl of pale green elixir. "Ah, the transformation, when essential oils bloom and the fairy is released. To quote Rimbaud—"

"A meandering, scatological French poet." Zander huffed.

Undaunted, Phaeton poured a last splash over nearly dissolved sugar. "As I was saying: 'the poet's pain is soothed by a liquid jewel held in the sacred chalice, sanity surrendered, the soul spirals toward the murky depths, wherein lies the beautiful madness—absinthe.' "

He settled down and lifted his glass. "I know what they say about me at the Yard. Eccentric, when they're feeling charitable, a menace or madman otherwise."

"That's not true. Gabe Sterling thinks the world of you."

"Then you and he are the only ones."

"Not me, just Gabe." Zander sipped a taste before taking a swallow. "Frankly, I can't say enough about a man who can step into a crisis situation and disarm a Fenian bomb without a care. I don't know where that kind of courage comes from, Phaeton, and neither do a lot of other agents who would rather call you mad than try to understand a man who invites death and fears nothing."

Phaeton shrugged. More pale green potion slipped down his throat. "I miss those small hours of the morning. You know as well as I do, from all our evenings on surveillance, the coldest chill of night happens at the edge of dawn." His hazy gaze landed on Zander. "The time when shadows are not deep enough for spirits and abominations to hide in."

Zander leaned forward. "I need you back on the job. Murdering hobgoblin, vampire—whatever or whoever the killer turns out to be. Take the assignment, Phaeton. But don't do it to prove the other agents wrong."

Taken aback, Phaeton blinked. "Why not?"

"Because they're right."

"Bloody, thieving pirate."

America Jones's gaze fixed on Yanky Willem's every movement as he moved across the polished wood floor of the shipping office. The vile ship snatcher paused between secretary desks and curled back an upper lip.

Up until this night, she had merely been an annoyance to him. A pestering fly he could easily wave aside. But his nonchalance had served only to embolden her purpose. She had picked the door lock, and he had caught her, dead to rights, searching for proof of treachery. Now, quite suddenly, her circumstances had grown perilous. Eyes darting, she calculated the position of Willem's other lackeys stationed around the workplace. His men had not bound her as of yet. No doubt they thought her a helpless, frightened twat. Thickheaded cock-ups.

"Miss Jones." The Dutchman exhaled smoke as thick as his accent. His breath reeked of the black cigar clenched between his teeth. "Words cannot express how pleased I am to have you in my company this evening."

The captain's gaze traveled over every inch of her. "And my great, great grandfather was a pirate, Miss Jones, but not I."

One day she'd wipe that smug grin off his face. Forever.

"I was obliged to take over your father's shipping business because he failed to make good on our loan arrangement."

She bit out a single word. "Liar." Quick as a strike from a snake, his hand lashed across her face. The blow jerked her head back, flooding her cheeks with heat. She licked dry lips and tasted blood at the corner of her mouth. Heart pounding, she blinked aside tears and retreated.

By the look in his eyes and the bulge in his pants, he would have her flat on her back soon enough. Then he would hand her off to his crew.

"I wager you'd all like a taste." She lifted her skirt and lace petticoats above the knee and made eyes at every surly mate. Her sashay about the room revealed more and more leg. When she reached the tops of her stockings, their mouths dropped open.

Seductively, she slipped her hands between her thighs. Eyes wide with feigned surprise, she looked down, then up again with a wink. "Silly me."

In one swift motion, she loosed a derringer from one garter and a bowie knife from the other. Falling back toward the door, she brandished both weapons.

"If you value y'er jewels, I wouldn't make a move."

Chapter Two

"Hold on, Mr. Black." The pretty harlot quickened her steps to match his longer strides. Phaeton grabbed her by the hand and wove a path between the fancy carriages and cabs queued along the Strand. Traffic would shortly become a mangle, as theatres began to let out. A frosty wind blew across the broad avenue forcing them both to squint and hold onto their hats.

"Come along, Lizzie."

He quite enjoyed Miss Randall, whether she was on the job for Mrs. Parker or retained as a night crawler. He often used her for reconnaissance, a spotter who ably worked the streets or public houses.

At the corner of Savoy Row, he parked the tempting doxy by a lamppost. "Right here, love." A fine dusting of snow covered the cobblestone. Not enough to turn the ground white, but just enough to reveal a curious impression of footprints leading off down the row.

He directed his gaze after a diaphanous, almost imperceptible, flurry of snow. "I mean to follow a trace of vapor down the alley. I shan't be far off."

"A trace of vapor?"

He paused to think about his answer. "Do you believe in ghosts, Lizzie?

The girl scoffed. "No, sir."

"Phantasms with fangs who can pierce a vein and drain your body of vital fluids in mere moments?"

Eyes wider. "No, sir."

Phaeton leaned close and brushed her neck with his lips. "You will."

She shivered. "No need to frighten a girl, Mr. Black."

"I need you to keep a look out. Act like a street whore— not terribly difficult. If any gents or goblins get too frisky, you scream bloody murder."

He swept a stray curl off her robust, pink cheek. "Lizzie dear, have I ever ventured into your lovely slit?"

She snorted. "A girl doesn't forget a poke like that, sir."

"Did I pleasure you?"

She batted dark lashes. "Yes, sir."

"I am so pleased to hear it." He tipped his hat and walked into the deeper shadows of the narrow lane.

The trail of impressions appeared cleanly made. Small feet, with steps placed far apart, as if whomever or whatever barely needed to touch ground. He followed the tracks down a curve in the row until the imprints grew so faint, they became all but invisible. He inhaled deeply. Snow and soot and something else, faintly . . . metallic. Again, Phaeton sniffed the air as he scanned the rooftops and lane ahead.

Aware of the faintest shift in atmosphere, he focused his search once more on the bricks below his feet. A tear-shaped drop fell onto the pavers.

Red. Warm. Ice crystals surrounding the drop melted.

There, another drop.

He looked up, but could make nothing out. A sudden spray of crimson drops scattered across the snow as a gust of wind blew off the Thames. A hiss of fine ice swirled into the air and traveled up past shop windows. A ghastly misshapen figure settled onto a window ledge close to the roof.

Phaeton froze. A large, birdlike entity formed out of ice crystals and grey speckled flakes, or were those feathers? Long, spindly legs, tucked against each side of a thin torso. As the creature struggled to gain its balance, a bloody appendage slipped off the window ledge. Pearlescent feathers ruffled as the rare bird retracted the crooked, gangly limb. A protective wing folded over the injury.

So, the owlish harpy appeared to suffer.

He stared hard at the apparition. Would the wraithlike specter ever fully materialize? The pale visage continued to reshape itself until it resolved into something more human than avifauna.

"Ah, there you are." He inched forward, mesmerized. "My high-strung, feathered"—the facial features were feminine, fragile; an enchanting, chimerical bird—"beauty."

The humanlike face swiveled and blinked. *Why do you not fear me?* The voice whispered in his head.

"You might try being more bloodcurdling. Bone-chilling. Hair-raising, perhaps?"

Another ruffle of ashen feathers. *Male, what is your name?*

"Phaeton Black." A wicked smile encouraged him to press forward for a closer look.

I do not like. The white bird hissed and drew away. Phaeton tilted his head to align his sights with her yellow-eyed stare. There, on the rooftop, the dark silhouette of a man gazed down on them.

He had to ask. "Friend of yours?"

A blast of air and cyclone of snow enveloped the harpy. A billow of white particles whirled off the ledge and vanished down the alleyway.

A chill shivered through his body. And a deep sorrow. Squinting through a tempest of frost, he swept the skyline for the stranger. Nothing.

Intrigued, he started after the small twister passing by several basement railings. He paused to stare at an odd finial post. The cast-iron head of a dog. Edging closer, he imagined the canine's upper lip curled back. How long had it been since his last glass of absinthe? Several hours ago with Zander. Any unearthly effects should have passed by now. He reached out his hand and the canine creature snapped.

"Ouch!" He put his finger to his mouth and sucked a very real scratch.

A faint tinkle of laughter. Crimson drops fell at his feet. Were they his? He guessed not. Wavering on the edge of hallucination, he traced bleeding drops of red over street pavers. Light snowfall dampened each footstep to a soft crunch. An icy stillness crept over the lane. Nothing but the sound of his inhale and exhale.

"Over here, lovey."

"Hav'a taste, handsome?"

A pair of street prostitutes stepped out of the shadows and beckoned to him.

"Evening, ladies." He noted a large dustbin just past the huddled women. Inexplicably drawn to the container, he reached for the lid and hesitated. A steady pulse of rapid heartbeats throbbed in his ears.

Lifting the cover, he examined ordinary contents. "Rags."

With a glance around the alley and a wink at one of the working girls, he edged closer. A rat leaped out of the pile of refuse. He dropped the lid, and it clattered to the ground. "Bloody hell."

Wait. Phaeton pivoted.

A presence lurked in the velvet black darkness of a niche between buildings. He leaned into the unknown. The cold steel of a large blade pressed against his neck.

"Do as I say, *mon ami*, and I won't cut your throat."

A feminine voice, with an accent. He swallowed. "I make it a point never to argue with a female wielding a knife." In the blackness, he could just make out luscious plump lips and almond-shaped eyes. Human. What a relief. And a good deal prettier than his recent encounters.

"Back me up—against the wall." She pressed the blade edge deeper into his flesh. A trickle of blood ran under his collar.

"Careful." Adhering faithfully to her instructions, he pressed her to the bricks.

"Any moment now, a number of pirates are going to round this corner. They wish to do me harm. I want you to convince them you are near to completing your satisfaction with a street doxy."

He grinned. He couldn't help it. "Allow me to do my best."

A clamor of hurried footsteps echoed off the row buildings. Racking up her skirt, he inserted a hand between her legs. "Hook a leg around me."

When she complied, he placed both hands under her buttocks and angled her against the wall.

"Oh my!" She cried. "What is that?"

Phaeton paused. "My cock, miss. What were you expecting?"

"But—" She gasped.

A few harried shouts came from several yards away. Quickly, he brought himself under her and worked her down onto his prick. He began his thrusts slowly. Not too deep, as yet, until he knew her body would receive him. "Make much ado, as if you are a pretty whore well paid for a quick tumble."

Buttons loosed, he nuzzled a firm, round breast and tasted salty sweat. He suckled a taut morsel of nipple through thin fabric and bit down. "Ahhh." She gasped. A flood of moisture drew him deeper.

"That's a girl. Louder. Tell me you want more." He drove in. "Do it."

Her words seethed between her teeth. "I will kill you for this."

"Must I remind you"—he gasped—"your blade remains at my throat." Gently, he began to withdraw from her. "In or out, love? Make up your mind."

A low mewl from this luscious alley cat accompanied a bold thrust of hips. Her cries were layered with mockery. "Oh yes, more of that—big man."

"I'll take that as a yes." This woman's sheath girdled him like some kind of heaven. "I have yet to play deep, miss.

How much of me do you want?" His arousal was huge and satisfaction precipitous. He pumped into her, closing in on his own finish. "This is going to be fast."

"Deeper, lovey." She cried, urging him onward. Phaeton could just make out the shapes of several men. Her pursuers paused to listen to their heated sighs and muffled groans.

"Yes, oh yes—give it to me." Warm flesh quivered as her words gave way to lusty exhales.

"Happy to oblige." As he growled his lust like some kind of wild beast, his fingers pressed into the flesh of her buttocks.

Heavier footsteps this time and the harsh, exhausted breath of hunters in pursuit of runaway prey. The men circled closer, near enough to make out her features or wardrobe.

"Bugger off." Phaeton barked over his shoulder. "Get your own doxy, mate." Inarticulate grunts accompanied his intensified thrusts as her pursuers changed course and ran off toward the Embankment.

Arousal heightened by their public exhibitionism, the little minx moaned a fiery incantation. "Jesufina, Marianna, Josephina."

He was close. On the very edge of climax. He opened his eyes to view the beauty who had captured him. Her eyelids fluttered. Momentarily, she was incapacitated.

A fierce wave of pleasure slammed through his body. Phaeton let loose.

His prick throbbed inside her. A long moment passed, before he remembered the blade. In one swift move, he grabbed the knife and twisted it out of her hands.

Those slightly exotic, almond-shaped eyes narrowed. "Get off me."

One last glimpse up and down the alley. "Very well." He kept her pressed to the wall and slipped out. "Lovely, unexpected diversion."

Pants buttoned, he looked up in time to avoid the blow of

her fist. The ferocity of her swing caused a temporary loss of balance and the lady tumbled into an iron basement railing.

Phaeton leaned over. "Blimey, she's knocked out cold."

He had little choice but to pick her up and throw her over his shoulder. The pirates might double back this way. Pirates? Was she daft, or was he? More likely she was some kind of common street thief. He retraced his steps out of the row and onto the busy thoroughfare of the Strand. Lizzie, dear girl, stood under the streetlamp right where he had left her.

Quickly, he settled both women into a waiting carriage. The coach lurched off, rocking Lizzie back and forth. She tilted her head and studied the young lady. "Who is she?"

"A mystery." Gaslight briefly lit the interior of the cabin. Enough for him to note his little cohort's sallow cheeks and red-rimmed eyes. "Lizzie, anything unusual to report this evening? Perhaps a flying phantasm or two?"

"Nothing much, sir." She hesitated.

Phaeton removed her gloves and chafed icy hands between his. "Tell me, Lizzie."

"Well, sir, a very beautiful woman approached me. Pale she was and stood real close, wanting a bit of warmth." Lizzie pulled at the collar of her dress and began a raspy struggle for air. "I don't remember much after—"

He pulled her onto his lap. Gently, he brushed back loose curls to expose a lithesome neck and two perfectly dainty puncture wounds.

A dull ache of drums nagged at the back of her head. She moved to stretch and found her wrists tied to the arms of an oversized upholstered chair. Her pulse throbbed under the bindings. Assessing her circumstances, she closed her eyes and feigned a long awakening.

"Good morning, my dove."

She sensed the unmistakable power of his essence. He was

a channeler. A mortal being haunted by demons, or enchanted by fairies. Hard to say which, perhaps both. Genteel society would likely call him a wretched man afflicted by a mental disorder. Wretched? Possibly. But a rare gent he was, and no doubt gifted in peculiar ways.

Aware of a bubbling tea kettle and the familiar clink of china cups set on saucers, she opened an eye to observe the dark-haired man from last evening. The man who had thrust into her woman parts. Deep inside, she could still feel the effects of his churlish prick.

The shadowed niche of the alley had afforded scant illumination. This morning she revised her assessment of him. A bit swarthy, he hadn't shaved as yet and wore no cravat. His waistcoat remained unbuttoned, but she could see enough to know he was nicely made. Genuinely handsome, if a bit untamed.

His nose was strong and straight, but in profile appeared slightly beakish. His mouth was full and, yes, sensuous and kissable. Hair much too long to be fashionable, but there was something about the mode. Bohemian, perhaps? She examined his body as he moved around the stove. He was a nice size. Large enough but not imposing. And that rude shaft was plenty of male.

"If you are quite finished with your assessment of me, I would like to begin one of my own."

She closed her eye. Blood accelerated through every pathway in her body.

"You must know you have nothing to fear from me."

Still, a throb of alarm surged in her ears. She shifted her head and forced herself to open both eyes. He stood close by, scratching a raised brow.

"If I have nothing to fear, why have you made me your prisoner?"

"Ah, the ties." He tugged a side of his mouth upward. "For my own protection."

She strained against her bindings as he circled the chair.

"While the Darjeeling steeps, why don't we revisit our precious moments together, last evening?"

He had a kind of unruffled, arrogant way about him. She squirmed in the chair. "I prefer an Oolong. Or a nice, smoky Lapsang Souchong."

His eyes crinkled, but his expression otherwise remained stoic. "You know your tea, Miss, but I shall not be diverted. Evening last, I was having a chase down Savoy Row after a pesky, flirty little phantasm when I was abducted by an equally trifling, yet forward olive-skinned maiden who put a dagger to my neck and proceeded to abuse me."

His gaze wandered between several undone buttons that exposed much of her flimsy chemise. "Care to explain?"

In the blink of an eye, she moved into a trance. Transporting herself back a few hours, she recalled a whisper of chimera and a tingle of demon. Her eyelashes dropped lower. "I sense unfathomable powers and yet almost unendurable exhaustion. Not death, but a weakness of spirit." She looked up into his eyes. "And great sadness."

He studied her. "You have abilities?

She nodded quickly and shook off the spell. "My mother had gifts. A Cajun witch, powerful, beautiful."

"A *Vauda*?"

She eyed him suspiciously before nodding. "You know the *sang mélangé français* ways?

"Your name, mademoiselle?"

"Why should I tell you my name? You hold me captive, sir. Why should I reveal anything to you?"

"Because I believe in civility." Caught in his own deceit, he shrugged. "Let's just say I prefer a name. If not possible before intercourse, after will do."

"I had no idea a man could get up a shag with a knife at his throat." Was that a smirk or a lopsided grin from him? "That wasn't a compliment," she growled.

"Honestly?" He tilted his head back. "Sounded like flattery."

"You raped me."

"You demanded it." He placed a hand on each chair arm and leaned forward. "Why didn't you cut me ear to ear?"

Her glare faltered. Why hadn't she killed him? The evidence of her knife was right in front of her. A fresh scar slashed across the side of his throat. If she had pressed harder, he would be dead.

She chose not to respond to his question because she didn't like the answer. How could she forget those intense waves of arousal? Pleasure that was both frightening and miraculous. She caught her bottom lip between her teeth.

His gaze lowered to rudely ogle her mouth. "Our first time was rushed, wouldn't you say?" Grazing the curve of her cheek, his lips brushed closer to her mouth.

Weakly, she parted her lips. "You took advantage of me, sir."

"I heard little protest." He held back, his words delivered as a soft caress. "Only oohs and aahs. Your hot, breathless words in my ear."

She curled the tip of her tongue over the edge of her upper lip. With his attention on her mouth, she furtively lifted a knee between them. "How could I complain with a band of filthy pirates after me?"

"Mmm, most taxing." His exhale buffeted softly over her cheek. "But, did you enjoy yourself, miss?"

"Yes." With one swift kick, she shoved him off.

He bellowed a hellish groan, as his hand flew to his crotch. Apparently she had clipped the jewels. Bent over, he walked off his agony by rubbing himself into impressive arousal.

"Happy now?" She braced for a beating. But none came.

Spurning the steeping teapot, he went straight for a bottle of whiskey and popped the cork. She gave him high marks for grog guzzling and pain tolerance.

He sputtered and coughed. "Delighted."

Chapter Three

SHE HAD NEVER MET THE LIKE OF SUCH A MAN.

After a few deep draughts of spirit, he kicked a chair out from under the table and straddled the seat. "The chair rails guard my bulging privates. Not to be confused with filthy pirates."

He took another swig from the bottle. "Tell me about these imaginary, cutlass wielding corsairs. Miss—?"

"My name is America Jones."

He set an elbow on the chair back and cupped his chin. He had a wary way of studying her, as if she were some kind of curiosity. "Are you incapable of answering questions in a truthful manner? Again, Miss—?"

She set her jaw and glared. "America."

"Is the name of a continent, or two. I can never remember if there are two continents designated north and south, or one continent designated south and north. Which is it?"

Why did he play the Mad Hatter? Leaning far back off the chair, he had to catch himself. The grog appeared to be having an effect. "And there is a new country, the United States of *America*."

Even with her arms tied down, she still managed a shrug. "It is my name, sir. America Síne Jones, and I have learned to live with it these twenty-ought years."

"I believe I may call you by your middle name." His mouth twitched. "*Sin—ay*. I do so admire the first syllable."

Her gaze narrowed to a quizzical squint. "Is your mind always in the gutter, Mr.—?"

"Black." Liquid sable eyes flecked with gold drank in every inch of her. "Only when I am interested, *Miss Jones*."

"And are you interested?"

"I once enjoyed a meal at the Langham Hotel, which I thought about repeating for weeks afterward."

"Is that what I am to you? A supper?"

He lowered his chin. "A banquet, my tempting dark dove." Hooded ebony eyes crinkled at the sides. He enjoyed taunting her.

Captivated for a moment, she mentally slapped herself. "I would love to stay and chat, really I would, but I must be on my way." She flashed the faintest of smiles. "Now that we are introduced, certainly you can release me from bondage?"

"One more thing, Miss Jones. If you would kindly explain about the pirates?" He tilted his head. "Your eyes are most extraordinary. Almost feline."

What an exasperating man! While he swigged from the bottle, she tugged again on her bindings. "Why do you insist on torturing me?"

She pressed her lips together and chewed the inside of her bottom lip. A force of habit when vexed beyond endurance. Well, she supposed two could play this silly, annoying interrogation game. "Are your parents still living, Mr. Black?"

He sat up and blinked. "Mother died of a virulent meningitis years ago. My father teaches advanced mathematics at Trinity College." He ran a hand through thick waves of dark brown hair. "He might as well be dead. We don't get on."

"I could not tell you if my mother is alive or dead. I've not been home to Louisiana in many years. Buried my father four short months ago. Charles Gardiner Jones." She leaned forward purposefully. "A decent and honest merchant trader. Acquaintances said he couldn't face his business failure—that he died of drink. People who knew him well told a very different story. My father's heart was broken by his lying, scheming business partner."

When her eyes threatened to tear, she lifted her chin. "After his funeral I vowed to bring Yanky Willem to justice."

"And how goes this pursuit?"

She frowned. "Not as well as I'd hoped. Last night Willem caught me rifling through a year's worth of cargo manifests."

He arched a brow. "Searching for—?"

"Proof of piracy, Mr. Black."

He smiled that maddening grin of his. "I knew if I was patient, we might actually get round to the original subject of my query—the filthy pirates."

"Chased me from the Docklands all the way down the Strand." She laid her head back against the padded chair and absently counted the cracks in the ceiling. "When you stepped into the sharp edge of my blade, I was clean out of bullets."

"Bullets? And where, pray tell, is your pistol?"

Now it was her turn to grin. "Untie me, and—"

"I think not, Miss Jones." From behind protective rungs, Mr. Black stepped over the seat of his chair and ventured closer.

"Shall we search together?" In a blur of movement he threw her skirt up over her knees and wedged himself tightly in-between her spread legs. The man moved like a panther.

"Sorry, no chance to knee me in the groin." He moved his hands under her skirt and over her legs. Even as she fumed, her stomach fluttered.

He slowly worked his way higher. "Did you reach your satisfaction last night?"

She gasped for a breath. "What satisfaction, sir?"

His fingers slipped underneath satin garters, skimming the tops of her hose. "Ah, a dainty derringer, very ladylike." He placed the weapon in the lap of her gathered skirt and cocked his head to one side. "When we coupled, brief as it was, did you experience arousal, Miss Jones?"

"Surely not from that large wanker of yours routing me out." She avoided eye contact. "Perhaps, there was some pleasure. Briefly."

A hand remained under her skirt and stroked the inside of her thigh. "I'm curious. Have you ever been satisfied from intercourse? Since there have been one or two before me—"

"One." She bit out. "And I don't find any of it very pleasurable. *Satisfied,* Mr. Black?"

"What if I told you that I could make it very pleasurable for you?" The man's free hand undid a few more of her blouse buttons. And he purposely swept a finger along the lace edge of her camisole. "No corset?"

A grim sort of grin tugged at her lips. "I hate them. A woman can hardly breathe."

He looked up from her cleavage. "Shall I make you a promise, *Sin-ay*? I will untie you *after* you allow me to pleasure you."

She chortled with laughter. "I'd rather take another wager."

Coffee eyes deepened to black. "This is not a wager; it is inevitable. You will be satisfied, and then you will be free to leave. I consider this a matter of—"

"You are arrogant and conceited Mr. Black. Why should I indulge you?" But he was also outrageous and appealing. And, she quite wondered if the pleasure he imagined possible, was . . . possible.

Phaeton picked up the pale grey ribbon of her chemise and pulled. Two satin brown nipples invited him to taste. He suckled one until she moaned and her belly shivered.

"Miss Jones, have I been a very bad boy?"

A sensuous pout of a frown caused a painful ache in his manly parts.

"You are playing some kind of game with me?"

"We are playing a game together." He unbuttoned his trousers, but stopped short of exposing himself. He spread

out his hands as though he was about to reveal a masterpiece.
"May I?"

She bit her lower lip. "All right, Mr. Black. You may remove that beastly tosser. But you must not stroke it."

He did as he was told, and became fully erect. "Since I cannot pleasure myself, may I touch"—his hand moved over the top of her skirt, pressing the fabric between her legs—"here?"

Eyelashes fluttered over exotic eyes. They were more grey than green.

"No touching." Those grey-greens fractured into dark emeralds. "Not until you express your regret for last night."

Smart, wicked little strumpet. Phaeton worked hard to suppress his amusement. "I am so sorry to have neglected your satisfaction, mademoiselle."

America said nothing, but moved her knees farther apart.

He reached under her skirt, and worked fingertips over hose and garters. He stopped just short of her feminine triangle. The inside of her thighs were like taut velvet, yet jiggly in all the right places.

His penis jerked, and he longed to toss up her skirts for a look. But he would wait until she squirmed, nay, ordered him to do it.

Softly circling smooth inner thighs, his hands brushed by moist curls. "May I?"

"I'm afraid you will have to apologize again. This time you will ask for my pardon with sincerity." Those almond-shaped eyes narrowed. "Only then will you be allowed to touch my cunny."

Phaeton pressed his lips together. His passion now elevated dangerously close to peak arousal. "My dear Miss Jones. I beg you to forgive my angry phallus, which I do now fully admit took advantage of your plight." His fingers slipped easily into heavenly warmth and copious wetness. And this young lovely had never known the glories of intercourse? He would make sure to remedy that.

Grazing her face with his mouth, he pressed his lips to the

tip of her nose. His tongue found the sensitive underside of her upper lip. "And yet—you did ask for it at knife point," he taunted.

Her eyes glared even as she gasped for air.

He easily found the rapidly burgeoning nub to her pleasure and circled. Her head fell back onto the soft padding of the chair as her sighs and moans urged him onward. Those lovely breasts, fully exposed, nipples taught, pointed at the ceiling.

"As I am nearly always up for it . . ." He stroked with his thumb, guiding one, then two fingers into her sheath. She answered him with a tremble in her legs.

A push of her skirt got him a peek at dark curls and glistening pink folds. A deep groan rose from his chest. "I do implore you to say yes and allow me the comfort of your sheath." He might die from this hellish prick tease. A game of his own making, which he now regretted.

Abruptly, he discontinued both his apologies and ministrations. After a sad look at his bobbing prick, he pleaded with her. "Might you grant me some relief, dear lady? May I press onward?"

"You may put it in, but only an inch." She marked the spot with her gaze. "Just to the end of the knob." He sucked air between his teeth. Clever puss, this one.

Capturing her legs, one arm under each of her knees, he tilted her bottom up to receive him and pressed in by an inch. "One more?"

Her lashes lowered over dark eyes. "Then no more."

Slowly he pressed inward, his thumb circling her pleasure. He added fingers to tickle and tap and flutter over the nub, coaxing the sensitive rosebud to swell and run wet with juice.

"Yes." She moaned and thrust her hips upward. "Don't stop."

He thrust deeper, circled faster. A dozen hard pumps, and she cried, "Yes." And again. "Yes." A strong wave of orgasmic ecstasy reached out and entered his body. The very sensation of her pleasure sent him into loud, growling release.

As his shattered world pieced itself together, he pondered the effect her arousal had exerted on his own. Phaeton raised his head from her shoulder. " *'Tis a fair thing to lie between a maid's legs.*" He returned his head to her chest and nuzzled a plump mound.

"I recognize the bard's words. Hamlet to Ophelia?"

"Yes, my dear."

"On long voyages, when my father owned just one ship, he would read to me every night from the plays or sonnets." His lips brushed over a nipple, causing a tremor. "What you did just then—the effect you had upon me. How exactly did you accomplish that, Mr. Black?"

He jerked upright and loosed the knot binding her arm. "Do not fall in love with me, Miss Jones."

He chafed her wrist between his hands to encourage circulation. "And please do not come knocking at all hours of the day and night requesting my services."

She snorted. "You are safe with me, for I do not believe in such affection. Men take love for granted; they do not prize it."

He unleashed her other hand. "You claim to be a woman with no heart?"

"A girl gives away the secrets of her heart, and a man is off down the lane for a toss up the neighbor's skirt." She rubbed her own wrist this time.

"Phaeton." The voice and footsteps came from the landing. "Might I ask you to sit with Lizzie for a spell?"

He bolted out of the chair and yanked up his pants. "Mrs. Parker, an unexpected but welcome visit."

Madam paused at the base of the stairs. The scene in his flat received an amused once over. "So sorry, Phaeton, it appears I have interrupted—"

"I was just on my way out, Ma'am." Miss Jones pulled her chemise over bouncing breasts and retied the ribbon. He tried to help with the buttons, but she slapped his hand away. With a curt nod, she straightened her skirts and headed for the stairs.

"Esmeralda." He offered a chair. "I'll just be a minute."

He launched himself upward, two steps at a time, and ran down the hall. An elderly gentleman chased after a giggling harlot in chemise and pantaloons. "Miss Jones."

She confronted him in the entryway leading out to the street. "What is this place?"

"Mrs. Parker's is a—"

"Bordello? Hooch house? Out with it, Mr. Black." Her hands fisted on her hips. "And what sort of role do you play here?"

Without waiting for an answer she turned and descended to the street. Oddly enough he followed after mumbling protests. "I don't play any sort of—do you think I work there? I assure you I do not."

"Perhaps you service the residents as an avocation of sorts?"

He grabbed her elbow. "Miss Jones, I work for—" Damn the woman, he was actually flummoxed. "I am only a tenant."

She pivoted on her heel. "Good day, Mr. Black." The flounce of her ruffled overskirt bounced along to the rhythm of her gait and the sway of her hips.

"Good-bye, Miss Jones."

Phaeton sprinkled the remaining garlic along the window ledge. "Would someone please explain to me how these tuberous bits of flora might ward off the chimera I chased after last evening?"

Lizzie sat up in bed, sipping hot bouillon from a cup. "Please tell me more about the creatures you encountered, Mr. Black."

"Why would I unduly frighten you, Lizzie?" Phaeton sank down on the edge of the mattress and examined her carefully. "Besides, I now strongly suspect those phantasmagorical events were a ruse. Meant to distract me while a truly vicious killer stalked after you."

The dear girl set cup to saucer. "She was quite beautiful. Pale and delicate, with lovely mesmerizing eyes."

"So, you have begun to remember."

She fingered the bandage wrapped around her throat and swallowed hard. "Will I become one, Mr. Black?"

"A lady of darkness. A nosferatu?" Phaeton lounged on his elbows. "According to the rules as stated forth in the *Feast of Blood*, Varney the Vampire was able to turn Clara Crofton only by draining her blood completely." His head rolled back on his shoulders as he studied the ceiling. "And I believe there needs to be an exchange of blood." He reached over and chuffed her chin. "You, on the other hand, have rosy cheeks. Far from the pale countenance of the undead, Miss Randall."

She smiled the first bright smile of the afternoon.

Esmeralda poked her head in the door. "Phaeton? Mr. Skimpole is here."

Unlike his spindly name, a rather good-sized chap entered the room with his cap in his hand. "Mr. Black."

"Mr. Skimpole." He stood up and approached the newly hired man. "Straight away, the wardrobe will need to be moved over here, against the window. And while I am gone this evening, you will station yourself against the door to this room and refuse any and all persons entry with the exception of either Mrs. Parker or myself."

Lizzie wrinkled her brow. "You are leaving me, sir?"

"I have been invited to the opening of *Aida*, and I never refuse an opera. I promise to check in on you later tonight." He leaned over and kissed her cheek.

Chapter Four

PHAETON CLOSED HIS EYES and held onto the last strains of the aria for one last glorious moment. Applause broke out in the opera house as he exhaled.

Someone tapped on his knee. "Glad you could make it." Zander Farrell's low voice barely registered. "I'm off in search of refreshment." He looked up in time to see Zander exit the box along with a handful of his in-laws.

Sophrinia Farrell turned and smiled. "Mr. Black, come keep me company."

He took a seat in the front and angled his chair to facilitate conversation.

"Are you enjoying the opera thus far?"

"Very much." Phaeton adjusted his waistcoat and lounged against gilt chair rails. Zander's lovely wife always brought out the devil in him. "I find nothing more restorative to my soul than good music or good sex."

A smile tugged at the ends of Mrs. Farrell's extraordinary mouth. A bit wide, with plump lips, dear God, a man could lose control of himself.

She sighed. "Alas, our brave young couple is soon captured and entombed alive. I find the poignancy nearly unbearable—to lie in your lover's arms forever."

"If one is to be sealed away in a dark vault, I do recommend finding a companion one can tolerate for eternity."

Sophie chuckled softly. Her hand stroked a swollen belly.

She was expectant again. He had not known that. This would be their second child in less than two years.

"Last night, my husband returned home inebriated on absinthe. Don't bother to apologize, Mr. Black, for I have quite forgiven you." While her gaze remained on the audience below, she leaned closer. "After we retired for the evening, Zander became so . . . imaginative." She flashed silver eyes, full of mischief.

He always enjoyed these flirtations with her. A woman of quality who amused him. So few did. "You never fail to delight me, Sophie. I believe I might consider marriage, if I could ever find a young lady as beautiful, intelligent, and as . . ."

"Wanton?"

"Lusty, perhaps?"

Her laughter wafted into the air, musical as the evening itself.

Sophie swept a hand over her rounded girth. "*Heavenly Aida* was most inspiring, don't you think?"

"Yes, lovely."

"Zander sang the very aria to me our first night together."

"So, it becomes clear there was never a chance for me. I can't manage a decent note."

She patted her midriff. "I am much too big to be out and about in public, but I could not bear to miss this performance. Zander helped to secret the bulk of me into the theatre hidden under a large cape."

Phaeton could not stem his fascination. Mesmerized by the perfectly shaped globe hidden beneath the delicate shirred skirt, he reached out. She took his hand and placed it on her belly.

Slowly, his senses submerged into a veil of membrane. A life form, suspended in warmth.

He sat straight up, eyes wide. "Does that hurt?"

She shook her head. "Not in the least."

He took a furtive look about. Should he try it? With a quick head duck, his ear came to rest upon the roundness of her. A gentle hand hesitated before stroking his temple. Yes, there was a *sympatico* with this woman.

"Can you hear the babe thumping away?"

"She is humming, Mrs. Farrell." He sat up. "*Se quel guer-rier io fossi! . . . Celeste Aida.*"

She smiled. "She?"

"Sorry I took so long. Dreadful crush of smokers in the upper lobby." Zander stepped down into their row and handed her a glass. "Seltzer water and lemon, as ordered."

"Thank you for braving the crowd, dear." She sipped her fizzy refreshment. "Mr. Black informs me our second child is a girl."

Phaeton nodded. "Most definitely, a she."

"Excellent. We can narrow down names to Camille or Fiona." Zander's affectionate, possessive gaze caused a momentary pang of loneliness, a sensation Phaeton quickly set aside.

Zander settled an arm across the back of his wife's chair. "My dear, has he been pestering you with unwanted advances?"

"I would never attempt a tryst with Sophie. It would break your heart." Phaeton winked at her.

Zander snorted. "Not before I broke off your privates and sold them to cannibals."

The chime signaled the end of *entr'acte.*

Opera aficionados drifted back into the auditorium. A tall, striking gentleman caught Phaeton's eye. Something familiar about the silhouette. It was obviously not Zander Farrell, for Scotland Yard's finest sat one chair away, publicly nuzzling the neck of his prodigiously pregnant wife.

He straightened his chair. The intriguing gentleman stepped into a middle row and found his seat. Without a scan or search of eyes, the stranger looked directly at him. Phaeton met his gaze. He had not seen this man since his Trinity days, but sensed a more recent encounter, he was nearly sure of it.

As the lights dimmed, Phaeton shifted his attention to the

stage. Disturbing recollections drifted in and out of his thoughts and the third act came and went before he once again immersed himself in the music and story.

By the end of act four, the entire audience was riveted. Radames is sealed in a vault below the temple and finds Aida hiding in the darkness. All the men readied their handkerchiefs for the ladies in the box. *La fatal pietra sovra me si chiuse.* Phaeton whispered the words, "The fatal stone now closes over me." *Morir! Si pura e bella.* He sighed. "To die so pure and lovely."

Outside the Royal Opera House, Phaeton tagged along beside the Farrells. With one eye on the front of the theatre, he held up his end of a lighthearted, informal banter. Zander stepped into the street and opened the coach door. "Can we drop you at home?"

He spotted the stranger. "Thank you, but no. A brisk walk will do me good right about now." The tall man turned in the opposite direction and headed for the Strand. Phaeton nodded a bow. "Again, a memorable evening enjoyed in the company of excellent friends."

Dodging pedestrians and a bustle of carriage traffic, he followed after a dark figure that appeared to alternate between genuine flesh and illusion. Wisps of cloud cover drifted across the moon, darkening the street ahead. Gas lamps flickered and shadows danced beneath the dim light. There, up ahead, footsteps echoed against cobblestone. Phaeton picked up the pace. He couldn't risk losing the man for the second time in so many days.

Yes, he was quite sure the elusive silhouette he chased after would turn out to be the rooftop phantom that had frightened off the snow harpy, or whatever the odd apparition had been.

A few cobbled lanes and alleyways separated the wide thoroughfare of Strand from the Embankment along the river. He was back in familiar territory. It pained him to think this small enclave south of the theatre district had become a place of terror and death, not unlike those fifteen square blocks of Whitechapel. He needed to get to the bottom of this riddle posthaste. Catch the fiend, stop the murders, and try to keep the press out of it.

His pulse accelerated at the very idea of chimera chasing. He caught a slim glimpse of an opera cape vanishing around a bend in the lane and hastened his step.

The race was on. Each time Phaeton quickened his pace, the man ahead seemed to pull farther away. Frustrated, Phaeton sprinted down one row after another, able to catch nothing more than an occasional glimpse of a shadowed figure. He turned into a narrow passageway and ran straight into a dead end.

Certain that he had followed correctly, he scrutinized the brick wall in front of him. He pivoted slowly, scanning rooftops to each side of the alley.

"I am here."

Phaeton jumped back. The man stood just a few paces away. Odd, he had not seen or detected the stranger's presence. "Yes, you are."

"Why do you follow me?"

He cleared his throat, hardly knowing where to begin. "I believe we have met twice before. Our first encounter was at Cambridge, eight years ago. Just outside The Green Dragon, I was accosted by a dangerous sort of creature with fangs and claws. Something between a dog and a wolf, but man-sized. I had more than a few pints in me, too bladdered to resist."

Could that be a glimmer of recognition? Phaeton couldn't be sure. "You came along and tossed the hairy beast off me as if it was a child's toy."

A faint, twisted smirk appeared on an otherwise perfectly chiseled and largely inscrutable face.

"I remember the incident." The man cocked his head. "I take it you have the gift. Unusual abilities that are helpful in—what is your line of work, Mr.—?"

"Black." Phaeton reached inside his overcoat. The stranger stepped back. This time it was his turn to grin. Slowly, he pulled out his card. "Scotland Yard. Investigating several murders down here along the Strand."

The man grabbed him by the coat and flung him against the brick wall. Dazed, Phaeton shook off the ringing in his ears. "Very impressive."

"You will never track down or catch this killer, Mr. Black."

The stranger leaned in close—sniffing the ether. They each inhaled frosty air with the faint metallic scent of the other's essence. "Yes, you have superior talents, but they are buried deep. A dangerous condition. You are both cunning and foolishly brave. These qualities attract the creature you seek, but you have not the experience to defend yourself nor the expertise to defeat her."

Phaeton smiled. "It is a female. An Empusa, perhaps?"

The gleam in his rich, golden-green eyes narrowed. "I warn you once more, leave this to me. Continue to pursue this ancient Kemet goddess and you will be soon be dead. Another victim found along the Strand."

Phaeton quickly ticked off his options. If there was a chance to catch this demonic virago, he could use a chap like this. "We could work together."

He released his hold and backed off. "I do this alone."

Phaeton was unconvinced. "Just a guess, but I think you could use some help."

The man took one step back and leaped into air. One moment he stood in front of him, the very next—nothing. Vanished . . . but to where?

Phaeton turned in time to observe a familiar shadow leap from the top of the wall to a window ledge to the rooftop in three swift moves. Good Christ, he was seeing things. And he hadn't had a drop of absinthe in over a day.

Curls of smoke and the crackle of blazing timber was all that was left of Number 67. Warehouse of the Seven Seas

Tea Company, owned by Charles Jones & Partner. The enflamed storehouse in Wapping Basin had been declared lost beyond saving. The fire brigade would continue to defend the other buildings surrounding the facility until it burned to the ground.

America sat on the back of the fire wagon and struggled to keep her composure. Until now, there had been no time for tears.

Months ago, she had quit the expensive town house and fashioned a small apartment for herself in the offices of the warehouse. Now all was lost. Her clothes, a cache of money she kept hidden under the file cabinet, and an old daguerreotype, the only portrait she owned of her father. Handsome and dressed as a sea captain, the way she remembered him as a child.

She slipped into the distraction of memories. No more than six or seven years old, standing on the dock. Her father sternly protested as her mother handed her off to him. How frightened she had been on that first voyage. The nightmares. Waking in the dead of night to an unfamiliar rocking sea. Crying out, "*Maman.*"

"You'll be needing to find another place to sit, Miss." When she didn't move, the fireman lifted her off the back of the hose wagon and set her on the steps of a nearby storehouse.

America stared blankly into the ruins. A blackened wood beam broke off and crashed to the ground, throwing a swathe of sparks into the air. She wrapped her arms around herself and rocked. The gentle motion returned her mind to that first trip across the Atlantic. Days away from making port, she had taken a fever. Her father had sat with her, wringing out a cool damp rag and forcing down a bit of broth.

"You are a survivor, *Amiee.*" Papa had told her so just before he passed.

She would carry on, all right. And if she ever laid eyes on

THE SEDUCTION OF PHAETON BLACK   37

Yanky Willem again, she'd murder him without so much as a "good day." She imagined her trial, and conviction, but not before blackening the man's name in public with the truth of his crimes. She'd march to the gallows whistling.

"Miss Jones?"

Her gaze moved from the huge building in flame to a mild looking gentleman with a thick tuft of unruly grey hair falling over his forehead. He wore a dark suit and a clerical collar.

"My name is Father Lowell, Covenant of the Faithful Angel. I work with the Reverend Mother, who runs the Night Home on Lower Seymour Street—you've heard of us? A safe place to sleep for girls of good character."

All she could manage was a blink.

"The fire brigade captain has informed me that your place of residence will be gone by the end of the evening." His gaze darted toward the flickering light of the blaze. "Will you be needing a place to stay, miss?" He reached out a hand.

Tears didn't come until a Sister of Mercy tucked her into a soft cot at the shelter and covered her with a scratchy, thin blanket. A copy of the New Testament rested on a small night table between two beds. At first she hiccupped and choked, her eyes unable to manufacture enough tears. Eventually, the soft rain of grief streamed down her cheeks and dampened the pillow.

America slept fitfully and awoke with a thumping pulse and a startling idea. Nothing much more than a notion, but the thought kindled something akin to hope, deep inside her. There might be one person in London willing to help. In fact, the man was at least partially responsible for her delay. If she had returned to the warehouse earlier, there might have been a chance to prevent the fire.

She bolted upright and dried her tears. From their first encounter, she sensed a powerful enchantment, something magnetic about him. *Le visage d'un grand esprit.* The face of a great spirit. Her mother's people were a mélange of French and slave and lived for part of each day immersed in the practice of great mysteries. They had taught her to recognize another of their kind when she encountered one.

But would Mr. Black have her?

Well, he would just have to. That's all there was to it.

Chapter Five

THE DOOR TO LIZZIE'S ROOM OPENED with a freezing cold blast. A swarm of ice crystals stormed past Phaeton and swooped down the stairs. Pressed back against the balustrade, he hesitated, torn between chasing after the frost wraith's tail and checking on Lizzie.

Squeaking bed springs and low moans, the hot-blooded cries of fornication filled the hallway. And a whimper of pain, straight ahead. He reached for an umbrella lodged against the entry molding and gingerly pushed the door open. In the center of the room, an iron bed spun in slow circles, inches above the ground. A cloud of frost swirled in the air. Lizzie lay like death atop a crimson splattered mattress, her shoulder and dressing gown soaked in red. The dear girl struggled to inhale a shallow breath of air.

The nebulous apparition floating above the bed frame slowly shifted into the form of a woman. Disturbing. Deadly. Flowing black hair and rounded breasts like alabaster globes were visible through gossamer robes. A chimera of pale, luminous beauty turned to stare at him. Her eyes glowed wide and golden, before turning into sparkling rubies. The vamp's gaze traveled down his body and then up again. She licked her lips.

Bone-hard and ready to please, there was no doubt about it—the seductress aroused him. And there was something else. What was it Miss Jones had said? A weakness of spirit and great sadness. He moved cautiously, as he quite plainly understood not to underestimate the powerful little succubus.

"I would like to help you." Nonsensical words, given the situation.

Instantly the she-devil dissolved into shimmering dust and reconfigured herself as a large, pale spider. The apparition braced legs to each side of poor Lizzie's dying body and swayed back and forth, unsteady. A fuzzy grey face with claws for a mouth and several sets of menacing yellow eyes swiveled to fix on him.

She meant to frighten him off.

He circled the bed, and moved closer, forcing her to withdraw. Several spindly limbs faltered under the bulk of a pendulous, misshapen body. Her retreat ended at the foot of the cast-iron bed rails. There it was again; he had noted a similar injury to the harpy in Savoy Row. This time the wretched shape-shifter dragged a leg, perhaps more than one.

The doors to the wardrobe burst open. Once again, the she-creature dissolved into a frenzied whirl of frost and ice. He lunged after nothing more than a specter, which disappeared through the large hole in the back of the armoire. Leaning into the darkness, through the ragged opening and broken window, his gaze swept every corner of Shaftsbury Court. Nothing out of the ordinary. The usual number of carriages parked along the street. Most of them awaited Mrs. Parker's clientele or customers of Blades, the gambling hell down the lane.

Phaeton retraced his steps, noting a spray of red drops over the floor and bed sheets. He had interrupted the end of her feeding. If he had not arrived when he did, Lizzie would certainly be drained. As it was, she teetered on the edge of consciousness. The labored wheeze of her breath caused him to doubt whether she would live through the night.

He moved to the door, stepping over the hulking man

who lay groaning on the floor. Out in the corridor, he leaned over the second floor railing and called for assistance.

Esmeralda peeked her head out the door of her apartment. He was quite sure her shoulders were bare. Her nudity irritated him. Was she working tonight? He wondered who the man was. In fact, he was stung with jealousy over it.

"Lizzie has been abused again. I'm afraid she's in a bad way. We'll need to call for a doctor, straight away."

Esmeralda nodded. "Give me a moment. We have a doctor in the house."

Phaeton returned to the room and pulled the hired man up into a sitting position. No discernible puncture wounds. Poking around through a tuft of hair, he found a large knot at the back of the poor bloke's head. Having pieced together most of what had transpired, he nevertheless asked the question. "Mr. Skimpole, can you tell me what happened here?"

"He will not remember anything."

Phaeton turned toward an eerily familiar voice. Stunned, he gritted his teeth to keep his jaw from dropping open. It was him. All six feet of the mysterious, imposing gentleman. Phaeton's gaze narrowed as it slid from unbuttoned vest to untied cravat. Mrs. Parker stood beside him in a silk wrapper.

So.

Esmeralda tightened the belt of her dressing gown. "Phaeton, this is Doctor—"

"Jason Exeter. We meet again, Mr. Black of Scotland Yard."

The director's office stifled, as usual. Phaeton squirmed under Elliot Chilcott's scrutiny, whose untamable eyebrows and muttonchop sideburns underscored the irascible nature of Scotland Yard's head man.

"He examined Lizzie briefly, and left. Returning not ten minutes later with a leather satchel filled with apparatus— medical equipage. He gave her a transfusion of blood."

"His own blood?" Chilcott appeared to be making a concerted effort to control disbelieving mannerisms like his usual roll or bulge of eyes.

"Mine, actually." He hated debriefings. They always made him feel like he was some kind of oddity, and certainly not to be taken seriously. "The doctor claimed his own blood was tainted in some way."

Steepling his fingers together, Chilcott's gaze slid from Phaeton to Zander and back again. "How exactly do they extract blood during these . . . transfusions?"

Phaeton unscrewed a cufflink and rolled up a sleeve. The incision was red, held together with a stitch, and there was a good bit of bruising around the wound. "My blood is drained into a receptacle. And in turn, this man, Exeter, posing as a physician—"

Zander flipped pages in a dossier. "His full name is Asa Alexander Exeter. Father British, Mother Persian. He has Anglicized his given name—now calls himself Jason Exeter. He took a science degree, a DSc, from Cambridge. I can find no address for a surgeon under the name Exeter. More likely he's in research." Zander closed the file. "All I could dig up at a moment's notice."

The director sank back into the comfortable, worn cracks of his leather chair. "And do you believe this Doctor Jason Exeter to be—frankly, I don't know any other way to put it—human?"

Phaeton stared. "I believe so. At least partially."

"You believe or you know?"

"Sir, he's quite agile for an average man."

"In what way?" Chilcott pulled on the long hairs of a side-burn and scowled.

Phaeton hesitated, his patience edging along the thin side.

Zander shuffled files and opened his report. "In your own words, Phaeton, you report the man was able to"—Zander double-checked the notes—"jump from the top of a six-foot wall to a second-floor window ledge to a rooftop in just so many effortless leaps. And rather quickly—'blink of an eye' it says here."

The chill sobriety of the room was interrupted by a quiet knock as Mr. Oliver opened the door. "I beg your pardon for the intrusion, gentlemen, but a young man from the mortician's office was just here with a rather unusual tale to report. Since Mr. Black is here, I thought—"

"Yes. Yes, Mr. Oliver, bring him in."

Chilcott's secretary shut the door behind him and inched forward. "I'm afraid the young man has run off. He requested that an agent follow along as soon as possible."

"What seems to be the problem at the morgue?"

"A dead police officer, sir, found near the Strand last night."

Zander leaned forward, "Mr. Oliver, we are aware of the murder. The very reason we called Phaeton in—"

"According to the mortician's assistant"—the pitch of Mr. Oliver's voice rose and he shuffled a bit on his feet—"the dead body sat straight up on the examination table this morning and attacked Doctor Meloni."

Oliver nodded a bow to Zander. "Sorry for the interruption, Mr. Farrell." The ordinarily polite and unflappable secretary turned to his boss. "I believe what remains of the police officer is still moving about, sir."

The only sound in the room was the squeak of Chilcott's chair as he leaned forward. "Well, what are we waiting for gentlemen?"

It took all six men to restrain the dead man.

Gripping a leg with one hand, Phaeton pulled a copy of *The Feast of Blood* out of his coat pocket. "We'll need a stake to drive through his heart."

Zander frowned. "I thought they were never able to kill Varney."

"Poor distressed old vampire threw himself into the crater

of Mount Vesuvius." Phaeton pressed a bit more muscle into service to quell a jerking knee joint. "However, I have here a long list of talismans, cures, and elimination methods we might try."

The body began another fit of violent shakes. Chilcott slammed a writhing forearm back onto the slab. "Someone find a stake, damn it."

After an exasperating bit of shuffling about, the coroner's assistant held a metal rod over the zombie's chest, and Dr. Meloni swung the hammer. A swath of blood erupted from the poor devil's chest, spewing over agents and mortuary workers. To make matters worse, the wretched corpse continued to twitch.

Phaeton saw no way around it. "Perhaps for good measure we should separate the head from the body."

A slightly wild-eyed Meloni got out his autopsy hacksaw and removed the head. "Let's hope this ends it." The mortician wiped stained hands on a lab coat smeared in red.

Droplets of sweat and blood dripped off Phaeton's brow. "Anyone for a bit of fresh air?"

Chilcott called a meeting in the small yard outside the morgue. Lowering his voice he eyeballed each and every man. "Not one word gentlemen. Neither to friends or family. If the press gets so much as a hint of this episode, Scotland Yard will be written about for years to come in the penny dreadfuls."

The director continued to scan the crimson-splattered men in front of him. His gaze came to rest on Phaeton. "I expect you're used to this kind of thing."

He hardly knew what to say to the man. "Gone on for years, sir. Since I was a wee lad. All manner of ghouls and grotesques."

"Yes. I suppose that explains you, Mr. Black. Chilcott exhaled. "I'm put off supper this evening. Anyone care to join for a pint or two?"

★   ★   ★

Phaeton staggered into Mrs. Parker's drunk and beat.

Esmeralda called down the corridor. "You have a guest, Phaeton, waiting in your flat. And please run upstairs and visit Lizzie, she's been asking after you."

He turned toward the sound of her voice. He had not forgotten that she bedded Dr. Jason Exeter. The room swayed slightly. "I might suggest you and Doctor Exeter sit by her bedside. He to hold her hand and you to hold the hard, manly parts." He braced the wall, which was badly listing. "A ghoulish little *ménage à trois.*"

"You're drunk."

"Very." He stopped himself halfway into a turn. "Whooze, waiting below stairs?"

Esmeralda shot him a look and a smirk. "That pretty little thing you had tied to a chair the other morning."

Phaeton squinted in an attempt to bring her bustled rear into better focus.

A pivot toward the stairwell proved challenging as he considered the uninvited female in his flat. "Pretty little—?" He groaned.

Descending one step at a time, the tantalizing aroma of exotic curry spices wafted up to greet him. He dipped down to take a peek and nearly fell head first down the last section of stairs.

"Mr. Black, I've been expecting you for some time. Come, have your supper."

The room smelled delightful.

She had the audacity to smile. "Esmeralda was kind enough to donate the spices, and I purchased a bit of sausage and lentils to make a potage."

"I'm not hungry." His stomach growled.

"Have a seat, Mr. Black, and a bit of stew. It will do you good. Quash the stout in your system."

"Why?" He plopped down on a chair and she ladled out a healthy portion. The blasted little tart bit her lip. To keep from laughing at him, he supposed, but it was alluring all the same.

She stood beside the table and straightened her apron and skirts.

Slurping a bit of hot broth, he sighed. "Miss . . . Jones. That is your name, is it not? I seem to recall a young lady with pirates after her." He looked up. "Why are you standing? Spoon up a bowl for yourself and join." He pushed out a chair.

She fixed a sober stare his way. "I've come to ask for a job."

He looked behind him. "From who?"

"From you, Mr. Black."

"I don't *employ* servants. Never have. Never will." He swallowed a lovely bit of sausage. "This is quite good."

She smiled. "I learned to bake and cook some, on voyages. Papa employed a wonderful Indian man he found in the Adaman Islands who taught me many dishes. And I am neat and clean by nature, so keeping house for you will not be difficult—"

He noted the basket of buns on the table. "Did you make those?"

She nodded.

Phaeton set down his spoon. "I am not going to engage you." He dipped a piece of warm bread into the stew. "Even if you do make heavenly buns."

"I'll work for two and six a week, plus room and board."

He concentrated on the bowl in front of him. It seems he had no choice but to frown his way through bread and broth.

"I need this job, Mr. Black."

"Did your father leave you nothing to live on?"

"All that was left of his property was a large repository in the Basin. Father formed a new business and named me as full partner." He distinctly heard a catch in her throat. "Everything burned to the ground last night. That warehouse was my living, what I could make off the rent to other traders."

Studying her a moment, he chewed on a crusty piece.

"I'm sorry to hear that, Miss Jones, but your misfortune has nothing to do with me."

"I believe it does, Mr. Black. If I hadn't been tied up all morning, I might have been able to prevent the break-in and the fire. I hold you partly, if not wholly, responsible. Therefore, you owe me."

"Hold on—"

"I won't take up much space. I notice you have a room, across from your own, that would fit a small bed."

Phaeton raised his voice. "How many times must I say no before you grasp my meaning?" Her persistent pestering caused a sudden onset of sobriety, greatly agitating his nerves.

"I need a job, Mr. Black, and a roof over my head, at least until I can find employment elsewhere."

"Not here. For a few extra bob a month, Mrs. Parker's housekeeper sends her daughter down to dust and pick up laundry. And I take my meals out."

For all he knew, she was a common street thief. This imaginary tea trader father of hers and now a burned out warehouse. She must think him a prize thickhead to fall for such a flimsy pack of lies.

"Get out."

She untied her apron and tossed it over a chair back.

"I will give you one day to reconsider, Mr. Black. I currently have a bed assigned to me at the Sisters of Mercy Night Home on Lower Seymour Street." She pulled on a dingy, grey coat with black velvet lapels. It might have been a very nice looking coat at one time, but it was singed and blackened now.

Phaeton leaned back in his chair. "Come here."

She circled slowly as he brushed off a bit of soot, "If I do not hear from you by end of day tomorrow, I shall be forced to take Mrs. Parker up on her offer."

Mrs. Parker? Phaeton smiled. "Now, that sort of service I do hire, Miss Jones."

Chapter Six

AMERICA KICKED A FEW CHARRED BITS OF RUBBLE as she picked her way across the burned-out remains of the warehouse. A shiny metal button caught her eye. She turned it over and ran her thumb over the letter *D*. A typewriter key of all things. The shape of the character form was *distorted*—now all she could think about were D words. She stepped over chunks of blackened timber. "Distressed, despairing, devastated, dejected, despondent . . ."

"Careful now, Miss Jones."

"Yes, Officer Wilkie."

Their district policeman patrolled the burn site to ward off the ragpickers. Scavengers, who would comb through the debris inch by inch, collecting anything they could sell to scrap dealers.

"My orders are to keep trespassers out, everything nice and quiet-like. An agent from Scotland Yard is coming to look about for evidence of arson."

She stopped in her tracks and slowly eased her way out of the wreckage. So, one of London's celebrated detectives suspected something. A faster rhythm beat in her chest, as her breath caught for an instant. The possibility that anyone, besides herself, suspected foul play gave America a measure of hope. Something she had given up on, as of late.

"What are you to do, lass, now that the business is gone?"

"I must find employment, Officer Wilkie." She sighed. "I

detest the idea of factory work, but I must labor at something if I am to afford a room in a boardinghouse. The Lucifer Match factory is always looking to hire."

"Ahh, girl, a bad lot o'trouble for your toil."

She nodded. Just passing by the dank, malodorous sweatshop made a person choke from the sulfurous air. A girl might contract the disease that gradually rotted a body's jawbone away. A shudder ran through her body.

Mrs. Parker had offered a job. Said she ran a clean house and encouraged the use of condoms. Still, America wasn't desperate or frightened enough to earn a living on her back.

A small bit of happiness tugged at the ends of her mouth as she fingered the large bill in her hand. She considered the rude, irritating man who likely planted the five-pound note in her coat pocket last evening.

You are a puzzle, Mr. Black.

Phaeton stood in the middle of Savoy Row and stared at the basement railing of the mercantile building. The lane was different in morning light. Day laborers pushed hand carts past bookbinders and printing guilds. Bustling, noisy. Completely unthreatening. He recalled a pretty, copper-skinned female with almond-shaped eyes. Out cold, right about— here. She had swung at him and missed, striking her head on the corner of the iron rail.

Had he helped the little minx escape justice? Those pirates she claimed to be hiding from were likely men she had stolen from. He could not shake the idea, however, that an experienced thief would have held onto her blade, taken money over sex, and knocked him, not herself, unconscious. He surveyed the small niche where he had thrust himself into the bonnie lass. There, the narrow outcropping of brick where he rested her plump derriere, just enough leverage to get in between those luscious thighs . . .

"Phaeton?" A pale-skinned young man wearing thick, dark spectacles struck a safety match and held it to his pipe.

Long tapered fingers curled around the bowl as full lips drew down on the stem.

A blush of tawny color washed over an elegant face shaded partially by a top hat. The glasses, which guarded light-sensitive eyes, gripped the bridge of an aristocratic nose. High cheekbones angled toward ears that were nearly elfish.

He smiled. "Sorry Ping, woolgathering." He shook his head and cleared his throat. "I ended up in circles, following a cold trail. I'm afraid any trace of the fiend has long melted away."

"Shall we double back and have another look at that dustbin and window ledge? I've a mind we might still find some evidence."

The sweet smell of opium wafted in the air. "Chasing the dragon?"

Ping arched a brow. "Mix in a bit with my tobacco. Helps to ease contact."

Phaeton retraced his route, staying a step ahead of the pale-faced creature wrapped in a long black coat and carrying a small satchel. The odd, enigmatic Mr. Julian Ping might be the very best forensics man in London, outside of Scotland Yard. He was also a most unusual crime fighter.

Ping used his extraordinary abilities to re-create the scene of a crime, through making some sort of clairvoyant link with the perpetrator. The strange lad connected to the rage, pain, and pleasure of the criminal mind. He saw through the eyes of the beast, even smelled the victim's blood. The use of opiates dulled the experience.

Phaeton could hardly begrudge the young man a bit of the pipe. He led them back to Savoy Row and into a labyrinth of connecting walkways that meandered from the Strand to the Embankment along the Thames.

Ping set down his instrument case and retrieved a blade the size of a penknife and a small tin. He carefully scraped dried blood off the window ledge and collected a gobbet of unspeakable slime from a nearby refuse bin. Notebook in hand, Phaeton sketched out a crude map of the area. "Three murders. Here. Here." He placed an *X* at each spot where a body had been found. "And here."

Sallow cheeks puffed silently as the rare gentleman studied the sketch. "Two of them quite close to the Embankment, actually." Ping lifted his sunshades and squinted. Bright winter light accentuated the hooded slant to his eyes. He used his bent briar pipe as a pointer. "Let's have a look down along the Thames."

A passageway between buildings led to an intersecting alley angled toward the river. A look of intense concentration marked the young mesmerist's face. "You're being rather methodical for a man of pseudoscience."

"When you wired about a walking corpse in the morgue and a possible Empusa, I admit I was skeptical. But now . . ." His nose sniffed the air like a bloodhound after a wanted criminal.

Phaeton's pulse accelerated. Ping sensed something. Rounding a bend, shades of silver-grey water shimmered through a break in the row buildings. "Ah, here we are."

They reached the corner where the first body was found. "This one was male, and the second—"

"A female, you found her just over there." Ping flipped down cobalt blue lenses, but his mouth gripped the pipe tight enough to cause a dimple.

The gentleman seer led the way to the second spot. Once again, in the broad glare of day, both crime scenes appeared less than threatening.

Mentally, Phaeton rifled through various field reports of the murders. The bodies had been found early in the morning, the first by a neighborhood policeman, the next by laborers, employed by a nearby engraver's guild.

Something about the Strand murders continued to niggle at him. An intuition surfaced every time he compared these crimes to the string of unsolved murders that had begun and ended last year in Whitechapel. They were nothing alike and yet there was something coincidentally mysterious about them, mismatched bookends, but a queer pair nonetheless.

Ping used an umbrella to forage about in a crate filled with shredded leather refuse. The eccentric sleuth had often proven himself to be more adventurous than many of the Yard's field detectives. Phaeton exhaled. "You are aware Chilcott fired me over the Ripper fiasco?"

"Wild conjectures fueled by opium and absinthe, wasn't it?"

He grimaced. "Close enough." He dropped his voice a register. "What if I told you that I sense some kind of linkage?"

Ping swiveled slowly toward him, puffing heavily on his pipe. "Between the Chapel murders and the Strand?"

"Let's have a stroll down the Embankment, shall we?" Phaeton turned away from the scene. "I'd like to review what we know, unequivocally, about each one of these homicides."

Ping nodded. "I'd like a briefing on the injured party, as well. A prostitute in your employ, I believe?"

Phaeton assembled a list of facts in his head and repeated them aloud. "All killed south of the Strand, most likely after midnight, but before daybreak. All were drained of blood, the bodies marked by scattered puncture wounds. Sometimes two, sometimes more. Always in pairs." He squinted as the sun broke through at bit of cloud cover. "Two corpses were found lying in a pool of blood. A third was not."

"The officer at the morgue." Ping rubbed his chin with the pipe stem. "The corpse you, Zander, and Chilcott stabbed in the heart and cut to pieces."

"Right." He took a deep breath. "Pure conjecture, but the poor bloke may have been drained of blood over time. Think of it, a bobby on his beat—about in the Row every evening. A regular meal for the fiend, if you follow. Lizzie has been attacked twice. She shows signs of a personality change. Often wants to sleep walk, as if she was being drawn away from us."

"What do you sense intuitively, Phaeton? Forget Chilcott and the rest."

He chewed on his lower lip. His warnings about the Ripper murders had been dismissed as wild talk—raving, unprofessional guesswork. Eventually, due to a mountain of pressure, Chilcott had called Phaeton into his office and given him the sack.

"There were apparitions the first night Lizzie and I worked the row. I have come to believe these were phantom visions—persistent hallucinations meant to lead me off, so the killer could go about her business."

A sudden brilliant glare off the water caused Phaeton to tilt his bowler forward. "I believe we are after a female. Cunning and powerful, but also injured in some way. I have seen the harpy weaken quickly and turn to frost." He waved a hand in the air. "A flurry of ice crystals, swirling into the air, much like the magic smoke from your pipe."

A trail of pale blue vapor wafted from the ends of a broad mouth, which tugged upward at the moment. "Tell me about the gentleman you spotted on the rooftop and later, at the opera."

Phaeton studied the talented clairvoyant. He had not mentioned the stranger, as yet. Which means Ping had captured the scene through the eyes of the harpy. What had Gaspar, the leader of the Gentlemen Shades, called Ping? A very muscular mesmerist.

"I have a moniker for you. Doctor Asa Alexander Exeter."

Ping got out a notebook and scribbled. "Believe I've heard the name about Pennyfields."

"Are the Shades courting him? No surprise there, I suppose." Phaeton grunted. "The man stuck needles in my arm and Lizzie's—ran a tube between us—transfused my blood into the girl. Then he disappeared. Haven't been able to get much out of Mrs. Parker."

"I've been meaning to ask you," Ping leaned closer. "What is it like living in a brothel?"

"Convenient." Phaeton winked.

Ping threw back his head as if to laugh. But he didn't laugh—he purred. The gentle sensuous rumble made Phaeton stop short. A long shank of black hair clasped neatly at the back of Ping's head came loose and flowed around his face and shoulders. His pale lips blushed the color of roses.

"Ping?"

"Jin." His voice was still resonant, but higher and softer in pitch. His face transformed into something decidedly more feminine in appearance. Phaeton froze, spellbound by the transformation.

He received the most alluring smile from this . . . female creature.

"Are you attracted to me?"

He clapped his mouth shut. So this was Jin. Phaeton had only heard rumors. It was said Ping could transmogrify himself into other sentient beings. That he was, in effect, a hermaphrodite. This sudden shift in gender was apparently no illusion.

A strong tug on his body pulled him closer to Jin.

"Will you kiss me, Phaeton?"

Echoes of the green fairy. How she haunted him. A swipe of pink tongue moistened Jin's lips. Phaeton managed a quick glance at his surroundings. Their walk down the embankment had brought them in close proximity to the landmark obelisk, Cleopatra's Needle.

"Detective Black."

Phaeton swung around.

Maxwell Fyfe, the chief forensics man for Scotland Yard, hustled down the broad thoroughfare toward them.

Phaeton cocked his head and feigned disappointment. "Perhaps another time, Jin."

"Best make myself scarce." Ping turned and walked away, his long black hair and coattails billowed with the wind off the Thames.

He called upriver after Ping. "When can I expect to hear from you?"

"Check your evening paper."

"Having a beastly day, I'm afraid," the lab director groused. Phaeton pivoted. "Aren't we all?"

"Can't stay long, but I can spare a lab assistant. Collect samples, comb the crime scene again." Maxwell glanced upward at the obelisk. "I understand they dug several pits before settling on this location. The excavations kept seeping river water. This whole section of embankment is pocked with holes covered over."

Phaeton craned his neck to see the top of the obelisk. "Odd bit of Egyptian plunder to erect here at the river."

The lab director checked his watch. "I'm afraid I have to move on. The technician should be along any minute. Show him the locations you want sampled. Try to keep me apprised of any progress."

He wondered, frankly, if Scotland Yard ever got its priorities straight. Still, he tried for an affable smile. "Certainly, Max."

"Good man, Phaeton. Have yet another investigation in Wapping Basin. A large warehouse burned down. The Fire Brigade's report suspects arson. Dexter asked me to have a poke around."

After his mouth fell open, Phaeton clapped it shut. "What is Agent Moore's interest in a warehouse fire?"

The director shrugged. "Working on a fraud case—some sort of double dealing. Several shipping merchants have complained about piracy, of all things."

For once, America was experiencing a pleasant dream. She sailed a small boat along a pretty waterway. "Wake up, Miss Jones." She awoke to realize the serene rocking of the boat was her mattress moving, and not so gently at that. She grabbed the sides of the bed frame as it jostled her about.

"We have excellent news. Your cousin Mr. Black is here to offer you a home and the comfort of family."

She propped herself up on her elbows and blinked. The rapscallion was standing at the foot of her bed, hat in hand.

"Thank the Good Lord I have found you. Esmeralda and I were afraid you perished in the fire. Imagine our relief to locate you here, with the Sisters of Mercy."

A consummate actor as well. His head remained tilted in a pious manner, but there was no mistaking the spark in his eyes. She looked him up and down. "I suspect you are pressed for time, and wish me to hurry along and collect my things?"

He cleared his throat. "If you would, *dear cousin*."

The sister on night duty rung her hands. "Oh, Mr. Black, perhaps you should come back in the morning?"

"No time like the present, Sister Germaine." He even sighed. "Just look at those wool welts on America's neck."

She felt the heat on her throat where the scratchy woolen blanket had rubbed.

Mr. Black reached inside his coat and removed his card.

"I work for Scotland Yard, Sister. Our benevolent fund will gladly provide you with enough means to purchase new bedcovers. Something warm that will not ravage the ladies' fair skin. Young women of fine, moral character they are."

He trained a smile on the sister, while his eyes signaled America to get moving. "The very thought of these poor innocents shivering under thin, felted blankets makes my heart—well, all this will be remedied with a sizable donation."

Sister Germaine blushed.

America rolled her eyes.

Mr. Black glared.

The cab ride to his flat was equally uncomfortable and seemingly endless. He stared straight ahead and hardly spoke. Finally, he turned his head, eyes narrowed. "Surely the warehouse had fire insurance. You can file a claim."

"Not when arson is suspected, Mr. Black."

"How is it you have no friends or relations here in London, miss?"

She shrugged. "Few worthy of my trust."

"You understand that your employment is temporary. As soon as you find work elsewhere, you will be gone. Is that clear?"

"As long as you grant me leisure time to look for suitable employment, I'm sure—"

He cut her off. "I'm too angry to chitchat. In fact, I cannot bare to listen to the sound of your voice."

America pressed her lips together, hoping to hide her amusement.

He growled, or was it a grunt? "I have never roomed with a woman. I am sure I will dislike it immensely."

"It seems to me you live with a houseful." She pressed folded hands into her lap.

"Clever, Miss Jones, but incorrect. I do not room with the ladies. I fuck them."

He jumped down from the hansom and did not release the retractable step. Instead, he grabbed her by the waist and held her against his body as he lowered her to the street. He stood too close, held on too long, and seemed reluctant to let go. A strange thrill ran through all her female parts, the ones he had already touched, intimately.

With his hand at her back, he swept her through Mrs. Parker's lobby and downstairs to his rooms. He disappeared for a moment, then returned with blankets and a sheet. "You'll have to sleep here on the chaise tonight. That large closet you have hopes of making into sleeping quarters can wait until morning."

He opened a cabinet door and removed a bottle of green spirit. "I believe I'll mix myself a bracer."

America went straight to work, spreading a sheet over the lumpy cushions of a low slung divan and laying the blankets on top. She sat down on the edge of the sofa and demurely tucked her hands under her skirt. "The stove keeps the room nicely comfortable."

"It does." He did not look up, but sampled the cloudy mixture in his glass.

"For the last two nights, I have slept fully clothed and shivering under a thin blanket. It would be heaven to—"

He savored another drop of absinthe. "Yes?"

She swallowed. "I will need to undress now."

He settled into his chair. "Indeed, you will."

"I will not be your concubine as well as your house maid, Mr. Black."

"No need to impose myself, Miss Jones. As you have already indicated, I live below a house full of women ready to service me."

"Very well." Off came her skirt, petticoat, and bustle, leaving on her chemise and pantalettes. A quick glance told her everything she needed to know about the state of Mr. Black's attention. Transfixed. And not by the muddling drink.

Neatly folding both the dress and undergarments, she sat down and unrolled her hose. Without an upward glance, she could sense his gaze travel down the length of her leg.

Slowly, deliberately, she slipped a stocking down one leg, then the other.

"You do that like a practiced courtesan, Miss Jones."

She wiggled her toes. "Good night, Mr. Black." A quick tuck of legs, and she slipped between sheet and blanket.

Phaeton poured another drink. Chilled water slipped over a crumbling lump of sugar, as clear emerald spirits dissolved into a swirling, milky green elixir. Holding the glass in hand, he studied the curvy shape under the blanket. Fleeting recollections of a mad, raving climax ran through his head. Their intercourse on the chair, the other day. If he was not mistaken, he had felt her pleasure, enhancing, stimulating his own. He reached down between his legs and adjusted his cock.

His life had suddenly taken a turn into Dante's trial in the

Inferno. Complete with an assortment of ephemeral beasts, including this flesh and blood she-cat. He exhaled a low sigh and eased back into his chair. At least he could take pleasure in a bit of peace and quiet.

"I can't sleep."

The hired help was up on an elbow, rubbing her eyes.

"I would so enjoy fetching you a hot milk, but there is no cream in the larder. Anything else, miss? Perhaps a fairy story?"

Her eyes narrowed. "Conversation will have to do."

He poured the last of the chilled water through a slatted spoon.

"Have you ever been in love, Mr. Black?"

"A very long time ago. I try not to think of it." He picked up his glass. "One needs to be careful about digging up the past. It can be a dirty business."

"I thought not." She huffed.

"Ah, you've had a thought. My congratulations. Do you wish to share it, Miss Jones?"

Those plump lips formed a pouty, lopsided smirk. "You've never been in love."

He tilted his head, considering her statement. "Well, that makes the two of us. I believe you informed me after we had intercourse for the second time in so many hours that you do not believe in love. Do I remember correctly?"

"There is no such thing as love. There are only proofs of love."

"Proofs?"

"You heard right, Mr. Black. Proofs of love. It is what my father taught me. Pay little attention to a man's words of love, he would say. But, watch closely his behavior. There, you will find the truth in his heart."

"Proof of pirates. Proof of love." He stretched his legs out in front of him and caught her ogling.

She swallowed. "You have very nice limbs, long and muscular from what I can see under the fabric of your trousers."

"Do you make a habit of studying masculine physiques?"

"It is important to know if a man is better suited to climb rigging or stoke a furnace."

He studied her quietly for a moment. "What sort of proofs suggest a man's affection?"

She smiled so sweetly he was taken aback.

A terrifying thought crossed his mind. "Oh no. Please tell me you don't believe—removing you from the parish home was a proof of—" He scoffed. "Proof of nothing but my own madness."

She pushed up on both elbows. The coverlet fell off her chest, revealing dark points under a thin silk camisole. The sight encouraged him to gape. "Mr. Black, you didn't have to come after me, now, did you?"

He wanted to rip the dainty lace off and suckle each dark tip until it stood at attention. Another erection pressed painfully against his trouser leg.

Phaeton leaned forward. "One chore unfinished, one task forgotten, Miss Jones, and you'll find out just how hard my heart can be. I'll toss you back on the street without a care."

The little hoyden flung herself onto the chaise and pulled the covers over her head. She mumbled something distinctly impertinent for hired help.

"Go to the devil."

He lifted his glass to the bump under the blanket. "Easily done."

Chapter Seven

A GREY DAWN FILTERED THROUGH HIGH-PLACED WINDOWS. America blinked. The room was unfamiliar and sparsely furnished. Where was she? Oh yes, Mr. Black's flat.

Groggy from sleep, she pulled the covers close and nestled deeper into the sofa. The terror and sadness of the past few days had eased somewhat, especially since last night. In a rather dramatic, middle-of-the-night maneuver, Mr. Black had rescued her from the shelter and given her work. The ends of her mouth tilted upward as she recalled his grousing in the hansom cab. Tolerable enough, even somewhat comforting.

The ill-humored male temperament didn't phase her in the least. Papa had been a cantankerous sort, but underneath his prickly, bearish demeanor she had always found affection. Good men, the kind who take their responsibilities seriously, were often cranky. America wondered if this was true of her new employer.

She closed her eyes and Mr. Black's calling card came to mind.

If what she had seen and heard last night was true, if Mr. Black actually worked for Scotland Yard, might he be able to assist her? She sat upright. The prospects of bringing Yankee Willem to justice, as well as having her stolen ships returned, suddenly seemed greatly improved. Tossing back blankets, she dressed in a frenzy.

She hesitated. Or was she just playing the fool? Without a doubt, Mr. Black had proved himself to be debauched as well as disagreeable. She found an apron in the closet and tied it on. But if he was a Yard man, well, that made him a godsend.

By the time the morning mist burned off, she had the small kitchen and pantry scrubbed to sparkling. There were also freshly made buns on the stove and a hot kettle ready for tea.

She tapped at his door quietly and the door swung open. "Mr. Black?"

He was pulling drawers up over chiseled buttocks. She did not cough or gasp. She stared.

Having grown up on a ship, America had caught glimpses of near naked men often enough, but this was, well, quite delicious. He grabbed his trousers and turned in her direction. She nearly choked. Naturally, he would have a broad, hard chest, dusted with brown hair.

"Looking for a bit of morning in and out, Miss Jones?" He yanked on pants. "Shall I leave these unbuttoned?"

Stop gaping. "Excuse me, I came to inquire—how do you take your tea, Mr. Black?"

He tugged a grin into a frown. "How disappointing." He tipped his head and buttoned his pants. "Spot of milk and sugar."

"Exactly how I take mine." She smiled and dashed down the narrow hall to ready his breakfast.

"I do not sleep in a night shirt." He stood in the pantry, lifting braces up over a newly pressed shirt. "If it bothers, I suggest you refrain from opening my door, leastwise before knocking."

"But I did knock. And the door opened on its own."

"An unlikely occurrence, but nevertheless, do take care in the future." He unfolded a sheet of paper and let it dangle between two fingers. "I take it you read, Miss Jones?"

She wiped her hands on her apron and took the note. It

was a list of chores, a very long list at that, and several tasks quite dreadful, filthy work. Then and there, she determined never to let him see so much as a grimace.

"Very good, sir." She set the note aside. "I borrowed a jar of milk from Mrs. Parker and she told me there is a bed frame in the attic along with several mattresses. I'm to have a look."

He retrieved a few coins from his pocket and pressed them into her palm. "You'll need to purchase a sheet, and a few personal items. The blankets from last night are serviceable enough."

"There is blackberry jam in the pantry, and I made more buns, the kind you like, Mr. Black. May I pour you some tea?" He studied her for a moment, before sliding a chair out from the table.

She set down his teacup, a plate of butter and buns, and a jar of preserve. She waited until he bit into a mouthful of hot bread dripping with melted butter and sweet berries.

"Do you really work for Scotland Yard?"

"At the moment." He chewed with enthusiasm. "Periodically, they discontinue my contract. Has something to do with the odd nature of cases I work on."

"Is it possible, Mr. Black—that is, might you assist me with my problem?"

He buttered the second half of the bun and ignored her presence. She tiptoed closer. He set the knife down and looked up, raising a brow.

She bit her lower lip before mustering a brighter look. "You remember, sir, the stolen ships."

He slurped a bit of tea. "Ah, the rude, unpleasant pirates."

America sighed. "You could help me if you wanted to."

"I could." He popped a last piece of bun in his mouth. "If I wanted to."

He disappeared down the hall and returned a moment later, cravat in place, vest and jacket donned. "I'm out for the day, won't be back until late afternoon." He nodded to the list on the table. "If and when you succeed in completing those—"

"Yes, Mr. Black?" She brightened.

"I'll think of more." He whisked by and gave her posterior a pat. "Those buns of yours are heavenly, Miss Jones."

Phaeton clenched his stomach to take the blows. After being pushed across the ring, Zander had him against the ropes. Dripping sweat, he held up a gloved hand to signal a break. Several months off the job, and he'd gone soft.

To relieve a kink, he lifted one shoulder, then the other, rolling his head side to side. A pale, trifling bit of illumination filtered through the skylight, which left the sparring arenas poorly lit. Above the glass panes, a thick black fog blanketed London. Shadows hovered in every corner and niche of the gymnasium. An attendant turned up a nearby gas lamp. The hiss mingled with the slaps and thuds of padded leather gloves smacking human flesh.

"Had enough?"

He shook his head. "One more round."

Barely winded, his sparring partner grinned. "Sure of that, Phaeton?"

What was Zander Farrell? Ten years older and in better condition. It rankled. He punched his gloves together. "Just give me two minutes and we'll go again."

Zander leaned against the corner post. "It was your idea to meet at my athletic club. Any news to report?"

Still breathing hard, Phaeton exhaled. "I may have a chance at the enigmatic Doctor Exeter this afternoon."

"So, the fisticuffs. A little late to prepare for that mysterious fellow, don't you think?"

Phaeton ducked his head and wiped away sweat with the back of his forearm. "Received a tip from one of the whores, a fairly reliable source. It seems a tall, austere gentleman arrives most every Thursday around teatime. He greets no one in the salon, but goes directly upstairs to Esmeralda's apartment and often stays well into the evening."

"You plan on interrupting the man's weekly coitus?" Zander's frown was formidable.

"Reports of my fearlessness are greatly exaggerated. I am not daft."

"Why all the mounting interest in Exeter?"

"Mounting? You'll have to ask Esmeralda about that. Besides the fact that he irritates, I get the feeling Exeter and I are both after the same culprit." He pounded gloved fists together. "Whether Chilcott cares to admit it or not, we're in over our heads. I believe we can use this man—I need to know what he knows."

Zanderx drilled into him with those deep indigo, all-seeing eyes. "I may have a bit more on the doctor for you, background mostly. It seems he is the only surviving son of Orius Exeter, Baron de Roos, Premier Baron of England. Ancient title, one of the oldest in the kingdom. And here's the rub, no one is completely sure the reclusive Baron is dead. There were reports last spring the old man succumbed to a wretched disease of some kind, but I could find no record of it. No death certificate or funeral notice."

"Nicely Gothic and ghoulish. Soon, I shall have enough material to write a novel." Phaeton absently studied an apparition sitting in a darkened corner, an ephemeral, greyish gargoyle. The creature perched on a stool, chin cupped in clawed hand. Whenever portals from the netherworld opened, he never knew quite what to expect. Would it be a hellish beast or a pestering fairy? Occasionally they lingered and were bothersome, like the fiendish trickster in the shadows. In due course, most demons dissolved into the mist, a gallery of faded ghosts from his past.

Zander bit back a grin. "If you insist on writing up your exploits, be sure to change up names and make yourself a hired detective, otherwise you'll give Chilcott an apoplexy."

"I'll use a *nom de plume*, Lavender Lavishe, no one shall be the wiser." Phaeton sashayed out into the ring and affected a flamboyant bow. "Youth before beauty, Mr. Farrell."

Zander pushed off the ropes. "As long as you concede I am the prettier one."

Phaeton slipped out of Lizzie's room and quietly shut the door. He leaned against flock-work wallpaper and massaged both temples. The girl was still not herself. Would the poor thing ever be right again? She had been a brave and sassy coworker, and he did not wish to think of her as half alive or half dead.

Every muscle in his body ached. Except for an impressive last minute show of courage in the ring, Zander had soundly thrashed him. He often marveled at what, if anything, the Yard man saw in him. At least this time he had a trustworthy man at his back, both in the field and at the office. Not so with the Ripper case. He had instantly clashed with CID inspectors, fools with brains in their bollocks. They had gone to Chilcott and accused him of acting raving mad.

The brothel was pleasantly tranquil in the early afternoon. He stole down the hall and stopped short of Esmeralda's door. A silent turn of the knob, and he entered more of a library than a parlor for socializing. Astounded by the number and quality of books, he nosed about the dimly lit room. Many of the tomes dealt with middle eastern mythology, history, religion. An avid interest in anthropology, perhaps? He recalled Layla's name, the aroma of curried dishes being prepared in the kitchen. There was much more to Esmeralda Parker than met the eye.

From behind a wall of bookcases, soft moans of pleasure lofted through the air. He imagined Esmeralda naked and writhing beneath—well, he would rather not think about who, at the moment. He took a seat beside a pedestal table piled high with pictorial books and entertained a brief fantasy.

Rummaging through the stack of oversized reference volumes, he found the perfect accompaniment to his rapidly burgeoning lower anatomy.

The Perfumed Garden of Sensual Delight. Translated from the French by Sir Richard Francis Burton.

He opened the book to a random illustration of a female. Sitting cross-legged, she reclined onto locked arms. Even though she wore exotic pantaloons, her breasts were bare. A man, her lover, knelt in front of her; one hand cupped a breast, the other held a nipple between thumb and forefinger.

He read the caption. "If you desire coition, cling first to her bosom; bite her, kiss her breasts, then suckle until you make her faint with pleasure; when you see her so far gone, then push your—"

"Mr. Black."

He clapped the book shut. "Doctor Exeter."

Phaeton perused the nude body of the man standing directly in front of him. Golden skin, lean muscle, impressive phallus even at half-mast. Magnificent. If he wasn't inclined toward the female sex, he would surely be aroused. Actually, he was aroused.

"Please be assured, it was my intention to wait until you both achieved satis—"

"That could take hours, Mr. Black." The man crossed his arms over a well-defined chest.

"Hours? Well, that is masterly of you, doctor."

Green eyes peered out from under a slash of dark brows. "Esmeralda deserves such adorations."

"I couldn't agree more." Both gazes narrowed, assessing, reassessing.

Phaeton sighed. It would be best to sidestep a cock fight. "I came to ask politely, one last time, if you would cooperate with Scotland Yard. You are elusive, Doctor Exeter, but not impossible to find. I could make your life quite miserable."

"You have already proven to be annoying."

"Well then, how about more of me? I can have the entire force brought down upon you. No matter how many interesting abilities you possess, you also have physical needs that require maintenance—eating, sleeping." He nodded toward the bedchamber. "Adorations."

Phaeton rose from the chair. "If what I surmise is true, this ghastly business has been going on for some time, and you've been going it alone. I recommend you consider reinforcements. Would it not be better to coordinate surveillance? Work together, rather than continually get in each other's way?"

Phaeton held his breath while the doctor deliberated.

"Tonight, Mr. Black. Above 91 Savoy Row. Anytime after moonrise."

"Draw me a bath."

He said nothing about how the apartment looked. America had scrubbed and washed until the flat smelled like spring and sparkled like a finely cut diamond. A serviceable bed frame and reasonably clean mattress had been carried down from the attic and set up in her room.

Esmeralda had encouraged her to borrow a few more furnishings, and she pulled together quite a nice little sitting room. She had also managed to get to the market, stocking the larder with sorely needed staples. Crossing off chores as she went, even the disgusting ones, the list shortened considerably by late afternoon.

He stood in the center of the room, scrutinizing every last detail of her work, but made only a single comment. "It appears you have been busy today, Miss Jones." He settled into a chair and opened the newspaper.

She jabbed her fists into her sides and bit her lip. Fine. If that was all she got, it would have to be enough. "Do you take a relaxer? Perhaps some sherry or—"

He barely looked up from his article. "Whiskey, neat. A good tumbler full."

"There's a wire message for you. Came tucked in the *Times*." She nodded at the pale yellow envelope that had dropped onto his lap, unnoticed.

America tilted her head and pursed her lips. "I doubt many Scotland Yard detectives receive messages inside their evening paper."

Phaeton read the wire and returned to the news. "A colleague of mine requests a meeting. Nothing clandestine about it, Miss Jones."

She exhaled a sigh and pivoted on her heel. Setting several pots of water on to heat, she soon had the copper tub by the stove filled with steaming water. She placed a cake of hard soap and several towels on the kitchen table.

"Your bath is ready, Mr. Black." She turned to leave the room.

"Stay where you are, miss." Gingerly, he rose from the deeply cushioned chair. "Went a few too many rounds with Detective Farrell, I'm afraid." Her drawn brows no doubt signaled confusion. "Pugilism, Miss Jones, at the athletic club."

"I see, sir."

With some effort, he stretched himself up to his full height. "A bit stiff, as you can see. You will need to undress me. And give me a bath."

A slight eye roll accompanied an open mouth. "Are those new duties, sir? They do not appear on the list."

He stood entirely too close. "You use the word *sir* as though you are prepared to obey me. Are you, Miss Jones?"

She uttered a sigh and removed his jacket and waistcoat. He made only small efforts to help with his disrobing. She pushed braces over broad shoulders and unbuttoned his trousers. Slipping his pants off, she could not help but notice there was also something rather stiff below deck.

It seemed Mr. Black wished to be stimulated, perhaps brought to pleasure. Well, two could play this game.

Slowly, she unbuttoned his shirt, making sure her fingernails scratched at the thin undershirt beneath. She removed both and stepped back to admire his chest and arms. They were larger, harder, more defined than she remembered from that morning.

"Your sport does you good, Mr. Black."

He sucked in air when she reached for the string on his drawers. Gently, purposefully, she worked her palms around his buttocks and slipped off the undergarment.

"I'll need you to step out of these and into the tub, then." She looked up to find his eyes fixed on her.

She pressed her lips together to avoid a grin. How easy men were. Give a man a bit of this and that, and he will begin to drool like a hound.

"Too hot?" She poured cool water into the bath to adjust the temperature. The man's penis jumped and twitched every time she drew near.

Eyes closed, he settled into the bath. With his bare knees out of the water, and his head laid back against the edge of the cooper tub, he looked like a painting she had once admired in Brussels. Such striking masculine repose.

Determined to treat his bath no different from an everyday chore, she scrubbed his shoulders and chest and kneaded arms knotted with muscle fatigue.

She soaped his hair and massaged his temples. He opened his eyes for a moment. "You are a goddess." She laughed off his adulation and tilted his head back, rinsing him with warm, clean water.

He lifted one leg at a time out of the bath, and she soaped the inside of each thigh, until he groaned.

"Care for a Mandalay foot massage?"

"Please do." He smiled with closed eyes. "Burma, jewel of the British Raj. You received quite an education in your travels, Miss Jones. Do you speak many languages?"

Both thumbs pressed into the arch of his foot. "Enough to make my way about any port in the world." She dropped his leg gently back into the water and tapped his knee for the other. "I miss the open sea. Sails snapping with wind. The Orient in my sights and England far behind me."

The sole of this foot apparently enjoyed her manipulations, for he groaned and mumbled something about divine pleasure.

Each individual toe received a massage, but her mind was off on a voyage. "The warmth of the sun and the taste of brine on my lips." This time, when he opened his eyes, his gaze moved to her mouth. And she returned his interest. He was a most sensuous man at rest.

She plunged his foot underwater. "Now for the private bits."

He grinned. "Use your hands and a cake of soap."

The nasty end of the job took a great deal of her time and attention. Those manly parts had to be soaped and made slippery several times. "Goodness, I believe that needs doing again."

A gurgling sort of growl rose from deep inside his chest. And when she left him to soak a few minutes, his eyes had gone black and glittered with lust.

She held up a warm bath sheet and wound it carefully around him. His close study, eyes filled with hot-blooded hunger, made her cheeks sear and knees quake. She half-imagined that large phallus rubbing inside her and nearly moaned. "Was your bath satisfactory?" She managed a shy smile.

"Most stimulating, but I cannot claim satisfaction, as yet." He surveyed her with hooded eyes. "Care to join me in my bed?"

"Why should I?"

"Because I make you tingle, Miss Jones."

With his hand at her back, he quite purposely steered her down the narrow passage. At the end of the hallway, she turned into her small room.

An iron frame bed, made up with clean bedding, filled a

good deal of the space. Bedside, a simple washbasin and pitcher sat on a plain wooden nightstand. Her shabby grey coat hung on a hook attached to the wall.

"I am your servant, not your whore, Mr. Black." She closed the door.

The door slammed open.

He pressed her against the wall. The towel fell off his body as he wrapped his hand around her waist and yanked her to him. The hardness of him pulsed against her belly as she gasped for air.

His warm breath fanned the heat on her cheeks. "I have kissed your breasts, but it occurs to me I have never kissed you there."

Chapter Eight

PHAETON STEPPED OUT OF THE HANSOM and pitched two bob up to the driver. He was edgy, more so than usual. He ran his fingers over his mouth. His body still burned from her kisses. Not figuratively. Literally. He had gone down hard on her lips, slanting back and forth, insisting she open to him. A brush with the tip of his tongue allowed him entrance and he penetrated deep. Even now, the sweet taste of her made him ache in every part of his lower anatomy. Soft lips surrendered the moment he teased them apart. Her tongue swirled up to greet his and encouraged him to delve deeper.

The woman was a torture to him. How—when, exactly, had this happened?

He had placed both hands on the wall, one above each lovely shoulder, and nipped at a luscious bottom lip, caressing raw flesh with his tongue. "I should be flogged, my dear, for I have wounded you." Her whispered sigh and moan fully engorged the shaft of his penis. He answered her with a growl that might have come from a den in a wood.

Rallying to his game of kiss and release, she caught the bottom ledge of his mouth between her teeth and tugged. "Exquisitely arousing, Miss Jones." She spoke in incoherent, musical utterances. And then his name. "Mr. Black?"

"Hmm." He brushed his mouth gently over hers.

"Please." Her sweet breath buffeted his face, delicate hands traveled down the flesh of his back, grabbing the muscle of his buttocks. "Yes, my dove?" Shifting her hands to his waist, she shoved him off. "You kiss expertly, Mr. Black."

"Not quite skillfully enough it seems."

Their little tête-à-tête had been explosive. Passionate. Like no kiss he ever remembered giving or receiving. Drat, the little minx was going to strain his libido to impossible new heights of discomfort.

What was it about this light brown belle that affected him so? Skin the color of coffee with cream. And that ravishing mouth, plump and inviting. The upper lip's peaked curvature formed a pout so alluring it distracted him beyond reason.

That she aroused him was a certainty. But her disposition puzzled. She went about her household duties with admirable vigor. He even found her impertinent directness of speech and manner rather refreshing. And it was not as though she didn't want him. He could feel the heat in her blood, see the wanton way she looked at him. So why such reluctance in matters of intercourse? Considering the way they had begun their acquaintance, her reticence to spread her legs seemed most disingenuous. Unless, of course, she toyed with him.

It really didn't matter what she was up to; the more he thought about Miss Jones, the more desirous he became. Phaeton exhaled. Just as well he hadn't bedded her this evening. It would have been a hard slog to leave home with that warm flesh pressed against his body.

He moved quietly into the crisscross of streets between the Strand and the river. Having set to memory every last intersecting byway of Savoy Row, he adjusted comfortably to the lane's poorly lit surroundings. The buildings, occupied mostly by tradesmen, were related to publishing, stationers, printers, and the like. He stopped at a corner book bindery. The lingering acrid fetor of leather stamping, gilding, and glue pots made his nose twitch.

In the darkness of the alley, he could only approximate an address. He walked around to the side of the building and decided to scale it from there. It was either that, or learn to fly. He pulled himself up onto the top of a large refuse bin, and shimmied up a drainage pipe. Inching upward, he found the occasional jog in the bricks for a toe hold, which greatly advanced his efforts. His fingers shook as he inched them into a mortar crack. The higher he climbed, the more rattled he became. Odd that heights unnerved him. Especially when any number of frightful apparitions had little or no effect.

As he ascended close to the roof edge, a face bobbed into view wearing bloodred goggles. "Mr. Black."

Losing his grip, he slid downward. Abruptly, his fall was stopped and reversed. Instantly, he was lifted up by a powerful, invisible force, until he stood on the rooftop, facing Dr. Exeter.

He blinked. There remained an odd buzzing noise in his ears, which didn't help an uneasy stomach as he tried to focus on the sparkle of the Thames drifting behind Exeter's head.

"How did you do that?"

The stoic man actually flashed a wry grin. "The physics are complicated. Not something I feel inclined to discuss this evening. You require a staggering amount of education, Mr. Black, but we are not here to conduct class in the manipulation of the physical universe."

The thick spectacles the doctor wore glowed a fuchsia-rose color, swirling into lurid hues of cerise and purple. Phaeton could barely see the man's eyes behind the tinted glazing. Exeter removed another set of goggles from an inside coat pocket. "We are here to catch a powerful manifestation, an incarnate soul."

He quirked a brow. "Is she not a vampiress—an Empusa?"

Exeter opened the ear armatures and locked them into place before setting the heavy glasses on the bridge of Phaeton's nose. "Remember your ancient history, Mr. Black. The immortals have always required blood—in copious amounts." The doctor scanned the embankment along the river. "London does not currently have a sacrificial temple in which to restore the ichors of the gods. Please correct me if I am wrong."

As Phaeton's eyes adjusted to the optics, he noted a shift in the spectrum of moonlight. Reflections of river current, the pale flicker of the gas lamps along the embankment, all glimmered in mysterious brilliant pink tones. "So our Empusa, for we might as well call her that, is forced to stalk the streets, seeking human sacrifice."

"Replenishment. It is a theory of mine." Exeter nodded toward the river walk. "These lenses will pick up the slightest illumination. Concentrate your surveillance around Cleopatra's Needle."

Phaeton scanned a stretch of Thames behind the needle as he listened to Exeter.

"As you have already witnessed, she travels in a flurry of luminescent particles. I have fashioned these opticals to enhance our abilities. There are often small precursors of essence, before any perceptible occurrence of her."

The doctor turned to Phaeton. "I felt no presence at Mrs. Parker's the other evening, but she drew you to her." Exeter lowered the odd spectacles on his nose and peered over the tops of the lenses. "I suspect she has turned her attention to you, Mr. Black."

Phaeton grinned. "Jealous?"

Exeter drew slanted brows together. "So carefree and glib, but not for long. You have no idea what you are dealing with—"

"Why don't you tell me?" Phaeton settled back against a chimney stack. "We have hours yet before dawn."

The doctor's gaze continued to narrow. "For my own edification and your safety, a bit about yourself, first. You appear to have contact abilities. Do you see as well as hear them?"

Phaeton nodded his head.

"And when did this all begin for you?"

"As a child I routinely conversed with magical beings. And there were night terrors. Mother understood, even encouraged the parts that didn't frighten me. Father never approved of her doting."

The river waters rippled a virulent shade of violet. "When she died, I was packed off to school. To avoid being buggered to death by the older boys, I hid my abilities, tucked them safely away. Gradually, the visitations became less frequent."

A faint droning noise caused Phaeton to focus on the obelisk. "A swarm of some kind is headed our way."

"Likely, one of her distractions." The doctor ran to one end of the building and motioned him to follow. They both ducked as a posse of small objects buzzed overhead. Large eyeballs, framed in black and sharply-pointed on the one end. "All-seeing eyes."

"With stingers." Phaeton tracked the buzzing pests back to the swarm. "Rather clever, how she fashions her minions."

"She knows we're here. We'll need to jump to the next building, then the yard below." From a standstill, Exeter leaped to the roof of the next building.

A swarm of flying orbs bearing knifelike points descended upon Phaeton. The storm cloud of dangerous wasplike creatures encircled him, stabbing from every conceivable angle. He braced himself for a stinging assault, but felt no pain. Phaeton held up a hand and pressed against a thick, invisible barrier. An invisible force field held the prickly monsters at bay.

"Jump, don't think."

"I can't."

"Why not?"

"Because I am—" Phaeton dodged several stingers that poked through the membrane. "Damn it, man, I don't like heights." Heart racing, palms sweaty, his entire body vibrated with obsessive fear.

"The shield will not hold much longer. Your choice, Mr.

Black, you can jump or be ripped to shreds." Cursing under his breath, Phaeton gritted his teeth. He took a half step back then vaulted over the dark void between buildings. For one long moment, time stood still as he sailed across the divide.

He landed next to the man, who actually chuckled. "A leap of faith by an agent of Scotland Yard. Follow me down to the lane." Exeter landed neatly on his feet while Phaeton's fall and subsequent tumble to earth was broken by another unseen shield. Stunned, he lay on the ground for a moment to let his stomach settle.

The doctor shrugged. "It takes practice."

Phaeton dusted himself off and took the lead. Inching along the rough side of a brick wall, they made excellent progress in the direction of the obelisk. Ivy hung down over a large niche in the barrier. They quickly took refuge behind a curtain of greenery.

Exeter nodded toward a wall fountain which featured the placid, sleeping face of a young goddess. Moss bloomed in the deeper clefts of the sculpture as empty eyes opened and blinked. She opened her mouth but did not speak. Blood gushed out.

They both stepped away.

"Ouch." An errant eyeball, a scout of some kind, took a stab at Phaeton, and he swung at the nasty pest. A cacophony of cricket sounds indicated the swarm was not far behind.

"Quickly." As the waspish eyes invaded, the doctor shoved him into the alley. They raced across the lane to the river walk. This time, Exeter signaled him away from the needle. They ran until they stood at the corner of Savoy Row and the Strand. Exhausted and out of breath, they slowed their run to a walk and waited.

"You and I, together, create some kind of magnet. In the future, we will have to make our observations from afar or split apart."

Phaeton paced in small circles as he sucked in draughts of air. "I take it you plan to locate her hideout and set some kind of a trap?"

Exeter shook his head. "Destroy the lair. She has another located somewhere else in the city."

"Ah, so one by one, we close in. How many are there?"

"Unsure. Three or four possibly. I destroyed the first."

Phaeton stared. "She'll just find more."

"The very reason we have to move swiftly." Exeter nodded toward the eastern cityscape.

A pale sky streaked with yellow and pink. Charcoal-edged clouds hovered above a row of waterfront buildings. Phaeton exhaled. "Dawn."

Dr. Exeter turned and walked away, dissolving into the grey mist of early morning. A voice traveled out of the fog. "We must find her hideaway, Mr. Black. Meet me at my laboratory late in the day. 22 Half Moon Street."

America caught his reflection in the looking glass as the door swung open. Mr. Black stood at the entrance to her room with the back of his hand raised, knuckles turned out, as if he was about to knock.

"Perhaps now you'll believe me." She turned around and stuck her chin out. "Doors open around here without the courtesy of a knock, Mr. Black."

"Most likely fairies." Eyes half open and shoulders hunched, he leaned against the entry frame. "Pester the devil out of me from time to time. On the subject of minor nuisances . . ." He pulled an object out of his pocket, and pinched the quivering oddity between two fingers. "Might we find a cage for this?"

Her eyes grew wider as she approached him. She reached out to touch the queer object and the rabid critter buzzed to life and angled a stinger toward her. She quickly retracted her hand. "Cheeky little pest. What is it?"

"Haven't a clue. Perhaps, after a good strong breakfast tea, Miss Jones?

At the pantry table, they each held a freshly brewed cup and stared at the little orb fluttering about inside an empty conserve jar. It was an eye all right, encircled by a ring of black, which formed a kind of pincher, or stinger-like shaft, at one end.

Mr. Black slurped a bit of Earl Grey. "We were chased off a rooftop by a swarm of these things." The irritable orb bounced off every side of the glass container. He picked up the jar and slammed it down, stunning the little fiend.

America tilted her head and leaned closer. "Port Said, in the bazaars. I have seen bejeweled gold pieces for sale with this image. Powerful amulets." She tilted the jar for a better look.

He stared. "Egyptian?"

She nodded and sat back to sip her tea.

"Keep the kettle hot." He sprang out of the chair and paused. "And could you possibly make some of those buns of yours, Miss Jones?"

She steeped a second pot and set about making a bit of breakfast. When her employer returned from upstairs, he carried under his arm a number of tomes on Ancient Egypt borrowed from Mrs. Parker's library. Combing through the illustrated books, they were able to decipher the symbology of the eye of Horus.

Mr. Black sliced through a rasher of bacon. "Horus' eye was shattered into six pieces, each representing one of the senses . . ."

As he read, America opened the last book in the stack. After a brief perusal of the illustrations, heat rushed from her belly to her cheeks. She clapped the book shut.

Her employer popped a last morsel of buttered bun into his mouth. The man could grin and chew at the same time. "Mrs. Parker has quite a collection of erotica. I brought that down for you, Miss Jones. 'Tis your reward for recognizing this Egyptian Horus fellow."

Damn the man for smiling that twinkly grin at her. She bit back a flirtatious repartee.

"A reward for me, Mr. Black. Are you quite sure? The book is filled with lewd pictures. I have no interest in pornography."

"Then perhaps, you might consider another reward." He studied her, anticipating, assessing her interest in his next offer. He reached into his waistcoat pocket and pulled out a card. "Yesterday morning, I had a brief discussion with this gentleman at headquarters."

The calling card stated Metropolitan Police, Scotland Yard, 4 Whitehall Place, and the name Dexter Ambrose Moore.

"It seems Dex is working on a case involving an outbreak of unusual thievery. Merchant ships, stolen by pirates, of all things." He winked.

America sprung to her feet and kissed his neck and cheek. He turned his face toward the warmth of her lips. "No need to wire. He will be expecting a Miss Jones."

She held the card close against her bosom. "Oh, thank you, Mr. Black."

"You have the afternoon off." He leaned back in his chair and stretched. "Run along, then. I am perfectly capable of washing a few breakfast dishes."

She emerged from her room wearing a pretty dress and coat, which caused him to turn away from his chores and stare.

"Very charming."

"Borrowed from Lizzie. I sat a few hours with her yesterday, at her bedside. Mrs. Parker says she is greatly improved."

He soaped a teacup. "I don't recall that chore on your list."

"You specifically stated . . ." America lifted her apron off the chair back and found the folded note paper. "Right here, Mr. Black. 'If you complete this list, do not hesitate to be of service to Mrs. Parker.' " She could not ignore the stack of dripping dishes. "Would you like me to finish up or may I leave now?"

"Watch yourself around Dexter Moore," he grumbled. "Comes off as quite the proper gentleman, but I have witnessed a kind of rampant sexual athleticism . . ." Phaeton clamped his mouth his shut. "Just be warned."

She nodded a quick curtsy.

"And, Miss Jones."

She turned back. "Yes, Mr. Black."

Drying his hands with a dishcloth, he circled around her. "In the next day or two, I expect you to pick out one of the delightful poses from the *Kama Sutra,* and I shall endeavor to please you." He leaned over her shoulder and kissed the exact spot on her neck that made her shiver.

Chapter Nine

AMERICA ENTERED AN OFFICE THAT CONTAINED TWO DESKS.

The secretary nodded to a chair. "On the left, Miss. Agent Moore will be here shortly."

She took a seat and perused the orderly landscape of the desktop. A neat stack of files sat to one side of an otherwise spotless, gleaming wood surface. She noted a blotter and pen set. The ink bottle was adorned with an engraved sterling silver stopper. Certainly not government issue.

She glanced at the disarray across the room. A messy desk indicated an agent who was busy in the field. A man of action, or just disorganized? She scanned the pristine surface of the desk close to her. A man who was conscientious and meticulous? She hoped so.

"Good afternoon."

She shifted in her seat to catch the back side of a reasonably tall, dark-haired man as he adjusted the door to the office. For the sake of decency, he left the door ajar.

Dressed in a perfectly tailored suit, his collar points high and cravat slim, the man was the very picture of fashionable. He straightened an otherwise perfect stack of files and twisted a gold cufflink at each wrist before sitting down.

"There now, how can I help you, Miss Jones?"

America tilted her head. Agent Dexter Ambrose Moore was attractive. A shock of black hair fell over his forehead, which might have given him a less imposing, youthful appearance were it not for the neatly trimmed beard that emphasized the man's best feature. Sparkling sapphire eyes framed by long velvet black eyelashes. Really quite dashing.

She cleared her throat. "Less than a year ago, my father owned a small fleet of merchant vessels and a thriving trading company. In rapid succession, several of his best, single-stack ships were lost at sea, along with their cargo. It was a devastating blow to the business." Her voice trembled as the words tumbled out. "Then one of his business associates claimed the remainder of his fleet as repayment of debt. One blow after another was too much. My father died recently, in November."

"Very sorry for your loss, Miss Jones." He appeared reasonably sincere in his condolence, though perfunctory. All business, this one.

"Those ships weren't lost at sea. They were stolen." She raised her chin. "At the moment, I have no proof of thievery. But I shall not rest until I catch whoever did this and make them pay. Bloody pirates." She supposed the upturn at the edges of his mouth indicated he was at least listening to her. The agent opened a desk drawer and took out several sheets of a paper. From inside his jacket pocket, he removed a fountain pen, unscrewed the cap, and shook it down.

"Your father's name, the name of his business and his investors?"

"Charles Gardiner Jones. Star of India Trading & Shipping Limited."

"British Registry?"

"All five ships."

He glanced upward as he scratched names onto paper. "Might the name of your father's business partner be either a Mr. Harry Poole or Captain Yanky Willem?"

Her heart flip-flopped inside her chest. "You know of Yanky Willem?"

"I hope to find the scoundrel a new home, preferably a cell in Newgate." He pulled a file off the top of the stack and flipped it open.

He smiled at her. "With your assistance, Miss Jones, perhaps we can expedite his change of residence."

"I'd like nothing more than to see a rope around his neck." She answered his raise of brow with one of her own. "The man can go straight to Hades."

"That would be a miserable change of address, wot?" A chestnut haired man stood in the doorway wearing a pleasant grin. "Sorry to disturb. I'll just collect a few files and work in the next office."

"Hold on, Gabe. Midway to his desk, the affable gent pivoted toward them. "Gabriel Sterling may I introduce Miss Jones." The slightest ring of acrimony edged Mr. Moore's voice.

She held out her hand. "America Jones, pleased to meet you."

"Miss Jones." He studied her for a moment. "You are American, then?"

"My late father, recently passed, was a British citizen. My mother is American." Both men stared at her, unwilling to ask the most obvious question. Brits could be annoyingly civil. She sighed. "My skin color and curls come from my grandmother, a freed slave, Mr. Lewis. My *Français* grandfather owned cotton plantations."

She looked from one frozen half smile to the other. "I am known as a high yellow Cajun in Louisiana."

"In England we would just call you beautiful." The one with the messy desk certainly had his appeal. "Would we not, Dex?"

Detective Moore sputtered out his agreement.

America studied the more punctilious man. "I find it peculiar, Mr. Moore, that you never met with my father regarding the piracy of his ships. As I recall, he made several trips to Number 4 Whitehall to report his suspicions."

Moore flipped through a number of files. "There are no records of any interviews, but then I recently took over this investigation." A hardened expression turned vulnerable as he met her gaze. "The agent working on this case went missing months ago, Miss Jones. He is presumed dead."

Phaeton stepped off the train and onto the platform. An engraved placard of a hand with an outstretched index finger pointed the way toward the Underground lift.

P-s-s-st. A draft of steam and a gust of wind whipped through the station. Phaeton glanced over his shoulder as he followed foot traffic up a narrow tunnel plastered with handbills.

A prickly, spine-tingling sensation coursed down his spine as he became aware of a figure trailing behind him. Pivoting on his heel, he swung around to confront—nothing. He scanned the station searching through the crowd of commuters. Imaginary? He thought not; he sensed something, someone.

"Phaeton."

There, in the corner, a slender man dressed in black emerged from the shadows to stand beside a match peddler. Julian Ping.

Phaeton dodged a few bustling pedestrians. "Hello, Ping. Thought we were to meet in the park."

"Turned out to be a lovely day topside." With the dark spectacles off, one could plainly see why the young man needed protection from the sun. "Easier this way. No need to cover up." Pale skin, silver eyes, nearly colorless, even in the dim light of the tube station. Exotic, liquid mercury orbs framed by dark lashes. Sable hair, pulled straight back and clasped tightly at the back of the head. No. Ping was decidedly not albino. He was . . .

"Immortal, potent energy."

Phaeton leaned closer.

"No ordinary fiend is stalking the Strand. You are dealing

with the remnants of a divine being's corpse. Relic dust and champagne."

He cocked his head and squinted. "Sorry. Did you say relic dust and champagne?"

"In-between matter. To the naked eye, one sees nothing but darkness. The substance, in-between other substance." Ping raised both hands and bounced a small, sparkling ball of violet energy between his palms. "But in a vision, she leaves a trace of sparkling effervescence."

"Yes, I believe I have a bit of in-between matter in this satchel." Phaeton lifted the bag.

Ping closed his hands in prayer, and lowered his voice. "Gods, reanimated. An ancient form newly risen, with hardly any control." The wan young fellow backed away.

He considered the message. "Thank you, Julian—oh yes, and Jin." He tipped his bowler. "So much simpler to call you Ping. Where is she today?"

Ping tilted his chin and swept a leisurely glance up his body. "Aroused, as usual, to see you, Phaeton." The young man drifted close, then angled away.

He rolled his eyes and called after the solitary figure. "Not Jin—the immortal she-devil."

An echo of feminine, flirty voice trailed after Ping as he headed back toward the platform. "Be careful, love."

Phaeton exited the tube station at Hyde Park corner and walked a few blocks to the tony Mayfair address of Dr. Exeter's laboratory. Half Moon Street turned out to be a charming block of elegant townhomes. The absolute reverse of any residence he might have imagined the doctor would occupy. The austere, greystone Gothic manse he had pictured in his mind's eye turned out to be a pristine white terrace house featuring elegant columns that supported a covered portico entry.

As he reached the top step, he noted tall palladium windows. A row of flower boxes beneath the sills sent up the first green shoots of spring's hardiest flower, the daffodil.

Before he could lift the door knocker, a stunningly attractive young lady opened the door. She wore a school uniform and a smile.

Dr. Jason Exeter, it seemed, attracted a number of lovely ladies. And what had he expected? A high-toned butler, large of girth with pointed nose in the air? Or some wizened, prickly old door opener?

"Mr. Black. I hope your journey across town was pleasant. The Underground can be terribly congested these days."

Since no cab or carriage sat at the curb, she must have guessed at his mode of transportation. Still, he was rather flummoxed. "Do we know each other, Miss—?"

"Anatolia Chadwick. Please use my pet name, Mia, if you don't mind?" After his coat was hung in a nearby closet, she led the way upstairs.

"I understand you are a detective—a Yard man?" Her eyes gleamed with interest. "All the girls at school positively swoon over the idea of a dashing Scotland Yard inspector."

"I can hardly think why, miss."

She looked at him as if he were mad. "Because you pursue evildoers and villains, because . . ." The young lady bit her lower lip as she searched for the right word. "Because you are heroes."

"I suspect your friends read too many harrowing tales of crime in the *Strand* magazine." A breathy giggle told him he could not be far off.

His young escort tapped lightly on the door before bursting into a large airy space that immediately struck him as both a study and a laboratory. Every wall except for a bank of windows facing the street was lined with shelves, spilling over with books, beacons, and an assortment of peculiar scientific equipage.

They approached a long table in the middle of the room. Glass tubes set over Bunsen burners bubbled mysterious liquid contents. Dr. Exeter sat at one end, bent over an instrument of some kind.

Mia spoke first. "Making progress, Oom Asa?"

"A frustrating day, I'm afraid." He looked up from the contraption. "Ah, Mr. Black. You have met my ward?"

"Indeed, Miss Chadwick. A lovely and hospitable young lady." Phaeton nodded to the girl who returned a shockingly sultry smile.

Exeter frowned at her flirtation. "Schoolwork finished?"

"A fiendish tract of Latin left to translate."

Before the doctor's glare narrowed further, the precocious chit excused herself with a flip of her skirt and a mutter under her breath. "Bollocks."

"You are not allowed to say that word, Mia." The doctor's perplexed grimace was rather amusing. "Smart as a whip but a bit of a chatterbox. Lately, she's taken to blurting out the most inappropriate words and phrases."

"Charming girl." He clamped back a grin. "Befitting her age, wouldn't you say?" Phaeton's interest returned to the odd apparatus in front of the doctor.

"You like my microscope, Mr. Black?"

"Curious." Phaeton set a leather satchel on the table.

"Come have a look." Exeter showed him how to adjust focus as a number of plump, brownish red objects resolved into view.

"My area of research is serology. The study of blood serum. I have a contract with the university to discover and identify blood groupings, a theory of mine, which I hope to someday be fortunate enough to publish."

Phaeton removed a glass jar from the briefcase. The doctor edged closer, eyes locked on the fluttering creature inside the container. "You caught one, Mr. Black?"

"Batted one off my arm and it fell into my pocket. I thought we might take it down to the Embankment and let it loose—"

"The malicious little irritant could lead us right to her den." Exeter raised a brow. "What could be simpler?"

"Yes, you brilliant types need us simpletons." Phaeton crossed his arms.

The doctor's eyes crinkled ever so slightly. "Brilliance is very often simple."

Phaeton ignored the compliment. "Care to tell me what significance the eye of Horus or Ra has on the case we are dealing with?"

"Ah, so you are studious as well as clever." The doctor closed a large file full of notes and opened another. "I have come to believe the perpetrator of this murder spree arrived in London nearly fifty years ago, when the obelisk was shipped here from Egypt."

Exeter turned over several pages. "According to what I have found, newspaper articles and several published articles from the dig, Cleopatra's Needle was packed in native soil and transported in a large custom-made tube.

"The cargo ship set out from Alexandria towing a barge carrying the obelisk. The voyage was unusually rough. Horrendous storms. At one point during extreme high seas, the obelisk separated from the ship and was considered lost for several days."

Phaeton scratched his head. "I've read an accounting of this tale. Didn't they pay a ransom to the fisherman who salvaged the barge?"

"A bloody fortune." Flipping through more notes, Exeter set the file down. "Details regarding the obelisk's installation is where the story gets muddy." He picked up a pair of spectacles and hooked an armature over each ear. "Ah, here it is. When the monolith was being readied for installation, two sarcophagi were found laying in the sand beside it. As much as I have been able to piece together, an accident happened. One of the stone caskets was broken and discarded."

Phaeton remembered standing near the obleisk, and Director Fyfe's words. "I'm guessing they used the damaged one to help fill-in the sinkholes along the embankment."

"Ah, you know about those." Exeter nodded. "And a likely postulate. I have not been able to trace the second, intact, sarcophagus. The British Museum claims to have no records of its existence. I'm afraid the reliquary may have ended up in a private collection."

"The significance of the broken sarcophagus, I assume, deals with its unusual contents?"

Exeter nodded. "It is my theory that each one held the remains of a god."

Phaeton took a moment to compare remarks. So far, nearly all of Exeter's conjecture confirmed Ping's vision. His gaze wandered over instruments as odd as the man beside him. "I am greatly relieved to know we're not chasing after the usual riffraff."

"Avatar or vampire, whichever you chose. My assumption is her ancient remains long ago turned to dust." The doctor slumped a bit. "Something must have occurred to reawaken such a dangerous Mesopotamian witch."

Phaeton absently scanned the lab. "I thought she was Egyptian?"

"All gods emerged from the confluence of two rivers, the Tigris and Euphrates."

"Even the Greeks?"

Exeter glowered. "Particularly the Greeks."

The lull in conversation was broken by the sound of bubbling test tubes. Phaeton rubbed his temples. "How does one go about eliminating a goddess?"

"Perhaps the best we can do is encourage her to move on."

He frowned. "Pass the problem along to another century, perhaps?"

"One step at a time, Mr. Black. First we must destroy her current nest and force her to move on—seek new refuge."

A shadow moved across the windows. Phaeton was aware

of something or someone in the room with them. He nearly jumped off the stool at the sight of a tall ebony-skinned gentleman. The striking fellow wore stark white pajamas and copious amounts of translucent, colored beads around his neck and wrists.

"Oom Asa, would you and your guest care for some tea or other refreshment?" Such a gentle tone of voice from the imposing character.

Exeter turned to Phaeton. "When at home, I take afternoon tea with Mia. Hot chocolate and biscuits. I sweeten mine with a spot of crème de menthe." The man actually winked. "Please join us."

"Here we are. 21 Shaftsbury Court." America no sooner recited the address when Detective Moore experienced a spasm of coughing.

"Are you all right?" She patted his back.

Moore had flagged down her cab as it turned out of Scotland Yard and insisted on seeing her safely home. Now, sitting beside her with a rosy red flush surging up his neck, the man seemed positively distressed. "Are you quite sure—"

"I work here, Mr. Moore." She had a good idea what he must be thinking. "Not for Mrs. Parker, but for Mr. Black."

"Mrs. Parker?" The man wrenched his neck to loosen his cravat.

Was the poor man going to try to feign ignorance? After 10 Downing and 4 Whitehall, Mrs. Parker's was the most recognized address in town. Well, infamous, anyway.

She grinned. "You must come in for tea, and I will not take no for an answer." On their way through a near empty house, they chanced upon several ladies in the hall who greeted Mr. Moore by name.

"I say, this is embarrassing." The man mumbled as she led the way downstairs trying very hard not to release a bubble of laughter that seemed determined to leak out.

"M-miss Jones"—he sputtered—"this not a proper situation for a young lady."

"Proper? When the warehouse burned down, and I was left without income or shelter, Mr. Black plucked me out of the Night Home, offered decent employment and a room of my own."

"No matter how well intentioned, it looks—"

"Whose looks, Mr. Moore? The refined, gently bred people of London who left me to fend for myself on the street?" Fists on her hips, she did her best to flatten him with a glare. "If you lost everything—a loving parent, your every worldly possession, and your livelihood—tell me, how much would you care about how things look?"

Shoulders hunched, he sighed. "Sorry to sound like such a prig. Please forgive me."

She studied glistening, vulnerable blue eyes. "Do you take cream and sugar in your tea?"

"A spot of cream." Mr. Moore swallowed. "You work for Phaeton Black as . . . ?"

"His housekeeper and that is all." She unpinned her hat. "You appear to be well acquainted with the companionship available above stairs." She eyeballed him. "There are a dozen women who would jump at the opportunity to be of assistance to Mr. Black."

Odd that her own remark would cause a pang of . . . what was that?

Mr. Moore moved closer. "If you would allow me, I could arrange for more suitable lodging—"

"I suggest you concentrate on my stolen ships and allow me to handle Mr. Black." America set the kettle back on the stove to hide a grin. "Although, I do confess the man is a Lothario, at times."

The glowering agent settled into a chair at the table. "Lothario? I'd say libertine, adulterer, profligate debaucher is more like it."

"Dex, since when have you taken a liking to me?"

Chapter Ten

PHAETON DESCENDED THE REMAINING STAIRS. "I'd say debaucher is something of an improvement. Up from raving mad at the very least. Have you forgiven me?"

Detective Moore shifted in his chair and delivered a glare just short of daggers. "Good afternoon, Phaeton."

A year ago, Phaeton had wooed a vivacious, willing widow right out from under Dexter's amorous designs. He then had enjoyed a rather rambunctious love life with the lady until a very rich lord proposed and she accepted. Within a month's time, she was married and whisked off to a country estate. But not before she returned to Phaeton for one last liaison. The remembrance caused a smile, which deepened the scowl from Moore. Ever since their falling-out, neither man had made much effort at civility.

America set another place at the table.

"I've had my tea, Miss Jones. A glass of whiskey, please, if you don't mind?" He shed his coat and took a seat at the table. "So, Dex, how goes the investigation?"

"Very well, indeed. With the help of Miss Jones, I may have one of the culprits behind bars soon enough."

Phaeton inhaled whiskey fumes before taking a swallow. "Tell me more."

Moore leaned forward. "Two ships of suspicious registry put in recently at different ports—one anchored off Portsmouth and the other is dry-docked in Millwall. Tomorrow morning, I plan to locate the original records naming Charles Gardiner Jones, principal of The Star of India Trading Company, as owner of the vessels. Miss Jones assures me that when the time comes, she will be able to identify her father's ships beyond a doubt."

America beamed. "I am to pay a visit to the sail maker's shop, as well as Matthew Brothers, dry dock repair. Patched up nearly all of our vessels at one time or other. They will surely be able to identify their handiwork."

"Sworn statements will be taken to help fortify Miss Jones's claim." Moore's self-satisfied grin widened as his gaze met hers.

Phaeton smacked the empty whiskey glass down on the table. "Out of curiosity, what is your plan, Dex, for boarding and searching these vessels in order to identify them as stolen?"

"I intend to press for a warrant."

"If the ships are currently registered to another country, a warrant will take time." Phaeton scoffed. "With no legal authorization to hold them, they'll up anchor."

He narrowed his gaze on Moore. "I suspect you will have to go in undercover. How exactly might that be done without placing Miss Jones in danger?"

"I assure you she will be safe with me." He stood up. "Thank you for tea, Miss Jones. I shall keep you apprised by wire of my progress with your registration papers."

Shrugging into his coat, Moore removed his hat from the rack. "And what about you Phaeton? Have you given any thought at all to what is best for Miss Jones, living here, in this situation?"

Phaeton slouched against the chair rails. "Miss Jones is comfortable here, if I am not mistaken. Are you not Miss Jones?"

"I did advise Agent Moore that I am satisfied with my circumstances." She picked up the empty teacups.

"There, you see? Miss Jones is as safe with me as you, Agent Moore."

A thin grimace creased the man's face. "Like to believe that." He headed for the stairs.

"Oh, Dex?"

The man paused a moment, and turned back. "What is it, Phaeton?"

"Layla was asking after you when I came in this evening."

The detective's eyes darted across the room to Miss Jones, who was otherwise occupied washing up dishes.

"Something about a bit of lolly for the old tosser." Phaeton couldn't help the grin. Really, he couldn't.

Moore issued a shriveling scowl and bound upstairs two steps at a time.

The man had just met Miss Jones and was already possessive of his lovely housekeeper. Phaeton could not fathom a clue why he found this disclosure so disturbing. He glanced over her way. She wore the attractive emerald green dress with the plaid overskirt. One after another, several clean plates were placed on the washboard to drain. She caught him admiring her backside.

Her smile, while always pretty, seemed a bit thin. "Please don't torture Mr. Moore. He has been very kind, and he happens to be the only man by my side at the moment."

"That's horribly unfair and untrue." He stood up and moved in close. Gently he rubbed against her bustle. "I am behind you all the way, miss."

She turned around, eyebrows drawn, lips in a bow. "Yes, but you're rather busy what with all this chasing about after a—*déesse qui suce le sang. Créature de vampire maraudant le Strand*—"

"Slowly, *lentement, mademoiselle.*" He found her eruption of French temperament stimulating. "You are very pretty when you are cross, but rather difficult to understand." He bent his head to make eye contact. "Try to keep me informed, and I shall do my very best to be of assistance on your case against the pirates."

She sighed. "Do you mean this, *monsieur?*"

"I rarely say anything I don't mean." He picked up her apron and dried her hands. They stood face to face and wonderfully close. "Now, I don't suppose you've had time to make supper?"

"I'm afraid not, Mr. Black."

"If you promise to read the *Kama Sutra* tonight, I shall take you out to dinner." Reaching around her waist, he untied the strings.

"The Cheshire Cheese offers fresh oysters and a baked fish most every Friday night." Eyes brighter, she tilted her chin.

"Mmm, very delectable." His gaze never left her mouth, the lips devastatingly pouty this evening. "I believe I lied to Detective Moore. You are not *entirely* safe with me, Miss Jones."

At the edge of the rooftop, Phaeton opened the case holding the Eye of Horus and shook the jar. The small creature sprang to life, gamely bashing itself against the curved walls of the glass container.

He could hardly imagine what kind of sorcery propelled the odd little pest rattling around inside the jar. Even though the netherworld was close for him, it remained elusive, out of his scope. To wake, in the dead of night, with a succubus heavy on his chest. Attend a gala event, laughing among friends as a demon's whisper shushed over his cheek. These were experiences he both tolerated and hid from the natural world.

After many years, he had learned to focus at the outside corners of his eyes. This way he could keep a watch over the fey creatures. Gargoyles with translucent wings and long slithering tails lurked in the dim shadows of his vision. Phaeton sighed, remembering a time when these shifts in awareness caused his spine to tingle. That didn't happen much anymore.

He had slogged on alone with these unusual visitations since childhood. The opium helped. Drifting along in a cloud of insensibility deadened the racing thoughts. Other times, he actually baited the green fairy to appear.

Phaeton settled himself against a chimney stack and waited for Exeter to set up a wooden tripod and attach some sort of biocular telescope. Quite unexpectedly, he had found a possible mentor, and he hungered for answers. It was rare enough to discover a human being with genuine gifts. London was filled to the brim with occult charlatans. Scads of crystal ball readers, séance holders, and sundry mesmerizers, all courting an easily deceived, zealous clientele. But Dr. Exeter, it seemed, possessed a number of quite astonishing gifts. A man of science and metaphysics. Rare, indeed.

A blanket of grey cloud cover hung over the jagged rooflines along the Embankment. Phaeton's perusal ended on the austere silhouette of the obelisk guarded by a bronze sphinx. A rise in pulse hinted at the mysteries he might uncover this evening.

Peering through the eyepieces, Exeter adjusted the instrument. "Mist rising from around the obelisk."

"Do we have a goddess on the hunt?"

"I believe so." The doctor straightened.

"If you don't mind my asking, what's to stop our little orb from following after its mistress?"

"Exactly why we will give her time to venture off."

While they waited, Phaeton ticked off their level of preparedness. The metropolitan police had a squadron of men stationed near the theatre ready to be called into service at a moment's notice. Once he and the doctor found and destroyed the nest, they would need the extra officers as well as the fire brigade on hand.

"Loose our pigeon, Mr. Black."

Phaeton adjusted his pair of red-tinted goggles before opening the jar. The flying nuisance bolted out of the container and hovered for an instant before swooping down along the river. It took both sets of eyes and Exeter's vision enhancing instruments to keep up with the fluttering little orb.

"I can't see anything but a trail of vapor." Phaeton followed a trace of shimmering glow as it flew circles around the obelisk. "I don't believe it. The damn thing can't find a way in."

A glowing red tail dashed over pavement and wiggled around the head of a sphinx before its peculiar homing device abruptly rose high into the air. Hovering at nearly the height of the monument, it took a dive toward the water and disappeared. Phaeton noted the approximate spot using a nearby lamppost as a marker.

They waited a moment to see if the eye would reappear. Nothing.

Exeter turned and leapt across the rooftops of several buildings and waited. "No time like the present." Phaeton took a deep breath. With each jump his racing heart rate slowed until he followed after the man with relative ease.

Both of them landed safely on the ground. "You are showing improvement, Mr. Black."

"I'd rather not think about it." Phaeton glanced around the alley. "Where's the petrol?"

The doctor nodded to a row of dustbins. Phaeton retrieved both cans, handing one off.

Side by side, they sprinted for the river, carefully searching along the water's edge for any sign of the little drone. Just east of the needle, Phaeton stopped at a gas lamp. "This is where the eye dropped out of sight."

He leaned well over the embankment railing. "Nothing but a grotty old barge tie-up and a storm drain." His gaze once again traveled over the retaining wall to an iron grate covering the flood control channel. "We're going to need a rope."

Exeter peered over the edge and studied the opening. "There's a manhole not far from here. I rooted about down there a week ago. There will likely be some sort of access to the storm drains from below."

Phaeton dropped down into the sludge of the sewer and

waited for the doctor to lower the cans of petrol. He removed a cylindrical metal object from his coat pocket.

Having no need for ladder rungs, Exeter landed beside him. "What is that?"

"You're not the only one with gadgets, doctor." Phaeton toggled the switch. "An experimental torch, compliments of Scotland Yard. Runs off dry cell batteries." He banged the apparatus in his palm and a strong circle of light illuminated the tunnel. "Ah, there we are."

Exeter motioned him forward. "Lead on, Mr. Black."

Slogging southward, they came to a T connection not two hundred feet from the Thames. Phaeton pivoted right, then left. "Any guess as to which way?"

A deep, howling moan echoed in answer. He flashed the beam and lit up the doctor's face. He suspected his own eyes were as bright as Exeter's—the thrill of danger and what not.

"No doubt she's left apparitions here and there to terrify intruders; it's best to go quickly now." The doctor nodded toward the river. "Try this passage."

They found a walkway, more like a narrow ledge, which allowed them to jog slowly alongside a trench of sewer sludge. The growls and moans continued to emanate up and down the tunnel, conveniently chasing off a few rats in their way. When the unearthly howls finally quieted, it was the silence that seemed unnatural.

Phaeton directed the torch over a crumbling patch of rock and debris. "Blimey."

A gaping breach in the sewer wall. Huge, irregular chunks of mortar and stone partially blocked the way ahead. Exeter sprang up onto one of the larger blocks to get a better look through the opening.

He turned toward Phaeton and gave him an assist up. Beyond the crevice, the light beam revealed a good-sized chamber, filled with sand and odds bits of carved stone.

"Hieroglyphs."

"The lair?

"Either that or close to it."

Phaeton was the first to climb into the opening. He dropped down into a soft bed of dry earth and waited for Exeter. Slowly, he swept the torch into each dark corner until he settled on the stone ruins in the middle of the space.

The doctor landed beside him.

"Now what?"

Exeter moved forward cautiously. "If I am not mistaken, the nest is straight ahead."

With every step, sand shifted underfoot. Carefully circling the remains of a stone coffin, Phaeton peered into the open sarcophagus. Nothing but a clean, dry bed of earth inside. "Not a glamorous abode for an ancient goddess. No wonder she's prickly." The torchlight flickered over a makeshift stone shelf. A row of glass jars and crockery lined up like a column of soldiers.

Phaeton took down a brown container and sniffed. "Eeesh." He pointed the light down into the mouth of the receptacle. "Dead rodent, perhaps?"

Returning the crock, he studied the clear glass jars. "If I am not mistaken, doctor, some of these bits of flesh appear to be human organs."

"When the great kings and queens of Egypt passed from this life, we know they were embalmed and mummified. Organs were removed and stored in jars." Exeter lifted up what remained of a simple reed sleeping mat. "Upon the pharaoh's awakening, the organs were to be returned to the body, as his servants readied him for the arduous journey into the underworld."

Phaeton took another glance at the contents of the jars. "Might the assumption be that she is collecting organs for herself? Or is this exercise in mayhem wrought for someone else? She is a goddess, after all. Do the gods perform these rituals on each other?"

"You ask for answers far beyond my ken."

Phaeton sucked in a breath.

"What is wrong, Mr. Black? Even in the dark, you are obviously distraught." The doctor's voice echoed softly off the walls of the chamber.

"The Whitechapel murders. Mary Kelly, the last victim. Found her cut to shreds, her own organs removed and lined up neatly around her body." Phaeton sensed a growing tension in the atmosphere. The doctor took a position to one side of the sarcophagus.

He pointed the torch directly at Exeter, who blinked under the harsh glare. "You two have been at this game for some time. What is this for you, doctor, round two? Abating or abetting, which is it?"

"Shall we save this discussion for another day? Right now we need to destroy the nest."

Phaeton kept the light steady. "The nest or the evidence, doctor?"

The man sighed. "What do you wish to know?"

A rush of wailing, hissing shrieks sounded from somewhere above.

"She returns. We have no time for argument." Exeter shifted his focus to the can of petrol. Opening the tin, he drenched the interior of the sarcophagus.

Phaeton hesitated, but only for a moment. He tossed off the gas cap and doused the chamber floor in petrol. The scratching, hissing noise returned. He flashed the torch upward onto the ceiling and froze. "At your first opportunity, take a glance at the object overhead."

Phaeton set a stick of dynamite in the sand and unwound a coil of fuse wire.

Exeter placed one foot behind the other and slowly traced his steps backward, toward the opening in the wall. "I know what I perceive. What do you see?"

He glanced upward and followed after. "A large black stain spreading—rapidly."

"I see an orifice, with large fangs for tearing and chewing." The doctor pointed to a number of pointed objects project-

ing from what was now beginning to look more like a cavernous hole.

"Ah yes, but is this muzzle real or illusion?" Phaeton unrolled more wire as the gaping mouth moved off the ceiling
and inched down the wall.

"Light the fuse. Quickly, Mr. Black, before we are swallowed."

The moment he lit the wire, his body was lifted out of the
chamber. The walls of the sewer sped by in a blur. He rock-
eted through the tunnel, passing ladder rungs as he flew up
and out of the manhole.

Phaeton stood in the middle of the lane. Dizzy.

He became aware of the clatter of horse hooves and the
creak of carriages traveling along the Strand. The thought
crossed his mind that it was not terribly late. Cloud cover
parted overhead and he could see several stars twinkle in the
ink-black sky.

"Come." Exeter appeared out of nowhere and encouraged
him to leap from garden wall to window ledge to rooftop.
Exactly as he had seen this strange man escape that first night
after the opera.

With his usual amount of trepidation, Phaeton sailed from
one rooftop to another with the help of the curious physician, who remained a first-class enigma. Tonight, at the very
least, he took satisfaction in matching Exeter jump for jump.

The dynamite detonated while Phaeton was in midair.

Chapter Eleven

A THUNDEROUS BOOM AND DISPLACEMENT OF ATMOSPHERE pushed his body through the air. Phaeton tumbled onto the roof and groaned. Rolling onto his back, his addled brain focused on the tall, indistinct man standing above him. An appendage with fuzzy fingers appeared in front of his face. He grabbed hold of a flesh and blood hand and was pulled to his feet. "Blast shock. You should fully recover in a few moments. Can you hear me?" It was Exeter's voice all right, only it came from the bottom of a barrel.

Propped against a chimney pot, Phaeton rubbed his eyes and the doctor came into focus. He signaled thumbs-up.

Rather quickly, he was able to survey the scene below as Exeter packed up his optical device. A plume of acrid, hissing smoke bellowed out of the fissure as the river flooded into the gaping breach in the retaining wall. Towering behind a curtain of vapor, he could just make out the Egyptian obelisk seemingly no worse for the explosion.

"Thank the Thames for coming to the aid of our lackadaisical fire brigade." At least he recognized his own voice.

Shrill police whistles joined the gasps and cries from the local onlookers. Jolted out of their beds by the explosion, a group of frightened, angry residents pushed back against the squadron of officers on the scene.

"What could be more inept? The Metropolitan Police appear to need protection from the citizenry." He swiveled away from the river. "Ready for home? Do impart my regards to your pretty charge, doctor."

Exeter's steady gaze met his. "I must say, Mia was quite taken with your detective stories at tea."

"Your ward is a clever conversationalist. A very bright girl." He shifted his full attention to his cohort. "She, as well as your African man, call you Oom Asa."

"An honorific of sorts. Oom means chieftain in Zulu." The doctor shrugged. "Mia's parents were unfortunate casualties of the Boer War—caught in a crossfire in the Transvaal. She and Mr. Tandi arrived on my doorstep five years ago." Exeter picked up his equipment case. "Mia is only distantly related to me, but they are both family now."

A new round of shrieks accompanied a deep rumble as another section of the Embankment gave way. Phaeton's attention drifted back momentarily to the chaotic scene at the river walk.

"Two dens down, more left to find," the doctor murmured.

"I am skeptical. You mentioned three or four, earlier. Why not a dozen? I continue to suspect you withhold information." He returned to Exeter. "I also harbor growing suspicions regarding this female necromancer. Shortly after the last homicide attributed to the Ripper November last, a fire was set on Dorset Street. It gives me cause to wonder if Mary Kelly's murder isn't somehow connected to nest number one."

His head ached. He rubbed his temples and considered his words carefully. "There has been a fair amount of conjecture given to the idea that the Whitechapel fiend might well be either a physician or a female. What if the Ripper turned out to be both a Jack and a Jill?"

Phaeton chewed a bit of inside cheek. "Before I retire, I intend to offer my assistance to the poor officers at risk from the unhinged locals." He studied the inscrutable man beside him. Exeter was hard to read, but this time his face was ashen. "I recommend you use what is left of the evening to prepare a confession or alibi. Your life expectancy depends on it, Doctor Exeter."

"When she raises both of her legs, and places them on her lover's shoulders, it is called the 'yawning position.' " America stared at the book illustration. The female engaged in the unusual congress displayed commendable flexibility.

She turned the page and tilted her head. "When the woman places one of her thighs across the thigh of her lover it is called the 'twining position.' " Two copper-colored bodies reclined on an intricately woven carpet. A tray of ripe fruits and cups of wine sat beside the amorous couple. She admired the size and apparent hardness of the man's member. According to the caption, he was about to plunge his *lingam* into his partner's *yoni*.

At least this pose seemed more feasible than the last picture. From the moment she had opened the book, there had been a stirring in her body. So far, her response to the drawings had been brazenly immodest. The *Kama Sutra* turned out to be utterly titillating. She squirmed at the sensation of moisture between her legs.

And her naughty imaginings and desires, with some constancy, involved Mr. Black. He had advised her to pick one of these ridiculous positions, and he would attempt to please her. She uttered an exasperated sigh. The man was a cad and a pervert. And she would never in a million years participate in a single one of these hopeless postures with him.

Earlier that evening, they had found a quiet corner in the cavernous old pub, the Cheshire Cheese. She had matched him swallow for swallow, devouring a dozen oysters each, before supping on seafood chowder and fresh baked bread.

He had sprinkled cayenne pepper and lemon juice over the plump, succulent meat before holding the knobby half shell to her mouth. She had swallowed the oyster in one gulp and licked her lips. *Mmm.* Underneath the table, he took her hand and placed it on his crotch. "You see what you do to me, Miss Jones?"

She had yanked her hand back and shot the rake a withering glare. He had chuckled over her indignation and prepared another oyster in apology.

A scurry of footsteps and a peel of high-pitched laughter filtered down from the brothel upstairs. The house was often raucous in the evenings. A comfort to her when Mr. Black so often worked late hours.

The clock on the mantel chimed a single stroke. *Where was he?* America yawned.

Sprawled out over the chaise, chin cupped in the palm of her hand, she turned the book upside down to view a difficult new pose. She could not fathom how the act of love could be accomplished in this tangle of limbs.

She absently twined and untwined her legs. " 'When a man, during congress, turns round, and enjoys the woman without leaving her, while all the while, she embraces him round the back, it is called the 'turning position,' and is learnt only by practice.' "

She snorted. "Impossible."

"Nothing is out of the question, Miss Jones, with enough discipline and rehearsal."

So, her employer was home.

To hide a smile, she didn't look up. "Perhaps not impossible but rather strenuous, if you ask me." She propped herself upright, leaving the illustrated volume open to the pose in question.

He tilted his head. "Ah yes, the turning position. Tricky, but I would be delighted to work on it with you." His gaze moved off the drawing to her. "Is this your choice?"

She puffed herself up with a huff. "Absolutely not, and I am quite sure there will never be a choice."

He turned away and hung up his coat and hat. "Has the

book not provided you with a wonderful selection of plea-sures?" He then removed his jacket and unbuttoned his waistcoat.

She cleared her throat. "What are you doing, Mr. Black?"

"Undressing." He lifted the kettle from the stove and poured warm water into a basin. He shrugged out of the vest and unbuttoned his shirt to the waist. With a soap cake in hand, he began to wash up.

"Please do pick a position of some difficulty. After a bit of scrubbing, I shall be ready to perform my duties."

He wet a dishcloth with water and rubbed it over his chest and underarms.

She snickered. "Difficult for which one of us? As far as I can see, the women in these illustrations do the lion's share of work."

He grinned that wolfish fornicator grin. Drat the man. Water glistened over his torso as he took a clean towel and dried off his very appealing ruff of chest hair. There it was again, the tingly sensation. The same one she had experi-enced when Mr. Black stood very close. Or took her hand. Or kissed her.

She whisked the erotic tome out from under him as he took a seat. "If I am not mistaken, you and I have already completed two of these positions." He tugged at the picture book. "May I?"

A half naked man pressed up beside her was most distract-ing. His upper body hard and masculine and—

"Do you recall our first time, Miss Jones?"

Leafing through the volume, he stopped at a page depict-ing a man standing upright lifting a woman onto his mem-ber by cupping her buttocks.

America glanced at the drawing and gulped. "Of course I remember."

The ends of his mouth quirked up. "The night you forced yourself upon me."

"I didn't—exactly . . ." She bit back a frown. Intolerable man!

His smile widened as he continued shuffling pages. "I'm looking for . . . ah, here we are. 'When she raises her thighs and keeps them apart and engages in congress, it is called the 'widely open position.' " He glanced across the sitting room at the overstuffed chair. "Right over there, wasn't it?"

Her bottom lip slipped out from under her teeth.

"Your inaugural zenith of pleasure."

"Hmm-ph, I'm not entirely sure about that zenith bit." The prickly, quivering sensation was back as she recalled his fingers swirling over her hidden female parts and his large phallus driving into her. She chanced to look at Mr. Black directly and found him studying her expression.

Warmth flooded her cheeks. All right, she had not been entirely honest with him. America relented with a sigh. "I do remember it being very agreeable."

"Would you like to feel agreeable again?"

She nodded. "Yes."

"Brilliant. We shall start at the front and work our way back through page . . ." He flipped to the back of the book. "One hundred and nineteen."

"All of them, tonight?" Her eyes bugged out.

He chuckled. "Not unless you plan on throwing my back out." With his index finger holding place, he closed the tome and reclined against the sloping arm of the chaise. He patted the space beside him.

Without much hesitation, she reclined.

"Are we a bit starchy tonight, Miss Jones?" He nestled close and turned her onto her side. "Put your arm around me." She rather enjoyed the sensation of his damp skin and the clean scent of soap. His upper arms were strong and muscled, and she liked holding onto them. He turned to an early chapter of the text.

"For the duration of this exercise, I shall call you *Sin-nay*."

He pronounced her middle name with an emphasis on the first syllable. He held up the book somewhere behind her head.

He shifted his body and moved his upper leg against hers. "This is called the embrace of the thighs." He turned her belly toward his and pressed his hips to hers.

Her belly trembled as he shifted his weight against her. His face, close to hers, reminded her of the first night she had laid eyes on him. She suddenly couldn't help herself, and before she could gain any control over her hand, she had reached out and stroked the dark temptation of unshaven whisker hairs. She traced a faint, nearly invisible scar that ran along the edge of a firm jawline.

Her gesture stopped his recitation midsentence.

She withdrew and managed an uneasy laugh but he caught her hand in his, and returned her fingers to his stubbly cheek and handsomely formed mouth. Gently, he turned her hand palm up and brushed his lips down to the faint pulse on the inside of her wrist.

He said nothing, but his sable eyes darkened into pools of desire.

After a lengthy perusal of her lips, he cleared his throat. "Navels." Arousal surged through her body as, one at a time, from forehead to shin bone, he pressed parts of his anatomy to hers. Sometimes rubbing, other times barely touching her.

He flipped the page. " 'Pressing, marking, or scratching with the nails'—some of my favorites."

Two of her fingers were selected. "Scratching." He placed her fingertips on his chest. "Press lightly." She ran her nails over the hard curve of his breast and followed a thin trail of hair past his navel.

"Again. Harder this time."

She pressed into taught flesh as he groaned. "Ah yes, Síne."

He unbuttoned his trousers, and placed one of her fingers on his groin. His voice grew husky. "Now, mark me."

His stomach muscles shuddered as her nail nicked into his flesh. A rose-colored slash emerged across his lower belly. His belly trembled

Her fascination began at the edge of his dark man curls and moved from his lower abdomen along a sinuous torso. She could not resist spreading her fingers through his chest hair. When her gaze met his, she caught her breath.

"Have a care, my temptress, or you will turn me into Wagner the Wehr-Wolf." He placed a kiss on each one of her fingertips, and then removed her blouse and camisole. Even as his body temperature warmed her flesh, the air chilled her breasts and hardened the tips. He ran his nails over each mound until her arousal became so great, she moaned and demanded more. Only then did he scrape harder over her nipples.

With his thumb, he marked her with a curved line. "A Tiger's nail."

Her female parts ached for his touch. She thrust her pelvis against him. Her desire, a heat wave of primal demands, danced along an invisible edge of pleasure. When her breath became rapid and shallow, Mr. Black ceased his ministrations and embraced her.

"Not yet." Holding on while her belly quivered, he stroked the small of her back, easing her sudden, ferocious arousal.

He swept loose curls away from her cheek. "You are a very responsive young woman."

Another shiver ravaged her body. "I have been debauched by you, Mr. Black, and all those wicked illustrations."

"Would it surprise you to know that I believe it is I who has been seduced?" His eyes crinkled as his attention turned to her mouth. "Place your lips here." He touched his mouth as she leaned closer. With her eyes barely open, she pressed lightly, but did not open her mouth.

"That is called the 'nominal kiss.'" His usual teasing grin softened. Even his ebony gaze, filled with hunger, seemed different. The reference book had slipped into a deep crack of the sofa cushion. She hardly gave a care as she continued her kisses.

America Síne Jones just might succeed with her enchantment.

When had this happened, exactly? Phaeton's memory poured over her initial week of employment and then dug further back. From their first encounter, she had captured him with more than a blade. Her delectable charms had woven a spell of some kind. Something he was unfamiliar with and shy of fighting.

"When I kissed you in your room the other night, I used my tongue." With his thumb, he brushed over her lips, parting them. Olive-toned cheeks, flushed with arousal, turned a pale rose. "Do your best, my dear."

Her tongue licked the inside edge of his upper lip and pushed inside. He answered her by surrounding her with his arms and pressing her body against his. When he finished, they both lay gasping for air. His rock hard cock throbbed against her belly.

A wild, prurient desire came close to overwhelming his manners. He wanted to do unspeakable things to her. Using his tongue, he would delve into the nest of curls between her thighs. Or perhaps redden her derriere with the flat of his hand and then enter and ride her like the beast he undoubtedly was.

At the very least, he wished to kiss each breast and suckle those pretty tips until they grew hard and pointed. But that would certainly lead to intercourse. With enormous difficulty, he shifted away and sat up. The act of coitus must be her idea this time.

For a moment, he thought to take her and be done with it, but that would mean risking . . . What would that signify exactly? He paused. Might her respect and affection be in jeopardy? Odd, that he would entertain such a concern.

If he made her his concubine, her resentment would grow even as his appetite for her mounted. Once he bedded her in earnest, he might never be able to stop. He wished her to experience every position in the *Kama Sutra* as well as *The Garden of Pleasure.*

That could take months—years.

"Enough lessons for one evening." Gingerly, he rose from the chaise, his erection painful and obvious. "Good night, Miss Jones."

She raised herself onto elbows and stared, openmouthed. "Good night, Mr. Black."

The soft timbre of her answer caused him to glance back at those exotic golden eyes and rounded breasts. Somehow he made his way to his room, closed the door, and undressed in darkness.

As bewitched as he was by her sensuous body and those amazing lips, his need for her stemmed from something deeper. Yes, her bold as brass, strong-willed personality captivated, but she was also a supernatural force to be reckoned with. Somehow this essence of hers heightened his own arousal. Did he have a similar affect upon her? He wondered.

On rare occasions he engaged in self-gratification. And this night, with his cock threatening to burst on its own, he thought it best to give it a whack.

The door creaked open. "I've nearly decided. It's between two positions."

Chapter Twelve

"Do not come in here, Miss Jones, unless you desire me inside you."

The lamp she held high illuminated one side of her shapely figure. The rest of her form disappeared into velvet blackness. Her thin wrapper, open in the front, revealed tantalizing details of her nude figure.

Placing one bare foot in front of the other, her strides were slow, erotic, mesmerizing. He could not take his eyes away.

"Either page twenty-eight or fifty-five, Mr. Black." The slightest pique in her voice enhanced her sensuous, provocative movements. She set the lamp down on the bed stand and turned the wick low.

Phaeton craved her.

His balls, a right pretty shade of blue, ached as her gaze roamed over his torso. His cock danced in anticipation of her nearness, her touch.

"You are naked and . . ." In the dim light her eyes widened. "The duke is quite large, isn't he?"

"I was just in the process of providing him some relief." He followed the narrow opening of her robe and lingered a moment on the dimple her navel made on a smooth belly. He then lowered his gaze to a shadow of triangle. "And you will be ready for him, when the time comes."

She slipped out of her robe and placed a knee on the bed.

"How could you leave me in such a state?" On all fours, she drew closer.

Until this moment, he had never seen her hair down. A thick, soft halo of waves fell past her shoulders. His fingers tangled in the mass of curls as he pulled her down for a kiss.

He grinned. "What kind of state? Describe it to me."

Brows drawn and lips pouted, she growled. "Squirmy and, and . . ."

"Frustrated?"

She nodded. "Exactly."

The aggressive little minx climbed on top and straddled him. He stroked nicely rounded hips and worked his way up to a dainty waist. His phallus smacked against a plump cheek of her buttocks.

Wheels turned behind sultry, almond-shaped eyes. She smiled. "Page twenty-eight. The position is called the woman acting the part of the man."

He cupped her breasts and rubbed thumbs over taut peaks. The wide spread of her legs beckoned, and he delved into her *mystères femme* until his fingers were soaked with arousal. "You are more than welcome to ride me, or enjoy being ridden like this—"

He lifted her up off his body, and encouraged her to support herself on hands and knees. "Page fifty-five. The jump of the tiger." He pressed up behind her and used his fingers to prepare her opening.

"The congress of the elephant." She groaned as he pushed into her.

"I shall go slowly." He nuzzled the nape of her neck and kissed the wings of her shoulder blades.

She took his hand and moved it back to her small spot of intense pleasure. "Already so demanding." He snorted a chuckle and used two fingers to tickle and swirl.

On his knees, he pumped into her, inching deeper. He was dangerously close. On the edge of his own climax, he rubbed her plump derriere, and experienced a sudden desire to smack both firm round globes. She cried out in surprise at the unexpected slap, but a flood of wetness gave her away. He massaged away the sting.

"Please." Her breath was soft and rapid.

"Please yes, or please no?"

"Please again," she gasped, and he paddled her ass and rubbed her arousal spot until she shuddered and moaned her release.

He soothed her with soft strokes over her female parts until she bucked and pushed his hand away. Her shattering climax had surged through him, rocketing his own arousal near to the precipice. He removed his cock and leaned over the mattress, opening a drawer of the bed stand.

"We're not done yet?" Her brows converged and her lips pursed.

He tucked her into his arms and opened a tin box.

"Condoms?"

"I beg your pardon, miss, these are called French letters." He kissed the side of her cheek. "And very expensive ones, I might add."

"Must we?"

"Unless you desire to bear my children, I recommend their use."

He lifted himself up and positioned himself above her. "You, my beauty, are assuaged, for the moment." He straddled her pelvis and stroked his long thickness, which remained large and threatening.

"I, on the other hand, will be coming along shortly." He smiled down at her. "So to speak."

He showed her how to roll on the thin, rubber prophylactic.

"Like hard velvet." She stroked his shaft and he sucked air through his teeth.

He took a turn with each of her breasts. He suckled and

bit and laved each nipple until she spoke through a sigh and a whimper. "Perhaps I am not finished, yet."

He spread her legs, grabbed her by the waist, and pressed into her. Easier this time. She hooked a leg over his arm, and he raised it to his shoulder. Slanting her pelvis upward, she lifted her other leg to his shoulder.

"Yawning position," he groaned. His hands slipped under her buttocks to help support her back. He increased his thrusts, careful not to plunge too deeply. At this angle, he might hurt her.

"Cup your breasts, for me." His eyes were intense, like his demands.

"Like this?" She teased. "Or perhaps something more like this?" She twisted the tips and he begged for more of her erotic play.

"Wonderful, desirable, wanton female."

His member, nicely thick and well lubricated, rubbed into places that were meant to pleasure them both. Her sheath became increasingly receptive, and she pushed up to meet him as he increased the speed and force of his thrusts.

He gripped her buttocks as his body shuddered from chest to throbbing shaft. One last drive. "Yes." He exhaled the growl of a predatory beast and collapsed onto the bed.

Awestruck or dumbfounded, he pulled her against him and exhaled. Never had he experienced such intensity of pleasure. His heart pounded inside his chest, pushing blood to every tingling fingertip. He jerked and shuddered a second time when she turned around and wrapped a leg around him.

"The duke was very deep inside."

"My penis has been called many things, Miss Jones, but never by his rightful title."

"I shall call him *le duc du plaisir*."

He angled his chin and lowered a kiss to her temple. "Always glad to pleasure you."

"And what do you call him?"

With the back of a knuckle, he scratched an itchy eye. "Which body part of mine might you be referring to, Miss?"

"Perched on the side chair," she whispered. "He's been watching us, since—well I suppose we put on quite a show."

He lifted his head, brows drawn together in a squint. The familiar grim-faced elfish gargoyle crouched in the deep shadows of his usual corner. "Edvar The Sneaky."

She dissolved into snorts of soft laughter.

"I was only four or five when I named him." Phaeton balled up a pillow and fired it across the room. The creature faded with the exception of pale yellow eyes that blinked in the darkness.

"Annoying little fiend follows me around. Pay him no mind, or he'll pester you into Bedlam."

"I don't believe he wishes you any harm." She swept a thick bunch of curls behind her shoulder. "In fact"—she peered into the black corner—"I sense protectiveness. Perhaps he is your guardian."

He propped himself up on an elbow and blinked, wide-eyed. "No one has ever seen Edvar, until now. Mother may have glimpsed his tail slither under my bed once."

"So your abilities come from your *maman*, as well."

Phaeton tugged her down beside him and kissed her several times. Soft, sensuous nibbles along her throat and over her chin. He pushed his leg between her thighs.

"Síne?"

"Yes, Mr. Black."

America's nose awoke to the savory aroma of bangers in the skillet. Another whiff confirmed sausage and a bit of scrambled egg. Mr. Black was making breakfast. Her stomach rumbled.

Something moved under the sheets and nearly caused her to jump off the mattress. A deeply satisfied groan came from beneath a pillow. A hand reached around her waist and pulled her against a hard shaft and warm body.

The man was ready again? She took a moment to admire his stamina. They'd had a go with nearly a half dozen positions last night. She sighed.

But if her employer snoozed beside her, who was cooking breakfast? "Mr. Black?"

"Mmm, what is it my dove?"

She quite liked the croak in his morning voice. "It's about breakfast."

He raised the pillow and sniffed. "Miss Jones, you are a marvel. Shall we eat in bed and have seconds? Or would that be thirds or fourths for us? I've lost count." He traveled a hand up her belly to cradle a breast.

"I awoke to the scent of sausage and egg, same as you. The point is—who is in your pantry?"

He shot upright and cocked his head.

"Perhaps one of the ladies from above stairs?" A disturbing thought. She did not relish the idea of anyone, other than herself, fixing breakfast for him.

He shook his head. "Late workers those girls. I'd wager most of them have yet to kick the last john out of bed." He slipped out from under the covers and grabbed his trousers.

"Do you suppose Edvar has taken a turn in the kitchen?"

"Wouldn't that be a score. No, if that was possible, I'd have turned the little monster into my valet years ago."

She wasn't about to argue with the man first thing in the morning. But she very distinctly remembered his clothing strewn about the floor last night. This morning, his pants were folded neatly and hung over the foot rails.

Finished buttoning his pants, he opened the door and peered down the hall. He swung back into the room. "I believe our phantom cook is Doctor Exeter."

America jumped out of bed and grabbed her wrapper. "What is he doing here?"

He took another peek. "Perhaps, he is about to be arrested."

She slipped into her room across the hall, hoping not to miss the excitement of an arrest or a bite of egg and sausage. She washed up quickly, tied her hair back in a ribbon, and dressed.

An elegantly attired, handsome man noted her entrance with a great deal of interest. "You have a guest, Mr. Black?"

"Doctor Jason Exeter, please meet America Jones."

She dipped a curtsy and lifted her arm.

"Delighted." He kissed the back of her hand.

"Doctor Exeter has been so kind as to prepare a breakfast. Please join us." While her employer returned to his room to finish dressing, America set about helping the doctor ready the table and fill three plates.

"Tea or coffee, Mr. Black?"

"We have coffee?"

The tall man took a seat at the table holding a carafe of aromatic, dark brown liquid. "Seems I can't start the day without it. Stopped by Mason and Fortnum on my way here."

Phaeton scratched his head. "How late is it?"

Exeter sipped and swallowed. "After ten in the morning."

Mr. Black scooped up a forkful of egg and changed the subject. "Have you an alibi or a confession for me, doctor?"

The gentleman glanced at her and raised a brow.

"Feel free to speak in front of Miss Jones. It was she who identified that spying little orb as Egyptian. She is a kind of . . . assistant to me." He winked at her.

Narrowly avoiding an ogle, the doctor returned his gaze to Mr. Black. "I have an offer."

"You don't believe I'll negotiate." Her employer sliced through a plump sausage. "Do you?"

"You are invited for a weekend in Twickenham, the family's estate. It is time you were introduced to my father, Mr. Black. If you are to understand what has happened here in

London these past few months, it is imperative you hear the truth from him."

"So, the elusive Baron de Roos is alive."

Exeter's unflappable demeanor chilled. "No doubt Scotland Yard would like to know one way or the other."

Mr. Black chewed on a last bit of sausage. "Scotland Yard is curious."

Exeter sighed. "My father is perhaps days away from his grave. If you would make your way to Roos House on the Thames you will learn the truth of the matter. Then, in due course, you can decide whether you want to have me arrested or not."

"Truth is a very good start." Over the edge of a coffee cup, his eyes narrowed on the doctor. "Answers, better."

"You will have both, Mr. Black." The dark, reserved man rose to leave. "I shall accompany Mia and Mr. Tandi. We leave this afternoon by ferry." He nodded to her. "Miss Jones is welcome to join."

POST OFFICE INLAND TELEGRAM
28 FEBRUARY 1889 9:00 AM
TO: AMERICA JONES

IN RECEIPT OF SHIPS REGISTRIES STOP
PREPARE TO LEAVE FOR PORTSMOUTH
AGENT MOORE

She read the telegram and nearly fainted. Perhaps all was not lost. If her heart could sing, it would be trilling an aria. Light-headed and breathless, she could barely contain the surge of hope and joy quaking through her.

Mr. Black read the missive over her shoulder. "I see Agent Moore wants to get cracking."

"Oh yes, I believe this is very good news, don't you?"

"You shall have a very relaxing, pampered weekend with me at Roos House." He kissed her neck which always caused a shiver. "Then, first of the week, we shall travel on to Portsmouth and reconnoiter with Mr. Moore."

Her eyes glistened. "You will go with me? Help me find my father's ships and arrest Yanky Willem?"

"I told you I would help you whenever possible." He moved around the table. "And you will not travel to Portsmouth accompanied by Dexter Moore. The man's a—"

"A roué and a seducer?" She lowered her eyelids and shot him a smoldering gaze. "Nothing like you, Mr. Black."

"He does his best to hide it." When he raised a haughty brow, she found it impossible not to scoff.

"Which would you rather have, my dear? A man who is honest and forthright about his proclivities or a profligate underhanded cheat?"

A sudden revelation caused her brows to furrow. "Oh, but I cannot accompany you to Roos House, Mr. Black."

"Why ever not? You received an invitation. I heard it myself."

She hesitated, bit her lip, and then blurted it out. "I have nothing to wear."

Chapter Thirteen

HIS WIDE-EYED STARE CAUSED AMERICA TO TURN AWAY. She carried their breakfast dishes to the pantry counter and filled a dishpan with water. Rare, to catch Mr. Black unawares.

"We'll go shopping."

She spun around. "I've not a farthing to spare on clothes."

"But you have a generous employer who can easily purchase a few dresses."

The man was positively wicked to obligate her in such a way. A terrible ache in her chest led to a rush of yearning. A new wardrobe was an agonizing temptation. "I cannot accept such an extravagant gift, Mr. Black."

His gaze narrowed to a squint. "Ah yes, you refuse to be my concubine."

"I will not play your simpering doxy."

He brightened. "You are on the brink of recovering your shipping business, Miss Jones. Once you get your sea legs back, so to speak, you can repay me."

She swirled soap flakes into a teacup of hot water and stirred with her finger. "An acceptable offer. But only if I include a reasonable amount of interest." She dried her hands on her apron. "I'll need the use of your fountain pen and a sheet of paper."

At the kitchen table, she wrote out a promissory note.

A small snort from over her shoulder meant he was annoyed by either the amount of interest or her atrocious penmanship. "Drop that to four and a half percent, Miss Jones. No sense in paying me any more than the short-term bank rate."

"I believe I wrote down exactly the going rate, but if you insist." She crossed out the number. "What about Agent Moore?"

"Keep him abreast by telegraph." He leaned forward to initial the note. "If we are to reconnoiter at Portsmouth Harbor, he can reach us at Roos House, Twickenham."

Not entirely returned to her employee role, America turned her head and kissed his cheek. "Thank you, Mr. Black."

He drew her back for a kiss on the lips. "Now, we can spend what is left of the day shopping along Oxford Street. Or there is Harrod's. '*Omnia Omnibus Ubiqat ue*—All Things for All People, Everywhere' is their motto. I'm told the store offers some very fine apparel, ready-made. Since time is a factor—"

"Harrod's will be fine."

After another stolen kiss, he let her go. "I shall arrange for transportation and wire Detective Moore."

A charge of elation tempered her every thought as she packed his suitcase and a leather satchel. She saw the bags as well as herself into the waiting carriage. She was actually traveling with the man.

He smiled at her from the opposite side of the coach, and she knew exactly what he was thinking. The memory of all those positions she and Mr. Black had accomplished last night made her fidget against the comfortable upholstered seat.

She tried setting aside a number of awkward and troublesome thoughts, until she gave up and blurted out her most pressing concern. "You may accompany me, and help select my new attire, but you must allow me to pay for these purchases on my own. That will require the specified loan amount in banknotes."

"Your purchases will be simple enough, I have an account—"

She crossed her arms under her chest.

"Very well, Miss Jones." Mr. Black tapped on the roof of the coach and used the speaking tube. "Slight alteration in plans. We'll be making a stop at Lloyd's Bank on Waterloo Place."

He replaced the cone on its hook. "Do not vex me any further." The carriage rocked and their knees bumped just to emphasize his point. An exasperated glare, meant to intimidate her, did not.

"One more thing. A question, really. Do you plan to refer to me as—what? Who am I to be, Mr. Black? Certainly not your housekeeper." She scraped upper teeth over lower lip. "Perhaps a long lost sister. Your father might have had an indiscretion with a woman of color?"

"The Princess Serafine al Qatari is here to replenish her western wardrobe." Phaeton nodded a respectful bow to the assembled salesladies and attendants. "Alas, a number of her traveling trunks have gone missing and are presumed lost or stolen." He handed his card to a mature saleswoman of accommodating expression. "Mrs. Boswell.

"Phaeton Black, Scotland Yard, assigned to the service of Her Highness for security purposes and fashion advice." He lowered his voice, drawing the shop girls closer. "The princess intends to make an ungodly amount of purchases and wishes to proceed immediately. Discretion is paramount. Call as little attention to her highness as possible. Now, if you please?" The ladies whisked the princess into a spacious, elegant dressing room.

Phaeton was shown to a seat in an adjacent parlor, which featured a full-length looking glass framed in gilt. Immediately, he was surrounded by a bevy of young women, who brought him an assortment of newspapers, and at his request, replaced the sherry on the table with a good Scotch whiskey.

He gestured to a lovely girl hovering nearby. "Her Highness has asked me to inquire about undergarments. Dressing gowns, pantalettes, lacy camisoles, and the like? Preferably French. And do make sure they are silk."

The otherwise pale complexioned sales assistant turned a lurid shade of pink and ran off in pursuit of said unmentionables.

Phaeton sipped his whiskey, opened up the *Times*, and waited for the parade of fashion to begin.

The first dress. "Too pink."

And the pale peach? "Lovely, but for all those ruffles."

A boldly striped carriage dress with a crisp white collar and cuffs and a cornflower blue fitted pelisse made him sit up. "Yes." And when the attendant added a jaunty, high crowned hat in cobalt blue, he added, "Very striking."

Next came a crimson concoction with a dazzling array of scarlet plumes. "Awful. Where exactly would you wear that? To a hog slaughter?" His remark drew a withering glare from Her Highness, and a harrumph from the matronly sales woman.

For her part, Miss Jones had adopted the most alluring accent. What was the inflection exactly? Some appealing patois of French Creole. She raised a noble brow. "Monsieur Black, *comment vous savez*—you know fashion?"

"I often accompany the Princess Louise and Princess Beatrice on their shopping trips." A boldfaced lie, but since the two royal women were well known for their fashion sense, Phaeton narrowly redeemed himself.

He quickly gave the nod to a confection of emerald green satin. The gown featured a narrow bodice held up by the daintiest small sleeves, which fell off her shoulders and threatened to bare all if she so much as exhaled.

How he hoped she might take a deep breath.

A navy skirt, with a high-collar blouse and a brass-buttoned jacket complete with epaulettes also received his nod. But it was the deep plum-colored evening gown with plunging décolleté that left him speechless.

The pretty shop girl entered the dressing room carrying an armful of lingerie. From the top of the pile he held up a pair of sheer pantalettes with dainty lace edging.

Mrs. Boswell drained of color.

"You wouldn't happen to have a few girls free to model, would you? Like they do in Paris?" The elder saleswoman snatched the expensive French drawers out of his hands and shooed her twittering staffers into the back room.

"How disappointing."

The selection of shoes, gloves, and various sundry items went on interminably, and Phaeton left the dressing room to supervise the loading of a half dozen hat boxes and a trunk filled with dresses and delicate underthings into the carriage.

He waited at the curb and checked his pocket watch.

Finally, Princess Serafine exited the celebrated department store in all her splendor. Phaeton took a moment to appreciate his vivacious traveling companion.

"Your Highness, I'm afraid we have missed our rendezvous at the river ferry. However, Mr. Milner, owner and driver of this fine transport, has offered to take us on to Roos House."

"I will trust your decision in the matter, Mr. Black, if you promise to never, ever make another comment about my wardrobe choices."

He followed her inside the carriage. A large stack of hat boxes and packages filled up the opposite seat of the cabin. "I happen to be very good at knowing what looks dreadful or appealing on a woman."

"Yes, but do you have to be so . . ."

"Honest about it?" He sat down beside her.

They bickered from Knightsbridge until the terrain outside the coach turned to countryside. Having escaped London's congested boroughs, they now made their way through the quaint hamlets and expansive parklands, whose estates lined the river.

"At least the air is healthy to breathe." She stifled a yawn.

Phaeton quirked a side of his mouth. "You must be exhausted, trying on all those pretty things."

"Some of them not so pretty." She removed a wad of banknotes from her reticule and began folding back corners. "What did you call that last dress? Perfect for a funeral dirge."

"The garment was drab. No, make that dreary."

"It was understated." She corrected him and resumed counting. "There is still quite a large sum here. I shan't require . . ." After tallying nearly three hundred pounds she looked up. "Are you secretly a wealthy man who deliberately chooses to live below stairs in a brothel? Please do tell, Mr. Black."

Dressed in a new striped traveling dress, coat, and hat, she was the very picture of pretty. He could hardly take his eyes off her. "Upon my majority, I came into a comfortable living bequeathed by my mother's estate. I have little use for the income. Parked most of the inheritance with bankers. I have also made a few investments."

He wondered what color undergarments she wore. The pale blue with the black satin bows and matching garters? He meant to find out.

From an inside coat pocket, he retrieved a small velvet box. "A little something I found in the jewelry department. If we are traveling incognito together, you'll have to start calling me by my given name, in earnest." A gold ring nestled in the satin lining of the box. A large oval sapphire surrounded by white diamonds sparkled in the dim light of the coach.

"You can be my fiancée. No, better yet, let's call ourselves married. Perfect cover and we can lodge in the same room together." He winked.

America raised a brow, but was unable to take her eyes off the ring. "My future, unexpectedly, is full of promise and adventure. And I am not about to ruin it with another quarrel."

"No objections? Lovely. You shall be my assistant during our stay at Roos House and married while in Portsmouth." He unfastened dainty pearl buttons along the inside of her wrist and removed a new kid glove. A bit of heat rushed to her cheeks as he slipped the ring on her finger for size. A near perfect fit.

She held up her hand and admired the beautifully cut deep blue stone before meeting his gaze. "I shall call you Phaeton if you conduct yourself as a proper husband. If you persist on acting the Lothario and pestering me with advances, it will be Mr. Black."

His grin appeared to irk her, no end.

"And do not think to use your wicked charm on me again."

"This husband has insatiable appetites for his wife."

"Mr. Black—"

His gaze narrowed. "Phaeton."

"Phaeton." The pout did it. Unable to control himself, he grabbed her up and set her down on his lap.

"You feel that?" He rested his head on the upholstered squabs of the back rest.

Her thigh rubbed against his burgeoning erection. "How could I not?"

"Mmm, such plump, moist lips, and the upper lifted in perpetual petulance."

"Perpetual petulance?" She smiled. "We might make a tongue twister out of that. Penelope plumped a pout of—"

"Perpetual petulance." He placed his mouth over hers and took soft bites. His tongue swept under her lip and pushed her mouth open. She greeted him playfully, their tongues intertwined, as desire surged through him.

"Unbutton me." Through eyes half closed, his gaze connected with hers. Glassy pools of green and gold sparkled in the late afternoon light.

He pushed up her skirt and set her knees to each side of his thighs. Reaching between her legs he found the slit in her pantalettes. "Ah yes, you wore the blue." Slick fingers signaled she was ready and he plunged into her. The coach did most of the work; as they rocked back and forth, she gradually took more of him inside her.

She grinned. "The Duke of Pleasure pumps his prick into—." She thrust against his groin and demanded more.

"Tonight, my dove."

"Why not now?" She kissed him quite savagely and flexed silky smooth inner wall muscles to further excite him. He groaned. "Because we have arrived." He retracted a window shade. "Have a look."

Her gaze turned into more of a gape. The immense edifice, no doubt considered a jewel of Gothic architecture, featured the kind of arched buttresses and steeply pointed eaves one would expect in a church. The stately manse was built almost entirely of stone, and appeared to incorporate a prayer chapel at one end.

"Blimey." She returned to him. "A good lot of rooms, aye, with all those chimneys?"

"No doubt haunted by both the living and dead."

She wiggled up against his chest to see more of the manse. "Hmm. I sometimes wonder which are more frightening."

"The living, of course." He planted a kiss to the fold of her jaw, just under her earlobe. Sheathed in warmth, his cock throbbed in protest as he gently lifted her off.

Exiting the coach, they were greeted by several footmen who straight away attended to their bags. America could hardly take her eyes off the impressive facade, every cornice of which was adorned by a monstrous stone gargoyle.

When she stubbed her toe on a shallow stair, Phaeton took her arm. "You sightsee, I'll steer." At the top of a sweeping set of ascending steps, a massive wooden door opened and a hunched over, wizened butler stepped forward.

Phaeton leaned close. "So this is where Exeter hides all the ghoulish characters from the *Strand* magazine's Ghostly Tales."

She nodded. "I do hope for a storm tonight, to top off the experience."

"Mr. Black and his assistant, Miss Jones. Welcome to Roos House." The elderly man straightened up as best he could before making his bow. "I am Grimsley."

"Yes, of course you are."

Chapter Fourteen

THERE WAS NOTHING TO DO BUT CLOSE HER EYES AND REOPEN THEM. Again, America swept an admiring gaze over the room's lavish furnishings. Walls covered in a pale blue *chinois* motif featured exotic birds alighting tree branches. Damask draperies of dusty rose brought out the cherry blossoms in the wallpaper. Her bedchamber was a work of art. A giant four-poster bed occupied the center of the room replete with sumptuous coverlets and plump pillows.

"My word, you did get the finer accommodations." Phaeton entered the room.

Mr. Grimsley stood at the door, his chest puffed out. The butler surveyed the décor as if he had personally chosen the wallpaper. "Miss Anatolia recently supervised the restoration of this wing of the residence." The elderly fellow motioned two footmen carrying her trunk into a sizable dressing room.

A blur of grey edged the corner of her eye as a shadow passed through the wall. The otherworld was busy and about, as well. "Should you require anything at all, Miss Jones, please use the bell pull." Grimsley backed out of the room, leaving the door open.

Phaeton's gaze roamed from the gaping entry to the four-poster. "Although my baser instincts tell me to throw you down upon this fine counterpane and have my way with you,

I do believe there is yet another marvel worth your attention." He turned her toward the window. "Look, my dove."

America followed his line of sight, through wavy panes of glazing, to an airship floating in the sky above the wilderness park.

"A vessel that sails in the air." Openmouthed, she moved to a set of French doors. The oval-shaped dirigible, decorated in lovely scrolls of color, drifted closer. Suspended under the magnificent balloon, she could make out a flat-bottomed, ornately carved gondola, large enough to hold a number of passengers. "She's fitted with spanker and jib sails." The equipage appeared to be rigged for steerage, as much as propulsion. "A fast slip of an air schooner, I'd wager."

"Aye, matey." Phaeton slipped his arms around her waist. "I believe if you asked very nicely, Doctor Exeter might take you up on a voyage."

She blinked. "Doctor Exeter?"

"Let's have a better look." He unlatched tall windows above the window seat.

Rimmed by golden afternoon light, the majestic aircraft floated over an expanse of lawn to the formal garden behind the house. A very pretty young woman stood beside Dr. Exeter. She began waving enthusiastically and called out to Phaeton. "Mr. Black. We saw your carriage arrive. I insisted Oom Asa turn around. Please come for a flight with us." Her gaze turned to America. "And Miss Jones, you must join, as well."

Unable to contain her excitement, America whirled around. "Oh yes, I have always wanted to fly."

He hesitated, before offering her his arm. "As you wish, Miss Jones."

Once they were in the garden, she did her best to control her excitement, although there was a bit of bouncing up and down. Phaeton called to the doctor above. "As you can see, Miss Jones is no wilting lily."

Exeter tossed one rope, then another overboard. Several servants helped lower the gondola to several feet above the ground. A dark skinned man dressed in exotic clothing directed them closer.

Phaeton nodded to the tall man, who wore a long white tunic. Matching white pajama pants were tucked into tall, soft boots, which appeared to wrap and tie around his legs. Hundreds of beaded necklaces emblazoned the man's chest. He nodded to Phaeton. "Mr. Black."

"Mr. Tandi."

The exotic man gazed curiously at her. "Miss Jones, I am at your service." His bow was reverent, deep.

"Thank you, Mr. Tandi."

The craft settled, and a set of retractable steps dropped to the ground. Phaeton steadied her by holding an arm while Mr. Tandi, his fingers covered in rings, held the other. She safely climbed up to the passenger deck with Phaeton behind her.

Enthralled by all the fantastic equipage, America returned her attention to Phaeton. Small beads of perspiration had formed along a pale brow ridge. "Are you feeling well, Mr. Black?"

"Mr. Black. Miss Jones." Dr. Exeter's severe gaze softened.

Phaeton hesitated. "I am not entirely comfortable with heights. Otherwise, I'm perfectly well." His eyes darted about the deck of the gondola. "What keeps this contraption afloat, doctor?"

"Steam, from a boiler below deck." Based on a simple enough principle—"

"Hot air rises." Phaeton swallowed.

The doctor seemed particularly amused by Phaeton's noticeable discomfort. "We'll make this a short trip along the river. Follow the Thames a mile or two and make our return. Does that suit, Mr. Black?"

Without waiting for an answer, the doctor, turned airship captain, put Phaeton to work retracting rope and setting the jibs. America smiled. It seemed Dr. Exeter planned to keep Mr. Black too busy to think about heights.

The craft lifted off, and soon they soared over the treetops of the park, drifting along with the gentle turns of the Thames. America leaned out over a side rail and traced a near perfect reflection of the airship in the surface of the water.

Phaeton came up behind her and held on. She placed a hand over his. "Pinch me, Mr. Black, for I am flying, am I not?"

"I shall reserve my pinch for later this evening, should we make it back to Roos House in one piece."

America watched the billow and snap of the sails and marveled at a gust of wind that came out of nowhere, a breeze she herself could not feel on her face.

She turned to Exeter and stared. " 'Tis your doing, doctor?"

Dr. Exeter didn't answer. He stood on aft deck, as if in a trance, and stared into a large round object mounted on a polished brass pedestal.

"Once the sails are full, I expect he will answer at least some of your questions. Although I cannot say for sure, as Oom Asa can be secretive, at times." The pretty girl placed her arm through America's. "Shall we take a turn around the deck, Miss Jones? I am Anatolia Chadwick, but everyone calls me Mia." She leaned close and whispered. "Doctor Exeter is my legal protector."

"America Jones."

Her eyes lit up. "You are American?"

"With a name like mine, it would seem likely."

Mia's laughter was genuine.

"My father was British; my mother is American." She found Mia's gaze rather penetrating for such a young woman.

"I sense you are a potent mix of many things, Miss Jones."

"Please do call me America."

"May I? America. I quite love the name already."

"And you shall be Mia." She smiled at the girl. No doubt there was enough psychic energy swirling among the four of them to propel this aircraft to Madagascar and back.

"Miss Jones, shall we put your sailing skills to the test?" Having returned to the living, Dr. Exeter gestured to America to join him.

She glanced around and found Phaeton, who had braced himself against a sturdy railing.

Her heart flip-flopped in her chest as she stepped up beside Dr. Exeter. Before she had a chance to ask her first of a thousand questions, he motioned her behind the large crystal globe. "Take the wheel, Miss Jones."

Instantly the ship took a sweeping dip in altitude, nearly skimming the surface of the water. Mia's laughter echoed through the air along with a growl from Phaeton as he held on for dear life.

"Are you all right, Mr. Black?" A bit green in the gills, her employer signaled a thumbs-up.

Calmly, the doctor showed her how to use the levers, not only to propel the craft but also to raise and lower the airship's nose.

"Gaze into the center of the looking globe. What do you see, Miss Jones?"

Through a swirling mist, she was able to make out a view of the river straight ahead. She had once attended a demonstration of moving, photographic pictures at the Théâtre Optique. She knew quite emphatically what she saw in the globe were images of the river, exactly as it lay before them.

Dr. Exeter showed her how to climb and level the airship high above water.

She bit her lip, almost afraid to ask. "And how might I turn us?"

"Merely focus your eyes to one side of the globe or the other. Follow the bend in the river, imagine a gentle turn portside."

She narrowed her gaze on the globe. The airship obediently followed the turn of the river.

"You are a quick study, Miss Jones, but then, I expected nothing less." Exeter's gaze wandered about the deck, landing on Mia and then Phaeton. "Between the four of us, there is enough energy to take this craft on a lengthy journey." His piercing eyes, seemed less daunting than usual. She might even say they teased her. "Perhaps even to Madagascar and back, yes Miss Jones?"

"We are all powering this craft?" Phaeton asked.

"We share our abilities with ancient gods as well as the high-pressure steam engine and the science of Hero of Alexandria." The doctor gazed far out ahead of the balloon. "Have you ever heard of an Aeolipile? Steam converted to motion as described as early as two hundred B.C. Science and metaphysics working together. Should you be interested to see more, Mr. Black, we can tour the boiler room below deck."

For the second time that day, a large shadow swept across America's field of vision.

Exeter took his position behind the steering globe.

A thunderous squawk trumpeted from above.

The doctor thrust brass levers forward and an electrical charge crawled up over the balloon. A force field, perhaps? Or shielding device? America steadied herself beside Exeter as the ship quickly gained momentum. "Can you see it, Phaeton?"

Shielding his eyes from glare, Phaeton craned his neck and squinted. "Directly overhead. Huge wingspan. A very great bird, with . . . at least three heads."

Exeter set his mouth in a thin grim line.

Phaeton stepped back from the railing. "About to make a dive at us, I suspect."

"From which direction?" Exeter shouted.

Phaeton pointed right, and she vocalized. "Starboard." Before America could stop herself, she blurted out orders. "Jib sails to port, Mr. Black. When she makes her dive, we'll slip around her."

Stunned momentarily, Phaeton actually followed her orders.

Exeter's eyes glowed. "Shall I take her lower, Miss Jones?"

"At your discretion, doctor." She widened her stance and fashioned a tight-lipped grimace. The sky turned dark as the creature blocked out the sunlight. After a deafening screech and a snort, the bird took a swipe past the craft and rattled the gondola. All she could see was a blur of crimson scales and a flash of necks and fangs. A great gust of energy tossed Mia over the banister, but she hung on long enough for Phaeton to grab hold of her hand. A wing tip caught the edge of the gondola and spun it round with such force the airship tilted dangerously and gyrated out of control.

Clinging to ship rails, America watched, frozen in horror, as Phaeton and Mia were both carried overboard.

A blur of movement.

Dr. Exeter dived over the rails and disappeared. The airship descended so quickly her stomach felt as though it moved from her belly to her throat. America pushed on levers as if she knew what to do. Invisible aid from Exeter. She concentrated on the globe and banked the ship further port side. Phaeton, Mia, and Exeter all tumbled back onto the gondola's deck.

America gulped in air. How long had it been since she remembered to breathe? The airship continued to hurtle downward, spinning out of control. They were headed straight for a large stand of trees by the river.

In the time it took her to blink and clear her vision, Dr. Exeter stood behind her and took over the globe. With seconds to spare he calmly raised the ship. The brush of treetops along the bottom of the gondola meant they had cleared the forest but they were still spinning.

America barked orders. "Cut sail, Mr. Black."

Sprawled out on the deck, Phaeton sat up and glared. "Aye, aye, Captain." He rolled onto his feet and staggered up to foredeck.

America smiled. Phaeton was back in fine, grumbling form, as he hauled in sail. "Where's the damn bird?"

Mia was on her feet again at the railing. "Far off the starboard bow and climbing."

America shaded her eyes. "Appears to be flying away."

"All I glimpsed were feathers and scales." Phaeton joined them aft, as the doctor brought the craft fully under control. "Perhaps the most formidable minion of hers yet. What do you make of it?"

Exeter squinted past the bow to the retreating bird on the horizon. "She either flaunts her strength or depletes her power. We will soon find out."

Phaeton's stomach growled. Neither he nor Miss Jones had eaten since breakfast. Still, the fact he had any appetite at all, after nearly ending up a puddle of bones and flesh on the bank of the Thames, was surprising.

Finished with his cravat, he adjusted his collar points. A tap came at the door, which he answered. "I do hope this is about dinner—"

Miss Jones stood in the hall wearing a cloud of plum-colored taffeta and silk. "Ah, the gown with the dazzling décolleté." His gaze traveled over silken mounds of flesh to a pretty throat and subtly rouged lips. Kissable, squeezable Miss Jones. "Even more lovely than I remember."

Her gaze slid over him more than once. "You are handsome, as well, in formal attire." She held up a simple gold necklace with an amethyst stone cut into a heart-shaped pendant. "I need your assistance."

She stepped into his room and handed him the choker. Standing behind her, he inhaled the scent of freshly washed hair, tamed into a simple chignon. Still, he missed those riotous curls of hers. He purposely fumbled with the catch. "I don't believe I will take dessert at table this evening. I will wait until we are alone in that great bed of yours."

He locked the clasp and kissed her shoulder. He slipped his tongue up the side of her neck to her earlobe. "I mean to taste you tonight, Miss Jones. I wish to savor all of your spice, your tang, your sugar."

His mouth traveled over the vein in her neck. Her heartbeat throbbed under his lips and she uttered the sweetest sigh. With his arms at her waist, he turned her around to face him. In this moment, he wanted her, perhaps more than he had ever wanted a woman. His gaze wandered down to her breasts, pressed into perfect globes of flesh. He slipped a dainty sleeve down her arm.

A loud knock caused her to jump. He returned the cap sleeve to her shoulder and glared at the door. Reluctantly, Phaeton backed away. "Yes?"

The door opened and Mia poked her head in the door. "Oom Asa has asked—" Her eyes grew wide. "Oh my word, Miss Jones, you do look ravishing, doesn't she, Mr. Black?"

The pretty girl looked down at her own frock and frowned. "I do hope I grow larger breasts—and very big ones at that."

"Why would you wish for such a thing, Mia?" He drew his brows together and studied her chest. Not large by any means, but no doubt firm and perky. "What is it the French say about breast size? More than a champagne glass is too much."

"Honestly, Mr. Black, 'tis all men look at." She turned to America. "Isn't it true, Miss Jones?"

"Please call me America." His lovely Cajun dove rolled her eyes in his direction, as if he didn't see or hear the coded exchange between the two women. "And yes, I have noticed the effect on occasion."

Mia stuck her nose up in the air. "I do appreciate your words of encouragement, Mr. Black, but it does a girl no favor to be mollified." She exhaled a small gasp. "Oh my, I am forgetting the very reason I was sent here. Oom Asa has requested your presence in the library before dinner. Please, come with me."

"Mollified?" Phaeton followed the two ladies out of his bedchamber.

Chapter Fifteen

"I SHALL TAKE UP THE REAR GUARD, LADIES." A most diverting view of bouncing bustles made his task a pleasant duty. Phaeton listened absently to snippets of female chitchat as he reordered and put to memory the layout of the great house. He could not be entirely sure, but he sensed Mia led them on a most circuitous route, avoiding an entire wing of the manse.

If he understood the layout of the residence correctly, a traverse through the older annex would have made the shorter route to their gathering place. Neck hairs prickled under his high-pointed starched collar. And a second wave of whispered sighs and moans wafted through his body. As usual, he shook them off.

America glanced back. She sensed the undercurrent as well.

Recently, he had experienced the most disconcerting thoughts about Miss Jones. The most disturbing of all was the impossible idea that he rather enjoyed having her around.

At the grand staircase, Phaeton threw his shoulders back and any thoughts of America Jones right out of his head. He returned to his analysis of the house. Ceilings painted with murals and austere arches, notwithstanding, he could not summon up a word like *resplendent* for the manse. He had just about settled on *stately* as the better description when a footman stationed in the hall opened a set of doors to the most impressive private library he had ever seen.

"Oom Asa says this room holds all the secrets of the world."

Hands behind his back, Phaeton craned his neck to take in all the ancient volumes that lined two stories of wall space. "Might there be an index somewhere?" When both young women raised a brow, he leaned forward. "To locate the secrets, ladies."

Mia giggled. "I shall ask Oom Asa if he has catalogued the secrets."

A door between the impressive stacks led to a cozier room, more of a study. He recognized Exeter's tall silhouette at the fireplace. A few pleasantries were exchanged as he and America settled to one side of the warm hearth.

"If you will, sir?" Grimsley nodded to the glasses of champagne on a silver tray. They were being prepared for a toast of some kind.

Phaeton removed two glasses of pale bubbly liquid, handing one to Mia, the other to America. The old butler passed the last glass to him and added a bow.

"Thank you, Grimsley." Dr. Exeter studied them each rather severely, before a twitch of mouth and a spark in his eye gave him away. "When early balloonists landed in a patch of farmland, they were likely to be attacked by frightened peasants heaving stones and wielding pitchforks. French pilots discovered the farmers were easily appeased when offered a glass of champagne."

"In commemoration of your first flight, Mr. Black and Miss Jones." Dr. Exeter lifted his glass. "Mother Nature has taken you into the skies and returned you gently to Earth. Welcome to the ranks of the Aeronauts!"

Phaeton swallowed a healthy gulp and admired the shapely cup of his glass. He could not help but wink at Mia, who blushed the prettiest pastel rose as she sidled over. "Please do not mention anything to Oom Asa about our little discussion earlier."

"I am easily bribed, especially by two lovely females."

Phaeton turned to America. "Does something come to mind, Miss Jones?"

"I would be most interested to know what kind of inappropriate discussion my ward is having with you, Mr. Black."

"Nothing too terribly risqué." Phaeton squinted at the bubbles running up the hollow stem of crystal. "Legend has it the shape of the champagne coupe was modeled on the breast of Marie Antoinette or was it Madame de Pompadour?" He shrugged. "Both enchanting French ladies, but I can never remember which one honors the distinction."

"A romanticized tale that is almost certainly false, Mr. Black. The glass was designed in England in 1663, preceding those aristocrats by nearly a century." Exeter turned to America. "May I escort you into the dining room, Miss Jones?"

She grinned at Phaeton as the doctor led her away.

He leaned closer to Mia. "Your guardian keeps the most insignificant facts and figures in his head."

She took his arm. "There was a time when I believed he invented the dates just to win an argument."

Phaeton grinned at the precocious girl. "I'm certain you checked and found he is never wrong."

"It's infuriating." Her lower lip protruded in a charming pout.

The dining room proved to be another immense hall. The formal table, reduced to a length that might seat eighteen guests comfortably, was most likely down from twice the number. The four of them were seated among five place settings. Phaeton could not help but stare, on occasion, at the very obvious empty setting of plate and silverware at the end of the table.

The dark, elegant room was lit by a few wall sconces and one chandelier. A set of windows at the end of the room was covered by heavy drapery to hold back the chill. The table itself was lit by two immense candelabras, each blazing a dozen candles. After two starters, consisting of a clear soup and a white fish, Phaeton finally had to ask about the extra place setting.

"The Baron has asked me to ask your indulgence. He will be joining us as we near the end of our supper." Exeter explained. "My father suffers from a rare disease of the blood, Porphyria, also known as the Vampire's Disease, which should have killed him months ago."

The doctor set a fork across the edge of his plate as the first entrée was served. "All of his body parts have begun to decay. He can no longer eat a meal as we know it."

Phaeton swallowed the last of his fish as a footman whisked the plate away.

Exeter shrugged. "No sense putting everyone off their supper."

Phaeton stared at a large slab of rare beef lying in a pool of blood-red juice. "Indeed."

America looked up from her plate, and they exchanged what he considered a private moment of mutual revulsion. Her eyes darted oh so subtly to the base of the silver candlestick.

The sculpted motif was that of a seashore, whose denizens all appeared to be in motion. A starfish crawled over the remains of a nautilus shell. Emerging from the twisted chamber was a strange canine-looking head attached to a length of rubbery neck. The starfish reached out and strangled the unfortunate creature. Phaeton shook out his linen serviette and snapped it over the base of the candelabra. Candles flickered.

Phaeton glanced at Exeter. "She's about."

Exeter calmly carved off a bit of rare meat. "It would seem so."

Mia glanced about the room. "Who is about?"

Exeter mouthed a forkful. "The Baron's lady friend."

"Please tell me she's not back again." Mia dropped her utensils upon the plate. "And I'll wager it was she behind that mischief on the airship this afternoon." She stuck out her chin. "Well, am I right?"

Exeter rolled his eyes and chewed. "Mia claims her abilities pale in comparison to mine."

"Both your ward and your guests are quite correct. We may yet have another join us for dinner this evening." A frail voice, made up largely of wheezing breath, managed to carry across the hall. The unseen entity barked an order. "Grimsley, have a sixth place set at the far end of the table, if you will."

The butler dragged a wheelchair backward across an expanse of Persian carpet. Both Exeter and Phaeton rose to stand.

"Please, do not trouble yourself Asa—Mr. Black." The elder manservant swiveled the chair around. A hunched over figure dressed in a tuxedo, head and hands swathed in bandages, arrived at the table. The head was completely wrapped, with the exception of two eyeholes and a slit for a mouth. Tied onto the face was a partial mask, the snout of a dog, presumably, where a nose formerly resided.

Phaeton experienced a collective shudder from nearly everyone in the room. And then a lessening of revulsion to something more akin to pity.

Shaded by gauze wrappings, the movement of dark, beady eyes could be tracked as two pinpoints of light shifted from one guest to another. "Good evening." The mummified entity listed to one side of the chair. "I am Oris Exeter, Baron de Roos."

Phaeton nodded his respects. "Premier Baron, of all England."

"We are an ancient family." The man's breath labored along with his pitch. "Asa will bear the title when I am gone. There are only days left to me."

"Do not speak of such sorrowful partings, Uncle. You have bravely resisted the Porphyria for many years." He read genuine affection in Mia's concerned gaze.

The Baron managed a stiff shrug. A glow in the small eyes roamed over the two young ladies. "Good evening, my gentle Mia."

"Great Uncle."

"And, Miss Jones. How lovely you are." With some effort, the Baron rotated stiffly toward Phaeton. "Excellent taste in assistants, Mr. Black."

"Invaluable." Phaeton shot an obvious wink across the table. "Bright as well as beautiful."

"You are too kind, sir."

He waited for the dimple to appear beside those pouty lips. Ah, there it was.

"Please excuse my appearance." The Baron raised carefully bandaged hands, missing a finger here and there. "I assure you without these wrappings I am an abomination."

Perhaps to ease their discomfort and to satisfy his own desire for stimulating discourse, the Baron expounded on a variety of metaphysical subjects.

"In his *Critique of Pure Reason*, Kant used the phrase '*ens imaginarium*' to describe pure space and pure time, preconditions of clairvoyance." A footman stood beside the Baron's chair. Occasionally, when the decrepit nobleman nodded, the manservant would raise a crystal goblet and angle two hollow straw blades through an incision in the linen.

A hissing gurgle preceded a slurping sound, as the Baron siphoned up his claret.

Phaeton raised his fork and knife, ready to attack his entrée. The slab of cow flesh inched along the plate. Did the odd sucking, slithering noise come from his meat or the Baron? He experienced a flash of vertigo.

"From a purely practical sense, would you say your second sight originates in the imagination or some other faculty, Mr. Black?"

He stabbed his fork into the undulating cow flesh and left it standing upright. "Educators and scientists may refer to my reality as pure space and time. I see it as a kind of open portal. A door of perception that is always open. I cannot chose to see or not see." Phaeton met the old man's gaze across the table. "I endure, if you follow, Baron."

"I know very well."

Their plates were retrieved and replaced by a second en-trée. A portion of succulent, well roasted pheasant. Phaeton dug in before the bird decided to take flight.

Forking down a quick mouthful of succulent meat, he experienced a gentle rubbing against his leg. A flirtation under the table? His gaze flew to Miss Jones who appeared to be otherwise occupied with her new dish. Wasn't she the clever tease.

Something gnawed on his shoe leather. Phaeton shot up out of his seat and pulled away his chair.

Everyone at the table stopped in mid-chew. He lifted the tablecloth and got a glimpse of a slithering, shadowed creature. The legless fiend clawed its way to the end of the table, where it rapidly merged into one of the carved wooden table legs.

He pulled up his chair and inspected the toe of his shoe, which bore the evidence of teeth marks.

Exeter leaned sideways to take a look. "As I told Mr. Black evening last, I suspect she has transferred her interest to him."

The Baron slumped into a reverie of weak moans and sighs. "Try not to fall in love with her, Mr. Black."

"I have no interest in love." Finally, a subject he could toy with. "Acts of love, however, are a different matter, isn't that right, Miss Jones?" Phaeton speared a string bean. "She calls them proofs of love, I believe."

America chewed and swallowed. "Acts and proofs are not equivalents, much as you care to think so."

Mia giggled.

Exeter glared.

Phaeton grinned.

The Baron wheezed. "Before I tire, I promised my son I would make my confession."

Exeter dismissed all the servants, with the exception of Grimsley.

The elderly man lifted a hand to scratch an eye. A spot of

blood spread over the fresh linen bandages covering his brow. "Some months ago, when I could still amble about on my own, I attended a play at the Lyceum. Afterward, I took a solitary stroll. It had been a perfect evening, perhaps the last of its kind. The Porphyria would soon see to the end of me. That night, I found my way to the river and decided to end my life."

"A great bird rescued me. Swooped down into the water and fished me out of the Thames." There was a weak smile in his voice. "My goddess not only saved me, but restored my body. At least, while the affair lasted."

His wrapped head drooped slightly. "I made a Faustian pact with a she-devil. As many ancient gods do, she required blood sacrifice and human worship. She would replenish her ichors by choosing victims from the streets of the poorest boroughs. All the veneration she needed, she received from me." The frail voice faltered in a sigh. "I adored her."

The Baron's gaze drifted far way. "After she drained her victims, I covered up her crimes—sliced throats and removed organs as she directed."

Phaeton sat up in his chair.

"You surmised correctly, Mr. Black." The barest pinprick of light remained in the Baron's eyes. "I am Jack Ripper."

Mouths fell open as both young women gasped. America's gaze shifted to Phaeton. "You knew of this?"

"I suspected the good doctor protected someone or some thing." Phaeton noted a pale green mist crawling under the closed door of the dining hall as the shocking revelation continued to reverberate around the table.

Exeter also tracked the rolling bit of fog along the carpet. "And now that you know the truth, Mr. Black, what do you plan on doing about it?"

"Nothing, for the moment." Phaeton matched the doctor's concern with a flinty gaze of his own. "What exactly might I report to Scotland Yard that I haven't already?

Months ago, I advanced the idea the Whitechapel murders were committed by a savage fiend not of this world. The allegation got my employment contract cancelled. A second assertion could land me in Bedlam."

He continued to study Exeter. "I take it your involvement stopped the murders. But the gods do need their ichors, and it seems you succeeded only in delaying her return to the streets. Which is where I came in, both of us chasing haplessly after the evasive little succubus."

A faint tinkle of laughter echoed through the room and grew into the robust laughter of a mature female. A goddess materialized at the far end of the table. An immortal nymph the likes of which Phaeton had seen only glimpses of in illustrated books on ancient archaeology.

She sat motionless on the chair, arms placed formally to each side, like the giant seated statues of Luxor. Exotic eyes outlined in kohl shifted slowly. The stunning beauty studied her subjects at the table.

"Where is my husband?" Her gaze landed on him. "You are not my husband."

"No, I am not. I am Phaeton Black. We have met before, Mrs.—?"

"*Fay-ton,* where is Anupu?"

"Anupu?" Phaeton repeated.

The Baron managed a strained whisper. "The designation early Egyptians gave to Anubis, god of the Underworld. To speak the name of the dead is to make him live again."

Dr. Exeter leaned closer and whispered in his ear. Phaeton repeated the word aloud. "Qadesh?"

An appraising gaze slid over Phaeton. "I am Qadesh, one who rules over nature, beauty, and sexual pleasure."

"Some of my favorites." Phaeton smiled at her. "So, Qadesh. You search for your husband."

"Long ago, I was like you. Not a god, but much desired. Anupu stole me away from two husbands, Reshep and Min, such a relief." Qadesh shifted her interest to the women at the table. "Two men are a great deal of work for any female. No?"

Her attentions did not linger long before returning to Phaeton. "I was put to death for my disobedience, but Anubis gave me new life. I was reborn as I am now. A powerful night creature fashioned to reign over the dead at the side of my husband."

"A rather sweet story, Qadesh. And where do you think Anupu might be found?"

All the fury of an unexpected, early spring storm rained down on the table. "This is what I ask you. Where is my husband?"

Phaeton reached out with his mind and connected with the temperamental vixen. Instantly she stopped her tirade and stared. He dared to probe, and she opened. A simple gossamer gown hid very little of her body. Phaeton's gaze paused at her breasts, high and round. Answering his interest, the translucent fabric parted, exposing a firm mound. A golden loop pierced the nipple.

He blinked upward and locked eyes with her. *Do you wish to be pleasured, Qadesh?*

"My dear boy, stay far away from her."

The fickle goddess shifted dark orbs. A rack of wretched sounding coughs split the air. The Baron gasped for breath as a gurgle of foaming pink liquid drooled from the bandaged mouth slit. A cruel, violent force strangled him. The Baron reached out and gripped Phaeton's forearm.

"Beware, Phaeton . . ."

Exeter motioned to Grimsley. Prying one finger back at a time, a joint snapped, and a finger fell off. The gasping, desiccated man still managed to utter a cry of fear and misery. Briefly, Phaeton held the Baron's hand in his, and then let go. The butler wheeled the chair away from the table.

Phaeton clearly saw the pale specter of death encircle the elderly man. With a certainty, the Baron was dying. His gaze lowered to the gauze-wrapped digit left on the table. He opened his palm and another piece of finger rolled onto white linen.

Exeter looked back. "I must see he is made comfortable upstairs."

Phaeton stood up. "I will see the ladies safely back to their rooms." At the far end of the table, the chair Qadesh had occupied was empty. The witch was gone for now.

The doctor nodded. "Remain vigilant, she will likely return."

Chapter Sixteen

"MMM," SHE MURMURED. How quickly this man could drive her to sighs and moans. He ran the tip of his tongue along the edge of her upper lip to accomplish his wicked goal. He made her tingle.

"Mmm, indeed, my lovely Miss Jones." He continued sampling, tasting. "I shall return with an assortment of prophylactics for you to put to the test." His words drifted over her cheek as he found the lobe of her ear and nibbled.

The door to her bedchamber opened behind her. She fell backward and would have toppled onto her backside if Phaeton had not steadied her. Startled, the little maid gasped. "Beggin' your pardon, Miss. I was just turning down the bed." She dipped a curtsey and slipped around them.

Undaunted by the interruption, his heavy-lidded gaze remained focused on her mouth. "Please change into the diaphanous little confection of a dressing gown and wear nothing underneath."

"A great deal of effort wouldn't you say?" She edged an eyebrow upward. "When you are just going to take it off."

"And leave your hair up." He kissed her briefly and reluctantly backed away. "I wish to take it down."

She closed the door. How had this happened? Like a ship adrift in waters too deep for anchoring, she felt unbalanced, out of control, even captivated. America sighed. She had never intended an amorous interlude with the accomplished roué. Calmly, she reviewed what it would get her. Well, for one thing, she stood a very good chance of recovering her ships, even if the sinful Mr. Black wished only to assuage his lascivious needs.

She pressed her lips together. He also did a rather expert job at seeing to her pleasure. Her cheeks flushed with heat at the remembrance of his touch. He knew where to caress and how long, the very strokes to use and the variance of pressure. Phaeton was more than adept; he played her body like a maestro. Damn the devil or praise God. She hardly knew which expression to begin or end with.

Still, she suspected he was a rare man.

A pull to a chord promptly brought a maid, who helped her out of her gown and petticoats, bustle, and corset. She took a deep breath and exhaled. How she hated corsets. She soothed and softened her skin with a calming lotion and tied on the filmy negligee.

The shameful fact of the matter was she enjoyed bedding him. And, well, it didn't matter. She would copulate with the devil himself in order to have her livelihood restored.

"You're a survivor, Miss Jones." She studied her reflection in the dressing room looking glass. There were hints of breast and a shadow of feminine triangle. She tilted her head. A freshly scrubbed face peered back at her.

She pinched her cheeks and bit her lips. Better.

Phaeton pulled off his cravat and unbuttoned his waistcoat. He yawned. Perhaps a short nap before venturing down the corridor was in order.

He sat on the bed and rolled onto his back. Thoughts of pleasuring his lovely assistant streamed in and out of his mind. Perhaps a kiss to each dimple above that round derriere. He could almost taste the salty sweet essence of her. He descended deeper into reverie.

Buttons popped and his shirt parted. He groaned as sharp fingernails scraped the length of his torso.

"Who comes calling at this late hour? Not the chamber-maid, I suspect."

He grinned, eyes closed. "The lovely Miss Jones, per-haps?" He sniffed. "No traces of lavender and the ocean at night—*le parfum du Siné.*"

Something closer to the smell of the air after a thunder-storm and sandalwood. An ephemeral breeze swirled the scent of burning incense into his nostrils as he breathed deep. A hushed voice whispered in his ear. *Fay-ton. Will you kiss me, Fay-ton?*

Large ebony orbs returned his interest. She lay prone, floating in the air just above him. Straight, dark hair inter-woven with hundreds of small gems flowed over her shoul-ders but did not cover her torso. His gaze lingered over exposed mounds, pointed nipples; rings of gold tempted him to use his tongue.

He propped himself up on his elbows. "Looking for a bit of relief? Can't say as I blame you. How long has it been? Thousands of years, I expect. Quite a long time for a god-dess who rules over sexual pleasure."

Her lips blazed a trail along the small hairs that led to his navel.

"Ahh. Qadesh."

Luscious ruby lips parted. Her laughter was musical, mes-merizing. The minx moved lower.

My desire sleeps. Her eyes traveled through him into his mind. Probing. Penetrating. *You will awaken me.* An unnatu-ral force pushed him down on the bed. *Close your eyes, Fay-ton, let me pleasure you.*

"So, you want to be on top. Very good."

The buttons opened on his trousers.

He sucked in air. "I am so easily seduced by a beautiful female—"

She hissed.

"Goddess."

Even though he was sorely tempted, Phaeton could not shake the discomfiting idea that he was about to be supper. "Delighted as I am to be the recipient of your amorous designs, may I offer a suggestion?"

He tried rolling off the bed, but he could not get his body to move. Unable to flex his arms or legs, he struggled to free himself from invisible bonds. He broke out in a cold sweat. All he could do was lift his head. The little minx wanted him to watch.

He gritted his teeth. "Qadesh, let me help to you find your mate—I believe you called him Anupu?"

She snorted and snuffled like a bull before she yanked down his drawers.

With his shirt thrown open and his trousers down past his hips, she had him pinned and exposed. Cast in invisible bindings, there was something delightfully erotic about his state of being. With great concentration, he tried to hold back an erection. A warm breeze of goddess breath blew over his bare chest, past his navel.

"You cunning little trifler." The beast sprang to life.

Qadesh appeared momentarily stunned. She turned her head, curious. "You are a god?"

Aroused and uneasy, he considered his answer. "Mother might have been the concubine of a god." He offered a hapless sort of grin.

"Ahh." Black eyes gleamed with lust. "Then your blood is of the gods." Her lips curled back to reveal sharply pointed teeth.

He thought about going back and correcting his answer. Her fangs extended. Too late.

She lunged in for the bite. A searing heat ravaged his groin as her teeth sank through skin and sinew. He gasped as she gouged flesh and ripped into his mind. His head dropped back onto the counterpane as a delirious, thick fog dulled his faculties. Drifting out of his body, above the bed, he watched her take hold of his manhood and suckle. A thunderous sensation of pain and pleasure shot through his body, and he lost consciousness.

He tumbled headlong into the darkest corners of awareness. Laid out on a shallow barge on a river beset by fire, he floated in vaporous crimson waters. To each side, he was guarded by serpents whose tails wrapped around his ankles and his chest. He gasped for air that scorched his lungs. Emerging from the inferno were all forms of otherworldly souls blackened and burnished like writhing bronze statues; they rose into the atmosphere buffeted by flames and clouds of smoke.

Was he a dead man? Had his time come to cross the river Styx? Phaeton lay prostrate on the deck of the barge. His body had no weight or other equilibrium. All he heard were the shrieks and bellows of pain.

He opened his eyes. A great vessel in full sail churned flames into froth as it passed his barge. A cool breeze wafted over his parched lips, the simplest, sweetest relief. High above, she stood at the bow. He caught a glimpse of her before the ship vanished into the underworld.

He rasped out a dry whisper. "Miss Jones."

America reached for another sweet from the box on the bed stand. Propped up in the sumptuous poster bed, she fidgeted in her new lace negligee. The gilt-edged card next to the truffles simply stated: For my chocolate dove. No signature needed.

She bit into an orange cream with a hint of cinnamon. Heavenly. Mr. Black had done a bit of shopping on his own at Harrod's. A sapphire engagement ring, chocolates, an exotic assortment of condoms, indeed.

And where was he? He had promised to return with the prophylactics. She wondered how one went about finding such an item in a sundry goods store. Was there a gentlemen's condom department? She thought it entirely more likely the man carried them about in his pocket, for that ever ready John Thomas of his. How utterly annoying.

She leaned sideways to turn the lamp down. A sudden shift under the bedcovers caused her to start. Lately, she paid close attention to those blurs at the corner of the eye. Holding her breath, she waited. A large lump at the foot of the bed inched closer.

She froze.

Something nibbled on her leg. She squealed. Drawing up her legs, she threw back the covers.

A serpentlike tail whipped about as the small grey gargoyle cringed. Golden eyes blinked. The creature emitted an odd whimper and panted softly.

America stifled a cry and swallowed. "Edvar?"

Before she could jump out of bed the little fiend landed on her knees. She could not help but let out a series of yelps as she wrestled the creature off her person. Its skin was cold and leathery and thoroughly off-putting. She recalled the snake handlers in Marrakesh as she gingerly removed his tail from her ankle with two fingers. Ick.

Feet tucked safely under her dressing gown, she stared at the fuzzy outline of the nearly transparent creature. She patted the sheet. "Sit."

A shadow curled up beside her. Slowly, the little savage revealed details of himself. His face was more like that of a hound with sharply pointed ears and a protruding overbite. And those yellow eyes like beams from a lantern, large and liquid. The little monster yelped a growl, leaped off the bed, and scrambled toward the door.

A rapping came from the hallway. The grey-skinned imp jumped aside as the door drifted open.

America narrowed her eyes. "So, it was you, Edvar."

"Are you all right?" Mia stood in the hall clutching her wrapper tightly around her. "I heard a scream."

She cringed. "I'm fine. A bit of a tussle with a gargoyle."

Mia hesitated, then cleared her throat. "I heard some strange noises coming from Mr. Black's room."

America pulled on a robe and hurried down the hall. At his door, ungodly human groans wafted into the corridor. Was the philanderer having a go with one of the upstairs maids?

Frigid air emanated from the room. Mia shivered. The gargoyle quivered on a hall table and wrapped a long slithering tail around himself.

"Cold enough to freeze the balls off a brass monkey." America read the energy clearly. This was Qadesh. No matter how much he might be enjoying himself, Phaeton was in trouble. She gnawed a bit on her bottom lip.

The gargoyle whined like a puppy.

"Hush!" She held a finger to her lips and glared at the puckish goblin.

Shivering, Mia looked behind her and back again. "It's her, isn't it?"

America nodded. "I am not sure if I can manage this alone. Run and get the doctor."

"I shouldn't leave you."

"Go!"

Mia scurried down the corridor.

She placed her hand on the knob and eyeballed the little devil. "And you stay out here." Who was she fooling? Mother had taught her well as a child, but she was no match for this powerful she-demon, who would quickly overshadow her feeble powers.

America took a deep breath and steeled herself. She would need all the *gris-gris* she had ever been taught by the voodoo witches of 'Nawlins.

"Never be afraid to fight dirty." She whispered the old seafaring advice and turned the knob.

The door was locked.

"Open up." She beat her fists against the door. "Let him

go, Qadesh." She rapped on the door again and rattled the knob. A pale grey shadow moved under the threshold. She held her breath and heard the latch move. Edvar.

America turned the knob and pushed the door open. Inching into the room, she disturbed thick clouds of low hanging pale mist. The two of them were splayed out across the bed. Phaeton lay in a stupor, incoherent and deathly pale, while Qadesh stroked the impressive mortal breeding weapon and replenished herself.

America's lips curled back. "Get off him."

She grabbed the closest thing to her, an expensive looking Chinese urn, and threw it at the bloodsucker. The ceramic vase bounced off the bed and broke into a thousand pieces on the floor.

The succubus turned her head and hissed. Red dripped from the sides of her mouth. Thick droplets stained the crisp white tails of Phaeton's shirt. The Egyptian goddess appeared euphoric—bloody stewed, all right.

America looked around for weapons. An iron poker leaned against the hearth. She placed one foot behind the other and backed her way over to the fireplace. She tried to remember the old vauda curse for a sorceress stick.

"Release him, Qadesh."

The goddess paid her no mind and moved up Phaeton's body, headed for his neck.

America tried shouting. "Get up—wake up, Phaeton!"

He remained in a deep trance. Lost, floating somewhere far away. Her stomach churned, the way it had when her father had whispered his last good-bye.

America grabbed the poker. She would use the baton as a *torche de charme*. She lunged forward. "Take no more. You will kill him."

The rod quivered in her hands. "*Protégez mon aimé contre un ennemi qui volerait son coeur et âme.*" Spoken in the French language, the ancient enchantment would protect a loved one from an enemy who tried to steal his or her soul. She thrust the poker into the goddess, who screamed in rage and retreated. The Nile goddess let go of Phaeton to examine a curl of smoke and the barest singe to gossamer robes.

Disappointed, America frowned.

Her female foe peered out from under black bangs. "You use children's magic on Qadesh?"

"A warning." America bluffed, meeting her glare. "I'll not ask again. Leave him alone."

Tossed into the air, her body sailed across the room. America's head hit the wall and a great number of stars flashed before her eyes. Her knees buckled and she slid down the wall onto the floor. Something like a groan emanated from her mouth as the scene in front of her blurred.

"If you drain him, Qadesh, Phaeton cannot help you find your husband." Dr. Exeter's voice.

America was lifted up and carried to a nearby chair. Hammers went to work inside her skull. She squinted and managed to bring the doctor into focus. Mia dropped back to stand close beside her.

"Three to one, powerful energy, Qadesh." Exeter picked up the dropped poker. A pale blue light emanated from the tip. Qadesh eyed the iron suspiciously.

A beam of pale blue light crackled out of the end of the poker. The goddess retreated on all fours. Like a strange sort of human crab, she crawled up the wall and onto the ceiling. Exeter released a bolt of lightning, which left the rod and instantly dissolved the goddess into a flurry of pale crystals. A flash of white light whooshed by the window as the apparition whirled past, traveling in the direction of the river.

Exeter held up the poker. A few sparks sputtered from the tip. "Handy."

America coughed. "*Le baton des secrets.*"

"We might exchange a few enchantments among friends, Miss Jones."

The doctor sat beside Phaeton and peeled back one eyelid at a time. He placed two fingers along Phaeton's throat. "I will need my transfusion kit." He turned to his ward. "You know the bag?" She nodded, eyes large and round. "Quickly, Mia."

America raised her head. "Will he live?"

Exeter examined the lower belly. "She gorged from his groin. He was aroused. She was able to ingest a great deal of blood rapidly." He leaned over the body and placed a hand to each side of Phaeton's head.

"May I . . ." America bit her lip. She pushed herself up off the petite chaise. "Does it hurt very much to give blood?"

Exeter frowned. "The danger is not that it hurts, Miss Jones, but that you will become squeamish and swoon."

America stuck her chin out. "I don't faint, Doctor Exeter."

He studied her. "Come, then. Lay beside Mr. Black and roll up your sleeve."

Mia arrived with his kit. The doctor unwrapped a folded cloth which covered a number of metal utensils and a length of tubing. He retrieved a small container of clear liquid and poured it over his hands. America recognized the sharp, pungent odor of rubbing alcohol. Mia held a white cloth underneath to catch the excess drippings as Exeter poured the disinfectant over a small, sharp-looking knife.

America grabbed his arm. "You must please explain everything to me. Only then will I not be afraid."

"Very well. I am going to cut your arm and insert a hollow needle into your vein. I will then attach a syringe to the end of the needle and a thin rubber tube will transfer your blood into a similar apparatus implanted into Mr. Black."

He held up the knife. "Try to think of something pleasant, Miss Jones."

Chapter Seventeen

"WAKE UP, MR. BLACK."

The sharp burn of ammonia caused a deep, involuntary inhalation of breath. Phaeton clawed his way to the surface of consciousness. He blinked, then blinked again. His vision remained hazy, obscured by a flutter of pale shadows—his eyelashes. A second waft of smelling salts lifted his head off the pillow. Racked by a spasm of coughs, he jerked upright.

His body thrashed violently from side to side. Sluggish, deep voices spoke to one another. "Get hold of his upper arm, throw your weight into it." Phaeton tried to twist out of the painful viselike grip that held him down. There was unbearable pressure on both shoulders. He exhaled, took another deep breath, and broke free of the noxious, cruel grip of the underworld.

He collapsed onto a mattress and pillows. An indistinct shape sat beside the bed, which stubbornly refused to resolve itself.

"Hold my hand." His own husky parched words sounded distant, foreign. Someone's fingertips pressed lightly on the inside of his wrist.

"Fond as I have grown of you, Mr. Black, I believe Miss Jones is the one you want."

He opened his eyes wide with a start.

Dr. Exeter. Phaeton attempted a grin of relief, but it hurt to smile. Excruciating soreness permeated every fiber of his body. He had seen what a steam-powered threshing machine could do to a man who fell into endless rows of scissorlike tines. If one could survive something like that, Phaeton supposed, they would feel something like he did at the moment. Vaguely, he was aware of fleshy parts in private places that were chafed and raw.

He decided against any sort of physical movement. Without too much difficulty, he rotated his gaze. Shapes were still faint, shadowy. "My eyes—are they moving together?"

"Well . . ." Another indistinct figure spoke, and he recognized America's voice. "Oh yes, now they are. Much better, Mr. Black." A gentle hand squeezed his. He knew it was hers.

The doctor swabbed a soothing cool solution into his eyes and wiped off the excess. Phaeton blinked many times before she came into focus. Those lovely golden green eyes crinkled at the ends, and a corkscrew of untamable curls fell down the side of her neck. He thought her smile was the most beautiful thing he had ever seen. "Hello, my dove."

"You require copious amounts of rest, Mr. Black. You nearly left us."

Phaeton answered Exeter, but his gaze never left Miss Jones. "So, I have not yet crossed the River Styx."

"Is that where you have been? Well, you are safely back among the living." The doctor turned Phaeton's head to one side and palpitated a wound on his throat. "Perhaps, when you are feeling stronger, you will give us a full report." The strong hands lifted the back of his head. "Drink and sleep peacefully. We will exchange notes later in the day."

Phaeton gulped cool water mixed with the bitter taste of a sedative. Laudanum. Another squeeze to his hand, and he slipped away into the merciful arms of Morpheus.

The worried brow on his drowsy face caused America to smile. Phaeton untied his drawers. "I'm afraid to look. How is the man Thomas?"

Gently, she brushed hair off his forehead. "The duke suffers battle fatigue, my lord, but he will soon recover."

His liquid brown eyes remained dulled by opiates, but that lazy curve at the ends of his mouth made her heart skip a beat. "And how do you know, my tantalizing dark dove?"

Phaeton was back. And it made her deliriously happy. She concocted her own version of a devilish grin. "Because I will make sure of it."

His eyes cleared enough for a rare bit of tenderness to shine through. "I wish I could have been there to see you duel with the treacherous little man-eater."

Her grin turned lopsided. "You missed a brief clash. Qadesh made short work of me. It was Doctor Exeter who managed to frighten her off."

"Your blood flows in my veins." He kissed the back of her hand. "Through my heart."

She lowered her eyes, folding his blanket down. "The doctor says we are a match. Not all transfusions go as well as this one."

His hands swept around her waist, and he pulled her close. He surveyed her through half-closed eyes, a look that made her shiver all over. His gaze flickered over every feature of her face. "Then it would be prudent, indeed sensible, to keep you near, to replenish my body in any number of ways." The surprising strength in his arms caused an extra tingle of joy.

She reached for a glass of sedative. Phaeton groaned. "No more."

America sighed. "Oh dear, unless you nap for an hour or two longer, I'm afraid I will not be able to remove of all your clothes to give you a sponge bath."

He pressed back into bed pillows and stared. Easy enough to read the lusty imaginings swirling through that randy mind of his. She pressed her lips together and feigned determination. "Doctor Exeter had ordered one more dose of sedative."

"You are a witch and a tease, Miss Jones." But he took the medicine.

★ ★ ★

Phaeton stood at the helm of a great ship, the salt air whipping through his hair as the sun burned a swath of warmth across his cheeks. Miss Jones stood beside him wearing an Admiral Nelson hat and a frothy white dress. Suddenly, they were fired upon by nearby vessels flying the Jolly Roger. Cutlass swinging buccaneers sailed across the sea on ropes and dropped onto the deck. Phaeton and America drew swords.

He found himself face to face with Yanky Willem. The schooner lurched to one side, and the filthy pirate nearly had him over the side rails. As the pirate leader drew close, his black-toothed grin drooled blood. "This day will be yer last, Yanky." Phaeton withdrew his sword from Willem's body and booted him into the drink. America stood at the helm, smiling at him over a pile of dead men.

A spray of salt water soothed his sun-kissed skin and Phaeton awoke with a sudden jolt.

A damp washcloth bathed his face and neck. Pale shadows in the room signaled late afternoon. Miss Jones dipped the cloth back into a basin of water and wrung it out. The tinkle of drops created a sudden powerful urge to urinate. Raw, recently scabbed wounds on his cock burned as the shaft enlarged. His eyes watered.

"I'm in desperate need of a chamber pot, Miss Jones."

She eyed the pitched tent under the bedcovers and brought a porcelain receptacle out from under the bed.

She helped him sit up and maneuver himself to the edge of the bed. A bit lightheaded, he positioned the bowl between his knees. Nothing. He looked up from the business at hand. "Are you going to stand there and watch?"

Hands on her hips, America snorted. "Priggish all of a sudden, Mr. Black?"

He glared.

"Oh, very well, I'm off to the kitchen." She turned on her heel.

"Warm buns and chocolate pudding, Miss Jones."

At the door, she turned back. "Pudding, Mr. Black?"

He tried a pleading, starved look. "Please."

She pivoted and nearly ran into Exeter. "Oh, hello, doctor."

"Miss Jones."

"I'm off to forage a meal for my patient."

Exeter paused to let her through. "I ordered a beef and barley broth for him."

She returned his raised brow with one of her own. "He fancies a sweet pudding."

The doctor brightened. "Cook makes a steamed chocolate pudding with chocolate sauce, Mia's favorite. But he must have the soup first."

Phaeton released a torrential stream into the chamber pot.

Exeter peered into the bowl. "Clear and nearly colorless. A good sign, indeed. Quite a remarkable recovery." The doctor pulled up a chair and took out a small journal and fountain pen.

Phaeton tucked his legs under the covers and adjusted a pillow.

"Now, Mr. Black, while it is fresh in your mind, might you relive your expedition to the other side?"

He exhaled a testy groan. "Why would I wish to do such a thing?"

Exeter opened his notebook. "Your odyssey will be recorded and stored in the library of secrets. One day your experiences will help inform another, who must undergo a similar trial."

His eyes narrowed on the doctor. "Very well."

Much to Phaeton's surprise, the better part of an hour slipped by with no ill effects. As he relived his journey, a veil lifted, and a burden eased. Occasionally, Exeter would ask a rather pointed question, but for the most part he left him to his ramblings.

Phaeton sighed. "There is a painting by Goya. I believe the work is titled *Saturn Devouring His Son*. It was here on loan at the National last year."

Exeter never looked up as he guided his pen across a ruled page. "I'm afraid I missed that one. Sounds frightful enough."

Phaeton rested his eyes while the brass pen point scratched indelible cursive letters onto paper. "A gargoyle of immense proportions holds his son, the size of a child's doll, in hand. His large mouth is agape, having already eaten one arm and torn off the head." Phaeton opened his eyes and met Exeter's stare. "I can tell you that Spaniard has crossed over."

A tap on the door signaled the arrival of supper. Phaeton's stomach growled. Exeter snapped the journal shut and smiled his now familiar close-lipped grin. "An appetite, very good."

"I should hope so, doctor." America's eyes were bright, full of sparkle. As hungry as he was, Phaeton hardly noticed dinner as the footman set up a tray table.

She removed a folded wire from a rather cleverly concealed skirt pocket. "I have received a wire, Mr. Black, but I cannot decipher a word of it." She passed it over.

"An encoded message." Phaeton borrowed Exeter's pen and tried several different letter substitutions. "Ah, yes, here we go." In moments he had the wire decrypted.

POST OFFICE INLAND TELEGRAM
16 FEB 1889 9:00 AM
TO: MISS AMERICA JONES
ROOS HOUSE ON-THE-THAMES

STEAMSHIP OF SUSPICIOUS REGISTRY IN
PORT STOP UPON ARRIVAL LEAVE WORD
WITH PERCY AT THE BLUE ANCHOR
INSPECTOR MOORE

"Dexter has a flair for the dramatic." Phaeton read the message a second time before handing it back to her. "You are not to go alone."

"Which is why I mean to get you well enough for travel." When the doctor raised a brow, America stuck Exeter with a grim stare. Those two were plotting something.

She steadied the bowl in his lap. Phaeton narrowed his gaze at the two conspirators and spooned up a wonderful beef barley broth. He opened his mouth wide as Miss Jones fed him a piece of hot buttered bun.

Exeter stood at the foot of his bed and observed. Presumably, he was concerned with whether or not Phaeton managed to keep the soup down.

America added a dollop of conserve to the next piece of bun. "Doctor says we have both made a remarkable recovery."

"You have a hard head, Miss Jones." Exeter's nod swept to Phaeton. "Mr. Black proves to have a strong heart."

As she leaned in, Phaeton inhaled the scent of her. Lilac and something else—lavender perhaps? She had fought the she-devil off him. And her blood flowed in his veins. A bolt of strange energy surged through his body at the very thought of her essence inside him.

America sat upright. "Your eyes have turned red again."

"Mmm. May I bite your neck?" Phaeton chewed the rest of his bun and winked.

Exeter moved around the side of the bed to get a closer look. "I found no evidence of an exchange of blood. Any residual spell from Qadesh will disappear shortly." The doctor clasped hands behind his back. "How do you feel?"

"Thickheaded."

Their laughter caused him to set down his spoon. "What is so amusing?"

The doctor continued to snort. "You decrypted a coded message in minutes. Hardly dull-witted."

America smiled. "Eat up, Mr. Black, so I can move on to your bath."

Exeter checked his watch. "Time to look in on my other patient."

"Doctor Exeter has been at your bedside or his father's for the better part of last night and today."

Exeter looked like he could use a few winks. Phaeton ladled up another spoonful of soup. "How is the Baron?"

"Comfortable, I hope. He is no longer conscious." The doctor nodded a bow and excused himself.

The moment the door closed, Phaeton pulled her close. "Nurse Jones. I believe it is time to examine the wounds on your patient's privates."

"I see that playful smugness is back in your grin." She returned the wicked glint in his eyes and left his wandering hands to wander. Without exposing any skin, she rattled off a report. "Bruising has gone from dark purple to pale green, and the scratches and bite marks are healed over. Wouldn't want to open up any wounds by forcing too much blood down there, now would we?" America laughed and pushed away.

He smiled and pulled her back. "I can take a bit of pain with my pleasure."

She easily read the sleepy sable gaze that perused her body. Shifting her eyes, a darker thought needled at her. She hadn't planned to mention anything about last night. He had been injured, nearly killed by that wicked pythoness, but the question escaped her mouth. "Did you enjoy her?"

His eyes met hers before rolling upward and to the side. "The simple, honest answer would be yes, for a very brief period."

Suddenly and most unexpectedly, she kissed him. His generous mouth opened and unleashed a hot tongue as he took control. How easily he made her body burn for him. She took his lower lip between her teeth and moaned softly. "Thank you for being honest."

A small corner of his mouth twitched. "I didn't know you cared, Miss Jones."

She reached behind her and lifted his arm from around her waist. "I believe I promised you a sponge bath, Mr. Black."

Phaeton's head fell into the pillow, as his belly shuddered. "Do not stop, Miss Jones." The washcloth sprang to life and began to wave. America caught hold of the dancing fabric and gently stroked the soapy cloth over his ready mast. Her hands soapy and slick, she abandoned the cloth and stroked the length of his shaft.

America had built up a fire in the hearth and removed his nightshirt. Carefully, she had washed every part, every appendage except the one he most wanted her to touch. She had taken her time, until the anticipation became unbearable.

Her fingers danced over his chest as she followed a narrow trail of hair past his navel to the proud member throbbing in her hands. "You are beautifully made."

As his arousal edged upward, he sensed she wanted him badly, but would not press for her own pleasure. The quick-witted, affable side of Miss Jones had always made her a pleasant companion, but this recent kindness toward him moved Phaeton, inexplicably.

She kept her fingers wet and soaped, so that she would slip over cuts and scratches. His euphoric demands increased in a frenzy of peaking pleasure. "You may grip tighter, faster."

The vixen purposely stroked slower, lighter. He opened his eyes and frowned.

She grinned. "A picture in the *Kama Sutra* comes to mind, Mr. Black." She leaned over and kissed, then licked him like a stick of hard candy.

He released a kind of trumpeting growl. For a moment, she must have thought she pleasured a bull elephant. When she jerked upright, her eyes were large and black with desire.

"You temptress, you—" He grabbed her up into his arms and lifted her skirts. "Lay on your side." She wrapped a leg around his waist and he found the slit in her pantalettes. His fingers moved into the damp heat between her legs. The light tickling she received continued until he made her cry out and her body tremble. He fingered deeper to see if she would receive him. He was nearly mad with passion. "Oh, my dove, you are ready."

He pressed into her. They shared a ripple, then a wave of fierce arousal, which moved directly through her body into his. He continually marveled at her ability to bring him such astounding pleasure. She answered each of his thrusts, and added more of her own, until she brought him to release. Sleepily, he used his fingers to play and stroke and circle until she tumbled over the edge of desire and into the Land of Nod.

The whining squeak of his bedchamber door roused him out of his own dream. A rustle of skirt and two sets of footsteps.

"Have you seen the way Mr. Black and Miss Jones look at each other, Oom Asa?" Phaeton very clearly heard Mia's whispered comment.

Phaeton opened an eye and raised a finger to his lips. Mia and Exeter stood at the foot of his bed, well aware America lay fast asleep, nestled in his arms. And he did not imagine the subtle lift at one corner of the doctor's mouth, even as he turned his wide-eyed charge away from the scene in his bed.

"Then"—the girl stammered—"have you any idea what is going on between them?"

"I believe I do." The repressed amusement in Exeter's voice was evident. "Come along, Mia." Soft footsteps padded over the carpet and door hinges creaked open.

"Oom Asa, please do not nanny me."

"I shall not and never will attempt to *nanny* you, my dear."

"Are you going to tell me?"

Phaeton smiled at the chit's tenacity.

"In a year or two you'll understand perfectly, Mia." Exeter closed the door.

Chapter Eighteen

A CHAMBERMAID PULLED BACK THE WINDOW DRAPERIES and opened the shutters. A beam of sunlight traveled over her cheek, coaxing America to wake. She yawned and rolled over to enjoy the view, a rather splendid aspect of the deer park. The subtly striped tonal walls meant she was in Phaeton's room.

Phaeton's room? She sat straight up.

"Good morning, my somnolent dove." Handsomely attired, Phaeton stood at the foot of the bed looking refreshed, if a bit pale. He tipped his watch just far enough out of his waistcoat pocket to check the hour. "You have barely enough time to wash up and change if we are to catch the early train to Portsmouth."

She rubbed her eyes. "You must not travel yet, Mr. Black. You need more rest. Doctor says—"

"Plenty of time to sleep on the train. Run along now, the carriage is waiting."

She swept back the bedcovers. Dear Lord, she had slept in her clothes all night. Uncomfortably stiff and feeling a bit grotty, she made her way to the door before questioning his orders. "Do you always get your way Mr. Black?"

"Used to." The man had the temerity to grin. "Before a certain young lady took up residence in my life. I barely remember what it was like to live the joyful unencumbered life of a bachelor."

She slammed the door and opened another farther down

the hall. Her trunks were packed and the boldly striped traveling dress and coat were laid out and ready for her to change into. It seemed Mr. Black could be exceedingly well organized when he set his mind to a task. Not that he was a frivolous man by any means. In fact, he had proven himself to be resilient and resourceful. She exhaled and yanked the bell pull. A large bowl of warm water and a quick wash up refreshed her. The kindly little chambermaid even thought to bring up tea and buttered toast slathered with wild strawberry conserve.

Growing up aboard ship, America had learned many useful things. How to ready herself in a wink, for instance. She was dressed and waiting at the carriage well ahead of Mr. Black, who exited the great house a few minutes later accompanied by Dr. Exeter. The doctor handed a lunch basket to a footman who packed the food stuffs inside the carriage.

"Some rare roast beef for Phaeton to build up his blood. And a jar of bouillon. I believe there are sandwiches and an apple tart as well." She had come to know Dr. Exeter as a thoughtful and kind man, whose severe demeanor did him no justice.

Exeter turned to Phaeton. "The Baron has only hours left. He has asked to make a written confession. I should like to deliver it to Scotland Yard myself."

Phaeton nodded. "A first meeting with Zander Farrell would be best. I'll wire him from the station to expect you. My advice would be to hand over the confession, answer any, well . . . I'm sure—"

"Yes, I am quite sure there will be questions." Exeter coughed. "Will he have me arrested for—what do you call it—harboring?"

Phaeton tilted his chin and squinted. "I don't believe so."

Beads of perspiration formed above the doctor's brow. America pressed her lips together to restrain a chuckle.

Phaeton grinned. "I wouldn't land the airship outside 4 Whitehall. Might get you locked up as a flight risk."

Once their carriage lurched off, she could no longer suppress a grin. "You weren't much solace to the doctor."

"I shall not lose a wink of sleep over Exeter. Scotland Yard will deliberate for weeks over that confession. I suspect, once the Baron is dead, which seems imminent, there will be no one left to arrest—no one they wish to admit to anyway." Phaeton shook his head. "No, I predict the document will be burned and the case will go on unsolved."

When she raised a brow, he grinned. "Can you picture Qadesh standing trial in the Old Bailey?"

"I suppose not." She studied the ready upturn at the ends of his sensuous, masculine mouth. Sometimes, she had to fight off the urge to jump in his lap and kiss him. "You do a great deal of grinning, Mr. Black."

Instantly, he turned the ends of his mouth downward, into a much exaggerated frown, which made her chuckle. "I confess you do have quite the charming smile, but—" She scraped a bit of lower lip under her teeth. "How is it I have never heard you laugh?"

He straightened up. "Because I never laugh, Miss Jones."

"Never?"

He shook his head. "Never."

She wrinkled her brow. "Ever?"

He exhaled. "I remember laughing as a child."

A bit misty-eyed, she nodded. "Your mother died—when you were just a lad."

He glanced out the coach window. "Fully recovered from her death years ago."

Aware she had hit upon a subject that caused him some discomfort, she folded her hands in her lap and waited him out.

Several long minutes passed before his black hooded eyes shifted to met her gaze. "Mother was barely cold in her family crypt before my father remarried. Ghastly woman, but he was deliriously happy—for a time. They used to laugh constantly. I would hear their laughter laying in bed at night, coming from either bedroom, outside in the garden, at the dinner table. Even as my sorrow deepened, the evidence of their happiness was in the air, everywhere." His glower grew darker still. "I vowed never to laugh again, and was greatly relieved to be packed off to school."

Her heart broke to think of Phaeton as a young boy, losing his mother, the only one who understood the fey, darker side of his troubling, extraordinary faculties. How alone in the world he must have felt. She well understood that kind of loss. Her own mother often said it was like learning to live with a foot in two worlds. Many born with abilities beyond the everyday sensory were unschooled and therefore unable to interpret the otherworld. Often, they were deemed insane and subjected to ice baths and horrific treatments in the dreadful prisons otherwise known as asylums.

She remembered a cautionary warning from her mother. Standing on the pier, she buttoned her coat. "Mark my words, child. Keep your essence secret and never reveal your gifts to those who know only the temporal life. They fear the power of the unseen and will often attempt to harm a *vauda* witch." She grabbed her shoulders. "Do you hear me, Síne?"

"*Oui, Maman.*"

She glanced across the carriage cabin and found Phaeton also lost in thought. She cleared her throat. "My mother handed me over to my father when I was seven. How old were you when left motherless?"

His downturned eyes met hers. "Eight."

She sighed, deeply. "Might I ask you how old you are?"

"Five and twenty."

Years younger than she figured. In fact, she was quite taken aback. It made sense though, with regard to some of the immature behavior. He was also wickedly clever about disguising his youth.

The glint in his eye acknowledged her reaction. "I was pushed ahead in school. Got bullied by my classmates for being clever. Then, when I moved up a grade, I got bullied because I was still clever and a great deal brighter than the older boys."

No wonder he was such a tough scraper. Brave as well as wicked smart. "I have no doubt of it, Mr. Black." Her admiring gaze did seem to please him some as he eased back into upholstered squabs and resumed an affable expression.

"Since the sapphire has never left your hand . . ." His gaze traveled to her ring finger. "I do recall we got engaged on the way to Roos House." Phaeton reached into his waistcoat pocket and pulled out a gold band. "Will you marry me?"

A heated flush ran up her throat and set her cheeks on fire. "You are joking, sir."

Phaeton's eyes crinkled. "Yes, of course I am, Miss Jones. Had you there for a moment, didn't I?"

America smiled, and didn't stop chuckling until Phaeton got the engagement ring and band on her finger.

She held up her hand. "Quite a lot of jewelry for one small digit."

Phaeton leaned forward and nodded toward the coach window. "We have arrived at Waterloo station, Mrs. Black. Shall we get ourselves to Portsmouth Harbor?"

It poured rain and sleet in Portsmouth. "No cabs at the moment, but I have paid a baggage handler to procure us a lift at first opportunity." Miss Jones sat on one of her trunks looking prettily rumpled and wonderfully content.

Their compartment had been empty for the last leg of the trip, and he had unmercifully teased, one hand under her dress, until she had nearly swooned from her semi-public climax. It had been hugely indecent of him, and unbelievably arousing.

"Any moment now, a stranger could walk through that door and discover us." He whispered the words as his fingers coaxed her to the brink, her moans of release muffled by his kiss. Afterward when the dear girl could speak coherently again, he got up to stretch his legs and unlock the door.

He waited for her to clap her mouth shut.

She had appeared unable to decide on laughter or a flogging. He held onto the baggage rack above her, swaying to the movement of the train. Her gaze had traveled down to the evidence of his enormous physical discomfort. Her eyes narrowed. "You shall atone for this, Phaeton."

"Slow and torturous, I hope," he had replied.

Phaeton smiled at her across the station platform. She now regarded him with the kind of sultry-eyed air women gave men who knew how to attend to their pleasure. He loved that look. Especially hers. He had every intention of tossing Mrs. Black onto a bed at the Dorchester Arms and having his way with her, as soon as possible. He pictured her fully naked flesh and that wild mop of curls spread over counterpane and pillows.

"Phaeton!" Inwardly, he cringed at the recognition of Inspector Moore's shout. He swiveled. "Thought I would check the afternoon train, just in case you made it." Dexter nodded to America. "Very good to see you, Miss Jones. I take it the journey was not overly taxing?"

Phaeton used his flat-lipped grin. "Only the arrival."

"How's that?"

He shrugged. "No transport, I'm afraid."

"Come along, I've got a hansom waiting." He bowed to the lady. "Miss Jones, let me escort you."

Peevish, but still well in control, Phaeton strolled after them, followed by porter and luggage.

"There's another cab now, Phaeton. We'll take the smaller bags with us, and you can follow along with the lady's trunk."

America feigned a pout and smiled at him. Dex offered his hand, and she climbed into the waiting cab. Phaeton glanced overhead. At least the rain had abated. The porter strapped the trunk to the back of the hansom and Phaeton soon followed along after his wife.

Alighting his cab at the Dorchester, a ready bellhop took care of the trunk, and Phaeton stepped into a small, well-appointed lobby in time to overhear the hotel clerk's question to the couple at the desk.

"Will you be wanting a suite, then, or a room, Mr. and Mrs. Black?"

Phaeton cleared his throat and spoke up. "I think, perhaps, a suite with an ajoining bedroom for Mrs. Black's brother." He approached the desk clerk. "I'm sorry. You appear confused, and no wonder. I'm afraid I was busy outside sorting out the luggage. I am the lady's husband." Phaeton swiveled to the right. "This gentleman is my brother-in-law." Phaeton squinted at the noticeable tension in Dexter's jaw.

America spoke sweetly but stabbed him with her eyes. "A suite would be the perfect arrangement, dear." She nodded to the clerk. "What might you have available?"

As the clerk sputtered, Phaeton removed his wallet from an inside coat pocket and laid several large denomination bills on the desk. "I'm sure something near to perfect can be arranged."

"Very good, sir." Immediately, the clerk tapped a bell, and they were escorted upstairs to a cozy suite of rooms. A pleasant-sized parlor sat between two bedrooms and featured a large bay widow. They waited for the bellman to stoke coals in the hearth.

"Since it's nearly teatime, shall we have a little something brought up?" Phaeton nodded to America and Dex, who ordered a sampling of cakes and sandwiches with their tea. "A bottle of whiskey for me. Something distilled in Scotland, if you have it." He handed the man half a crown. "And a glass."

At the window, he pulled back a sheer drapery, careful to shade himself from anyone on the street below. A mist of light rain tapped gently at the glass. Past their quiet street, a vast expanse of harbor stretched out to an invisible grey horizon line. The bay was dotted with ships of all makes and sizes, including two huge battleships anchored far offshore. "So Dex, fill us in on what you have uncovered thus far."

"Ten days ago, we received a wire from the Gibraltar office about the *Draakster*, bound for this harbor. The ship made port late last week. Extremely suspicious registry, manned by a Dutch crew."

America settled onto a camelback divan. "Yanky Willem?"

"A syndicated shipping company is the owner of record." Dex removed a pipe and pouch from his coat pocket. "The Dutch are a cagey lot. We believe Willem is the owner of majority, but we can't get them to confirm. Mind if I smoke?"

"Not at all, Mr. Moore, please do have your pipe." That beautiful bow of a mouth of hers fell open, slightly, her eyes riveted on Moore. Phaeton suddenly wanted nothing less than all her ships returned to her. By the look on his face, it was clear Dexter felt the same way.

Her straight posture softened as she leaned forward. "Do you have a description of her?"

"Two masts and a single smokestack, near the tonnage you described as the vessel presumed lost in the Bay of Bengal, Miss Jones."

Phaeton settled down beside her. "How do we plan to get access to the records?"

"We have a man in Rotterdam knocking heads with the registrarship. You called it earlier, Phaeton; we have no time to wait for records or warrants. The ship remains tied up at dock, transferring cargo." Dex tapped down the tobacco in his pipe. "We go tonight, or risk losing this one."

"I'd know the layout of this ship in the dark, if that helps. My father's first steamer, a right beauty she is, I practically grew up on her. If this is the *Ruby Star*, I can identify every scratch and repair on her."

A thrill ran down Phaeton's spine, which quickly turned into a chill as he watched America brighten with anticipation. "Dangerous work, Dex. Besides you and I, do we have any other trained agents here? Who are your contacts?"

Dexter's description of the local police force and the Harbor patrol was interrupted by a knock at the door. The blessed tea and whiskey had arrived. Phaeton sampled a few sandwiches and washed them down with a good tumbler full of spirit.

"We can't bring any of these men in unless we are in some kind of serious trouble. We can't even alert them to our plans." Phaeton mulled over their circumstances. Drat it all, they were in a tight corner. "Any local blokes on the pay ledger?"

"Just Percy, at the Blue Anchor. I have a room above the pub—"

"Keep it." Phaeton was beginning to formulate a plan. Albeit a perilous one. "We can't do much of anything before nightfall."

Dex leaned forward, eyes alight. "You mean to board her? It will be risky. The crew goes ashore most every night, but there's a watch. Several men patrol the decks at regular intervals."

Phaeton looked up from his empty glass. There would be no more whiskey this night. "We'll need clothing. Whatever vestments merchant sailors wear these days and the loudest, most conspicuous doxy frock we can find."

America rose to leave.

"You must remain in the hotel, Mrs. Black." Her brows gathered as her bottom lip protruded. "Whatever for? I would be most helpful picking out a wardrobe for you and Detective Moore."

"I have no doubt of it." He sighed. "I think it is safe to assume we arrived unrecognized. I would like to keep it that way, until this evening." Phaeton took her hand. "Trust me, my dove, you have a very important role to play, but it must wait until tonight."

He kissed her knuckles. "And do not bother unpacking your trunk. We will likely have to quit town in haste."

Chapter Nineteen

AMERICA STUDIED HER REFLECTION IN THE VANITY LOOKING GLASS and sucked in a breath. A pivot sideways revealed an alarming profile of bosom. Phaeton had some sort of ruse planned for the evening and her body, poured into this skimpy red dress, played a feature role. Her pulse raced in anticipation of the unknown, adventurous night ahead.

A knock at the door signaled help had finally arrived. She let the top of the dress fall to expose her new strapless corset.

"Come in." America took up a tin of loose powder and puff. "I need assistance with my corset and gown, please."

Adept hands loosened strings. She trembled at the light touch of fingers moving under the silk and whalebone undergarment to cup her breasts. She met his gaze in the vanity mirror. "Dear husband, I fear you misunderstand. My garments are to be fastened, not undone."

He nuzzled the side of her neck and earlobe as his fingertips played over nipples. "Mrs. Black, have I ever told you how enchanting you are as a common pub trollop?"

America shrugged off his kiss with a grin. "Not too tight, you know how I hate being trussed up like a roasting hen."

Those talented fingers pulled on laces, which magically tucked in her waist and pushed up her breasts. "As appealing as this undergarment presents your wares, I do believe the corset is unwarranted."

"If you have any hope of closing up this gown, sir, the

stays are required." He helped her pull up the top half of the dress. As he fastened many small cloth-covered buttons, she examined the roughneck sailor standing behind her. Phaeton wore a short wool jacket open over a heavy cloth shirt and corded trousers. Wide, striped braces held up the pants. A woolen scarf wrapped loosely around his neck reminded her of the chill in the air. He needed a shave; the dark shadow along his jawline completed his disguise to perfection. She shivered. "You make a rather handsome seaman, Mr. Black."

He shot a flirtatious grin back in the mirror. "The exulted duke of deckhands will be in sore need of relief later this evening. I do hope your door remains open."

She rose from the vanity seat. "Are your rooming arrangements with Mr. Moore cramped? I hope not."

His gaze traveled over burgeoning bosom, up her throat to a pout that she would soon form into a frown if he did not stop his ogling.

"Come here."

She tilted her chin in defiance, and he yanked her close, covering her lips with his. He entered her mouth with his probing tongue and a great deal of vigor. A tingle shot through her body and he did not relent until she returned his ardor. She wrapped her hands around his neck and tussled the short waves at his nape. He spoke softly against her lips. "The gentlemen's accommodations are tolerable." He kissed the tip of her nose. "Two narrow single beds, which prevent me from accidently nuzzling up against Dex in the middle of the—"

A rap came at the door. She caught a flash of annoyance in his eyes. He stole a quick kiss before crossing the room. Detective Moore, Greek seafarer cap in hand, stood at the threshold with a bit of a glower on his face. "We should get down to the pub."

"What's the dinner fare like? I'm starving." Phaeton turned to America. "Hungry, Mrs. Black?"

America covered her outrageous attire with a warm black coat. "Famished."

"Love a woman with healthy appetites." Phaeton carried on in his usual carefree jovial manner, but America could not help but attune herself to the nervous undercurrent in his demeanor. She very clearly sensed him steel himself for the evening ahead as he and Detective Moore jockeyed to escort her down the servants' stairs and out the back alley of the hotel.

America sighed. As amusing as both these handsome men's attentions were, their relentless male posturing quickly proved tiresome. Her hopes and attentions were focused on a bigger prize. A nine hundred ton freighter moored dock-side. When they reached a narrow concourse between a crisscross of streets, she could stand it no longer. "If you two continue to act like smitten schoolboys competing over the headmaster's daughter, I shall be forced to—" She tried to think of something to threaten with, but these Yard men held all the cards. Except one.

Phaeton's churlish grin did not help matters. "Forced to what, luv?"

She nailed them both with a sultry look. "Withhold my affection." She backed away and slowly opened her coat. "The man most likely to receive this gift will be the one who gets down to business." After a sufficient period of leching she buttoned the coat up to her neck and clarified. "For the rest of the evening, we shall concentrate on my stolen shipping business. Gentlemen?"

Phaeton's sable eyes narrowed into thin slits.

Dexter swallowed. "The Blue Anchor is just round the corner."

Several pints washed down a plate of chops and two baskets of fried fish. The hot meal put them all in better temperament, ready for news. Detective Moore went after another pint and returned with word from his informant,

Mr. Percy. "Several of Yanky Willem's men have been spotted in Weippert's casino—on the canal walk."

"I know where that is," America piped up.

Phaeton shushed them both and signaled for Dexter to sit down. He spoke in no more than a whisper. "Excellent news. We can make more of a show of Miss Jones in a saloon dance hall than stuffed away in a grimy dockside pub."

She spoke up. "I'm to be the focus?"

Phaeton set his mouth in a grim line. "Never believe I relish the prospect of using you as a live decoy, but if all goes well, your presence will serve to roust Yanky Willem and most of his crew out of that ship and scatter them about Portsmouth in search of the enticing Miss Jones."

Both she and Moore grinned. Dexter leaned further into their small circle. "And while Willem's men run about town, we will be—"

"Searching the ship."

"Might be brilliant, if it weren't so bloody dangerous." Moore groused a bit more, but his eyes sparkled with excitement.

America set her shoulders back. "How much time will we have, before they start to suspect something?"

Phaeton shook his head. "We can't count on much more than an hour. Two at most."

She turned to Moore. "In order to make my claim, how many proofs do I need?"

"Three should do it, witnessed by myself and Phaeton."

She thought about the size of the ship and the areas she needed to locate and examine. "It's not enough time."

Phaeton rose to leave. "It's going to have to be."

Unlike the more elegant establishments in London, Portsmouth's casino turned out to be more of a fancy public house with a stage for musicals and a band for dancing. The gambling hall would be located in the rear of the building, one presumed.

Phaeton made something of a show of removing her coat.

A number of heads turned along with a rude gesture and a few lurid queries. "Pay no attention to them." Phaeton held her firmly by the shoulders. "How many pirates might you recognize on sight, my dove?"

Glancing around the room she lifted her chin. "Very few. And I am not afraid."

He studied her resolve. "Well then, we shall flush them out of hiding."

A number of couples assembled on the dance floor as the band struck up a popular military waltz. Phaeton removed his scarf and jacket and tossed all the coats into Moore's arms. "Hold these."

"Whatever for?" The detective frowned.

"I am going to take Miss Jones for a spin around the floor. You will station yourself at the door and observe who takes note of the young lady and dashes off toward the harbor." Moore appeared far from resigned, but obeyed orders.

Phaeton returned to her. "Shall we?"

She hesitated.

"You do the waltz?"

She frowned. "Not this queer jig."

"Three beats with skips rather than gliding steps." He grinned that cajoling, winning smile of his. "Come, let me show you."

Under the brightest chandelier, in the middle of the floor, Phaeton swung her up off the ground and into the waltz. He apparently thought to make a spectacle of them. And damn, if the man wasn't an accomplished dancer. He led in such a skillful manner, she easily followed the faster paced steps.

The dance featured a hesitation before a turn, and he would lift her up in the air as he completed the rotation. The sudden elevation had the effect of raising her petticoats, which received a great deal of attention from the gents on the sidelines. Otherwise, he led her in lovely circles about the room as she relaxed in his arms.

"Now we will wait for them to show their hand."

She managed a dainty shrug. "I can't very well identify pirates while occupied in bawdy saloon dancing."

"But are you enjoying yourself?" His eyes crinkled as she locked onto his cheerful gaze and leaned into the next turn. She lifted the corners of her mouth. "I am."

A loud jerk of chairs and a grumble of customers alerted them to several large bodies moving through the casino in a hurried manner. Phaeton tensed slightly as he spun her along the dance floor. She watched him sneak a glance through the couples surrounding them. "I suspect you have been recognized, my dear."

Her heart thumped an erratic beat inside her chest. "Where are they now?"

Phaeton maneuvered them deeper into a thick group of dancers, and craned his neck. "They're at the door."

"Does Inspector Moore see them?" She pressed dry lips back and forth to moisten them. Phaeton lowered his chin in a nod aimed at Dexter.

"Now what?"

His attention returned to her. "We finish our dance, my dove."

She stepped down hard on his toe. "Ouch." He winced. "You little virago."

She chuckled. "Surly, cock-up."

He pulled her close. "We'll meet up with Dex outside. First, we need to make this look good, like we're headed upstairs for a quick tumble."

Phaeton hauled her off the dance floor, tossed a man half a shilling for a room, and chased her up a flight of stairs. She giggled and carried on, until they reached the end of a long hallway with no exit.

They retraced their steps and found a side door that opened after Phaeton gave it a hard shove. A zigzag of wooden stairs led down to a narrow side yard. The sound of a safety match being struck revealed a spark of light in the dark.

She turned to Phaeton. "Mr. Moore?"

He nodded. "After you, my dove, with the elephantine feet."

She chuckled softly all the way down the stairs. They found Moore behind a large refuse bin. "Glad you two are having a jolly good time." Dexter handed over their coats and hats.

Phaeton wound the scarf round his neck. "In which direction did they head?"

"Two of them took off at a run toward the harbor, two others spread out. I suspect one is in the alley behind us and the other is stationed somewhere out front."

He shrugged into his coat. "Pull your cap low and stay hunched over until we cross the street. If you spy one of the blokes, give us a sign." He turned to her. "As far as anyone knows, you're tasting the better part of me in an upstairs room. Keep that pretty head down and don't fall behind."

Single file, with Phaeton ahead and Dexter behind her, they snaked their way up the side yard and slipped across the street.

"Up ahead on the corner." Dexter jogged around her. Things moved rapidly as the two men greeted the lookout and asked for a light. Phaeton knocked the man up against the wall. She had no time to grit her teeth before she heard a head crack against brick. He signaled her to keep watch while he and Moore pulled the half conscious seaman down a narrow arcade of shops. They left him tied and gagged in a dark corner.

"Let's get to the harbor."

Dexter nodded, wild-eyed and out of breath. "She's in the great basin, north of Queen Street."

"Lead the way, Mr. Moore."

Shaking off a tremble, she inhaled a deep breath and coughed. Phaeton checked on her. "Are you all right?" She nodded. His arm went around her, gentle and soothing, before he nudged her up ahead. Once again they wound their way through the irregular streets of the port town, keeping to the shadows and away from streetlamps.

Dexter led them along the stone wall of an HMS storehouse and halted. "Round this corner, a number of casks are stacked on a large pallet. When I give the sign, make your way there as quickly and quietly as possible."

She nodded and Phaeton signaled a thumbs-up.

Just as they were about to make a dash, Moore turned around and herded them backward, into an old carriage passageway. He placed his finger to his lips.

A clatter of footsteps and shouting could mean only one thing, Yanky and his crew had taken the bait. At least she hoped so. She could just make Phaeton out in the deep shadows of the niche. He winked at her.

When the footsteps faded, Phaeton edged his way to the entrance and took a peek. He waved them forward and once again, they made their way to the corner of the building. "Ready?"

She scurried after both men and took up shelter behind a large barrel. The familiar scent of brine and smoked wood made her eyes water. She found a break between casks where she could view the main deck. A watchman passed by the gang plank and made his way aft, past the chimney.

The very sight of her caused America to suck in a breath. A sleek two-masted schooner, the *Ruby Star* also flaunted a tall smokestack thrust up from her midship. She'd recognize those lines anywhere, despite the fact that the dark crimson hull trim had been freshly repainted marine blue.

"Do you recognize your ship, Miss Jones?" Inspector Moore asked the question, but Phaeton leaned in close to hear the answer.

"I'd wager a hold full of black tea it's *Ruby* all right." She supposed her eyes glistened with a tear or two. "Let's go aboard."

Phaeton caught her coattail and pulled her back. "Hold on, there, Miss." Even when she growled, he smiled rather sweetly. "Dex and I will go aboard and disable the guard. You will wait here until we give a whistle." Phaeton nodded at Moore. "Ready?"

"Wait." She grasped his arm. "Check for damage on the far side of the chimney funnel, near the top. A spar let loose in a storm and left a nick on the rim. The lady may have a new coat of paint, but I doubt Yanky went to the expense of fixing a dent."

Chapter Twenty

PHAETON GRABBED A BELAYING PIN and tapped the guard on the shoulder. "Avast there, Davey Jones." The pirate swung around. *Thwack!* The seaman wavered, then crumbled to the ground. Dexter dragged the man behind the funnel while Phaeton searched the unconscious guard and pocketed several useful items. "Yo ho, heave to, a-pirating we go."

Dex nodded upward. "Take a look above when you get a chance, Long John Silver."

Phaeton craned his neck. "Thar she be—a good-sized mark near the chimney rim." He peered around the side of the smokestack and gave a whistle.

The light-footed Miss Jones walked the gangplank like a cat. Monitoring her stealthy progress across the ship, he grinned. Nimble all right, when she wasn't otherwise occupied stomping his toes. She drew close, and he pulled her behind the funnel. Her eyes were bright with excitement and something more akin to nerve, or courage. Dog's bollocks, she was appealing. He resisted the urge to toss the wench against the stack and impale her, much like that first night in the Savoy Row. Quashing his insatiable appetite for the young lady, he continued to marvel at just how pleased he was to have her around. "Where to, me beauty?"

"Captain's cabin below, through the wheelhouse."

He placed his hands on her waist and swiveled her about.

"Make your way carefully; I'm right behind you." Dex fell in step behind them.

"Keep a tight group." They scurried aft and slipped into the deck housing. A shaft of moonlight and the hollow tick of a clock permeated the control room. A huge iron ship's wheel, tipped with brass handles, dominated the space. America waved them past a high desk, covered in nautical charts. When they reached a narrow, spiral ladder, Phaeton caught her arm. "Any crew quarters below?"

She shook her head. "Passenger cabins and captain's quarters."

Phaeton positioned her between Dex and himself and took the lead. At the bottom of the stair, he craned his neck fore and aft. No duty guard. He waved her ahead, and she led them to a glossy lacquered door. She lifted a finger to her lips and pointed to a dark rectangular spot on the wood where a name plate had been removed.

Gingerly, she tried the knob. "Locked."

Phaeton held up an iron ring and dangled a set of keys. "Thought these might come in handy."

She fumbled through the bunch, fingers trembling. "Dear God, I know these keys." She fit one to the keyhole and jiggled. The door swung open. A single lantern, low on fuel, sputtered above. Rich dark wood paneling covered the walls of the cabin. America pointed to a built-in secretary. "Second drawer down, there is a false bottom compartment accessed from underneath."

The desk's roll-top cover didn't budge. America bit her lower lip. "Only the captain keeps the key."

On his knees, Phaeton wedged a knife between the writing surface and cover. He angled the tip and lifted the latch. He nodded to America. She rolled back the slated wood and exposed a bank of small drawers and pigeonholes along the back of the desk.

Phaeton removed the second drawer and turned it upside

down. The lantern sputtered a last gasp of light, plunging them into darkness. "Bollocks." A dim pool of moonlight poured through the porthole. "Dex, have you a torch on you?"

"Right here." Dex retrieved a long metal tube-shaped device from his coat pocket. He toggled a switch and slapped the gadget against the palm of his hand. "Only, the damn thing won't—" A beam of light shot across the room, as the torch tumbled to the floor. Several small cylindrical shaped objects rolled out of the bottom. "Jeezus, Dex, get them back in before the wires detach and we lose the light."

Tentatively, Dex picked up the small batteries and tried fitting them back in. Phaeton exhaled. "Come on then, pretend it's cock alley."

"Stuff it, Phaeton."

"I assure you, mine won't fit."

America elbowed her way in-between them. "If you're going to act like schoolboys—" She deftly pushed the two cylinders back into the tube and screwed on the end cap. She pointed the torch at the small storage compartment. Phaeton moved his fingers around the drawer's edges.

She steadied the beam. "What is this thing, anyhow?"

"Experimental. Electrical light generated by dry cell batteries." Something shifted under his fingers, and he slid back a wooden peg. The bottom dropped down along with a packet of papers. America angled the circle of light over as Dex untied the stack.

"Several letters here, of a personal nature, written by . . . appears to be a lady." Moore turned over the note paper.

"Abigail." Her voice, little more than a whisper, faltered. "Captain Jackson Starke's fiancée."

Dex looked up from the signature and nodded. "All my affection, Abigail." He unfolded another loose sheet. "Looks as though this was torn from a journal."

"12 July 1888." Dex read on in a low whisper. "Two days

out of Rangoon, we were fired upon and boarded by men who took over ship and cargo. I remain locked in this cabin, and do not know what fate lies in store for me. In the event the pirates do not scuttle the *Ruby Star,* I record here, my experience of these dastardly events. It is my greatest wish this accounting might one day assist in bringing the blackguards to justice." Dex read on silently for a few more sentences. "If this note is discovered, then rest assured, I am dead. Please tell my mother, sister, and my dear fiancée, Miss Abigail Fisher, they were in my last thoughts."

Tears streamed, and Phaeton dabbed a handkerchief over her cheeks. "You now have written testimony, my dove."

She blinked and turned to Dex. "Need we go further with these proofs, then?"

His thin-lipped grin appeared hopeful. "Hardly seems necessary to go on with the investigation." He refolded the papers and stuffed them inside his coat. "Captain Starke names the ship several times, and I am in receipt of a copy of her English registry. No magistrate in the land would not recognize the ship as yours, Miss Jones."

Phaeton nodded upward. "Well then, shall we wake the harbor master?" As if in answer, several loud thumps and a shuffling came from above. Phaeton switched off the torch and stuffed it in his coat. "Is there another exit?"

America nodded. "Forward, past the boiler room."

"Dex, you go with Miss Jones. I'll wait here. Ready yourselves near the main deck, close to the gangplank. I hope to make quite a din." Swiftly and quietly, they exited the cabin and closed the door. He caught Moore's eye. "Wait for a commotion, then make your dash down the plank."

America shook her head. "We'll not leave without you."

Phaeton turned her around and shoved her in front of Moore. "Do not wait for me. I'll join up with you at the harbor patrol office."

Dex took her arm and pulled. She resisted.

"I shall hold dear your adorable and worried glare, Miss Jones." Phaeton eyeballed Moore. "Muzzle and carry her off if necessary. Now go, the both of you."

Phaeton waited in the narrow corridor, until he completely lost sight of her. He sensed activity above in the wheelhouse and climbed the spiral of stairs high enough to get a glimpse of several men entering the control room.

He poked his head higher and still the dullards paid him no heed. Finally, he climbed near to the top of the stairs and leaned back against the curved rail.

He cleared his throat. "Might any of you bilge rats tell me where the whiskey is located? Devil take it, I can't seem to find a drop of grog in the captain's quarters."

All three men spun around and stared, openmouthed.

"And where's that bloody bottle of rum you blokes sing about?" Phaeton crossed his arms across his chest. "I'll take a noggin o' that matey."

"Here now, what have we got—?" One of the stunned seaman finally came to his senses, while another found his voice and yelled out the door. "Found one of 'em."

Three crewmen lunged at once, and Phaeton slid down the banister. He headed straight for the captain's cabin and pressed his shoulder to the door.

He threw the latch, backed up and waited. How he might extricate himself from these scurvy pirates, he had no idea. If caught and captured, which seemed imminent, his only hope rested on Dex and America. They would have to find a way to marshal the harbor patrol—and be quick about it.

A battery of shouts and scuffles had every man on deck headed for the wheelhouse. Dex nudged America. "That's our signal." He pushed her ahead, and they skittered down the plank and slipped behind a stack of dockside barrels. Between casks, she angled a view to the ship. "What will become of him? If they—"

"No time for worry, Miss." Dex checked behind them. A

full moon lit up the docks like it was twilight. He grabbed her hand and they ran for the deep shadow cover of the looming warehouse.

Plastered against the brick wall, he exhaled. "We need to make our way to the harbor patrol office."

She nodded, licking dry lips. "Somewhere near the gates, I believe. Do you know which way?"

"Not sure, exactly," Moore pointed across the street. "When I give the signal, run for the corner shop front." He waited for a lone carriage to pass by. "Now." Gingerly, they made their way in the direction of a wire office, where a single lamp lit the window. He tried the door and found it open.

America stepped inside. The office appeared deserted.

Dexter ventured ahead. "Hello?"

"Finally, got you!"

She sensed Moore stiffen as they both instinctively backed up. A red-eyed clerk with a great shock of orange hair sprang up from behind the counter. The man held a growling tabby cat by the scruff of its neck. The struggling feline swung a paw at the telegraph worker.

America exhaled. Dex cleared his throat. "Sorry to intrude, but could you direct us to the Harbor Patrol station, please?"

"There now, out you go." The wiry man swung open a Dutch door and exited the counter area. He chuffed the neck of the longhaired cat and sneezed. "That'll be the last of you for the evening, Mr. Chubbs." He opened the door and tossed the snarling puss out.

The clerk pulled a cloth square from his pocket and snuffled. "Two blocks south, past the gunwarf. Patrol office is straight across the way from the Harbor Master's Lodge, just this side of the Victory Gate." The man gasped for air.

Dex tipped his hat. "Be sure to take a powder for that wheeze."

They made a run for the Harbor gates and found lamps

ablaze inside the police station. Dexter's calling card got them ushered into the sergeant's office. A rather young man for his station, he listened intently to their story, with few interruptions. America, for her part, took a moment to catch her breath. When the sergeant eyeballed her chest, she took the opportunity to unbutton her coat, show a bit of cleavage.

She noted that Inspector Moore left out certain significant parts of the story. Namely the fact that a full accounting of the act of piracy had been found, signed by the deceased captain. "You must tell him about Phaeton."

"Indeed. Detective Phaeton Black, also of Scotland Yard, may well be in trouble. If he does not meet us here, within the hour, we must assume he is captured."

The young officer leaned back into his chair. "Certainly the crew will believe him to be an intruder and bring him here to the police cells?"

Dear God, was the man a bit thick? America bit her lip. "No. They are pirates, Sergeant–?" She searched her memory for his name.

"Nathan James."

She inhaled a deep breath to calm her racing heart. "Sergeant James. These men stole half of my father's merchant fleet in order to force a bankruptcy. Yanky Willem is a desperate man. He will stop at nothing to end this investigation. I fear for Mr. Black's life."

"A rather sophisticated plot for pirates, don't you think, Miss . . . Jones, is it?" The man had the gall to plunk his booted feet onto the corner of his desk. "Searching a foreign registered ship without a warrant is a serious breech of maritime law. Might well have to wait for a ruling by the magistrate."

The sergeant's nonchalant demeanor was beyond bearing. All manner of suspicious thoughts ran through her head. She turned to Moore, out of the policeman's view, and raised a brow.

Moore blinked a nod. "I'm afraid this incident could

quickly escalate into a life and death matter. Might we chance disturbing the Harbor Master at this hour?"

The sergeant shifted black eyes to the clock on the wall. "Near to midnight, if ye wake him, he'll not be kindly disposed to your plight."

She noted a phone box mounted on the wall, and posed an innocent question. "Oh my, is that a telephone? I have heard so much about them."

Feet whisked off the desk, he leaned forward and widened a grin. "Yes, Miss. Installed just last month, connects us to a substation in the basin and across the street to the lodge."

She brightened. "The Harbor Master's lodge?"

The captain's grin faded to something icier. "Yes."

"Lovely. Shall we call him straight away before he's off to bed?" She glanced at Dex, whose mouth twitch pleased her to no end.

The young sergeant's eyes darted from her to the telephone box. "Well, I suppose . . ."

She batted her eyes enough to make them water. "I don't believe the Harbor police of Portsmouth would let down a fellow officer of the law. If Mr. Black is injured or killed in the line of duty . . ." She squared her shoulders and lifted her chin. "Well, I would hate for anything to reflect poorly on the Harbor Master."

The sergeant cranked up the phone and waited. "Yes. Hello. Might I speak with the Harbor Master? If he's abed— No? Yes, I'll wait."

The sergeant rolled his eyes and grinned. "We're in luck, he's—"

"Captain MacLeod. Yes sir, quite late to be calling, but there appears to be an incident brewing." After a heated exchange with his boss, there quickly developed a noticeable shift in the sergeant's demeanor. "Yes sir, she claims to be the daughter—a shipping merchant, named—?" He quirked a brow.

"Charles Gardiner Jones."

The sergeant dutifully repeated after her. "Her name? Jones, as well, sir. Right away, sir." Incredulous, he held out the telephone's earpiece. "He wishes to speak with you, Miss."

Tentatively, she took the cone-shaped device and held it to her ear.

"Say hello."

"Hello?"

The sergeant positioned her closer to the box on the wall. "Keep the listening end to your ear and speak here."

"Oh yes, I see." She leaned close to another black metal cone and spoke. "Hello?"

"Am I speaking with the daughter of Captain Charles Jones?"

She nodded to the thin, metallic phantom voice. When she heard no response, she remembered to speak into the black metal cone. "Yes, sir. I am America Jones."

Openmouthed, she returned the listening end to the sergeant. "He says he'll be here straight away." She glanced at the clock. A great unease surged through her body, not unlike the night she had discovered Phaeton laid out prone beneath Qadesh. Just two nights ago, he lay deathly still, as the Nile queen drained the life from his body. He was in no condition to fight off Yanky Willem's bruisers.

America took a deep breath and jumped back as an imposing gent hurled the bulk of his frame into the room. He lifted his hat to reveal a wavy head of hair that merged seamlessly into a fuzzy wealth of grey muttonchop sideburns.

The gleam in his bright blue eyes sparked a memory. His face, a crisscross of seaman's wrinkles, was lined from years of salty air and sun. The man was older now, but his essence somehow oddly familiar. She inched forward as recognition burst forth. "Alastair MacLeod?"

"The very same." The man's cheeks grew rosy as he took in the sight of her. "Great guns, it is you, lass." He lifted her into a great bear hug of an embrace and whirled her about the room. Setting her down, he took a longer look at her. "And what a beauty you've grown up to be."

While she gasped for air, the Harbor Master sized up her companion. "Used to be a scrawny little mulatto child scampering about the ship. Into plenty of mischief, as I recall."

"I imagine she was quite the . . . scalawag." Dex stepped forward. "Inspector Moore, Scotland Yard."

"So my sergeant tells me." The large Scot examined both their faces. The sort of examination one sensed whenever being questioned by a law officer of some experience. He watched their eyes, looking for any tell-tale physical twitch that might indicate a falsehood. "By the looks on both yer faces, you'd like me to arrest a few pirates, dockside."

America wrung her hands together. "Captain MacLeod, might we go over the details as we make our way down to the ship? Another Yard man on the case, Detective Black, was to have met us here at the station, and I'm afraid he is long overdue. Inspector Moore and I believe he is in grave danger."

The hulking Harbor Master eyeballed his second in command. "Show a leg then, Sergeant."

The younger man barked an order down the hallway and bobbies came running from every corner of the station to assemble in formation. "Get yourself and every man on duty to the wharf." MacLeod turned to Dex. "What pier?"

"Not sure. Just past HMS Storehouses."

"That would be Pier 9 in the old basin, sir." The sergeant turned to leave.

"Hold on." The elder man barely had to raise his voice to halt his men. "Surround the ship, stealthy-like, and wait for my arrival."

"Yes, sir." Someone unlocked the armory cabinet and each man took a weapon as they filed out.

MacLeod turned back to her and Detective Moore. "Have ye any proofs these claims you make are true?"

America eyeballed Moore's inside coat pocket. With a reluctant sort of half smile, he removed the stack of letters and unfolded the journal pages. "We found these."

MacLeod braced himself against the heavy oak desk and donned a pair of spectacles. "I'll not be asking ye any questions about how ye came into possession of these documents so don't go offering any answers." Peering over the rim of his glasses, he gave them a stern look that softened into something more akin to a wink.

Dex grinned. "Yes, sir."

He read through the first half of the captain's recounting of the piracy before he refolded the document and returned the pages to Moore. "Keep these safe; I'll be wanting to study them further. For now, I've seen enough."

He smiled at her. "Under the special power of the Local Authority Act granted me by the Naval Office, any ship or cargo suspected of being taken by illegal means may be detained by warrant and searched, until such time as sufficient evidence of guilt or innocence may be established."

Relief welled up in her eyes. "Thank you, Captain MacLeod."

"Your father was a fair trader, Miss. I was greatly saddened to hear of his passing last year. Captain Starke, as well. Both men were well thought of in these waters."

America swept an errant tear or two away with her hand. "I don't mean to be rushing you, Captain, but might we?" She nodded street side.

The hulking man eased himself off the edge of the desk, and limped toward the door. She hadn't noticed the hitch in his walk until now.

"Touch of the gout, lass. Might ease a bit as we take to the road."

It was all America could do to keep from breaking away and running down the cobbled lane ahead of Detective Moore and Captain MacLeod.

Chapter Twenty-one

"Damn ye, bilge-sucking scurvy dogs." Phaeton tightened his midsection against a battery of punches. The sharp, rapid-fire blows did not relent until he wheezed for air and his knees buckled. The men on each side of him tightened their grip. A teeth-chattering blow to his jaw ended in a brief respite into merciful senselessness.

"Where is she?"

A trickle of red spittle dripped to the floor. Hundreds of bloody mallets throbbed a drumbeat inside his skull. He lifted his head. "She?"

The burly seaman drew back his fist. "Seems like he wants more of this." Poised to strike, the man waited for the order.

Phaeton tried moving his jaw. A nice pipe of opium would be just the trick right about now. His partially swollen eye failed to blot out the angry man who spoke from the doorway.

"What are you? A fellow confederate? No, I think not." Words uttered in a thick accent. The unattractive, probable leader of this motley crew sauntered closer. "Lover, perhaps? Much more likely, I think."

So. This was Yanky Willem.

"If I were you, I'd give Miss Jones up."

Eye-to-eye, Phaeton returned the man's stare. "If I were you, I'd be rather homely."

A hard slap across the face roused Phaeton into alertness.

"The ladies do like to climb aboard, if you take my meaning, Cap'n."

"Not for much longer." Willem nodded to his men and Phaeton braced for more. Pummeled by a barrage of jabs, he nevertheless managed to rally. At some point, one simply became inured to the pain. He ran his sore tongue over loosened teeth. A swollen lip stung when he licked away blood. After a few shallow breaths, he lifted his chin to face his captor.

A billow of smoke curled up one side of Willem's mouth. Pale eyes twinkled as the Dutchman's skeptical gaze traveled over him. "You were seen dancing with Miss Jones."

Phaeton shut his eyes for one glorious moment. Flickering candlelight whirled about her pretty face as he waltzed her around the room. "That bonny wench?" He shook his head. "A might too rich for this Jack Tar's pockets."

Willem rolled his eyes slowly over the low-vaulted ceiling before settling his gaze on Phaeton. "Do you know what a keel haul is?"

He muttered a few curse words and lifted his chin. "Surely you don't need me to explain . . ." At Willem's nod, a swift fist met the side of his torso. Phaeton gasped the answer. "A sailor is tied to a rope that loops beneath the vessel; he's given the toss overboard and dragged under the ship's keel to the other side." He sputtered out a cough and forced a grin. "That what you have in mind for me, Cap'n. Shark bait?"

"Scraped along the bottom, quick-like, and ye'll be cut to shreds by barnacles." Willem pressed forward, crowding his chest. "Pull ye slow, and yer own weight will drag you down. Dead men tell no tales." Pleased with the idea, the captain's eyes glowed.

Phaeton examined the mole alongside the man's nose. He counted three hairs before shifting his gaze. "A fine old Dutch Navy custom."

A flash of suspicion registered on Willem's face. "Take him above."

His hands were bound before they shoved him up the ladder. Phaeton staggered across what felt like a mile of deck to the ship's bow. Cool air wafted over his cuts and bruises but offered little relief from his injuries. Nothing but shivers and chills.

"Catch a line under the bowsprit, Mr. Cheever, and tie him up." Willem's pale eyes, bright as moonbeams, gleamed in anticipation.

Phaeton stole periodic glances toward the pier. Any time now the harbor patrol would arrive. What was keeping them? No doubt there were more of Willem's men still about town. If Dex and America were captured, he was a dead man, and they'd soon be joining him. Phaeton winced at the thought of the lovely Miss Jones at the hands of these filthy pirates.

She had never lied to him. Not even from their first meeting. She had been chased down Savoy Row by these blaggards and by some queer stroke of fortune, he had been selected to partner her that night. Oddly, he had no regrets.

Odder still, his mood brightened. What if she and Dex had made it to the harbor patrol station? He inhaled a deep gulp of air. There might still be a chance to catch these knaves in the act.

"Who are you?" So, the Dutchman was going to give it another go.

He had nothing to lose. "Phaeton Black, Scotland Yard. And you are under arrest for piracy and murder." He flashed a winsome smile that stung.

Willem stared, without so much as a twitch of expression. Then he began to laugh. Uproarious, hearty laughter. His crew joined him.

From the corners of his eyes, Phaeton perceived the faintest flutter of movement. A scurry of footsteps behind the barrels on shore. "Mind my advice, Cap'n."

"And what might that be, Inspector Black of Scotland Yard?"

"Detective Black, actually."

Willem glared at his crew. "Hurry up with those ropes."

"There is an important distinction." Phaeton raised a supercilious brow. "Metropolitan police—that is, CID and the like, use Inspector. Whereas Special Branch agents—"

Willem pulled out a pistol from inside his coat. "Take a walk up the bow and onto the boom."

Phaeton tilted his head. "Why not shoot me? A lot less bother—"

Willem's eyeballs nearly burst from their sockets. He grabbed Phaeton by the coat and shoved him onto the bowsprit. "And now, Detective, you shall die."

He glanced at a smattering of stars before squinting at the captain. " 'To die would be an awfully good adventure'—who wrote that?"

Willem seized the line and pulled Phaeton off the boom. A high-pitched scream came from the direction of the pier as he fell through the air and plunged into the frigid water of the basin. Gun shots rang out.

Shocked into keen awareness by the icy water, bindings cut into his wrists as he was towed farther under the bow. He waited for a bit of slack in the line and reached for the knife strapped to his leg. In the inky blackness, he could see nothing, all he could do was feel his way along the ship's keel. He tried walking the underside of the boat until all movement ceased. Under fire from the shore patrol, Willem's crew must have abandoned the job and left him tied under the keel.

Death by drowning appeared imminent.

The echo of pistol shots rang in his ear and an odd zing of bullets zipped through the inky blackness of the water. The heavy *swoosh* of bodies plunging into the water meant some members of the crew had jumped ship.

His lungs, starved for air, began to burn. Phaeton angled the knife through the coil around his wrists and sawed through the rope. In another minute or so, his windpipe would close off, and soon thereafter, he supposed, his heart would stop.

And she was there, omnipresent in his thoughts. Just one more kiss, before he lost consciousness.

A last jerk of the knife finally unraveled rope, and he tore at the rest of his bindings. He had no more than seconds to come up for air before his lungs burst.

He stroked again and again. Was he swimming up or down? For a terrifying moment, he lost his equilibrium.

Amid a spray of bullets, he burst to the surface of the water and gasped for air. He spun around in the water to get his bearings. Advancing on him was a small crew boat holding several men making their escape. Phaeton lunged for the craft and grabbed hold of the skiff. An oar lifted in the air.

Thwack.

A spray of stars crossed his vision before everything went dark. His fingers lost their hold and let go. The dark, smothering chill of harbor waters engulfed him once more. Air left his lungs.

Just one more kiss, my dove.

America had just about chewed her bottom lip raw. Phaeton was below the keel and drowning. Fearful thoughts raced through her mind. She prayed he had somehow worked loose of the ropes when the crew abandoned their punishment and returned fire. She would haul in those lines herself if they would ever let her go aboard.

"Hold yer fire."

She strained against Moore's hold on her. Out of bullets, the crewmen who remained aboard came out from behind barriers, hands in the air. She wanted up the plank. "We must get to those lines." She wrenched herself out of his hold and slipped in a slick puddle of red. She sniffed the air. The smell of Portuguese port was everywhere. The burnished crimson wine dripped onto the dock from barrels shot full of holes.

A gathering of sailors and citizenry, roused out of the pubs by the gun battle, crept forward for a closer look.

"Hold on there, Miss."

"Captain MacLeod, we must go aboard and haul in the line. Detective Black is—"

"Is dead, my girl, if he hasn't freed himself by now."

The look on her face said it all, she supposed. "There now, lass, we'll be hauling in the lines straight away."

"Now," she demanded.

His frown relented. "Come aboard then—if yer sure you wish to witness what we dredge up."

A shiver caused her to pull her coat together. She followed alongside the patrolmen who walked the ropes back toward the bow. The keel haul line was dropped from portside and hauled in quickly, hand over hand. The job was too effortless—too swift. Her heart quickened. There was no dead weight hitched to the line. "He is alive. I feel it. I know it as sure as I breathe in and out."

Wait. Something clung to the frayed edges of a coil of rope. The same coil that had fastened around Phaeton's wrists and held him to the line. She squinted. Pray God it was not a severed limb or some other ghastly part of him. Her eyesight blurred.

One of the patrolmen unwound the item and held it up. A length of knitted wool.

"That's his scarf." Dexter stood behind her. She spun around. His mouth formed a thin, grim line. "I'm sorry, Miss Jones, he—"

She shook her head "He is not dead."

He reached out, and she pulled away. "He is not!" America walked around the deck rails, stopping to inspect every wretched piece of flotsam and jetsam in the water. Crewmen who had jumped ship during the gun battle were being hauled out of the basin. She studied each drenched man closely.

No Phaeton.

She made her way around the deck a second time as the harbor police captured the last of the crew and led them off to the brig. Captain MacLeod and Mr. Moore approached her again, no doubt concerned about her state of mind. "There now, I shall be needing you to make out a claim of ownership. In the meanwhile, I will confiscate the—"

"The *Ruby Star.*" America sniffed, her eyes scanning the harbor landscape for any sign of him.

"*Ruby Star* it is. I'll hold her cargo, as well, in the name of the crown."

"I cannot leave, as yet. Not until we have found Detective Black."

The harbor master's forehead furrowed. "Ah, lass, we'll not be able to send a man underwater till well after daylight."

America glared. "He's not dead." She shook her head. "He cannot be dead. I would know if he was dead. We have—we have a kind of—" Her gaze darted about the ship and beyond, into the darkness of the surrounding waters. She searched for him, and for words. "I'm not sure what to call it."

The looks on the men's faces said it all. They believed she had suffered a hysteria of the mind, no doubt brought on by the terrible duress of recent events. Shoulders squared, she faced the two of them. "You go ahead Captain. I would like to remain here for some time." She dragged a raw lower lip under her teeth. "Just in case."

The harbor master widened his stance, folded arms over his chest, and shook his head.

"Perhaps, if we give her a bit more time." Dexter stepped forward. "I'll stay with her."

The big Scot scrutinized Moore, then herself. Any other time, she would have been amused, even touched by his fatherly protective manner. "Inspector Moore has always conducted himself a gentleman, Captain."

MacLeod grunted. "Mind you have her back to my office afore sunrise."

"Yes, sir."

The captain stationed two patrolmen at the gangplank and

left the ship. Detective Moore turned back to her. "Quite a stroke of luck you knew the Harbor Master, wot?"

"For me, perhaps, but not for Mr. Black." She ripped her gaze away from the horizon line to Moore. "There is a pontoon landing, just aft of the stern. We need to find the down ladder and have a look."

Moore didn't budge. "You're soft on him, aren't you?"

His scrutiny made her eyes water. "Don't make me cry, Mr. Moore. Detective Black has been very kind to me."

"Yes, so you say. Took you in when no one gave a care." His lips pressed into a thin line. When he opened his mouth to speak again, America turned away.

"I have no time to refute your rude insinuations."

He caught up behind her on the gangway. "Miss Jones, I would never suggest—"

"I know what you were thinking, Mr. Moore." America set a brisk pace along the pier. "Ah, here it is."

The inspector peered over the edge to the narrow strip of landing built to moor launches. "Perhaps I should go first, in case you slip or fall?"

She eyed him suspiciously. Even decent men got ideas about a woman with lax morals. "Very well, Mr. Moore."

The way down was slow. Twice, her foot slipped from the slick rungs and Moore held her until she regained her footing. When they reached the bottom, he did not remove his arms from around her waist. "Might you ever accept my attentions, Miss Jones?" He held her from behind, his voice just a whisper in her ear.

"Take your hands off me, Mr. Moore."

He released her with obvious reluctance. "Why Phaeton Black and not me?"

She spun around. "How could you ask such a thing?" Her eyes filled with tears she could not control. Tears that welled up and poured down her cheeks.

"I'm sorry." Moore hung his head. "I'm sorry, the man

laid down his life in the line of duty"—he hesitated—"to protect you."

America uttered an otherworldly shriek. "I am telling you he is not dead."

She turned and walked to the end of the landing. "Phaeton Black. Do you hear me?" She repeated the cry over and over, until she became hoarse from tears and shouting. "I am here, Mr. Black, can you make your way toward me? Please, please, Mr. Black."

Could he really be gone? Dear God, this could not be happening. A wave of guilt nearly leveled her to the ground. For his part, Dexter Moore at least had the decency to hang back and wait for her to collapse onto a column of coiled rope. She buried her head in her hands and sobbed and sobbed for what seemed like a very long time. Eventually, there were no more tears left, just a running nose, puffy eyes, and hiccups.

Moore moved up behind her and touched her shoulder. Tentatively, she reached back and placed her hand on his. Far off in the bay, she heard the lonely ring of a bell buoy and the bark of a harbor seal.

"Are you about ready, Miss Jones?"

Her heart broke under the pain in her chest. She sucked in air and exhaled a sigh. Rising slowly to her feet, she inched over to the landing's edge. The basin sparkled periodically as hints of moonlight shone through wispy clouds. She could barely see the outline of ships, stark ebony silhouettes anchored far out in the bay.

As the fog drifted closer to shore, the lapping waves turned dull and dark. Fisting a hand on each hip, her gaze drifted out past the gloomy water. "Phaeton Black." She hiccupped. "You find your way back to me this minute!"

Chapter Twenty-two

Was he dead or alive?

Alive, possibly. Phaeton was not entirely sure. He opened his mouth and belched out sea water. Lifting his head, he managed to look about. Hints of moonlight edged the undulating surface of the bay. He blinked to clear his vision and traced the narrow platform he lay on around the circumference of a bell buoy. A loud clang nearly sent him off his precarious perch.

Something ticklish snuffled over his neck and ears. Gingerly, he shifted onto his back, enough to meet the liquid brown eyes of a harbor seal who appeared to take a most startling interest in him. The creature rocked back and forth between flippers and sniffed farther down his body. The eyes of the animal glowed amber then shifted to gold. The musky smelling sea beast barked a jarring bellow.

"Edvar?" He hardly recognized the croaked query as his own voice. A bit groggy brained, Phaeton contemplated whether the annoying gargoyle was some kind of silkie, or could he be imagining things? The hovering harbor rat let loose a series of ear deafening barks.

"Mr. Black. Do you hear me?"

Stunned by the clarity of her voice, his heart beat an erratic pulse as he listened for more. Again, her call carried over the silent bay water. "I am here, Mr. Black."

He lifted his head to rasp out a response, but his breath had no power. A deep inhale caused a spasm of coughs. Everything came back at once, a barrage of events. Pushed off the ship, he had plunged into the bay. Bullets had zipped through the water. He was trapped in darkness under the keel. He was dead, wasn't he? So why was Miss Jones calling after him?

The dung of harbor sea lions and rotted fish drifted into his nostrils and caused an involuntary spasm of retching. Chilled to the bone, he tried moving a limb or two. Yes, there appeared to be legs and arms attached to his soggy torso.

Phaeton patted coat pockets inside heavy, waterlogged clothes. Every move he made took enormous effort, as if his body was only half alive. He felt around for the long metal cylinder. The battery powered torchlight. His hands shook as he removed the gadget. He toggled the switch. Nothing. Drenched, most likely. He banged the cylinder against his chest.

A light beam appeared then faltered. "Drat it all." He shook the torch again and once more a brief flash drilled into the darkness. Phaeton continued to shake and toggle until the torch flew out of his trembling hands into the drink.

He craned his neck. "Fetch, Edvar." The pesky seal slid off the platform and slipped into dark waters.

Another spasm of coughs racked his chest and there was a sensation of choking. Perhaps he wasn't dead yet, but his body felt like it wanted to be. He coughed up more sea water and strained to hear the sound of her voice once more. He rested his head on the platform. Another spasm of chills ravaged through his body, then faded. Eyelids heavy. Less painful now.

"Phaeton Black. Give me a sign this minute!"

The sea lion emerged from the water, torchlight in mouth. A sputtering beam of light bobbed about in the blackness. Phaeton drifted into unconsciousness.

★   ★   ★

America peered deep into the blackness of the bay. "Look, a flash just above tidewater." She pointed. "There it is again."

Dexter Moore squinted. "Ah yes, I see it now."

"It's him. I know it." America lowered herself into a crew boat tied to the landing.

"Miss Jones. We don't know if it's Phaeton. Could be more of those pirates—some jumped ship—Yanky Willem among them." He untied the mooring line but held on.

"Inspector Moore, climb aboard or I shall push off without you." She lowered both oars into the water.

Dexter Moore climbed in, mouth drawn into a thin, unhappy line.

"Coil that rope and sit yourself down." She adjusted oars.

"Are you going to row?" His look couldn't be more incredulous.

She snorted. "I learned as a young girl, Mr. Moore. Think you can best me?" She angled the skiff away from the landing and pushed off. "I'd rather get us there quick and silentlike, just in case you happen to be right about those pirates."

America dipped the oars into the bay and leaned back. The small boat skimmed over calm water. After a few strokes, Dexter's shoulders dropped a bit. "I say, rather deft of you, Miss Jones." He removed a pistol from inside his jacket and retrieved a handful of bullets from a woolen waistcoat pocket.

He loaded the weapon and spun the cylinder.

During the gun battle, Moore had shot and wounded several of Willem's men aboard ship. "You appear to know your way around a gun, Inspector Moore."

He pocketed the weapon. "Four years with Her Majesty's Scot's Greys."

"Are you a sharp shooter?"

The barest semblance of a grin. "I hit the target, more often than not."

The bell sounded close by. At Moore's gesture, she stroked an oar in a starboard direction and headed for the buoy.

A grey nose, covered in whiskers, popped up alongside and tossed an object into the boat. Moore jumped slightly, rocking the skiff. America grinned. "A harbor seal, Mr. Moore. Harmless enough."

"Sorry." He felt around the boat bottom and retrieved a metal cylinder.

"I believe Phaeton was the last one with the torchlight." She read his face, as he did hers. Grim at the thought he might be at the bottom of the bay, hopeful he still could be stranded somehow, somewhere. And alive.

America pulled in the oars. The buoy emerged from a wisp of fog. Her gaze traveled over the looming structure. Nothing.

The seal honked and swam to the other side of the floating metal tower. America dropped an oar down and skimmed the surface, turning the rowboat slowly around the buoy.

Dexter squinted through the rusty metal beams. "There on the ledge."

The lonely form of a still body. No movement.

"Mr. Black, is that you?" She nodded to Moore.

Dexter stood up in the boat and set his feet apart. He leaned portside and grabbed ahold of the narrow ledge, then the body. He tugged on the damp, bulky clothing until he managed to tilt the lifeless torso toward them.

America gasped. It was Phaeton all right, but was he dead or alive? "Quickly Mr. Moore, lower him down. It took all of Moore's strength and balance to get the bulk of Phaeton onboard. They laid him down and stretched him across the center seat.

"Facedown, Mr. Moore, angle his mid-chest across the bench."

America's own pulse soared when she found a heartbeat in his neck. It was thready, but he was alive. "On my signal, you will press on his back with all your weight, Mr. Moore." America took hold of Phaeton's arms like they were oars and leaned back. She pulled them forward, over his head, and then signaled Moore to press on his back.

"The prone pressure method. Very scientific." She pulled on his arms. "Onboard ship, we put a man over a barrel and roll it back and forth."

With each pull and press, seawater shot out of Phaeton's nose and mouth, until a sputtered cough gave up nothing more. With an involuntary jerk, he came to life and began to shiver. Her own body ached under the fatigue of tension. A deep exhale released hours of emotional strain and tautly held muscle. She looked up and returned Moore's smile.

"Well done, Miss Jones." Moore took off his coat and covered the trembling body splayed across the bottom of the dinghy. Phaeton's moan came from the depths of hell, but it sounded like heaven to her.

"Seems you've got more lives than a cat."

Reluctantly, Phaeton shifted his gaze away from America to the man speaking. Dexter Moore stood at the foot of his bed holding his hat. After a change into dry clothes and two pots of hot tea, he almost felt himself again. Except for the bruised ribs, the sore jaw, and the swollen eye. A sharp pain shot up his side as he spoke. "Bugger off."

Moore checked his watch. "As a matter of fact, I'm off to town. Yanky Willem will likely reemerge somewhere east of the Tower, where he has yet another of your ships in dry dock, Miss Jones."

America sat bedside and closed the book in her lap. "A few alterations and a fresh coat of paint to disguise appearances, perhaps?"

"Awfully bold of Willem." Phaeton pressed for details. "What are your plans, Dex?"

"Contact London Port Authority. Between Scotland Yard and Thames patrol, we should be able to cast a net from the Isle of Dogs to Limehouse."

She grabbed her bottom lip with upper teeth and slowly

released. He loved that adorable nervous twitch of hers. Perhaps too much.

Dexter rattled on. "Not to worry, Miss Jones, a man on the run makes mistakes."

She managed a smile. "Let us hope so, Mr. Moore."

Dexter cast a longing gaze her way. Phaeton didn't much care for that look of his. "Well, I'm off then." Fingering his bowler, the man backed away from the bed. "Don't want to miss my train."

America rose to see him out of the hotel suite. Phaeton listened absently to snippets of conversation. "We'll be following along behind you, Inspector Moore, as soon as Mr. Black takes his rest."

She stood at the bedroom door with her hands on her hips. "Phaeton, you really must try not to glower at Inspector Moore." She sat on the edge of his bed and swept a palm over his forehead. "He quite bravely defended me from the pirates and stayed on when I would not give up on you."

"Ah, there you see." Phaeton hissed a bit when she pressed gently on his taped ribs. "Sorry." She withdrew her hand only have it caught up in his. He pressed his lips to her knuckles. "It was you, Miss Jones, who insisted on staying behind. The rest of them would have left me out in the drink to rot like a bit of leftover sea lion dinner."

"Indeed, you may well have expired, Mr. Black, for I do not believe the harbor seals have any experience with artificial respiration."

Phaeton grinned. "Speaking of which, I believe my buoy companion to be none other than Edvar the Sneaky."

"Aha!" Her smile warmed his entire body. "More proof I am right about your powerful little ally."

"These proofs of yours." He tut-tutted. "Proofs of piracy, proofs of Edvar, proofs of . . . love?" He pulled her close, kissed her softly, and pressed for more.

She broke off the kiss to stare for a moment. "I was so afraid I had lost you."

Heavy-lidded, liquid brown eyes crinkled. "And I you, Miss Jones."

She climbed on his bed and readily returned his affection.

America opened her eyes. The pale walls of the room glowed a rosy hue. She estimated the time close to sunset. They had slept the entire day away. She smiled, listening to Phaeton snore peacefully beside her.

Her affection for him had grown tenfold during the few weeks they had known each other. A disturbing thought, given Phaeton Black was completely unsuitable. Suitable as a lover, perhaps, but not as a suitor.

She pushed a few stray hairs off his forehead, and he pulled her close. Could she possibly be in love with this man? She trembled at the very thought. He would break her heart if she allowed any further emotional attachment. Inwardly, she steeled herself for the days ahead. With two of her ships returned to her, she could begin to build a new life for herself. There would be no time for a man whose happiest pastime was bed sport.

No, the theft of the fleet, her father's death, and the loss of the warehouse had taught her a painful lesson. Count on no one. Only that simple notion wasn't exactly true. There had been one man.

A soft tapping at the parlor door launched her up off the bed. A hotel page stood in the hallway holding two telegrams addressed to Mr. Black. She asked for a bath to be readied and ordered a huge, hearty breakfast.

While Phaeton read the wires, she removed a package of perfumed bath salts from her toiletry case and swished the fragrant powder into the steaming tub.

"Seems Dex wasted no time briefing Zander Farrell on my presence in Portsmouth."

She sat down on the edge of his bed. "Undo me?"

His fingers deftly played over a row of covered buttons.

"Corset, please."

"Demanding little fishwife."

She snorted while he dutifully unlaced. "Will you be in a great deal of trouble at the Yard?"

"No more than usual."

She stood up and stepped out of the dress; the corset fell forward and released her breasts. She folded the red doxy dress over a chair and removed the corset. Stripped down to chemise and pantalettes, his gaze followed her around the room. "And your other wire?

"The Baron is dead. Internment is set for later in the week." Phaeton refolded both missives. "Doctor Exeter delivers his father's confession to Farrell and Chilcott late tomorrow morning."

"Such an odd old man, the Baron. I felt both pity and revulsion for him." She untied the ribbon on her chemise.

His gaze moved to the edge of lace barely covering the tips of her breasts. "I should try to be there."

"Well then." She stepped forward. "After a good warm bath, a hearty meal, and plenty of sleep, we shall make the early morning train." The chemise dropped off one shoulder.

He swallowed. "Bath?"

She smiled. "You and I, in the tub together. What do you say, Mr. Black?" She helped him stand up and removed his bed clothes. The thin, linen shirt tented from arousal.

"I see the duke suffered no serious injury." She stood by the polished copper tub and admired his erection.

His eyes turned feral. "Come closer." He tore off her chemise and ran his hand down into the back of her pantalettes. Her body quaked in response to his urgent, sensuous touch. The cake of soap fell from her hand and plunked into the water.

He pulled her back onto the bed and yanked off her underwear in one swift move. Like a beautiful injured god, he stood above her, panting. He opened her legs and stroked until she moaned. He kissed and suckled each nipple, trailing his tongue past her navel. He stopped just short of the curls below. "Someday, I mean to taste all of you, Miss Jones."

A surge of heat rose from her chest to her cheeks. What devilish sort of lovemaking did he speak of? Vaguely she recalled an illustration in the *Kama Sutra*. A man's face buried between a woman's legs. She bit her lip. "Now?"

He tilted his head. "I shall save it as punishment. When you have been a very, very bad girl." She threw back her head as he whipped her desire to a new frenzy with fingers soaked from her arousal. He placed one then two inside her and stroked while his slippery thumb circled her swollen nub. Her hips jerked and she trembled to the rhythm of his fondling. "Yes," she gasped. "More."

"Might this demand of yours involve my cock?"

America reached up and placed a hand on the hard, rippled surface of his bruised torso. "Does this hurt?"

He guided her hand down to the rigid staff that slapped against his belly. She massaged him softly and his eyelids lowered over a sable-brown gaze. "All I feel is pleasure."

His fingers changed to a rapid cadence and caused an untamed spasm of arousal. She mewled a wild cry and he growled a deep snarl. On all fours, he crawled across the bed and mounted her.

Chapter Twenty-three

A SOFT RAIN PELTED THE ROOF OF THE TRAIN STATION. Phaeton waited for a porter to check the lady's trunk and gazed absently at the gabled skylight. The light drizzle washed a layer of soot down glass panes. He collected the luggage tickets and joined the Harbor Master and America on the platform.

"A copy of the magistrate's seizure order and request for an immediate hearing, lass." Captain MacLeod handed her two envelopes. "Ye'll file the first with the courts and the other is yours to keep. Scotland Yard will no doubt wish to share these with London Port Authority, aye, Mr. Black?"

Phaeton sprung his watch cover and checked the time. "A formal accusation of piracy should motivate the Thames patrol."

The big Scot scrutinized the bruises around his eye and the swelling along his jawline. "If yer ever in need of employment, do not hesitate to call me. Any man who takes a beating, a keel haul, and shows up for work the following day—"

"Due in large part to the nursing skills of Miss Jones." Phaeton smiled at her.

The man's eyes twinkled. "Aye, a pretty lass and a glass of whiskey. Lovely cure."

America blushed a peachy tone. The same color her pale copper skin had flushed last night, from chest to high-set cheekbones. Once before bath and supper, and again after. He had taken his time when he pleasured her a second time. Phaeton ran a finger inside his neck collar and pushed the memory away. A nagging disquiet gnawed around the corners of his mind.

"Several steamers made port last night." The elder gent nodded to a number of travelers crowding onto the platform. "Best ye climb aboard, morning train always leaves on time."

America flung her arms around the captain's great bulk and kissed both of his ruddy cheeks. "I cannot thank you enough."

"There isna' much I wouldna' do for you or yer father, lass." As the train pulled away, MacLeod called out to America. "I can have her crewed and ready for service the day she's yours again."

Stuffed with passengers anxious to get to London, the compartment suddenly became warm and humid. Phaeton lowered a fogged window as the train chugged out of the station, and America leaned out to wave.

Phaeton snaked an arm around her waist and settled her beside him. They were only seconds out of the station before a new wave of uncomfortable, disturbing sentiments nearly overwhelmed him. Truth be told, he was more than taken by her. Soon the little minx would capture him body and soul. From the very start she had wormed her way into his life and now he could hardly believe it himself. He was soft on Miss Jones. What a horrifying development this was.

Despite his cautionary frame of mind, he studied the charming mole on the side of her neck as she conversed in French with a passenger across the aisle.

He lowered his voice. *"Un baiser entre vos jambes, Mademoiselle?"* She turned and raised a brow. The way she looked him up and down and licked her upper lip was a joy to behold. Instantly blood rushed from his brain to his lower extremity. "You wish to kiss me where, Mr. Black?"

"Slipped out. Pay no mind." He tapped his temple with a finger. "The keel haul mangled the faculties."

"Hmm." Her grin feigned a playful curiosity. "I do hope there's no permanent damage."

He really had to cease these debauched, lurid flirtations with her. Phaeton sighed. Perhaps their return to London would put some distance between them again. He would return to his pursuit of Qadesh and she, as well, could expand on her suit against the Dutch pirate.

Phaeton could not help wondering if he was in as much danger from Miss Jones as Yanky Willem. Not that she wished to see him locked up in Newgate prison, but there were other ways to leg shackle a man. His gaze dropped to her hand and traveled over slim fingers. The large blue sapphire sparkled above the gleaming gold wedding band.

"Mr. Black, you are perspiring." America opened her reticule and removed a delicate handkerchief.

Phaeton's leg tapped nervously. "Miss Jones, might I . . ." Great saint's bollocks, he had to change the subject. "Might I ask how the Harbor Master came to know you and your father?"

"Captain MacLeod was my father's first mate for several years." She patted his forehead with the cloth square. "Not sure how he came to be employed." America drew her brows together. "He came aboard in Port of New Orleans, under some duress, as I recall. The very day *maman* abandoned me to my father."

She shrugged. "*Maman* promised me I could watch the parade that year. Then she gave me away." America's gaze drifted past him to the rolling green countryside of Surrey. "I missed Fat Tuesday. *Mardi Gras.*"

"And your father never explained?

"Never." She sighed. "After a few years, I stopped asking."

The rail car lurched a bit as the locomotive braked to a stop in Petersfield Station. She straightened up and met his gaze. "You would enjoy the Lent festival in New Orleans, Mr. Black. There is much drinking and dancing along Canal Street. Women bare their breasts for doubloons." Her full lips turned up a wry sensuous smile.

He almost forgot he didn't laugh.

She cupped his hand with hers, but kept her eyes lowered. "While I have the chance, I mean to mention your act of bravery the other night. In the face of a very real threat to your person, you distracted the pirates so that Inspector Moore and I could safely make our escape from the ship. And you endured great pain and hardship for your trouble." She lifted dark lashes to meet his gaze. "You are my hero."

He hardly knew how to react to the sweetness of her sentiment, so he pressed for more. "And?"

"And?" Her quizzical brow caused him to grin.

"And, I make you tingle."

She inhaled a breath before she smiled. "Yes. You do."

Her eyes were pale green this morning, flecked with bits of rust and gold. At the moment, he could not think of anything more hellish than having to say good-bye to America Jones.

Mercifully, he survived the remainder of the commute into town by training his attention on two disturbing newspaper reports in the *Telegraph* and the *Times*. The bloated corpse of a middle-aged male had been found facedown at the edge of the Branch Hill pond in Hamstead Heath. With no signs of assault to the body, it was assumed the man, likely inebriated, had taken an accidental fall and drowned.

He pieced together all that he knew, thus far, of the naughty and dangerous apparition known as Qadesh. With the old Baron gone and her nest on the Thames demolished, he and Exeter found themselves back at the first square of the game board. He spent the remainder of the trip, from Whitley to Waterloo Station, lost in a puzzlement over the case.

★ ★ ★

America waited by the hansom as the porter fastened her trunk onto the back of the cab. Phaeton handed the man his gratuity and joined her. "Do you still have those bank notes on your person?"

"Of course." She loosened reticule drawstrings and withdrew the cash.

"Keep them. Use the money to get a flat for yourself. At least until your ships are returned."

She stepped back a bit and gulped for air. "An unnecessary expense, don't you think, Mr. Black? I am perfectly comfortable with my small—"

"Dexter Moore is correct, Miss Jones. It is unseemly for a young woman to share an apartment with any bachelor, particularly one such as myself. I want you to find a quality rooming house for young ladies as soon as possible."

"I thought we were getting on well, Mr. Black." She bit her lower lip. "Have I done something to displease you?"

"Just the opposite, Miss Jones." His gaze shifted away then returned. "I find you entirely too pleasing."

She frowned. "Then, I don't understand."

"Not long after our first encounter, you called me a Lothario, libertine, adulterer, and a profligate debaucher."

She swallowed. "I believe most of those opinions were Mr. Moore's."

He met her gaze, steely-eyed this time. "They were also accurate." He placed his hand on her arm and helped her into the cab. Once inside, she released the clasp and lowered the window.

"Neither a precise nor faithful evaluation of your character, Mr. Black."

"We are two people tossed together in a moment of time. I caution you not to make any more of our friendship, Miss Jones."

Phaeton nodded to the driver and the cab lurched off into a mangle of traffic. Something knotty and off-putting roiled in his stomach. Shoulders slumped, he made his way toward a queue of cabs at the curb. He coughed to relieve the tightness in his throat.

"Frankly, Miss Jones, I do not foresee a vacancy in the near future." Mrs. Horsley shook her head and set a fast clip down the corridor.

They passed a sitting room papered in a cheerful yellow rose pattern with comfortable furniture and a lovely set of windows that overlooked the lane. It would be very pleasant indeed to live in such a place while she waited for her ships to be returned to her.

"There is such a shortage of suitable accommodations for young ladies in the city." The very tall woman with the elegant neck and long pointed nose paused at the door.

Apparently, there was not a single room to let a young woman in all of London. America bit her lower lip and quietly evaluated whether there truly was no room available or this turn away had something to do with her copper complexion. "Might I inquire again, in a few weeks time? It is possible a tenant could leave unexpectedly."

The boardinghouse mistress fashioned a thin, wane smile. "It isn't likely, Miss Jones. You might try a rooming house a bit farther east. Spittlefield, perhaps?"

The woman referenced one of London's poorer working-class neighborhoods. America looked away and exhaled softly. So it seemed there would have been a vacancy available for the right sort of young lady. She raised her chin and met the woman's gaze. "I believe I take your meaning, Mrs. Horsley."

America sat in the hansom and stared straight ahead. Mentally, she checked the last rooming house off her list and sighed. Mr. Black would just have to tolerate her presence a while longer. And how utterly infuriating he could be at times. As if she wanted him around, pestering her for favors day and night. She sniffed and blinked back a few angry tears. It might require a bit of ferreting about, but she would find a very posh rooming house, even if it cost her double the rent. She would be glad, indeed, to be rid of him.

"Arrogant, conceited . . . bloody cockswain." How easily he could make her laugh or cry. And the worst of it was, she would miss him terribly. Had he not shown himself to be a worthy protector in Portsmouth? Proof of his surprising gallantry, perhaps, but certainly no assurance of his affection. She inhaled a deep breath and exhaled nothing but woe.

Phaeton stood safely behind the tall, slight frame of Mr. Oliver as he tapped lightly on the office door. According to the director's secretary, Dr. Jason Exeter had arrived promptly at ten o'clock and was already in conference with Chilcott and Farrell.

"Yes? What is it?" The growl in Chilcott's voice was almost a comfort.

The clerk poked his head in the door. "Mr. Black is here."

"Is he indeed? Please do send him in, Mr. Oliver."

Phaeton stepped around the secretary and through the door. As he might have predicted, both the director and Zander Farrell wore decidedly grim expressions. "A bit pale around the gills are we? I take it you've been told the worst of it." He nodded at Exeter who appeared relieved to see him.

"Do you ever arrive anywhere on time, Mr. Black?" Chilcott's lips returned to a thin white line.

Phaeton tossed his hat on a nearby rack and shrugged. "Caught the first train out of Portsmouth this morning." He stepped close enough for all the men sitting around the director's desk to get a good look at his face.

Zander lifted a brow. "Good Christ, Phaeton, you're quite worse for the wear. Chasing down pirates in Portsmouth, I hear."

Chilcott bristled. "Pirates in Portsmouth? What the hell is going on, Mr. Black? A blood thirsty apparition prowling about town should be quite enough assignment for any agent to manage." The director shifted his glare to Zander, who masterfully handled the man with a good natured grin.

"Phaeton lent his assistance to Inspector Moore, a last minute substitution. Short of manpower over the weekend."

Chilcott motioned to Phaeton. "Pull up a chair and tell us what you know of Baron de Roos and the lovely, poisonous—I believe she calls herself—"

Zander referred to the notes on his lap. "Qadesh?"

"Nearly had my soul as well as my privates." Both Yard men leaned in to hear the story. Whenever possible, he enhanced the more prurient aspects of his encounter with Qadesh until Exeter rolled his eyes.

Phaeton straightened. "Had it not been for the doctor's ability to transfuse blood, I might have crossed over the River Styx."

Chilcott dropped back into his well-worn leather chair. "As to the current status of your investigation, Doctor Exeter tells me you have yet another rock to find and turn over."

Phaeton nodded. "There's a lead I'd like to follow up on—several actually."

"And what might those be? Trail seems dead to me. After destroying a sizable chunk of Victoria's Embankment, what other havoc do you plan to wreak on the city?"

"For one thing, I'd like to pursue the missing sarcophagus."

When Chilcott raised a brow, Phaeton turned to the doctor. "What exactly do they know?"

"I'm afraid we got to very little of your case. We spent the majority of our time on my father's confession."

"And how goes that revelation?" Now it was Phaeton's turn to scrutinize the top Yard man. "Does Scotland Yard call the Ripper case closed?"

Chilcott didn't blink an eye but he lowered his voice. "For the time being, the case will remain open, perhaps indefinitely, to the outside world."

"And internally?

"I am prepared to believe the Baron's story." The director rocked back in his chair and the leather squeaked predictably. "I owe you an apology, Mr. Black. You had all the right instincts on the investigation—"

"Hard to believe in a monstrous shade stalking the Chapel, sir."

Chilcott's mouth actually twitched upward. "Generous of you, Phaeton, but nevertheless, I mean to have your lost wages restored, and we can arrange for a permanent desk here at the office, if you like."

The great, imperturbable but always irascible Chilcott had just made an apology. Phaeton was almost unnerved by the director's humble admonition. He glanced across a corner of the desk and caught Zander's wink.

"Thank you, sir." Phaeton swallowed, then cleared his throat. "Now, about the missing sarcophagus . . . ?"

"Yes, what about it?"

"Qadesh appears to be searching for an errant husband. What if we were to take the vicious little virago at her word?" Phaeton nodded toward the doctor. "According to Doctor Exeter's research, a pair of sarcophagi was found nestled in the sand beside the obelisk transported to England."

Exeter opened a carrying case and retrieved his notes. "One was damaged and broken, presumably used to fill in sinkholes along the Embankment."

Chilcott steepled his fingers against a drawn mouth. "And you feel confident you have destroyed the Empusa's primary resting place?"

Phaeton grimaced. "Yes and no. There was a nest of sorts in Whitechapel, burned to the ground by the doctor here. We can only assume she has others."

Zander looked up from his scribbling. "The Dorset Lane fire? As I recall, the murders did soon cease after the blaze."

Exeter managed a thin-lipped smile. "Before Phaeton left for Portsmouth, we thought we might take a new tack. Find the object of her desire and lure our dark goddess out of hiding."

"The missing sarcophagus. More specifically, whatever remains under the stone." Chilcott grunted. "A clever as well as prudent idea. I very much dislike the alternative, which is cleaning up after your wake of destruction through the city."

Zander opened a folder and set pencil to paper. "Do tell us your plans, Phaeton. I take it Doctor Exeter has been of considerable assistance to Scotland Yard thus far?"

"Invaluable." Phaeton gave a nod to the doctor. "There may be records of both public and private collections in the British Museum Library. We plan to make a start there. Perhaps a good poke around the museum's warehouses and storerooms is also in order. I'll need your assistance to get their cooperation."

"Easily done." The director signaled Zander. "Mr. Farrell, see to it the museum is informed and ready to assist the investigation. You will continue as supervisor, but I want you in a more active role, working directly with Phaeton and his—" He turned to the doctor. "Shall we call you a consultant?"

Exeter nodded and Zander closed his file. "I will clear my schedule."

For a moment, Chilcott almost appeared jovial. "Will that be all, gentlemen?"

Phaeton hesitated. "There is the matter of Hampstead Heath, sir."

"Ah yes, the dead body found floating facedown in the pond. An accidental drowning, wasn't it?" The director leaned forward. "What about it, Phaeton?"

Chapter Twenty-four

AMERICA TURNED THE PAGE. Her gaze swept over the words of the novel to the clock on the wall. The timepiece chimed its twelfth and final stroke. Where was he? She was more than ready for a rollicking good argument and would like to get it over with.

Earlier this evening, she had nearly worn the carpet runner bare from vexation. Why on earth was it necessary for her to move out? It seemed perfectly sensible, indeed prudent, to stay right here and wait until her ships were legally restored to her.

With her speech duly rehearsed and prepared, she settled down with Poe's *Tales of the Grotesque and Arabesque*. It was obviously a childhood tomb of Phaeton's. He had even scribbled enthusiastic notes between lines. It appeared, even as a boy, Phaeton exuded a nonchalant, devil-may-care attitude. She marveled at the spirited youth who idolized fearlessly cocky heroes, encouraging them on to reckless, dangerous behavior. In one revealing margin notation he had written a line from *Macbeth*.

Screw your courage to the sticking place!

An odd, hollow pain gnawed in the pit of her stomach. She slipped her finger out from between the pages and closed the book. She would promise to remain quietly to herself and pay never mind to his comings and goings. He, as well, would allow her to go about her business with no interference. Of course, once the intimacies between them ceased, rooming with Mr. Black would almost certainly present challenges.

She squared her shoulders and sat up straight. He would quickly resume the carefree bachelor life, which included drink, opiates, and a parade of harlots in and out of the flat. But in fact, this sort of depraved, routine behavior of his might be the very tonic needed to cure her of this wretched infatuation. Oh, he was more than charming, all right, and brave beyond measure. She would keep in mind his less admirable side. What had Inspector Moore called him? A profligate defiler of women.

A commotion of footsteps padded noisily from the stairs above. Some kind of chase, it seemed, for there was a great deal of pounding down the treads. And a female's laughter. America tilted her head toward the racket. Layla proceeded him by a few steps. As the two rounded the landing, Phaeton reached out and caught the harlot by a large bow fashioned above her bustle.

America shot up from the chaise and faced them.

Taken back at the sight of her, he staggered then lurched upright. "I thought I made myself clear, Miss Jones. You were to find yourself a very nice room in a quality boardinghouse." He swept a hand upward in a furious gesture that nearly tipped him over. "Out of my presence." Layla grabbed hold to steady the wobbler.

She could barely stand the sight of him. Near to blind inebriated, she could smell the drink from across the room. A glare she couldn't quite control darted from Phaeton to Layla to Phaeton. "I'm afraid there was no room at the inn." She lifted her chin. "Not in Knightsbridge, Mayfair, or Kensington. Not even here in the city."

His head jerked back. "That's ridiculous. London is full of—"

"Not for me, Mr. Black." Her gaze traveled to the pretty copperish-colored doxy beside him. "Layla, why don't you take him to bed, and as you ply your wares, would you kindly explain to your customer the most obvious of reason for such a curious lack of vacancies?"

Quite without warning, a dizziness came over her. As if a rug had somehow slipped out from under her feet.

The doxy towed him in the direction of the bedroom. Phaeton curled an upper lip. "Care to join?"

"Good night, Mr. Black." America turned away and collapsed onto lumpy cushions. Their voices wafted through thin plaster walls, and she covered her ears. The soft, deep rumble of his voice and Layla's high-pitched murmurs blended into a mélange of whispers. She tucked her knees under her chin and rocked back and forth. She wouldn't let herself cry. She wouldn't give him the satisfaction. "Surly, wicked libertine."

When his bedroom door crashed open, she barely noticed.

"You did not introduce yourself as the Princess Serafine al Qatari? An excellent ruse—" Her heart skipped a beat at the sound of his voice.

"Because I do not lie with the same kind of aplomb you devise so effortlessly. Besides, I had no entourage or Scotland Yard escort to enhance such a clever plot."

Phaeton rounded the chaise. "No, you just want to stay long enough to make sure I am entirely miserable." His bellow ended in an angry growl.

"Do not raise your voice to me." She grimaced at her own shriek.

"You little harpy." Hands on his hips, he shook his head. "I'll yell if I please."

"And that would make you a bully, Mr. Black." She thrust out a bottom lip.

Phaeton turned away, then back again. He strangled the air with his hands and kicked up a corner of the rug. "Out of my flat." He pointed at the stairs. "Immediately."

She blinked. "At this hour?" Maddened beyond reason, her eyes darted up a pair of long limbs. Phaeton stood in front of her with his shirt unbuttoned. Besides the fact that he appeared a bit flushed, he looked sleepy and adorable and very . . . she swallowed.

"Must I pack you up and move you myself?" His eyes were red-rimmed but surprisingly clear and focused. He glanced at Layla whose smile seemed to only grow brighter as she backed out of the flat and up the stairs.

America sighed. "Would it be such a terrible inconvenience if I stayed until at least one of my ships is returned? You can come and go as you please, Mr. Black, and enjoy whatever female entertainments you might—"

"Do you think me a fool, Miss Jones?"

"Of course not."

He leaned in. "Let me see if I take your meaning. While I waltz doxies in and out of my room, I am to ignore your insults and pretend you are not here."

She searched for a spot in the room to land her gaze. Anywhere but his face where those piercing black eyes caused a prickling on the back of her neck and her arms.

"You called me a surly, wicked libertine."

Her gaze lowered as she faltered a reply. "I'm very sorry you heard that, Mr. Black."

"Pardon me if I question the sincerity of your regret."

She took in a deep breath and held it. When he didn't continue on, she was forced to exhale, loudly. "I meant every word of my apology—"

"Unlike you, Miss Jones, I would feel entirely uncomfortable taking pleasure with another woman while you reside in such close proximity. In fact, I wouldn't think of it." Phaeton looked away then quickly returned his gaze. "I'm disappointed."

"I don't understand."

"I thought you actually cared for me—a little."

She bit her lip to stop the tremble. Her throat ached so acutely, she could not speak. "Look at me, America."

She kept her head lowered. Any sudden movement, even

a blink, would send a wash of tears down her cheeks. "I must say I find it rather endearing you don't seem to notice my color." She hardly recognized the whispered croak in her voice.

Phaeton exhaled a deep, gentle sigh. He descended to his haunches and lifted her chin. "Of course I notice." From what she could make out through a veil of liquid, his gaze softened. "You are beautiful, Miss Jones. In fact, I often find it quite impossible to look away."

She smiled and the flood gates opened.

"Come." He led her into his room and removed a clean pocket square from a dresser drawer. He patted her cheeks before covering her nose. "Blow."

She took the handkerchief and sniffed, while he unbuttoned her dress. "I am inebriated and exhausted. And quite regretfully, I am no threat to your body this evening."

He undressed her completely without much caressing, then removed his shirt and trousers. He climbed into his bed and patted the mattress beside him.

She studied the many discolored marks on his torso and face. The magnificent bruised warrior in repose. And there was the most alluring cut on his upper lip, another humble reminder of his heroism. A wave of tender affection hit her, as well as weariness. She was fatigued in the extreme; they both were. She climbed up into the bed, and he pulled her under the covers, against his hardness.

"The duke seems ever the ready man."

"Pay him no mind." Phaeton nuzzled her neck. "Until morning."

Phaeton weaved his way past the main exhibit room and found the doors to the courtyard. The British Museum Library, a large Georgian rotunda, occupied the central focal point of the gardens. Weaving a path through a labyrinth of flowerbeds, he inhaled the spicy scent of roses. A slight ache in his groin reminded him of how lovely she had looked in her sleep, despite the dark circles under her eyes. He had not awakened her, even though his cock would have enjoyed a lovely start to the day.

At the moment, his scheme to recover his life was in shambles. Overnight, the idea of America moving out had become at least as painful as the thought of her staying. He gritted his teeth until his jaw twitched. Well, if she could stand it, he could. A few more days or weeks, what could it hurt? Phaeton prayed for the former—not the latter.

He climbed a set of curved stairs and approached a wooden balustrade. Under a vast glass-domed ceiling, a number of library tables were surrounded by an ever-widening, concentric circle of bookshelves. The great reading room of the British Library. Other than the occasional jerk of a chair or the turning of a page, the chamber was silent. One could almost hear the air circulate in the room.

"Inspector Black?"

Phaeton swiveled. A tall, balding man of gaunt appearance crept forward. "Detective Black, Scotland Yard." Phaeton flipped open his card case. "I take it you have been briefed on the nature of my investigation?"

The gentleman removed a pair of pince-nez from his waistcoat pocket and examined the calling card. "We have prepared a private room for you and your consultant, a Doctor—"

"Jason Exeter. Has he arrived, as yet?"

"Oh, yes, he arrived quite promptly at nine o'clock, the moment the museum opened." The man slowly, precisely adjusted the spectacles on the bridge of his nose. "Allow me to introduce myself. Alfred Stickles, library curator."

"A pleasure, Mr. Stickles." Phaeton nodded at the elderly man whose hollow-cheeked appearance and slow, deliberate bearing reminded him of an old headmaster he and his schoolmates had dubbed Sir Bugsley Headmantis. "If you would kindly point me in the right direction?"

"I shall escort you."

"That won't be necessary."

"De rigueur, Mr. Black. I can't have Scotland Yard poking about, asking questions and the like, disturbing serious research."

Phaeton tightened a smile. "Lead the way, Mr. Stickles." He took a deep breath and slowed his pace. After a leisurely stroll through the reading room, they passed through a set of neatly concealed doors which led to a comfortable, well-appointed meeting room. The doctor sat, engrossed in a large, handwritten ledger, at one end of a long table.

"Ah, Mr. Black, pull up a chair and have at one of these volumes." Phaeton looked at the tall stack piled on the table. "Any one in particular?"

"The barge carrying the obelisk was towed into the Thames Estuary in January of 1878. The needle was erected in September of that same year. I asked for all inventory records from 1878 through to the present date."

Phaeton removed his coat and tossed it over a chairback. "Why all the extra years of records?"

"If the sarcophagus was sold to a private party, it may well have been stored for a time before resurfacing." Exeter leaned back in his chair and nodded to the librarian. "Mr. Stickles informs me that artifacts believed lost or stolen often make their way to the museum after a number of years."

The librarian handed Phaeton a ledger from the top of the pile. "For some time, the museum has quietly let it be known to less scrupulous dealers in antiquities, we would pay handsomely for certain missing artifacts."

Phaeton raised a brow. "No questions asked?"

"As long as the object is genuine and its provenance *bona fide*."

Phaeton thought about the Hall of Mummies packed with rows of stone coffins. "Would a sarcophagus dug up in Alexandria, connected to the obelisk, be of interest?

Stickles' eyes rolled upward. "That would depend, Mr. Black."

"On what is inside?"

The curator's gaze returned something that vaguely resembled a wink. "When is content not important?"

"Coffins carved with great artistry, death masks of gold, a stunning array of jewels, perhaps? And mummies of course." Phaeton saw no reason to trouble the elderly man by adding essence of Anubis, jackal-headed god of the afterlife.

A young page poked his head in the room. "Shall the gentlemen be needing anything, sir?"

The curator swung back toward him. "Care for some tea? A simple request to have refreshment brought up from the kitchen."

He hadn't stopped for breakfast. "Might there be a few biscuits with that?"

When Phaeton's stomach growled, Stickles raised a brow. "Perhaps something more substantial. A bit of toast and egg?"

Phaeton opened his ledger. "Lovely."

Stickles turned to the doctor who looked up from his ledger. "Tea would be fine, Mr. Stickles."

"I believe I'll have a spot myself." The assistant nodded. The curator swung back toward Phaeton. "Shall we get cracking?"

"You're staying?"

"For the duration, I'm afraid." The wily man actually grinned. "Just give me a moment." The curator accompanied his assistant out of the room.

Phaeton's gaze locked on Exeter. "You trust him?"

The doctor looked up from his ledger. "I know he's an odd duck, but I have a feeling he may prove useful."

Phaeton grabbed a blank sheet of paper and notated the number of an object listed in his log as a stone receptacle. He added a question mark. "Perhaps you're right."

Exeter flipped the page. "Mr. Stickles has offered to help us slog through the records. We're bound to have questions—"

The elderly man reentered the room with a bit more spring in his step. "At your service, Detective Black, Doctor Exeter." He carefully removed a flat, wide tome from the stack and took a seat at the table.

Phaeton continued to examine the logs in front of him.

"As you can see, gentlemen, every line begins with a date, followed by a description of the artifact. A donor name, if known, is then listed, as well as the initials of the receiving clerk who took receipt of the object. Lastly, each item is given a number and tagged so it can be stored and retrieved at a later date."

"I assume there are records of some sort that will tell us where a numbered item might be found?" Phaeton mused aloud.

Exeter looked to Stickles, who nodded to another pile beside the tall stack. "The smaller ledgers are assigned to the museum's archives, either one of the basements or the warehouses. Once numbered, the artifact is stored and recorded in one of these ledgers."

"I never realized the circumlocution office was located in the British museum." Phaeton leaned into his chairback. "We'll be here until the turn of the century."

Stickles peered over the rims of his spectacles. "I am not a trained investigator, Mr. Black, but might I suggest we concentrate on single entries? I would not spend much time with long lists of sarcophagi recorded on the same date. These would mostly likely be finds brought in from ongoing digs."

The man had a point. The sarcophagus they sought would very likely be a lone entry.

After an exhaustive, tedious day in the library, Phaeton was quite relieved to be on his way home. Pressed back into the leather seat of the hansom, he made a few mental notes for the day ahead. The Baron's funeral and internment would take the majority of the morning and then he would return to the British Library for another slog through the remaining inventory ledgers with Mr. Stickles. Exeter, of course, had been right about the odd gentleman. The curator had proven himself a most useful and enthusiastic investigator. He had half a mind to bring him in on the facts of the case.

If Qadesh had begun to feed again, he would consider having Stickles deputized. The elderly man had ordered the most promising sarcophagi identified in the ledgers brought up from storage for examination. With any luck, the morrow might end on a note of excitement. He exhaled. Well, one could hope.

Phaeton removed a notepaper from his inside coat pocket. He had found the folded up paper on the floor of his room this morning. He could only assume the list must have fallen out of a pocket in America's gown. Six different boarding-houses were crossed out with a few remarks penciled in.

Nothing until the summer or early fall. Let the last room just yesterday. No room at the inn. Ever. The script of the last entry was crudely underscored by several dark lines. He could feel the sting in her pencil marks. The words were written beside Horsley's Home for Young Ladies, Bloomsbury.

The words grew fuzzy as he recalled her choked words of last evening. He had never considered the color of her skin, nor her situation as untenable. America was such a fine, capable young woman, and she possessed the most startling independent and adventurous nature. He desired her like no other woman he had ever had the pleasure of—knowing, so to speak. Phaeton shifted in his seat, uncomfortably. And this rather disturbing attraction did not end with that sensuous, voluptuous body. Her candid wit and odd, charming speech patterns, part proper young English woman, part French sailor. She often took his breath away.

He checked the address again before he refolded the paper and slipped the note back into his pocket. Well, as long as he was in the neighborhood.

He rapped on the cab's roof and redirected the driver. "51 Applegate Lane."

The boardinghouse was a very charming home indeed. Mrs. Horsley, no doubt a fine, upstanding woman of the community, raised a brow when he offered his card.

"Scotland Yard? What can I do for you . . ." The tall,

severe-looking woman scrutinized the raised black letters on the card.

"Detective Black." Phaeton surveyed the cheerful sitting room off the elegant foyer. "Just a routine security check, Mrs. Horsley. The Princess Serafine al Qatari had noted your boardinghouse to be on the very top of her list of possible residences, while she extends her stay here in London."

"I do believe I would remember a princess, Mr. Black. Are you quite sure you have the correct address?"

Phaeton flipped open a pocket-sized notebook and just as quickly snapped it shut. "Positive, Mrs. Horsley. The young lady is somewhat exotic looking, a very pretty copper color to her skin and lovely green eyes as I recall. She does sometimes take to the streets on her own. I'm afraid she's given our bodyguards the slip on more than one occasion."

He watched the woman's reaction carefully. Wheels turned inside eyes that grew wide in horror. Yes. The boardinghouse mistress appeared to recall America's visit.

"The princess has recently gotten the oddest idea in her head. Wants to experience the city as if she were any young lady of privilege."

Phaeton leaned forward and lowered his voice. "Which brings me to the reason for my inspection. We have on our hands the rather sticky business of a possible visit from Victoria."

"Victoria, you don't mean—?" The woman's stutter was interrupted by the worst sort of twitch in her right eye.

Phaeton surveyed the silk striped wallpaper and gilded hall furnishings. Yes, America would have been very comfortable living here. Point of fact, she deserved a beautiful home and a kind and decent man to look after her. He returned to the boardinghouse mistress and narrowed his gaze. "I do not wish to alarm, but yes, I do refer to Her Majesty, Queen Victoria."

He rather enjoyed watching the color drain down that unusually thin, long neck.

Chapter Twenty-five

"SHE'S ONE OF OURS, ALL RIGHT." America sat beside Inspector Moore in a closed carriage just off the boat basin known as Millwall Docks. From the shadows of a covered passageway, she watched the loading of supplies and cargo onto their oldest square rigged clipper. Her heart swelled at the sight of her.

The sleek cut of her bow was unmistakable. The ship moored dockside was definitely the *Topaz Star*. The smallest gem in the fleet, but the most highly regarded. She had bested the East India Company's fastest cutter in her day. About the time circumstances had begun to run afoul for The Star of India Trading Company, her life in service was nearing its the end.

"She once made Australia in sixty-five days." America smiled. Oh yes, the *Topaz* would be retired, but not yet.

Dexter seemed satisfied with her reaction. "Not hard to locate this grand old girl. Thames patrol was able to identify every mark on her based on the legacy you provided, Miss Jones."

"I do hope they haven't given us away?"

"God no, at least, I hope not. They went aboard citing a routine inspection. Since then I have recognized at least two crew members from Portsmouth lurking about, dockside."

"And what of Yanky?"

He shook his head. "Nothing yet. Zander has assigned

two more inspectors; they're searching flophouses and brothels between here and the Tower."

She supposed Dexter grinned at her inability to stop starring at the elegant ship. "I cannot thank you enough, Mr. Moore. She barely carries some 600 ton, but the *Topaz* will have an important role to play in reestablishing my shipping business."

America itched to get aboard and back to the business of operating her small fleet. Even if she never had another ship returned to her, two would be enough to start over. With fair winds and a bit of luck, The Star of India Trading Company could be back on a paying basis by year's end.

"Miss Jones, you plan on operating the company?" A frown creased the ends of his mouth. "Please assure me you will not take a ship out on your own."

"I intend on doing exactly that." She pressed her shoulders back and lifted her chin. The Isle of Dogs was a chaotic, bustling peninsula of commerce. Briefly, she trained her sights on the ships being towed in and out of the West Indian Docks, a glorious cobweb of masts and rigging.

A quick dart of her eyes caused a sigh. Dexter had pressed his lips into a thin line almost as stubborn as her own. "Don't look so nettled, Mr. Moore. I am perfectly capable of captaining a ship, at least until the business returns to the profit side of the margin. Besides, I trust no one. In fact, I'm quite sure I will never trust anyone again."

Except, possibly, there was one man. But she didn't wish to think about him right now.

Mr. Moore opened his mouth but at the last second seemed to decide against further protest. "It's getting late. Allow me to take you to dinner and then see you home?"

Supper was pleasant enough as long as conversation remained on the business at hand, the discovery and claiming of her ships. The moment their discourse veered onto other matters, say, her current living accommodations or her arrangement with Mr. Black, she changed the subject. Frankly, she was relieved when their dinner fare arrived promptly at the table. Much to the amusement of the inspector, she made quick work of her supper.

"What?"

"Nothing. I do hope you are getting enough to eat below stairs at 22 Shaftsbury Court."

She chewed and stuck him with a glare. "Mr. Black enjoys watching me tuck into a plate of chops."

Moore's jaw twitched. "Yes, I recall Phaeton saying he appreciates a women with appetites."

She set down her knife and fork. "Take me home, Inspector Moore, or change the subject."

Moore stared for a moment before he reached across the table and placed her fork in her hand. Gently, he closed her fingers around the handle. "There is a ship—a two stacker, recently registered to a Dutch holding company associated with Yanky Willem. She's due into Portsmouth the end of the week."

She held her breath. The *Star of Bombay*. The crown jewel of their fleet. Named after the enormous and splendid 563-karat star sapphire. "Legally, she'd still be Yanky Willem's. When we were forced into default, he purchased the note on her for pennies on the pound."

"A conviction of grand larceny or embezzlement, whichever you wish to call it, will put all joint assets into review by the courts. With the right business partner and a bit of refinancing, she'll be yours again."

She sawed off a piece of meat and lifted it to her mouth. "Go on, Mr. Moore."

The rest of dinner passed pleasantly enough, as he finished his assessment of her missing fleet. His news was so uplifting she even shared the trying tale of her boardinghouse interviews, which he listened to with a great deal of interest as well as sympathy.

The ride back to Mrs. Parker's was made in relative quiet and the inspector saw her inside the brothel and downstairs to her flat.

America held her index finger to her lips. "I believe Mr. Black has fallen asleep in his chair."

With the evening paper folded over his chest, Phaeton appeared almost angelic in repose, until he spoke. "Quite the contrary, Miss Jones. I could hardly fall asleep when I had no idea where you were. I take it you went adventuring with Inspector Moore."

She ignored his remark and turned to the inspector. "Thank you for dinner; I feel quite restored."

"It was my pleasure."

Phaeton refolded the newspaper and rose from his chair. "Dinner?"

"I'm afraid I collected Miss Jones rather late in the day to identify a ship in the Millwall basin." Dexter's gaze shifted away. "I thought a bit of supper was the least I could offer."

"Indeed, and how was—supper?"

She brightened. "Lovely plate of chops and ale."

"Well, I'd best be on my way." Dexter patted his jacket until he found what he was looking for in a waistcoat pocket. "Mrs. Hingham's card. The woman runs a respectable boardinghouse and would be happy to take you in straight away."

America stared at the raised letters on the ivory cardstock. "Very kind of you, Mr. Moore." She removed a glove and slipped the card into a small pocket of her fitted jacket.

Phaeton crossed the room to stand uncomfortably close to one side of Moore. "Can't wait to get Miss Jones removed from my sphere of influence."

"Nearly as anxious as you are to see me out of here, Mr. Black." She pursed her lips.

As the inspector edged away, he shot her a look of concern. "Will you be all right?"

"Never mind Mr. Black. He's often disagreeable when—"

"Yes, never mind me, Dex."

"Good night, then." Dexter nodded to them both and lit up the stairs.

America whirled around to face him. "At least Mr. Moore has made an effort to find me appropriate shelter."

"Ha!" Phaeton pressed forward. "Dexter Moore can't wait to nose around under your skirts."

"And which is worse, Phaeton? A man who is interested in my favors or one who would toss me out with the dogs in the middle of the night?"

For a moment his body appeared to sway toward her. "I was going to say happy to see you, my dear. And very glad to know you weren't raped and maimed by pirates, perhaps lying injured in a gutter somewhere down in the Docklands." He pivoted abruptly and turned down the hall. She winced when the door to his room slammed shut moments later.

Hardly knowing where to turn, she headed for the pantry, where she shifted the kettle onto the stove plate. While she waited for the water to boil, she unpinned her hat and removed her jacket, folding it neatly over a chairback.

Drat the man. She sighed. His warnings about Inspector Moore were almost certainly correct. But she could handle Moore easily enough. And if she was not mistaken, Phaeton actually appeared to worry about her. The thought almost erased a frown. She poured steaming water into a teapot and took a seat at the table.

Greyish bits of fuzz and particles took shape on a chair beside her. Chin in clawed hand, the gargoyle blinked orange-yellow eyes at her. Mimicking the pose, she rested her chin in a cupped palm. "Lately, I hardly know what to make of him, Edvar." The creature emitted an unearthly whine.

"Hello?" Layla dipped her head to peek into the room before descending the last set of steps. "Thought I heard you speaking to someone, Miss Jones."

"Just mumbling to myself." America managed a grin. "What is it, Layla?"

The girl handed her a wire. "Arrived minutes ago by special messenger. Must be important, forwarded from Scotland Yard." She nodded at the envelope's addressee.

TO: PRINCESS SERAFINE AL QATARI
c/o DETECTIVE PHAETON BLACK

PLEASE INFORM THE PRINCESS STOP FINEST
SUITE IN THE HOUSE AVAILABLE END OF
WEEK MRS. HORSLEY

She read the message twice. There could be only one explanation. For the second time in two days, her throat ached and her eyes watered. "Thank you Layla."

The girl nodded and returned up the stairs.

America headed down the hall to his room, hesitating before she knocked. "Phaeton?"

No answer.

She pressed her ear against the door and rapped once more. She fell forward as the door opened.

Disheveled and half-dressed, Phaeton leaned against the doorjamb and stretched his naked torso. Her gaze wandered across a mat of chest hair and down a flat, trim stomach. The bruising around his ribs had turned to pale shades of green and yellow. Nearly healed.

"What is it, America?"

She jerked her attention upward and pushed the telegram into his hand. "It's addressed to me, or rather, the princess, in care of you."

He rubbed his eyes and squinted at the brief strips of words pasted on paper. A spark flashed in those deep liquid brown eyes before he crumpled the paper.

She raised a brow. "Well?"

"Popped in on Mrs. Horsley to do a security check on the

residence. Might have mentioned something about Victoria paying a call."

"I see." She pressed her lips together but could barely hide her delight. "And this rare visit by the queen wouldn't have anything to do with the princess, would it?"

A curl at one end of his mouth proceeded the familiar lopsided grin. "I may have"—his eyes moved to her lips—"mentioned something about a meeting with the princess."

Even though he made no move to hold her, a wave of desire swept through her body. She inched closer. So close her lips actually touched his when she spoke. "How might I find a way to thank you, Mr. Black?"

Still, he did not reach out for her, but his eyelids grew heavy and his lips parted.

She played the tip of her tongue along the underside of his upper lip. "Like this?"

He pulled back and tilted his head. "Should I allow myself to be seduced if you are only going to throw me over for the finest suite in the house?"

She placed several soft kisses on his lips and he leaned in for a long taste. "Why on earth would I ever invite the queen to tea at Mrs. Horsley's?"

His smile warmed her down to the tingle in her toes. "You caused me to worry, going off like that."

She bit her lip. "I am very sorry. I did not think—" She broke off her speech and lowered her eyes.

He lifted her chin to make eye contact. "Did not think what?"

A blush warmed her cheeks. "That . . . you cared."

He took her in his arms, his sensuous mouth covered hers, pressing her lips open. She played a blazing game of chase with his tongue as his hands tightened around her waist. His kisses, raw and impassioned, caused a surge of desire that spread through her entire body.

"Take off your clothes and have a seat by the four-poster."

She swallowed. "I beg your pardon?"

"You require proofs of affection, do you not?" He did not wait for her response; instead, he inched by her and headed down the hall toward the pantry.

She disrobed slowly, folding her clothes neatly on top of his dresser. Her body shivered in anticipation of what, she had no idea. But whatever Phaeton had in mind, she was very sure it would make her tremble and moan. Down to chemise and pantalettes, she sank onto the small upholstered chair and began to roll down her hose.

America sensed something and turned. A shadow appeared in the doorway, lit from behind she could not make out a face. She grinned. "Do not consider a ménage with Edvar, Mr. Black, even though I believe he's rather sweet on me—"

"Your mate cannot hear you."

America started. The amorphous shape standing in the hall refashioned itself into that of a tall, slender female. The apparition floated into the room.

America rose slowly and backed toward the dresser. She grabbed her dress and quickly stepped into the gown. "Where is Phaeton? What have you done with him?"

A tinkle of laughter traveled around the room, disembodied from the shifting form in front of her. "Your man is sleeping for now."

She tried to find a pair of eyes to—ah yes, there they were—glimmering ebony orbs. How lovely and strange this powerful goddess was. "I don't understand. What do you want with me, Qadesh?"

"*Fay-ton* will awake and find you gone. He will come looking for you." The chimera moved in close and sniffed her. "Fertile."

"I beg your pardon?" America backed away.

Chapter Twenty-six

PHAETON JOGGED THROUGH THE ENTRANCE OF HIGHGATE CEMETERY and down a grassy corridor lined with stately ivy-covered crypts. The pristine row houses of the dead.

His jaw ached from grinding his teeth. America was missing. Vanished in the night leaving behind a pair of high-button shoes on the floor of his room. The sight evoked dainty feet and small toes that curled when he touched her most sensitive places. Wearing nothing on her feet, left cold and shivering. Somewhere.

He shook his head to clear the cobwebs. His head felt thick, even after the powder Esmeralda had administered this morning. At first, he suspected pirates had stolen her away, but not one of the doxies had witnessed a single seafaring thug enter or exit the building. Brothel business had been unusually slow last night, and the girls insisted they would have noticed a new man enter or exit the residence. He questioned the kitchen staff. Cook insisted there had been no intruders through the back door.

Now, he very much suspected the damned little harpy was behind this abduction. Lizzie had sensed something. Wild-eyed at the very thought of a fiendish Empusa wandering about inside the house, she had begun to chatter nonsensically. The poor dear still wasn't right. Phaeton lifted the back of his collar against a cold chill of the morning mist.

His own experience of last evening was a jumble of impressions. He recalled a hurried scrounge through a bin of writing implements, digging about for an old ostrich quill. He intended to torment that beautiful beige flesh with the wispy strands of a feather, elevating her arousal to such a state that she would beg for something very naughty, indeed. A pleasant, burgeoning erection one moment and the next, he was out cold.

He awoke slumped over in the closet, the pantry door wide open. A vague lingering miasma had settled over the flat and a disturbing memory, or was it a dream? A face lunged at him, red lips parted, fangs exposed and a cloudy mist exhaled into his lungs. The wicked little goddess had conjured some sort of venomous sleeping potion. A simple enough way to overpower her prey. And it made sense; there had never been any signs of a struggle with her victims.

Phaeton caught a glimpse of a funeral procession just ahead, round the curve. He recognized one of the pallbearers as Dr. Exeter and slowed his pace. Lost in thought, he went over and over the facts of the case thus far. Why would Qadesh abduct Miss Jones, unless she wanted something from him? So preoccupied in thought, he barely noticed the vicar's internment prayer or the closing of the crypt.

"What is wrong, Phaeton?"

He looked into Exeter's steady gaze. "Miss Jones is gone."

Exeter appeared more curious than surprised. "You seem hard hit. Did you not tell me you were quite desperate to see her settled elsewhere, or am I mistaken?"

"Changed my mind." Phaeton quickly related the events of last evening. "I came to pay my respects and rummage about Hampstead Heath. I wired a colleague and asked him to meet me at the pond, perhaps nose about where the body was found and try to pick up a trail to her new lair."

"So, you believe Qadesh has spirited away Miss Jones." The space between Exeter's brows furrowed deeply as his expression changed to one of grave concern.

Phaeton nodded. "There is no time to lose."

"It would seem imperative to find her before Qadesh needs to feed again." Exeter gestured toward the south gate of the cemetery. "Push on, Phaeton; I'll join as soon as I can."

"Surely you have a wake reception and—"

"My father should have died a year ago. The majority of his peers are gone and buried. For the sake of propriety, I arranged a dignified, quiet burial service, but there will be nothing more." Exeter politely acknowledged several mourners, and returned to Phaeton. "What if this was Mia she had taken? Is not America a most cherished, living being?"

Stunned, momentarily, by the veracity in Exeter's question, he gasped a reply. "Very." Indeed, America Jones had become immensely precious to him.

Phaeton stumbled past the tall iron gates of the cemetery and found a connecting corridor, more of a bridlepath, which led onto the grounds of Hampstead Heath, a vast and ancient wilderness park. After a brisk walk through a pleasant glen, he came to a crossroads. A sign pointed him in the direction of the men's pond. He found Ping standing at the water's edge, leashed to a fearsome black-haired creature sniffing among a clump of tall reeds. He gave a wave as Phaeton approached.

"Good morning, Ping. I see you brought a . . ." Phaeton tilted his head. "Dog?"

"Tasmanian Devil. Has a nose for blood and feces." It was clear that Ping admired the animal. "An accomplished scavenger as well, enjoys a tasty piece of rotting human flesh."

"Charming." Phaeton leaned over to give the creature a pat on the head.

"Watch your fingers." Ping tugged on the collar. The beast snarled and pawed at a patch of grass beside the path. Phaeton dropped to his haunches and pushed back blades stained a reddish-brown color. A number of dried drops spotted the tufts of green.

Ping pulled out a cloth evidence bag. "I'd like a sample of that."

Phaeton took out a penknife and dug out a clump.

The creature strained at its leash and growled. "Blind Harry may be on the scent. Shall we?"

Phaeton shot upward. "Blind?"

"Sinclair found him on holiday in Australia. Abandoned in the wild. Someone had tortured the small cub, and left him for dead. Gaspar nursed him back to health and raised him as a pet." A breeze rustled along the edges of the glade. Ping pressed his top hat down lower on his head. "Come along, Harry."

The snuffling, groaning animal led them straight off the main course and into a stand of trees. They took several turns through a deep wood, past knurled, mysterious ancient oaks, no doubt formidable trees even when Henry VIII hunted in the heath.

Harry lurched to a halt and froze.

Phaeton prodded a blackish sort of lump with his foot, and used a stripling branch to wipe away leaves from a dead body.

The man lay facedown in the rich, brown mulch of the forest floor. "Poor chap."

Ping leaned in. "Let's have a look at him."

Careful not to disturb the grounds, he rolled the body over. Blank eyes stared straight into his. A number of ants and a translucent centipede crawled over the lines of a vacant expression. "Middle-aged. By the looks of his coat and suit, clearly well-dressed. A man of professional station."

Phaeton coughed. "By the smell of him, he's been here longer than the bloke in the pond." He tilted the man's face to one side, and swept bits of twig and leaf away from the neck. Two barely noticeable pinpricks. "Dainty but deadly, aye? It's no wonder no one ever notices."

"Perfectly centered over the carotid artery,"

Startled by the comment, Phaeton and Ping swiveled

toward the tall imposing figure behind them. Dr. Exeter stepped closer for a cursory examination of the body, paying particular attention to the color and length of the fingernails. "Qadesh has been feeding for some time." Exeter's gaze scanned the mounds of debris and damp leaves carpeting the small enclave. "Loose the creature."

Harry nosed about free of his leash and in quick time watered several tree trunks and uncovered another corpse. This one was fresh. Dead for just hours, the young woman appeared to be a street doxy. Ping straightened up. "One of us should alert the Yard. Ask for a few more men. We'll need to comb the wood and surroundings."

"Yes, excellent idea." Phaeton's attention never left the devil-dog, who moved out of the glen and up the path toward the street above. "Would you mind, Ping? I believe we'll just follow along after Harry." He and Exeter set off after the animal, who occasionally stopped to sniff the ground. As they approached the street that separated the north grounds of Hampstead Heath from the cemetery, Phaeton paused.

"Blimey, he's headed back into Highgate." The animal stopped to lift his leg at a shrub, and he slipped the leash onto the panting creature.

The eager beast released a bloodcurdling shriek and set a rollicking pace through the gates and onto cemetery grounds. Most uncharacteristically, Exeter began to laugh.

Phaeton glared over his shoulder. "I fail to see what is so amusing about this."

"Take a look where you're headed." The doctor's gaze moved higher.

He pulled back on Harry's leash. A deep archway lay up ahead, surrounded by columns fashioned to look like tall papyrus. The motif was famous and unmistakable. They were headed down Egyptian Avenue, one of the more eccentric areas of the cemetery.

He gasped. "First Cleopatra's Needle and now this?"

Exeter's wide grin turned rather grim. "Qadesh taunts us, Phaeton. She hides in plain sight, waiting for us."

Harry led them deep into a labyrinth of crypts, before the whining and whimpering began. Turning a number of tight circles, the wild dog stretched his forelegs and lay down with a groan.

"No time to nap," Phaeton lectured. The hound's dangling tongue whipped a bit of drool over his shoes. "Fine. Have it your way." He handed the leash to Exeter and explored the entrance to a moss-covered tomb. He shook the locked barrier and the rattled padlock clicked open.

"Hypothesis moves toward certainty." Phaeton eyed the doctor. "She wants to be discovered." Lock and chain removed, he pushed back the creaking gate and gestured man and dog inside. "Gentlemen?"

America lay on top of a cold stone slab in complete darkness. A shiver started in her toes and didn't stop until her teeth chattered. She turned onto her side and tucked her knees to her chest.

The apparition would soon reappear. She had counted the number of turns Qadesh had made through the crypt. The flighty succubus appeared to be semi-lucid, in some kind of trance. Her transparent, ghostly body flew in restless circles overhead, passing through stone walls, reappearing seconds later. With each brief visitation, scant flickers of luminous vapor revealed her surroundings, only to be plunged back into darkness once her captor disappeared.

Her soft sigh became amplified, echoing through the chamber. What came back to her was harsh and rasping, Qadesh's sigh. America covered her ears.

Fay-ton will come for you.

Yes, he would come. Hopefully, before she rotted away in this stinking crypt. To block out the hissing, whispered voice in her head, she closed her eyes and concentrated. Restless, she rolled onto her back.

The apparition hung in the air above her. Eyes the color of onyx, the black orbs grew oversized and blinked. "You are mortal flesh much favored by the young demigod."

America tried to move and got slammed back down onto cold marble.

Her voice faint, nothing much more than a parched whisper. "Who are you talking about?"

Once again Qadesh sniffed and uttered that odd declaration. "Fertile." Abruptly, the strange she-devil pulled away and vanished.

He is near.

Her heart raced as the words resounded in her head. She wasted no time, calling on every ability she had ever practiced as a child. She tuned her senses to the surrounding walls of the tomb. Yes, she sensed his presence. She did not dare to breathe. Listening, probing into the darkness until the faint scratch of footsteps against cold stone reached her ears.

America slipped off the stone slab and stumbled her way through the pitch blackness. She forced herself to slow down and let outstretched hands find the wall. With some relief, she lay her cheek against smooth marble.

Dear God, let it be him.

She tried to make out a faint murmur of conversation. Like a caged tigress she prowled the length of the wall until she finally let loose. "Phaeton, are you there?" She pounded the walls and cried out again for him.

A block of marble, not much larger than a bread loaf, moved. She pushed harder, but her prodding had little or no effect this time. "Phaeton, I am here. Come for me, Phaeton."

Phaeton pivoted slowly about. "Did you hear something?"

Exeter nodded. "Stone against stone, perhaps?" Simultaneously, he and the doctor turned toward a nondescript, blank wall of the mausoleum.

He attuned his senses and waited. *Phaeton, I am here.*

Was her voice in his ears or his head? Exeter pointed at a good-sized stone block protruding ever so slightly from the smooth, near seamless barrier in front of them. With one hand, the doctor gripped the edges of the block and pulled. The same unmistakable grinding noise as the block effortlessly slid toward them, but by not more than an inch.

Exeter pulled again several times, but with no results. He dusted his hands off.

"I'll give a heave ho from the bottom." Phaeton angled himself under the block. "On the count. One. Two. Pull."

A tremor ran through the crypt.

The hound whined and pulled on his leash.

Phaeton backed away and signaled Exeter to do the same. The floor of the tomb began to move under their feet. A faint rumble rapidly grew into a roar as a long block of stone blasted out of the partition and crashed into the opposite wall.

A cloud of minute marble particles filled the passageway. He and Exeter were forced to exit the crypt for a time, least they suffocate.

Dressed in a formal mourning suit, Exeter dusted off his top hat.

After a small coughing fit, Phaeton checked on Harry. The creature's muzzle had gone white with a clotted, greyish-white powder. He cleaned off a most prized nose with a pocket square. "Are you all right, Harry?"

A small nub of a tail whipped back and forth.

"The wild beast version of a thumbs-up, I believe." Exeter returned his hat to his head.

Phaeton straightened out. "Shall we?"

They picked their way through a pile of rubble to the square hole centered on the wall. Phaeton leaned over for a peek down the dark shaft.

"Where the hell have you been?" A dry, scratchy voice greeted him. But she sounded wonderfully unafraid, even plucky.

He experienced an odd sensation, as if his chest swelled, which he ignored. "I half expected a 'lovely to see you dear,' or perhaps a 'thank God you are alive, Phaeton.' " A very discernible harrumph echoed down the shaft. Still, he could not help a grin. "Had to let the dust clear, my dove."

Exeter leaned in. "Ask about Qadesh."

"Darling, where is the destructive little goddess hiding—right at the moment?"

There was a pause.

"Darling?"

He heard a sigh. "Oh she's about, all right. Seems very agitated, a bit off her game."

"She hasn't—fed recently, has she?"

"You mean me?"

"Yes." Phaeton held his breath and waited.

"No. At least I don't think so."

He exhaled. "Do you have any idea what she's after?"

"Difficult to say. She communicates in pictures and riddles." America's shallow nervous breaths seemed amplified across the thick expanse of stone between them. The wall had to be nearly five feet thick. He reached into the shaft and a moment later her small fingers found his. Her hand was like ice. He wrapped her palm in his and held on.

Phaeton turned to Exeter and kept his voice low. "I wager Qadesh wants us to see she is alive."

"It will take time to open a passage large enough to extract Miss Jones." Exeter scanned the opening in the wall and the stones surrounding it. Phaeton ducked his head again. "I take it you are breathing reasonably well?"

"Better now, with a bit of fresh air."

"Food? Water?"

"Water. And quickly, please."

Phaeton slipped his hand from hers, but gave her fingertips a squeeze.

"Don't leave me."

"But, I—"

Exeter tapped him on the shoulder and shook his head. "Stay with her. I'll organize a rescue team and bring water." Phaeton grinned. "You tell her."

Exeter dipped lower. "Miss Jones?"

"Doctor Exeter?"

"Yes, Miss Jones. Do try to stay calm. Phaeton will stay here while I'm off—"

Exeter's body left the ground, tossed like a paper doll across an expanse of passageway. Simultaneously, stone and dust rose into the air, drawing every particle of rubble into a cyclone of whirling matter.

"Phaeton?" America wailed.

Like clouds crossing in front of the sun, a cyclone of debris blocked out most of the daylight in the crypt. He checked on Exeter, who lay crumpled on the ground. A garbled moan was reassuring.

Phaeton rose slowly and turned. The little necromancer of the Nile had taken on huge proportions. She sat with her hands gripping the arms of a throne formed instantaneously by marble fragments. Tiny particles of silver dust shifted around her, floating on an invisible current of air.

A small voice traveled out of the hole in the wall. "Answer me, Phaeton. What is happening?"

"Qadesh."

Chapter Twenty-seven

PHAETON EDGED AWAY FROM THE OPEN SHAFT to help the doctor to his feet. "All right?"

"A few bruises." Exeter brushed off his coat and straightened his tie. "She's a bit tetchy, however."

The beautiful goddess stirred. Regal, powerful, and deadly, she awoke from her transfiguration with the barest hint of a smile. "*Ogai, pai pe nishti, Fay-ton.*"

He nodded a bow. "We meet again, Qadesh."

Exotic, kohl-lined eyes swept over the tall, stoic man standing beside him. "This one is also the issue of a god?"

"Doctor Exeter?" He swiveled to examine his comrade. "Why yes, I believe so."

She turned her head and tilted her chin. A slight lowering of those mesmerizing orbs left no doubt as to which part of the doctor's anatomy interested the she-devil. "Where is the sword he uses to insert his seed? Qadesh would like to see it."

Such a wicked, ribald little goddess. "As a rule, English gentlemen do not go about brandishing their . . . weapons in public." Phaeton did not attempt to hide a grin. "But I can vouch for the doctor's rapier, myself. Very impressive."

Exeter stepped forward. "Almighty Qadesh. Why do you steal the breeding vessel of the demigod beside me?"

Several piercing blasts of light struck the floor at their feet. A sizzle of electrical current crawled up the walls of the room and reverberated through his spine. Phaeton had no idea lightning bolts flew from the eyes of gods. "Try not to get us killed."

The doctor's usual frown strained upward. "If I am not mistaken"—he flicked a tiny fragment of marble off his lapel—"she needs us alive."

Smoke wafted around the edges of her eyes. "Bring Anubis to me, and I will release the cow."

"Cow? Did she just call me a cow?" A very disgruntled voice echoed out of the hole in the wall.

Phaeton threw back his shoulders. "On behalf of the lovely Miss Jones—"

Exeter grabbed him by the arm. "A compliment, Phaeton. The goddess of fertility assumed the head of a cow. A symbol of great power."

An onset of vertigo overtook the scene surrounding him. Phaeton's attention melded with the temperamental goddess. A question had been niggling at the back of his brain all day, and he wanted, nay, needed her to confirm his suspicion. The second reliquary to arrive with the obelisk must be the resting place of her husband, but . . . *the sarcophagus that broke apart, that was yours, was it not, Qadesh?*

Ten thousand pieces of me were thrown into the ground beside your river of life.

A whirlwind of visions passed through his mind's eye. Pictures of a frightened, angry goddess sifting through grains of sand, desperate to form herself—to make her body whole again. Pieces of the puzzle, though not fully explained, began to fall into place. Those odd, misshapen creatures she transfigured into, nearly all of them malformed in some way. He recalled the bleeding, injured limb of the harpy perched on the window ledge. Phaeton turned to Exeter and softened his voice. "She can hold herself together only for brief periods of time."

Great sadness and desperate isolation hung over the room

like a heavy cloud. It seems the goddess was also lonely, and profoundly so. Phaeton sighed. The gods so needed to be loved.

Jerked back to consciousness, he looked up into her eyes. For the briefest moment, he experienced an understanding with her. "The doctor and I are on the trail of a missing sarcophagus—we believe it to be the companion to yours, and the possible resting place of your husband."

In a swirl of light and dark particles, she disappeared, leaving a horrid serpent in her wake. A fiend covered in scales stood upright, and strode into the chamber. The reptilian creature sported a large snout and a set of razor-sharp teeth. A long sleek tail cracked through the air like a whip. Useless forearms dangled awkwardly as the monster paced back and forth across the crypt entrance, blocking any escape. Another blinding quick swipe of the spiked appendage forced Phaeton and Exeter to duck, least their heads be severed from their bodies. The tail slammed into the wall. Bits and chunks of polished stone cut a swathe of marble dust through the chamber.

So much for the vulnerable, softer side of Qadesh.

The goddess spoke from the elongated mouth. "Between moonrise and moonset, you will bring me Anubis. Only then will you have your Miss Jones returned to you."

"Do nothing to harm her, Qadesh." He dodged another lash of furious tail.

She slipped a long blood-red tongue over pointed fangs. "By moonset, or she will die."

Exeter leaned in. "You've got to charm her, Phaeton."

In no mood to curry favor, he took a deep breath. "Lovely goddess of the Nile—"

The strange serpent disappeared. Vanished. Nothing but a sparkle of relic dust and champagne.

"You charm her next time." A bit dazed, Phaeton turned to the doctor. "Moonrise to moonset, how long have we got?

"I believe the moon rose around eleven o'clock this morning."

Phaeton sprung the cover to his pocket watch. "Less than fifteen minutes ago. When does it set?"

"To be safe, we should return here with Anubis, no later than three in the morning."

"Christ. Even if we find the sarcophagus, who is to say we'll be able to raise this rogue husband of hers?"

Exeter met his gaze with a sobered grin. "Let us hope Mr. Stickles has made progress."

"We seem to have misplaced poor blind Harry." Phaeton spun around. "Harry!"

"Here we are."

The pale, elusive young man pushed back the iron gate. "Found him snuffling about Egyptian Avenue. Led me straight here."

"I'd like to introduce you to someone." Phaeton led Ping over to the square hole in the wall.

"Are you there, America?"

"Where else would I be Phaeton? I can't exactly go out for a stroll now can I?"

Phaeton grinned. "My little turtle dove. I would like you to meet Julian Ping, who works as a consultant on our more challenging cases." He drew Ping over. "Julian, please meet Miss Jones."

Incredulous, Ping removed his dark glasses and ducked his head for a look. "Oh yes, I see." He tipped his hat. "Good day, Miss. Julian Ping, at your service."

"Mr. Ping."

In rip-fire fashion, Phaeton explained the situation as best he could, including the more fantastic bits. "In short, Ping, I need you to stay here with Miss Jones." Phaeton bit his lower lip. "Can we expect reinforcements soon?"

Ping nodded. "I wired nearly everyone at 4 Whitehall Place."

"Good man."

Ping looked a bit wild-eyed without the spectacles. No doubt he was overstimulated. Phaeton suspected the quirky mesmerist led a relatively isolated existence. "Will you be all right?"

Ping ducked his head and peered into the opening. "We'll be fine, won't we Miss Jones?"

"Of course, Mr. Ping."

"Do not attempt a forcible escape of any kind." Phaeton clenched his jaw. "If Doctor Exeter and I fail to meet the exchange demands, then and only then will we attempt a rescue of Miss Jones. Do I make myself clear?"

"Perfectly, Phaeton."

"Excellent." He swiveled, then turned back. "No press. If they so much as get a whiff of this operation, we place her life in jeopardy."

He removed a calling card from a hard leather case, uncapped and shook down his pen, and scribbled a few words. "Show this to any officer or detective who might question your duties here."

" 'Believe anything this man says. Obey any order he gives you.' " Ping tucked the card away.

"I'm trusting you to take charge of this operation." Phaeton stared at Ping for a long moment, then reached into the small passage. He wrapped his hand around lovely small fingers. "I have to leave now. Do you understand why?"

Her voice trembled through the shaft. "Yes, Phaeton. Please do hurry back."

Outside the crypt, he turned to Ping. "Miss Jones is quite desperate for a drink of water, and she will need something to eat and warm clothing."

"I will see to it personally." Ping patted his waistcoat and removed his timepiece. "Shall we synchronize our watches, gentlemen?"

Phaeton grinned. "I believe you'll do quite well, Ping."

★　★　★

Mr. Stickles met them at the library entrance and escorted them down the backstairs to a length of underground passage that traveled beneath the gardens to the south wing of the museum.

"All four sarcophagi have been brought up to this level from storage below us."

"How many floors of basement are there?" Exeter dipped his head to avoid a length of low-hanging pipe.

"Three. Most of it used for storage."

Stickles led them through two sets of doors and into a room that could almost be described as sunny. Light poured into the space from a number of skylights positioned along the side of the building.

Four sarcophagi sat in the middle of the room, surrounded by long tables covered with ancient pottery fragments and artifacts. Lab workers sat about engrossed in what appeared to be cataloguing and puzzle solving.

With the aid of several assistants, they removed the lids from three of the vessels. The fourth coffin had no cover. Even from a cursory examination it was plain to see, there was no jackal-headed god to be found in any of the oblong stone reliquaries.

Phaeton peered into the bottom corners of the last sarcophagus looking for what? A grain of sand? He chewed a lip. "Blast it all."

"Cheer up, Mr. Black. I wager there are at least a hundred more possibilities." Stickles seemed unduly high-spirited, which Phaeton found mildly irritating.

"I do not wish to unduly alarm, Mr. Stickles, but there has been a nasty turn of events. A young lady's life now hangs in the offing." Phaeton drew his mouth into a thin line. "It is imperative we find the sarcophagus by midnight tonight."

Stickles blinked. "Oh dear. Well, we'd best get back to the ledgers, wot?"

"There is no time to identify and locate a hundred coffins." Phaeton worried aloud.

Exeter set a brisk pace back to the library. "What we lack is a key piece of information. Something that will narrow the search quickly."

On their way back through the labyrinth of underground corridor, Phaeton quickly deputized Stickles. "The information you are about to hear is privileged—of the utmost secret—never to be discussed or shared with anyone outside of Secret Branch. Is that understood?"

"My lips are sealed." If he was not mistaken the old man's eyes sparkled with mischief and adventure. "I had no idea Scotland Yard had a Secret Branch."

Phaeton rolled his eyes at Exeter, and held the library door open. "Precisely, Mr. Stickles." Once inside the private meeting room, each man settled down with a ledger.

Pages turned.

Hours passed.

Notes were scrawled onto pieces of paper.

Sarcophagi were located and brought up to basement level one. Trips were made to the workroom to examine empty stone boxes. Each time, Phaeton returned to the library dejected, but even more determined. He checked his watch. "It's nearly seven. What time does the museum close?"

Stickles removed his pince-nez and squinted across the table. By now they all suffered from eyestrain. "The museum closed over an hour ago."

"And the hired help?"

Stickles sighed, looking about the table strewn with crumpled papers and open ledgers. "We'll just have to locate them ourselves."

Phaeton glared. "I hope you know your way around."

Stickles brightened. "Not to worry, Mr. Black. I began my career at the museum, cataloguing artifacts."

Stickles' assistant arrived carrying a tray of sandwiches, cakes, and tea. A very late tea, but welcome sustenance. The lad handed a file to the curator. "The articles you asked for, sir."

"Ah." Stickles returned his spectacles to his nose. "I asked Mr. Darling to rummage about in the newspaper files. Anything in the way of articles written about the construction and installation of the obelisk." Sifting through a number of aged clippings, the elderly gent peered over the top of the folder. "I hope you don't mind?"

Phaeton dropped a small lump of sugar into his teacup and stirred. "Let's have a read through, straight away."

They went over all the clues again. Stickles' file was mostly a repeat of Dr. Exeter's notes, with a few exceptions. Each man took a turn reading to allow the others the opportunity to down a few sandwiches and have a piece of cake.

Exeter leaned back and tilted his chair. "A small tidbit here, mention of a stone mason who worked on the granite foundation. William Henry Gould, resident of Lambeth—"

"Lambeth, you say?" Stickles patted a few crumbs off his lips and picked up a pile of recent notes. He shuffled back and forth between papers. "Ah, here it is. A single sarcophagus brought in some years after the installation. No donor name recorded but a residence in Lambeth was notated. I thought it odd enough to make a note of it."

Exeter leveled his chair. "Lambeth is a working-class neighborhood—seems unlikely anyone there would have a spare sarcophagus laying about unless—"

"Unless a resident stone mason happened to be working on the site when those two coffins fell out of the packing and onto British soil. Hard to say how this chap—Gould—ended up with the relic." Phaeton leaned forward. "Let's say he tucked it away for years. Perhaps something happened, a financial difficulty, he needed the income. The stone cutter asks about, contacts an antiquities dealer, who brings the item to the museum's attention."

Stickles nodded. "Black market acquisitions are often anonymous; usually an alias is used, but not always."

Phaeton nervously fingered the edges of a ledger. "So gentlemen, what does our intuition tell us about this clue?"

★ ★ ★

A man's face, lit only by a flickering torch, appeared at the end of the open shaft. "Miss Jones, Detective Investigator Farrell, Scotland Yard. I take it we have not much time to settle this unusual exchange. I would like to ask you a few questions, if you don't mind?"

Phaeton had been gone for hours now, but she was grateful for the company she had received from Mr. Ping and the small contingent of police surrounding the crypt.

"Pleased to meet you, Detective Farrell. I believe Phaeton receives messages from you, though we've never met."

"And you are the young lady who is helping Inspector Moore hunt down and capture a bad lot of pirates."

"I do hope so, sir."

"Looks as though you've gotten caught up in a bad lot of business. How are you getting on?"

"A great deal more comfortably now, Detective."

"Splendid." The man lowered his voice to a whisper. "Can you hear me, Miss Jones?"

"Perfectly, sir."

"Very good. Phaeton and Doctor Exeter have gone off—on an important errand, I'm told. Might you know where they are?"

"Oh, Mr. Black rarely says much about his comings and goings." She thought for a moment. "I believe yesterday he was about in Bloomsbury."

"Bloomsbury?" The detective exhaled a rather loud sigh. "Nothing much up there, except the—" The man suddenly cut off his speech. America strained to hear bits and pieces of muffled conversation. She caught the tail end of a barked order. "Have Director Chilcott meet me at the museum." He tipped the edge of his hat. "Thank you for your assistance, Miss Jones."

A flurry of mist and miasma floated through the chamber. She did not have to turn around to know what caused a chill to run up her spine. "Detective Farrell?"

"Yes, miss?" The man's brows furrowed. "Is everything all right?"

She gave him a quick nod, but signaled otherwise with a roll of her eyes. "If you find Mr. Black, tell him to take care and please hurry back."

Chapter Twenty-eight

THE BRITISH MUSEUM, BASEMENT LEVEL THREE. A vast dark space thick with the dust of antiquity. Dismal enough. Vaguely, Phaeton made out the dim outline of objects, great and small, crated and stacked neatly in rows. He toggled the switch, hoping to add more light to the flickering lanterns held high by Exeter and Stickles. Impatient to get a better look, he slapped the torch against his palm. A swath of illumination sprang to life and cut through the endless black pit of the museum's underground depository. He swept the beam across a woefully barren storage compartment. "Bollocks."

"Let me check the warehouse address once again." Stickles rifled through the pages of a small ledger. "We are in aisle thirty, and this is indeed where item—"

The doctor squinted at the numbered placard. "Four fifty-one—"

Phaeton shifted the beam to the brass frame tacked to the floor. Exeter dropped onto his haunches and brushed a layer of dust off the numbered card. "Dash S."

"See here." He swept the circle of light along a near perfect outline of fine powder. "An object was moved recently." His jaw twitched. "So where is the blasted box?"

Exeter's gaze traced over the rectangular shape. "Are we on the right floor? In the correct warehouse?"

"Ahead of you there, doctor." Stickles clapped the ledger

shut. "We are in the correct spot, gentlemen, but I'm afraid the sarcophagus is not."

"Could the ledger be wrong?" Phaeton swiveled toward the elderly gent. Despite the blinding beam in his eyes, the odd curator smiled. "What's got you so amused, Stickles?"

"Unless the artifact is stolen, there can only be one other explanation."

Phaeton wracked his brain. He thought of several possibilities, each one worse than the last. He needed to find the resting place of Anubis and raise the dead. Right. All in a day's work. A deep breath and a slow and purposeful exhale helped. Perhaps the piece was on loan to another museum. Dear God, not off premises. He went with his last thought on the matter. "It's on display."

"Very good, Mr. Black."

After a clamor up three sets of stairs, they faced yet another looming staircase on the main floor of the museum. Phaeton sat the wheezing curator down on a bench and loosened the man's cravat. "Don't die on me now, Stickles."

"Gave up the pipe last year. Not soon enough, I expect." The curator managed a weak grin. "You both go ahead. Number four—the mummy room."

Phaeton swiveled, then turned back. "How will we tell one sarcophagus from another?"

"Find the placard. Every artifact on display has one. In the bottom left corner you will find the item number."

Cool blue illumination poured in from the domed skylight, dappling the marble floor with a cobweb of shadows and light. The edge of a great white sphere slipped below the curvature of glass, a reminder the moon was setting. In the entry hall, two colossal stone heads, placed side by side, guarded the mummy room. Phaeton stopped to stare into the imposing, sightless eyes of Amenhotep and Ramses II. "We Brits do know how to loot and pillage."

A staccato of hollow footsteps followed them across the

great room filled with glass cases, inner coffins, and the tortured frames of withered mummies. At the end of a long display of funerary masks, he and Exeter hesitated. A sea of sarcophagi lay straight ahead. The stone reliquaries were placed in an orderly circle, surrounding an impressive display built to resemble a royal barge. Phaeton opened his watch. "Nearly one fifteen."

Exeter's demeanor, usually stoic and difficult to read, was transparently grim. "If we divide the job—"

"No." Phaeton shook his head. "We'll never find the damnable coffin in time." After a few tentative paces forward, he shut everything out but the hollow rasp of his own breath and tattoo of heartbeats. He moved among the hollow-eyed dead and listened carefully to the faint whispers that were always with him.

Exeter followed several paces behind. *Lead the way, Phaeton.*

He distinctly heard the doctor's voice in his head. So, the enigmatic Exeter was a fair telepath himself. Excellent, his cohort might attune to something he missed.

A slither of grey tail and an unpleasant sniveling whine alerted Phaeton to his annoying nemesis.

"That unpleasant creature, the one I always see skulking about you." Exeter perused a reliquary. "Might the gargoyle be of any assistance, as say that hound of Mr. Ping's?"

Phaeton had lived nearly his entire life with the pesky beast lurking in the shadows of his world. Now, in a matter of weeks, he had made acquaintance with two people who were clearly aware of the ephemeral little monster. "Pay no attention to Edvar the Sneaky."

"Edvar"—Exeter glanced up from his examination of the coffin—"the Sneaky?"

Phaeton cleared his throat. "Miss Jones believes Edvar to be my protector."

The doctor's gaze narrowed on the cloud of grey matter assembling itself on a nearby display case. "Rather small, for a guardian."

Phaeton shrugged. "Quite a talented shapeshifter, actually."

Exeter stepped past the newly assembled gargoyle. "Hmm. If you say so."

Walking a zigzag pattern, steadily circling displays or statuary, he and the doctor closed in on the center of the room. Along the way, Phaeton placed a copper tuppence on one or two closed sarcophagi. Remote possibilities.

Once they reached the barge, he turned back to Exeter and shook his head.

"Nothing?"

Not exactly nothing. There was a niggling speck of something. More of a foggy suspicion, really. As if some sort of unknown entity, powerful and dangerous, lay hidden deep inside a grain of sand, out of reach. Words flowed from his mouth, whisperings, really. "We are close."

"The ancient Egyptians held a great reverence for the jackal-headed god Anubis, overseer of the weighing of souls." The words jarred Phaeton out of his musings. He pivoted toward the plaque as the doctor read aloud. "The heart of the deceased was balanced on a scale, against the feather of Maat, or truth. If the heart was lighter than a feather, the dead person was allowed to pass into the underworld."

Exeter turned to Phaeton. "If I recall my ancient Egyptian mythology correctly, should the applicant fail the weighing of the heart test, the Eater of Souls devoured the departed."

"This isn't some royal barge, designed for an afternoon scull down the Nile." Phaeton nodded to the signage hanging above the impressive display. "This is a model of the sun boat. The ark of Ra."

The long sleek lines of the elegant barge all came together at the center of the craft. A rather plain, undistinguished looking stone sarcophagus had been placed upon a dais. And yet, he sensed . . .

Phaeton's gaze wavered, then returned to the coffin. "Shall we go aboard?" He didn't have to glance at Exeter to know the doctor, as well, focused on the reliquary.

"Note the cartouche, here on the end." Exeter ran his fingers over incised lines, carved eons ago. "The eagle feather and crown signify god or ruler, followed by the symbol for a door and the ankh." Exeter straightened. "The door opens to death."

Phaeton scratched his head. "I thought the ankh represented life?"

"Life, death, eternal life. Three stages of being, one symbol."

"Ah-h. N. Oo-o. Phu-u." The doctor sounded out the letters and vowels of the cartouche.

"Anupu. The ancient name for Anubis. God of the dead." The thrum of his heart pounding in his chest stirred the murmurs in his head. *Yes-s-s-s-s.*

He moved to one end of the stone reliquary, fingering the coffin lid. "On the count, then?"

After several tries, the sarcophagus cover shifted. Both he and the doctor gained a better grip and were able to move the heavy slab to one edge. "Ready?" After a deep breath, they tilted the lid, straining every muscle as the stone ground down the side of the coffin.

"Try not to destroy the display." Exeter gasped, just as the cover slipped from their grasp and hit the floor. Decking snapped, wooden planks splintered and flew into the air.

Phaeton ducked and stepped back. When the dust cleared, a large portion of the ship's decking appeared to be dislodged. The open sarcophagus teetered on the edge of several broken floor boards, which sagged dangerously and made the most worrisome creaking noise.

To get a better look inside, Exeter placed a tentative foot forward.

Phaeton nodded. "Might as well have a go."

They both leaned forward. An earthshaking tremble proceeded a loud crunch, as the floor gave way all around them. Phaeton, the doctor, and the stone resting place of Anubis all crashed to the ground at once.

Having landed on his posterior, Phaeton rolled over and pulled a nasty splinter out of his rear. "Ouch." He rubbed his backside. "What happened to those gravity defying powers of yours, doctor?"

Exeter grinned at his discomfort. "We barely fell four feet."

The coffin, however, lay broken in several pieces.

Phaeton clapped the dust off his hands and peered inside. Nothing but a few inches of sand covered the bottom of the sarcophagus.

Exeter caught his eye. "Disappointed?"

"Not sure what I was expecting." A whiff of ancient miasma filtered into the air. Phaeton sniffed. "Bitter almonds."

The doctor raised a brow.

"A scent I often experience before—" He broke off in midsentence. Whatever it was, the essence was strong. Phaeton sank back down onto the floor. "Odd coincidence. More than ten years ago, Qadesh arrives here, in England, in a similar condition. Sleeping peacefully through the centuries, her stone housing is suddenly dropped and broken."

Exeter appeared mesmerized by sand pouring out of the broken corner of the stone receptacle. Piercing eyes shifted to Phaeton. "So, what awakened her?"

"The Whitechapel murders." He sat straight up. "When did they begin—approximately?"

"You know as well as I do, the date depends greatly on which victims you count. My involvement began sometime after Mary Ann Nichols, in August of last year."

"But what if the murders began earlier, with Emma Smith? That would put us in spring. Shortly after the Thames flood."

A spark lit in Exeter's eyes. "The sinkholes. No doubt one of them was her lair."

Phaeton nodded. "The Thames overflowed her banks late last spring—by nearly four feet in some spots." He recalled a newspaper photograph of Cleopatra's Needle rising up from the floodwaters.

"The ankh, the eye of Horus, powerful symbols, certainly. But the Egyptians' greatest symbol, the mother of all life . . ." Exeter dusted sand and debris off his coat sleeve. "If you lived in a desert, Phaeton, what might you call the elixir of life?"

"The Nile." Phaeton grinned. "Could water be the catalyst?"

Exeter shrugged. "Perhaps, not any water. With regards to its life-sustaining properties and importance, the Thames is not unlike the Nile."

Exeter reached inside his jacket pocket and retrieved a flask of whiskey. "I'm afraid all I have in the way of liquid is a dram or two of Talisker's." He unscrewed the cap, pulled a swig and passed it over. "There's a good drop left."

"Cheers." Phaeton tilted back to empty the flask as Stickles head popped into the deck opening overhead. "Dear me, it appears you have found item four fifty-one dash S."

Phaeton coughed, wiping his mouth with his jacket sleeve. "You wouldn't happen to have a queen's gallon of Thames water on you, old man?"

"Afraid not." Stickles continued to view the carnage below with bewilderment. "Would a spot of tea help? I brought a refreshment tray up, thought you gentlemen could use—"

Phaeton turned to Exeter. "Tea is brewed with Thames water."

The doctor flashed a weary, devil-eyed grin. "Might as well give it a go."

Phaeton turned back to the curator. "Mind pouring what you've got down into the sarcophagus? The tea, I mean."

A small stream of pale brown liquid hit bottom and puddled in a hollow of sand. The moisture was quickly absorbed by the dry fine particles.

They waited. Staring at the light brown stain of dampness.

A column of white steam and bluish smoke arose from beneath the grains with a scorching hiss. Exeter and Phaeton moved back as a diminutive funnel began to cyclone, simultaneously throwing off and drawing in bits of dust and flying debris.

Something small and black emerged from the whirling particles of sand and silica. Phaeton leaned closer. "What is it?"

"I can't tell much from up here. Appears to be a rat standing on two legs." Stickles held the teapot poised over the sarcophagus. "Shall I continue to pour?"

Without taking his eyes off the queer creature, Phaeton signaled for more. "A few sips."

Stickles tilted the pot a bit too far and the lid fell off. A splash of hot, brewed tea drenched the animated entity. A shrill screech tore through the little beast as it spun itself into a whirlwind.

"Oh, dear," gasped the curator.

The twister drew itself through the hole in the deck, expanding ever higher toward the high ceilings of the mummy room. Parts of barge and pieces of stone coffin lifted into the air as the winds grasped up Phaeton and Exeter. After a dizzying ride to the top of the glass ceiling, Phaeton caught a glimpse of the city through the panes of the circular dome. The glow of the moon's orb lay low on the horizon. *Dear Miss Jones.*

As swiftly as he and Exeter were transported to the heights of the museum, they were just as abruptly flung across the room. Phaeton's body slammed into the wall behind two colossal statues and slid down the wall. He fell feet first, landing quite neatly on the shoulder of a seated pharaoh. His jaw loosened and his mouth dropped open. A Lilliputian-sized Mr. Stickles ran to take cover as the monstrous giant arose.

Anubis.

Half man, half jackal, a magnificent ebony-furred figure stood eye to eye with Phaeton. Sleek as a black panther, the creature surveyed the wreckage of the room that surrounded him. A snarling mouth featuring sharp fangs dripped foam and saliva. A low growl rumbled up from a powerful chest and blew out a velvet snout. Phaeton held onto the curve of Amenhotep's ear, as the god of the dead's snort blew a sultry breeze his way.

The fearsome god took a few steps back, arms flung wide open. Stretching a clawed hand holding a flail. The whip struck a length of cabinetry set against a wall and the entire display shattered and crashed to the floor. Anubis appeared to steady himself.

After a nauseating tinge of vertigo, Phaeton turned to Exeter, who crouched on the shoulder of a neighboring statue, fascinated by the spectacle before them. "Please tell him not to destroy the place."

The sable-coated god tilted toward Phaeton.

Covered in a loincloth and a gold-striped headdress, Anubis raised his snout and opened his mouth. Glistening fangs flashed in the moonlight as the jackal head let loose a howl that finally brought the night watch on duty into the mummy room. Several hundred glass panes splintered into tens of thousands of shards, which rained down onto the checkerboard of marble squares below.

"All right down there?" Phaeton counted three men and Mr. Stickles, who appeared no worse for the wear. Both the curator and the guards cowered behind a few battered sarcophagi. A shaky up-turned thumb worked its way above the crumbled stone.

Deadly and fearless, the towering man-beast stood with legs spread. The jackal's cunning gaze slid over details of the room. Black orbs hesitated on Exeter, then Phaeton. Still a bit unsteady, the towering creature shifted back and forth, and leaned forward. A swipe of each clawed hand scooped them both up.

The colossus of dogs strode off, crushing everything in his path. Sights and sounds were a blur. Phaeton struggled against a crushing grip and was vaguely aware of some sniffing and snarling. Anubis stalked after something. Poking his head between dangerous looking claws, he caught a glimpse of Stickles and the guards. Two of the watchmen ran in terror, the other appeared to have fainted dead away.

Near the entrance to the mummy room, several display cases featured mummies. The demigod halted in his tracks. Anubis set them down on top of the carved head of Ramses. Actually, it was more like a gentle toss. Phaeton sat up and rubbed the nape of his neck.

Exeter was grinning. There were good reasons Phaeton had actually grown to like the man. "We may be mistaken about everything. Empusas, vampires—all of it."

"You're going to tell me something I'd rather not care to hear at the moment." Rising to his feet, Phaeton chanced a quick glance at the doctor. "Something really crushing—"

The monster's snout nearly blasted them off the statue. A large wet nose sniffed over Phaeton.

The doctor lowered his voice. "He senses her blood in you."

Phaeton edged away. "In all honesty, I haven't touched your woman—exactly."

Exeter turned to the beast. "*Masa El Khair.* Anupu, son of Set, protector of the dead, your woman, Qadesh, awaits you in a crypt not far from here."

The jackal curled back a lip and tilted his snout upward. His howl shattered the glass in another round skylight above the foyer. The invisible force took hold of Phaeton and carried him behind the stone headdress, where he flattened himself against the neck of Ramses.

A million tinkling shards formed a roar, as a great waterfall of sharp glass slivers crashed to the stone floor, bouncing and breaking into yet smaller pieces. Finally there was quiet, of sorts. "Jesus, my ears are ringing." Phaeton poked his head around a very large carved ear.

Gingerly, he and Exeter ventured out into the rotunda. "We seem to have lost Anubis." With the moon nearly set, the upper foyer was dim. The grand, stoic faces of Ramses and Amenthotep cast long shadows across the chessboard pattern of marble squares.

An errant piece of glass, a late comer, hit the floor. From behind the colossal head, footsteps ground into brittle shards. A strange gentleman dressed in formal attire emerged from the shadows and approached them. *"Bu nafret su em bu bon."*

Phaeton stepped forward. "Sorry?"

"A state of good has become a state of evil."

He and Exeter pivoted toward the voice behind them.

Chapter Twenty-nine

"THE GREAT GOD OF THE UNDERWORLD TAKES ON HUMAN FORM." Stickles picked his way through glittering debris. Phaeton read the curator easily enough, the elderly gentleman's eyes gleamed with an uneasy amalgam of fear and regard. They all felt the same way. "He asks you to take him to her."

Phaeton blinked. "You speak his language?"

"Smatterings." With a great deal of reverence, Stickles approached the ever shifting god-form. "An ancient dialect of Egyptian Coptic. I never dreamed—"

"Hmm, yes, none of us did." Exeter grabbed hold of the entranced curator's arm. "Best keep a good length away, Mr. Stickles."

Odd popping and stretching noises emanated from the humanlike figure as Anubis struggled to hold onto his new size and shape. A strong pulse beat under thickening flesh as a blanket of fur remerged. The proper, rather strikingly handsome British gentleman now sported an ebony head, emerging snout, and long pointed ears.

Jackals, Phaeton observed, looked rather dapper in a tuxedo. "Have a care." He pointed to the lapels. "A bit of drool on the suit." Anubis tilted his head to eyeball the damp stains.

Exeter leaned in close. "His request does fit neatly into our plans."

Phaeton turned to Stickles. "Tell him we must leave this place to find his mate."

"And the name of his goddess, again?"

"Qadesh."

The mere mention of her name perked both ebony ears forward. The elder curator spoke in halted speech as Phaeton motioned to Anubis. "This way, your Grace."

Exeter led the way as he and Stickles walked beside the struggling demigod. There was a brief delay as Anubis negotiated the staircase. They stopped to steady the wobbly creature. Such a powerful being, living proof of the eternal life force, and yet so vulnerable. Peculiar? Perhaps not. Phaeton shivered. There was an enchantment connected to these gods.

Once outside the main building, the jackal's faltering steps rapidly gained in strength and coordination. Anubis stopped to sniff the night air and take in the museum's architecture.

"He asks if we are in Alexandria."

"Anubis references the ancient city of Aegyptus built under Græco-Roman rule." Exeter appeared happy to indulge the demigod.

Phaeton tried to be patient. "No doubt the pediment and columns remind him of home."

The doctor's eyes crinkled. "He likely has no frame of reference for England. Please explain that we mean to reunite him with his wife and return them both to their homeland."

Anubis appeared to listen carefully to Stickles' words and answered with a long exhale and snort. The jackal head contorted into something more humanlike. A swarthy, masculine face with a wet, black nose.

"Looks a bit like you, Phaeton." Exeter tilted his head. "Except for the nose."

"That chin cleft is the very picture of you, doctor." Phaeton dashed ahead. He made his way toward Exeter's waiting carriage. "Where's your driver?"

The doctor opened the door and grunted. "Likely off behind a bush relieving himself."

Anubis, almost fully human, stood beside the horse team

nuzzling equine noses. Phaeton looked about for shrubbery to call after the driver.

A clatter of hoofs and the creak of carriage springs signaled visitors. At this late hour? Phaeton backed away from the coach. Two carriages dashed through the gates and up the drive. The lead barouche pulled up behind, while the other quite effectively cut them off.

Director Chilcott and Zander Farrell debarked, one from each vehicle.

"Bollocks." Phaeton muttered.

"Phaeton—" Zander eyed the odd creature snuffling over the horses.

"What's going on here?" Chilcott finished the sentence.

Stickles stepped into the fray. "Mr. Black, he wishes to know which chariot is his."

"He? Who is he?"

"Might you introduce Detective Farrell and Director Chilcott to Anubis?"

Both men turned toward the odd gentleman standing beside the team.

Phaeton leaned closer to Stickles. "Tell him they are emissaries sent here to escort him safely to his wife."

An abrupt shift in atmosphere put them all into a hazy, bleary-eyed trance. When they came to their senses, moments later, they discovered Anubis climbing into Zander's carriage.

"Dear God, Sophie is in there."

Phaeton sprinted off with Zander. "What the hell is Sophie doing up and about with you at this hour?"

"Can't sleep. Never can when she's this far along."

Zander leaped into the carriage prepared to do battle.

"Please God." Phaeton rolled his eyes and stuck his head inside the cabin. Their mischievous demigod had changed into a most handsome and proper Englishman. Oddly enough, not far off in looks from Zander Farrell.

Anubis sat close beside Sophie, whose wide eyes appeared calm enough. Actually, he thought she was handling the terrifying scenario quite well. Phaeton nodded to her. "Easy does it, Sophie." She appeared to sense this most irregular event was something quite extraordinary.

Phaeton sucked in a deep breath. "Sophie. Zander. Listen carefully to me." Phaeton proceeded to explain, in the fewest words possible, what they were dealing with. He backed out of the door long enough to motion to the curator. "Mr. Stickles, we are in need of you."

Zander sat opposite Anubis with fists clenched. "If he touches her—"

Phaeton shook his head in warning. "Ah, our translator arrives." He climbed in and made room for the curator. "Mr. Stickles, please inform Anubis that Mrs. Farrell is no temple priestess, and therefore she is not to be ravaged. In fact, she is the much cherished and esteemed spouse of this—" Phaeton caught a glimpse of Zander's clenched jaw.

Stickles raised both brows. "Pharaoh?"

Zander frowned. Phaeton turned up a grin. "Perfect."

Anubis appeared to listen to Stickles, even though his eyes never left Sophie. The demigod answered in a husky, guttural speech.

Stickles swallowed and shot a desperate look his way.

Phaeton sighed. "Share the less prurient remarks, Mr. Stickles."

"He calls her a fertile goddess, ripe with child. She will soon be in need of more . . . seed."

The moment Anubis leaned closer and sniffed Sophie, he was confronted by Zander, who leaned forward in a most aggressive posture. "My woman."

A force threw Zander back onto the opposite bench. Anubis snarled.

Phaeton nudged Stickles. "Please remind Anubis about the goddess, who impatiently awaits his services. Tell him how much he is missed by Qadesh and how she longs for his affection. Or seed. Whichever works."

Chilcott stood in the open door of the carriage. Having

pieced together a reasonably coherent picture of their bizarre circumstances, Scotland Yard's director shook his head. "Obsessed with sex, aren't they?" He sputtered. "Zeus, always taking on strange forms. Sneaking into a man's bedroom. Now this one—Egyptian, I take it."

"Indeed." Phaeton tapped on the cabin roof. "Marvelous topic, Director Chilcott, but might we take up the subject, postmortem? I've got a damsel to rescue and two gods to reunite."

Luck appeared to be with them. Anubis discontinued ogling Sophie's prodigiously fertile belly and sat upright. Zander managed to stop glaring at Anubis long enough to instruct his driver. "We return to the cemetery, Mr. Quint. With all possible speed."

Phaeton rocked with the motion of the carriage as it took a sharp turn. He checked his watch. A few minutes past three. At least there would be little traffic at this wee hour of the morning; they should make excellent time. He let down a window and gulped in the damp, night air. A rapid staccato of hooves and wheels meant Exeter and Chilcott followed close behind.

He experienced an abrupt shift in atmosphere and a blur of motion. The jackal-faced god sat beside him. Zander, just as suddenly, had been placed beside Sophie. The Yard man wasted no time sweeping his lovely wife, protectively, into his arms.

The strong pulse of his heart beat ever faster. Three chariots raced through London's northern suburbs in the dead of night. Anubis poked his head out the window and yipped like a dog.

A trail of phosphorescence looped through the small dark cavern. Qadesh circled the room like a roman candle let loose inside a barrel. The slightly deranged goddess had grown steadily more unstable since sundown. America sighed. Where, oh where was Phaeton?

She could just make out Julian Ping, her one and only contact to the physical world, steadfast beside the small opening in the crypt. Even beyond packages of clothing and sustenance, he had proved himself excellent company, passing the time with bits of conversation and comic accounts of the goings on.

Moonset approached, and the atmosphere in the narrow passageway, including the police guard, shifted to a more somber, resolute mood. Lamps flickered in the passageway. The snap and hiss of burning flames came from farther outside the crypt as torches were lit on cemetery grounds. The silence did not have a calming effect; in fact the hush over the scene set her on edge. An echo of instructions from Mr. Ping filtered back to her. "Make another sweep, shoo off any curious onlookers."

Qadesh had remained quiet for most of the day. By late evening she had begun floating about, circling in and out of the crypt. America had followed her trail until she became dizzy. As yet, the demigoddess had not made any further public appearances, not since Phaeton and Dr. Exeter had gone in search of her husband.

America whispered into the hole in the wall. "I believe she may be working herself into a state, Mr. Ping."

The now familiar face of Julian Ping dropped into view. "No doubt the goddess is restless." Ping's strange silver eyes peered past her. "Mind if I try to catch a glimpse?"

America nodded and backed away from the opening.

"Can't see much, nothing but black—" The young man let loose a yelp.

America sprang into view. "Sorry, Mr. Ping. She can give a person quite a scare."

Ping smiled. "Stand back, Miss Jones."

A huge forked tongue with two giant eyeballs at each end pushed through the shaft and waggled at the goddess, who promptly answered in kind.

The brief entanglement, punctuated by loud slurping and sucking noises, left a trail of effervescent slime down the shaft. America squinted. "I believe she got you on the cheek, sir. You might—"

He dabbed a pocket square on the side of his face and turned his head. "Better?"

America managed a closed smile. "Much." What a very odd character, yet, there was something about this young man that appealed, sans the rude tongue.

Ping exhaled a sigh. "I'm afraid we've only a few minutes left until moonset."

She bit her lower lip and nodded. "I do hope Qadesh allows for a grace period. Mr. Black makes a point of never being on time."

He grinned. "He has a reputation for it."

"Not when a damsel is in distress, Julian." After a bit of jostling, Phaeton dropped into view. The most handsome, most wonderful face in all the world. "Especially my damsel." He winked at her.

Her heart pounded heat from her chest to her cheeks. "Hello, Phaeton."

"Hello, my dove. You look healthy. Warm and well fed. No molestations, I hope, from our"—Phaeton peered behind her—"disgruntled goddess?"

Was it his glib manner or the lateness of the hour that sparked a rumble of discontent? All at once, she couldn't help herself. The strain and stress of the day let loose a fury of pent up anger. "Where the hell have you been, Phaeton? You could have returned to find a drained and lifeless damsel by now." Clenched fists landed on her hips. "And where is this husband of—"

A huge force from behind tore her away from the small square opening. Flung through the air like a child's doll, she hit the opposite wall of the crypt and collapsed onto the floor. Stars spun as her vision dimmed, then returned.

"America, are you all right?"

The very best she could do was a mumbled moan. "Give me a moment, Phaeton."

"Qadesh." Phaeton spoke in a low tone. "I have your husband with me. But you must be polite to Miss Jones or—"

So much for patience. Blocks of stone flew through the air and crashed down around her. America smacked away a piece of flying mortar and took cover behind the coffin. Time passed in the blink of an eye as a frightening tumult of marble stone and mortar smashed into every crevice and corner.

As swiftly as her fury began, the maelstrom ceased. America gripped the coffin lid and raised herself up for a peek. The atmosphere in the crypt was a fog of soft and silvery marble dust.

Qadesh had fashioned an entryway in the crypt wall narrower at the top than the base. The goddess stood just inside the opening, resplendent in gossamer robes and jeweled necklaces. Everything was visible, brown nipples centered on melon-sized globes. Her dark feminine triangle beneath a softly rounded belly. Haloed by light, Qadesh stepped toward the doorway.

America should have ducked at the sight. Instead she trembled, unable to tear her eyes from the monstrous figure that approached the goddess. Sleek, indigo fur covered a creature who appeared more beast than man.

Following after Phaeton, several of Scotland Yard's finest inched up behind the . . . figure. America chewed a bottom lip. This entity was her husband. The figure walked upright on long muscular legs. Part human, part dog or wolf? The male figure, for it was every inch a male, approached Qadesh with an erection that caused nearly everyone surrounding the reunion to gasp in unison.

"Dog's bollocks." Chilcott blinked. "Built like a stallion."

Phaeton tugged up a side of his mouth. "Mmm, yes, more horse than hound, I believe." The crypt steamed with curious onlookers.

Phaeton turned to Anubis, who stood transfixed by the sight of his mate. "Before you enjoy a few eternal moments alone with your wife, might I extract Miss Jones?"

Qadesh backed away from her husband. Slanted, kohl-lined eyes narrowed into slits. She spoke in low tones, ancient words bitten out in barely controlled anger.

Phaeton swiveled. "Mr. Stickles, over here."

"I'm afraid she is quite perturbed with her, ah, mate." The man called Stickles gulped. "I am here for many moons, abandoned in this awful city. Alone. Starving. Injured. You come to me after eons and the first thing you want from me is—"

The goddess turned on Stickles. "He thinks to mount me." She took another long look at the massive staff that shot up from between folds in her husband's loin cloth.

Anubis answered in a husky, gentle rumble. "I have crossed the rivers of eternity to find you."

Phaeton edged away from the testy couple. "America." His arm went around her waist, and he pulled her to him. Purposely, he dropped back into a dark corner of the crypt, where they watched, mesmerized.

Qadesh faltered, taking a quick backward step to catch herself.

"See, there, how she favors one leg. I have never seen her walk." Phaeton whispered in her ear. "She most often appears in a sitting position, or floating overhead."

America nodded her head. "Something is wrong, Phaeton."

Qadesh lay back on the top of the stone coffin and moved her legs apart. Slowly, she raised one side of a gossamer robe to reveal a shapely, caramel-colored leg. Every man jack in the crowd gulped.

Then she raised the other length of the robe and revealed a spindly, tortured leg, part human, part animal. The grotesque appendage could barely be functional.

Even with his mouth open, Stickles appeared moved. "She asks—entreats him to heal her."

Larger in stature than the tallest man in the room, Anubis pressed close to his wife. Angled dark eyes studied the injured leg. Low snorts rumbled like distant thunder from the dog-headed deity. Mumbled words, though unintelligible, were soft, calming. Large, clawed hands moved gently up and down the malformed leg. Gradually, before their eyes, a shape took form; the leg reconfigured itself. Elongating, taking on flesh. The demigod rubbed and smoothed her skin as a sculptor might polish the marble statue of a beautiful goddess. Two beautiful legs opened wide.

America fanned herself with a hand. "Well, this is stimulating."

"Mmm." His lips brushed the back of her neck. "No argument there." As the atmosphere in the small crypt warmed, gentlemen retrieved pocket squares and loosened starched collars. Anubis reached further under his wife's skirt and the goddess flung back her head and moaned.

Phaeton pressed her hard against him. "I have to have you." His cock stiffened, no doubt along with every other man's in the room. America turned enough for him to see the edge of her grin. "Randy lot, you Brits."

Slowly, he bunched up the back of her skirt. She waited, in anticipation of his caress. She got the distinct impression he was taking his sweet time. He wanted to make her long for the slide of his hand up her trembling thighs. And then it came; softly his fingers played along the inside of her leg flesh, sliding under French pantalettes. He was about to take her from behind, right here, in front of God and everyone.

She pushed away. "Mr. Black, we're in public."

He pulled her farther into the dark corner. "Not so public."

She couldn't quite stifle a giggle. "You are completely mad."

"Ah, you've been warned about me." Phaeton licked the underside of her earlobe. A string of tingles prickled her skin. Weak in the knees and lustful, she rested her head back against his shoulder. His hand wrapped around her breast. A thumbnail rubbed through silky fabric, pricking up a nipple. Another surge of arousal shot through her body. The more intimacies she allowed this man, the more she desired him. And worst of all, there were these new, nagging affections for him.

In one swift move, the god-creature grabbed hold of spread legs and pulled his goddess to the edge of the sarcophagus. The beastly ebony sword bobbed in anticipation. Jaws dropped around the room. America had overheard sailors boast of sights not half this prurient in the pleasure houses of Macau.

Wickedly, she rubbed her buttocks back and forth across Phaeton's throbbing cock.

Anubis groaned.

Phaeton groaned.

Stickles coughed. "Beg pardon, sir."

Phaeton straightened and let down her dress. The elder gentleman's gaze traveled up into the cobwebs crisscrossing the corner above them. "What is it, Stickles?"

"I am told there is a messenger outside. An urgent wire for you."

For a moment, Phaeton appeared as though he might explode or cry. Instead, he took her by the hand. The older man trailed after them. "Oh, Mr. Black?"

"What is it now?"

Stickles cleared his throat, gesturing toward the spectacle on top of the sarcophagus. "Should I ask for privacy?"

Phaeton halted their exit. The goddess wrapped both beautiful legs around Anubis and trust upward. "Do they look like they mind an audience?"

Chapter Thirty

SUSPECT LOCATED IN LIMEHOUSE STOP CAN
YOU SPARE A FEW MEN FOR DAWN RAID
STOP THE WHITE SWAN

"Dex has your pirate cornered." Phaeton passed the wire to America, who read the words by lamplight. Slanted green eyes flashed over the words pasted on paper. Her face animated. Such a game young woman. He quite enjoyed that about her. Bright. Spirited. Vengeful. And, oh yes, exceedingly beddable.

"You will help him, won't you Phaeton?"

He smiled. Dear God, how he would miss her. Hair a bit wild, cheeks flushed a peachy copper hue. She took his breath away. He thought about the long carriage ride across town, alone, with Miss Jones. Without taking his eyes off her, he spoke to the elderly gent nearby. "Mr. Stickles, might you wheedle Doctor Exeter away from the risqué burlesque going on in the crypt?"

He smiled at America. "No reason why this operation can't spare a few men. Anubis has agreed to settle down for a good long ocean voyage back to his—port of origin—shall we say?"

"You got him to agree to that?"

"Easily done. I promised him sex."

She rolled her eyes, lips pressed into a thin line. "Are all men so bloody simple?"

"Yes." His lip twitched. "Gods and jackals as well, it would seem." He lifted the folded telegram from her hand and shoved it in his pocket.

"I do hope this is important, Phaeton. He's got the flail out." Exeter approached with a wink.

Phaeton stared at Exeter. "You don't say." He leaned backward, for a glimpse down the triangular shaped passageway. "Miss Jones and I are needed in Limehouse."

Exeter folded his arms across his chest. "You want me to see those two safely entombed inside the sarcophagus, while you and Miss Jones go chasing after pirates?"

"Exactly. We'll also need the use of your carriage."

Was that a growl from Exeter? Certainly there were narrowed eyes. "Very well, Phaeton. How do you want me to handle this?"

"Anubis made a covenant. Gods, generally, abide by their promises. His mate, as well, finds London dreary. I don't think you will get much resistance from either one." Phaeton removed his hat and scratched his head. "Make a ritual or ceremony out of it. Might ask Zander Farrell to sing a refrain or two from *Aida*—wife claims he's a lovely tenor." He tried a grin to further cajole. "Soothe the savage god-beast, wot?"

"Leastwise, a fitting aria." Torrid moans echoed from the crypt. All three of them craned their necks for a good long, openmouthed stare down the corridor. Strands of whip feathered over Qadesh's trembling bottom. Phaeton wiped the sweat off his brow and adjusted for an uncontrollable surge of blood below the belt.

"Is that our plan then?" Exeter's eyes never left the spectacle on the stone. "Chilcott asked if we had one."

"Pray tell, what did you advise?"

The doctor faced him. "I told him—" A subtle lift edged a thinly clasped mouth. "You're going to have to learn to trust Phaeton."

He tore his eyes off the lusty scene at the end of the passageway. "You said that?"

"I did." Exeter stepped farther into the crypt. "Don't make me regret it."

Phaeton called after him. "Have Zander send a few men on to The White Swan, Commerical Road." America tugged at his arm. "Soon as possible."

They made a hurried dash through the cemetery to the carriage. He lifted America into the cabin and jumped in after. He yanked her into his arms, but stopped short of plundering her mouth. Instead, he bit down and tugged on a plump lower lip. Tasting, savoring her for several blissful moments. He hardly recognized the husky voice that spoke softly to her. "Something dangerous is happening, Miss Jones."

A mysterious smile formed on the unfathomable mouth he continued to nip at. Sensuous, moist lips teased, returned his ardor, made him wonder if she took his meaning. Did she, as well, feel this growing attachment between them? A tremble shuddered through him, enough to shake off the soppy romantic reverie. He jerked himself back to the task at hand, his aching prick.

"As much as I would enjoy ravaging you here on the spot, I'm going to have to ask you to undress, Miss Jones."

Reaching behind her, he pulled down the widow shade. "Slowly."

A quirk of mouth. A darling smirk. He fought an urge to rip that pretty bodice right off those pert— "The buttons on your dress. Are they decorative, or functional?"

"Functional, and don't you dare." A tantalizing hesitation proceeded a wicked smile. She began to unbutton. A deep breath revealed lovely rounded mounds. He nuzzled into her cleavage, trailing his lips past her collarbone and along an elegant bend of neck.

She exhaled a heavenly sigh. "I suppose all you men are a cock-up bunch tonight."

He covered her mouth and she opened. After a stimulating chase of tongue, he eased back. "Mrs. Chilcott might have a surprise coming." He winked.

Even her chortle of laughter aroused him. She pressed him back onto the leather-covered bench, hiked up her skirt, and straddled his torso. A breast escaped from her loosened chemise. He pulled her close and caught the nipple between his teeth.

There was a rap at the coach door. "Need a bit of privacy, Mr. Black?"

He grabbed the front of her dress and held it together. Carefully, he lifted her off his belly and angled himself toward the coach door. Christ, they weren't even moving. In his haste to make love to Miss Jones, he had forgotten to give the driver directions.

Phaeton sighed. "Decent, my dove?"

"Comme il faut." Her whisper musical with amusement.

"You speak near perfect Parisian French; certainly you did not learn that from your Cajun *maman*?"

"Pas Paris, monsieur, Brugge. Three horrid long years in a Catholic boarding school."

"Ah, no doubt you ran away."

"A young priest chased me around the Rectory one afternoon." Her gown rustled from a shrug. "I'd had enough."

"Gave his bollocks the boot, I hope. You're rather good at that, as I recall."

Another maddening rap at the door. Phaeton kicked the latch and the door swung open.

Several men, Metropolitan police, stood outside the carriage. His eyes narrowed into slits. "What is it, officers?"

"Detective Farrell ordered us to Limehouse. Sez you requested a few men. Mind if we catch a ride, sir?"

He cursed under his breath. Damn his bloody soul to Hades. One hellish hard-on and the worst case of the devil's blue balls he had ever experienced. He had no idea how the words escaped between clenched teeth. "Get in."

Phaeton held a hand out and tightened his grip on her small fingers. Dexter Moore led them into the blackness of a narrow alleyway. Still hours to go before sunrise. "The Chinaman's shop faces out onto Pennyfields, but the opium parlor is here, in the back."

Phaeton took cover beside Moore, keeping America close beside him. "You're quite sure Yanky is still inside?"

"I've got men stationed outside the shop, in the lane and the alley. He was spotted hours ago." Dexter's eyes never left the door. "I wager he's had a pipe or two and is off in dreamland."

"If that's the case, we can nick the mattress and carry him off to the lockup." Phaeton winked at America. "Hardly need the extra men."

Dexter's grin flattened. "A precaution. In case the den is a hideout."

In the dim light of a single gas lamp, a freshly painted orange door belied the squalor around them. Not ten feet away, farther down the alley, Phaeton noted a brightly colored green door and beyond that a sleek, black enameled entryway with the address *55 Pennyfields* etched upon a polished brass mail slot. "None of the dens have names in this part of Limehouse."

Moore snorted. "You would be the one to know, Phaeton."

Indeed, there were a great many goings on in this alley, too disturbing to reveal to the average citizen. Especially the odd persuasion of gentlemen secreted behind the elegant, numbered door at the end of Pennyfields Lane.

America's slanted eyes rounded. "Are you infatuated with opium, Phaeton?"

"Nothing compares to my fascination with you." He slipped an arm around her. *"Ma petite colombe."*

Moore frowned at them both. "I rather wish you had not insisted on bringing Miss Jones on a raid."

Phaeton's jaw clenched. "Send your men in, Dex. We'll follow along once you've got their backs to the wall."

Dexter swallowed. "You're not coming in with us?"

"Get Yanky Willem in cuffs and give us a yell. I'm sure Miss Jones would love to get within spitting distance."

An urgent, ebullient kiss brushed his cheek. Liquid eyes glittered as she nodded her head.

On Dexter's signal, two men approached the door with crowbars and made short work of the locks. Dexter and several others followed the men into the opium den.

Phaeton held a hand up and ordered their reinforcements to take cover. "Across the alley and keep a lookout." He nodded to the second floor of the building.

America sidled closer. "What's going on Phaeton?"

He removed his pistol from his jacket pocket and a number of bullets from his waistcoat. "Ever since we took cover behind this dustbin, a window curtain across the way has parted several times." Phaeton nodded upward. "Second floor."

"They've spotted us." Wheels turned behind her bright green eyes. "Once Dexter and the others are inside, they'll try for an escape."

"Pick your skirts up, lass." Phaeton grabbed her hand, and they crossed the alley. At the last possible moment, he shunned the doorway of the opium den and made for a covered walk between buildings.

A few shouts and a number of loud thuds emanated from behind the broken down door. A struggle was on. America's nostrils twitched. The distinctive, sweet odor of burning opiates suffused the static air around them. "I want you to run like the wind down this walkway. Send any officers you find out front to the alley entrance. Do not accompany them, Miss Jones." He looked up from loading his gun. "Promise me."

She nodded her head and received a buss on the mouth. Even in these perilous circumstances he made her toes tingle. "I promise, Phaeton."

She peeked around the corner. Several men dropped to the ground from a second story window. Phaeton pulled her back against him. "If you find yourself in trouble, use this." He pressed a knife into her palm.

She gasped. "This is my knife."

"As I recall, you wield it well." He stepped out into the middle of the alley, pointed and cocked his pistol. Two more of Willem's men jumped to the ground. That made four. Even numbers.

Her heart pounded inside her chest. She remembered to breathe and gulped in air.

"Halt and surrender to arrest." Phaeton stepped closer.

When the pirates turned to run, the hidden officers stepped into the alley, blocking the exit.

She did not recognize Yanky Willem among them. America leaned out for a better look.

Phaeton glared. "Go, America."

She backed down the walkway into something hard and hulking. An arm snaked around her waist and a hand covered her mouth. She struggled and almost escaped before she was slammed against the brick building. She blinked at the sight confronting her.

He'd shaved off the stubble and now dressed the part of a gentleman. But she'd recognize those pale eyes and that tobacco breath anywhere. He pressed her between his body and the wall. "You again, Miss Jones?"

Shots rang out from the alley. She tried to wriggle away, but Willem leaned harder. "Meddling little whore. I should have killed you when I had the chance."

Even as his words tore into her soul he sought to muffle her curses. His hands raked through her hair, and the back of her head collided again with the brick wall.

Shots. A battery of ricocheting bullets rang out from the alley. Willem's eyes darted back and forth. Holding her against him, he retreated farther down the dim passageway. He meant to use her as a shield. Her fingers edged along the handle of the knife hidden in the folds of her skirt. She had never killed a man before. She had cut a man once. No, twice. She recalled the thin red slice across Phaeton's neck.

She dragged her heels and stomped on his boot. Scratching at his hand, she tore his hand off her mouth and managed a feeble cry. "Phaeton."

"Yes. My dove?"

Willem froze. America felt the cold barrel of a gun against her temple. The silhouette of a man stood in the passageway framed by morning sunlight.

She swung the knife backward and plunged the tip into her captor's thigh. A hot gush of blood spurted over her hand, and a cry of pain. A blur of movement surrounded her. A gun fired, then another. Willem staggered backward, taking her down with him. The metallic stench of blood and gunpowder. A million shooting stars passed in front of her eyes.

She felt no pain.

"America?" She focused on his face. His chin and jaw all handsome angles and dark stubble. Phaeton smiled at her. "Can you stand darling? Let me help you."

Phaeton swept her up and held on tight.

She snuggled against his chest, trembling from shock, taking in one shallow breath after another. His hand stroked her back, soothing her, and he rocked her gently in his arms. She looked up at him. "I'm alive."

"Yes, of course you are." He had a lovely, long dimple to one side of his face when he grinned broadly. She had never noticed.

A jumble of men surrounded Yanky Willem. She lifted her head off Phaeton's shoulder for a curious peek. "How is he?"

Inspector Moore examined the crumpled body on the ground. "Got him square in the shoulder."

Phaeton's grin flattened. "Disappointing."

Dexter wiped the stain of blood off his fingers. "Crack shot, Phaeton."

"I wanted him dead."

Chapter Thirty-one

A MUFFLED LAUGH AGAINST THE SOFT WEAVE OF HIS JACKET LAPEL ushered a myriad of scents. Woolen coat dampened by fog, the faintest trace of blood, and the man scent of Phaeton. She wanted to smother him in kisses. No worse. She wanted to do unspeakable things to him. Things like those wonderfully indecent strokes and caresses he had taught her in bed.

She would grasp onto his hard prick, pitching and bobbing like the main mast in a storm, and taste velvet in her mouth. She placed her hand flat against his waistcoat and imagined the lovely ruff of hair hidden underneath that tapered down his torso. Absently, a finger trailed the buttons of his shirt.

Phaeton caught her wandering index finger and brought it to his lips. "Soon." She buried a grin in his shoulder.

Wrapped in a police issue blanket, the blackguard was hauled away moaning. Dexter motioned to several sturdy young officers. "If St. Bartholomews has no room in the locked wards, take him straight to the Yard and call a surgeon."

She lifted her head. "Thank you, Inspector Moore."

Phaeton nodded. "First-rate police work."

"Hardly, Phaeton. They almost gave us the slip. You brought down Yanky Willem with a single shot."

America frowned. "I heard two shots."

"You dogged the bastard, tracked him down. He's your

collar." Phaeton rubbed her back with a stiff arm. Was that a shiver or a tremble? Something was wrong. She stepped away to examine his shoulder. A smoke-tinged hole through the arm of his jacket. "Phaeton, you've been wounded."

Odd, the way he stared at her. Something hidden, behind those soft, deep brown eyes. "A mere scratch, my love."

The man was clearly out of his mind. He called her his dove, yes, even darling, but never my love. She caught her breath and ignored his slip of tongue. She nosed about and located a fresh bloodstain on his shirtsleeve. "There's a medical kit onboard the *Topaz*. I could patch you up right enough. We're close by."

Moore patted his coat pocket. "Slipped my mind entirely. There is hearing set for the morning. A formality, really." He handed a folded document to her. "Both ships are yours again, Miss Jones."

She hardly knew what to say, so she gasped. "I wasn't expecting—"

"My brother is a barrister. Works for the Chief Crown Prosecutor. Asked him to push it through the circumlocution office." Dexter Moore grinned. "Why not take Mr. Black aboard and minister to his wounds? I wager you'll both be safe enough, with Mr. McCafferty on watch."

She was quite sure her mouth dropped open. "Ned McCafferty?"

"Yes, that's the name. A rather crusty bloke approached me, asking after you."

"Are sailors, by nature, either crusty or salty?" Phaeton mused.

Inspector Moore ignored the jibe. "Says he's a Boatswain. Worked for your father for many years."

America pressed both lips together, her pulse raced. "Where might he be found?"

Phaeton groaned.

She stabbed him with a look. "I need a crew, Mr. Black, and he is just the man to put the word out. Muster the right sort of sailor, if you take my meaning." The strain and fatigue from her day and night in captivity vanished into the misty air. With exhaustion all but forgotten, her thoughts whirled with the possibilities of taking on a crew and cargo.

"I allowed McCafferty a berth aboard ship, in exchange, he keeps watch," Dexter explained. "Leave it up to you whether you want to keep him on or not."

America threw her arms around the inspector. "I don't know how I shall ever repay you for all your hard work and kindness, Mr. Moore." An arm slipped around her waist. "I can think of a few welcome favors, only Phaeton would gladly plug a bullet into my skull if I tried."

A bubble of giddy laughter rippled to the surface. She glanced at Phaeton, and confirmed a flinty gaze.

"No more bullets, Dex," Phaeton reached out with his good arm and pulled her close. "Dismemberment."

She grinned at them both. "*Chacun à son goût.* Everyone to his taste, *oui?*"

"*S'il vous plaît, monsieur.*" Her entire body shuddered in want, in need of him.

"You will call me Bonaparte." He pulled back and smacked the switch against his boot. Her entire body jumped. The French pirate lifted a corner of his mouth and narrowed his eyes.

Phaeton stood in front of her, legs spread wide, chest bare. His trousers outlined muscled legs and hard cock. Even the bandage around his shoulder and arm played a role in this titillating theatrical.

With the crop in one hand, a tumbler full of whiskey in the other, he tipped the glass. "Pirates keep such good grog." He winked at her and guzzled a dram more.

Just as soon as they boarded the *Topaz*, the pirate games had begun. After she washed him off and bandaged his wound, *Bonaparte* had found a riding crop in the aft cabin and put it to good use on his captive lady.

"*Touchez-moi*. Harder." Her pleading little more than a breathy whisper.

"And what will you promise in return—for Bonaparte?" He gestured low, toward the bulge in his pants.

Her gaze lingered on the impressive ridge beneath his trousers, then swept up his body. She ran her tongue over upper, then lower lip. "Which part of me do you most desire?"

Ebony eyes gleamed. He lowered his chin. Slowly, he circled her naked form. When he reached her backside, his fingers entered the crevice between buttocks and circled. He did not touch her in any other way. "Here, perhaps, my little courtesan?" The most delicate pressure tantalized her opening.

Lustful, wanton passion shuddered through her body. All her clothing was off with the exception of a brief chemise. He had paddled her bottom until the heat from his slaps radiated through her body.

He yanked off her camisole.

"I am going to give you exquisite pleasure, Miss Jones. So you will obey my every word." Phaeton tightened the soft cords around her wrists and looped the ropes through a ring in the low-slung ceiling. He pulled her arms up, and tied the cord in a pretty bow.

Vulnerable, raw, and unbelievably aroused, she waited for his next move. "If you are not compliant, nay, zealous, my wicked little *cocotte*, I will have to use this." He held up a riding crop. "Again." With her arms pulled overhead, her entire body shivered in anticipation of his next stroke.

"*Fouettez-moi*. Sting me." Her eyes flashed with need; she would beg, gladly.

The swat from the whip radiated warmth from her pink, naked bottom to the arousal pooling between her legs. Her naked buttocks shivered with each stroke.

"G-r-r-r." He so loved to growl.

"Or is it, a-r-r-r-r-gh?" He stalked around her again. Eyes

on her nude body, taking in every inch of exposed flesh. Memorizing her.

The cool air of the cabin traveled over exposed flesh. Thrilling, titillating her, peaking her sensitivity to his every touch, She gulped in air and swallowed. The excitation, mixed with expectancy, was intense, delicious.

Her eyes swept the cabin. More than any other place on earth, these quarters were home to her. The only home she had ever really known. So many memories. It would not be long before this love play would take its place among those recollections. Something to keep her warm on cold nights at sea.

Phaeton adjusted the Admiral Nelson hat, setting it sideways, on his head.

She tilted her chin. "Yes, much more French—my Napoleon pirate."

"Ah, oui, ma petite—how do you say, dove?

"Colombe."

He approached her slowly, tapping the whip on the side of his leg. *"Ma belle colombe."* Pointing the whip end at a breast tip, he circled her areola, which obediently gathered into a hard peak. "Beautiful dark nipples." She moaned as the whip traced the outline of her ribs and belly. Dipping further down, he slid the crop along the sensitive inside flesh of her thigh. He tapped the braided leather tail against her triangle of curls. Juices flowed down the inside of her legs.

He leaned in and laved rosy-beige peaks. "More?" He waited, his mouth inches away. Impatiently she arched her breast into his mouth, urging him to suckle. To caress, to nibble, to lick until he held her in suspension. She did not wholly understand how he knew. But he always moved on, just before she tumbled over the edge of desire.

No man would ever know her body as he did, or be able to hold her, indefinitely, at the brink.

He turned his back, flung the naval hat onto a coat hook, and set down his empty glass. Content, even lackadaisical

about her confinement, he made her want him beyond reason. He studied her from across the room. "Spread your
legs."

She returned his gaze.

"Pleasure or pain, Miss?"

She widened her stance.

The cabin floor whined as he sauntered toward her. He
used the crop to swat back and forth between her thighs.
"Farther." The bindings strained and her arms ached.

He dragged over a chair, sat between her limbs and pulled
her up to his face. He kissed her belly. "Bend your leg at the
knee." He lifted a trembling limb and placed her bare foot on
his shoulder. Cupping her buttocks, he drew her close.

His mouth pressed against the inside of her thigh. What
sort of wicked pleasure was this? Dear God, she knew where
he was headed, but he took his time. Feathering his kisses
along soft, quivering flesh.

He parted curls, his tongue sweeping long laps between
delicate folds. He delved deep inside her passage, inserting
one, then another finger. While he thrust in and out, his
tongue circled her swollen place, the slippery nub that always
demanded more and more excitation. Her pulse throbbed,
pounding blood under her skin. She reveled for a moment,
at the tipping place, deliciously on the edge of climax, and
then toppled into oblivion. Only when she thrust her hips
into the air and screamed her satisfaction, did he release the
ropes.

A rag doll fell into his arms. He swept back wild curls and
nuzzled her neck. "Bonaparte is pleased to give you pleasure,
mademoiselle." His voice soft, thick with desire.

He lifted her onto the captain's bed and climbed in beside
her. She stretched out like a cat, and smiled up at him. His
hands roamed over her body, soothing overstimulated skin,
kissing her softly, cooing his words.

He rolled her over and massaged her bottom. "Sore?"

"In a lovely, spent, sort of way."

He bit her bottom.

She smothered a laugh in the pillow, rolled over and took his face in her hands. His beard stubble was still moist from her pleasure. She guided him lower for a kiss.

Heat burned her cheeks. "My scent is everywhere."

Dawn filtered through the slat-shuttered porthole, shafts of light fell across his face. His eyes squinted a golden brown. "I would rather wear your scent than any cologne."

She listened absently to the faint lapping of basin water against the hull. The familiar stirring of dock workers on the pier. "There is a story a schoolmate loved to tell, very French—"

He placed her fingertip in his mouth and sucked, gently. *"Oui, cheri?"* He swirled his tongue then moved to the next.

"Henri the fourth reputedly wrote to his young mistress, Gabrielle d'Estree, 'Do not bathe my love, I'll be home in eight days.' " She angled her head to watch him nibble a ring finger.

"You are supremely responsive, sexually."

"Is that shocking?"

He laid back and raised a brow.

"No, I suppose nothing shocks you, Mr. Black."

"Mr. Black, is it?" He toyed with a long tangled strand of her curls. "You were rather disappointed with your first sexual encounter. Made a point of telling me, as I recall. But then, what maiden isn't?"

She closed her eyes and conjured a handsome young man with nut-brown skin and high cheekbones. Dark eyes like Phaeton's. "Suraj."

"Suraj?"

"Punjabi." She remembered with a smile. "A Sikh, who wore a crimson turban and kept a curved, gold-handled knife in his belt."

"Wonderful costume. Not much of a lover, I take it?"

She drew her mouth into a bow and wrinkled her brow. "Perhaps, I wasn't receptive. We were both very young." Phaeton leaned close to suckle a nipple. A pang of arousal shot through her body. "He was a passenger aboard ship, making his way home from school in England." She lifted herself up on elbows. He nibbled and released, teasing one rigid tip, before moving on to the other.

"No doubt the son of a maharaja." He bit down.

She moaned. "Jealous?"

Phaeton let the nipple slip from his mouth. "The next time I bind your wrists, I shall wrap a sheet round my head and you will beg Prince Alwar to whip your bum."

Her snort of laughter only encouraged him. Unbuttoning his pants, he straddled her torso and cupped her breasts, He pressed her swollen mounds around his burgeoning shaft and took slow deliberate strokes. He tweaked both nipples and she bucked and trembled under him. When he grew fully erect, he leaned closer.

"Take me in your mouth." His husky demand urgent with desire.

She raised her head, her eyes ravenous, admiring of his bobbing prick. A pink tongue moistened tawny plump lips. "No." She sank back into the pillow.

He blinked. "No?"

Her gaze narrowed into that beautiful almond shape. "Take off every stitch of clothing."

"Ah, a new game." Phaeton grinned. "Very well."

He swung his legs over the side of the bed and shed his clothes. Her breasts pressed against his shoulder blades as her arms came around his torso. Fingers splayed through his chest hair, rubbing, swirling, then moving down ribs and belly. The muscles in his abdomen quivered. Had she driven him mad with all that provocative talk? Or was this pure lust?

Her fingers closed around his cock and stroked. He forced himself to stand and turn around. America was on all fours;

that lovely round ass wiggled as though it might have a tail. "Wicked little minx." Taking her by the hair, he presented his turgid cock to her mouth. "Take it—all of it."

His penis felt the hum of her laughter as her lips covered the tip.

Very soon thereafter, speech abandoned him, replaced by the guttural, inarticulate sounds of a growling, wild beast.

On the brink of climax, he released her head and pressed her back onto the bed. She opened for him and he drove deep into the slick warmth of her sheath. Long legs wrapped around his body. Her breath was rapid again, coming in short gasps. She made sweet mewling sounds and ran kisses over his chest. Her licks and small bites to his nipples caused a gasp. "Again."

With firm, deliberate strokes, he concentrated on her pleasure while building his own fervor a little at a time. He dropped legs down between hers and without missing a single stroke, reached under the small of her back and lifted her upright onto the tops of his thighs. He set back on his haunches. "I hold you impaled upon the ducal sword."

Lips, swollen from bruising kisses, smiled. And those feline eyes, wide and colored with passion, nearly sent him over the edge. Drawing her tight against his chest he showed her how to rock her hips. He took a mouthful of breast and kept his thrusts slow. With each withdrawal, he pulled out enough to rub her with the tip of the royal weapon. As her love cries increased, he pressed his fingers into the flesh of her buttocks and brought himself deeper inside.

The blissful gasp of her release surged through his body. There it was again, her pleasure increasing, enhancing his own. His thrusts grew rapid and violent, until his climax exploded into her. "Dear God, you have bewitched me."

Chapter Thirty-two

PHAETON OPENED THE SLATED SHUTTER OF THE PORTHOLE and blinked away shafts of light. Well past dawn. Last evening was perhaps the most astonishing erotic experience of his life. And it had happened with America. He had given her a taste of unusual love play and what a game enchantress she turned out to be, responding with a kind of creativity and enthusiasm that was nothing short of dazzling. He already longed for more of her tempting flesh.

The enticing, seductive female lay stretched out beside him. A long, shapely limb straddled tossed off linen and blankets. Gently, he rubbed a rounded hip and buttock cheek, receiving a slumberous murmur in response. His cock twitched. Ah, the added stimulation of a little early morning arousal. Asleep or awake, he had the urge to take her from behind.

She had encouraged him to explore every part of her. His mouth, fingers, it mattered not. He, in turn, showed her how and where to explore. He took a deep breath and recalled curious questions and how intimate her examination was.

A rapid onset of heartbeats urged to him to run.

He had gone round the bend this time. Allowed a pretty, exotic, clever young woman to get close. Much too close. A bit of pressure squeezed his chest. She was after his heart—his very soul—for God's sake.

Phaeton bolted out of the warmth and comfort of the captain's berth and dressed. He paused to kiss an exposed derriere and pull up the covers. Topside, he ran directly into Ned McCafferty.

"Mr. McCafferty. She's sleeping rather soundly at the moment."

The gruff man eyed him in a wary sort of way. "A good thing, I expect, sire."

"Very good. Miss Jones has been through quite an ordeal these last twenty-four hours. See that she sleeps as long as possible."

McCafferty nodded. "I take your meaning, Mr. Black. No interruptions."

"Good man." Phaeton tipped his hat and was off down the gangway. Weaving a path through the bustling basin traffic, he hoofed it down Ferry Road to the West India Docks. Somewhere among this mob of drayage carts and carriages, he would find a cab.

"Phaeton." A voice in the crowd. He whirled around to find Dexter Moore climbing out of a hansom. "Just the man I was sent off to find."

"No doubt the director wants a full report."

Dexter shook his head. "Just a meeting. Nothing in writing,"

A side benefit of Secret Branch operations was the dearth of deadly dull paperwork. So he would debrief his superiors, have a pint or two with a few of the lads at the Rising Sun and then make his way home. Interesting enough day, he hoped, to keep his mind off America Jones.

"Volunteered to come after you. They need you back in Whitehall as soon as possible." Dexter opened the door of his cab. "And the lovely Miss Jones?"

"Asleep." Phaeton hesitated before stepping inside the hansom. "She is not to be disturbed."

"But—the hearing. She was to be at the Old Bailey in"— Dexter checked his pocket watch—"just short of an hour from now."

Phaeton pulled Dex in and leaned out of the hansom. "Turn us around—Millwall docks."

When they hit a snarl of traffic, Phaeton leaped out of the carriage and ran for the *Topaz*. He crossed the gangplank and nearly knocked over McCafferty in the wheelhouse. "So sorry." Worst of all, he did not think before flinging the cabin door open. A nubile, light brown Venus stepped from her bath. Phaeton's jaw dropped.

"Good God." The voice behind him was Dexter's.

"Phaeton." Her smile turned to something more akin to alarm. "And . . ." She grabbed for a bath sheet to cover herself. "Inspector Moore."

Phaeton clapped his mouth shut and slammed the door in Moore's face. "Get dressed, Miss Jones, you have a hearing to attend."

Her eyes grew large and round. "Dear God, I quite forgot. How long have I got?"

"One minute to get fully dressed." Phaeton gladly helped with stockings and garters. "Inspector Moore." He raised his voice.

A muffled answer came from behind the door.

"Get that hansom turned around and headed for—"

"No." America tied up her petticoat. "At this time of day, it's faster by water. Have McCafferty find us a water taxi."

"Bollocks." Phaeton struggled with the tiny buttons on her shoes. "Did you hear that, Dex?"

"On my way, Phaeton."

He set her foot down. "Ready, my darling?"

America twisted her curls into a knot and pinned up her hair. Her eyes darted about the cabin. "Where are the papers?"

Phaeton searched table and desktop. Amber eyes blinked at him from a shelf above the desk. He grabbed a neat stack of documents under the grey gargoyle.

He turned back. "Well done, Edvar."

Topside, in the blink of an eye, he grabbed her by the hand and they raced across the basin bridge. "There they are." McCafferty and Moore stood beside a low-slung watercraft which featured a tall smokestack and wheelhouse aft. The three of them scrambled aboard and the steam-powered taxi chugged away from the docks.

Moore opened his watch. "We've got a bit less than half the hour."

"Cracking good call, my dove." Phaeton leaned back toward the open steerage compartment. "Full steam ahead, Captain."

"How blasted long does it take to get from the Docklands to Whitehall?" Chilcott groused as Zander shut the door.

Phaeton's answer was a deep sigh of relief. He and Moore had been on the run for a solid hour or more. Now, finally in the dim light of the director's office, he eased into a side chair and stretched out his legs.

Hat in hand, Moore prepared to humble himself. "Sorry for the delay. Phaeton and I had to see Miss Jones safely inside the Old Bailey." Moore beamed. "Her ships are being released to her."

Chilcott returned to his desk chair. "This young lady is both Phaeton's abductee and your merchant ship owner, am I correct? Would someone please explain how Miss Jones got entangled in two different operations?"

Phaeton exchanged a quick glance with Moore and cleared his throat. "Rather a complicated story, sir."

Wild eyebrow hairs merged as Chilcott nailed him with a flinty stare. "I've got the rest of the morning, if needed, to sort this all out." The director's well-worn leather chair squeaked a groan as the boss settled in. "Do make this a ripping good tale, Phaeton."

He and Moore spent the better part of the next hour recounting the salient events of each case, breaking only to answer or clarify questions, when asked. As Phaeton gave an accounting of his and Exeter's investigation in the British Museum, and his story became increasingly Gothic and sensational, Chilcott turned to Moore. "Mr. Moore, need I remind you Phaeton is a Secret Branch operative."

"Secret Branch, sir?"

"A name I coined, recently, but you will find no mention of it anywhere outside of this office." Flat-lipped as it was, Chilcott actually grinned. "Mr. Farrell here keeps a false accounting of Phaeton's cases. For the record, what was Mr. Black working on these past few weeks?"

"He's been assisting Mr. Moore on his piracy case." Zander looked up from a stack of files. "Try to keep it as plausible as possible."

"Secret Branch cases are subject to the highest level of security and are never to be discussed. Not even with other agents." Chilcott leaned across his desk. "In point of fact, Mr. Moore, they do not exist."

Moore swallowed. "Yes, sir."

The director remained forward, hands steepled together, under his chin. "Were you finished, Mr. Black?"

"Near enough, sir."

"Right, onto new business. The British Museum has a rather lucrative proposition for Miss Jones."

An amused exchange between Zander and Chilcott made his hackles rise. "That being?"

Nose out of folders, Zander explained. "An Egyptian sarcophagus must be returned to sacred ground, to a location near Alexandria, I believe. And it appears Miss Jones will soon be in need of cargo."

Phaeton shrugged. "Keeps everything neatly under wraps."

"Precisely." Chitcott nodded to Zander. "That will be all gentlemen."

Zander tapped Phaeton on the back. "You might drop by and assist Exeter. Last I heard he's waiting on Anubis and Qadesh."

Phaeton shook his head. "Don't tell me they're still at it?"

Zander yawned a chuckle. "I believe so."

Chilcott stood up. "Tell them your news, Mr. Farrell"

"Oh yes. Last night, a little after four in the morning, Sophie delivered a healthy child. Quite a set of lungs on her. Kept us up the rest of the night."

Something oddly familial and oppressively warm affected Phaeton as he pumped the man's hand. "Good God, Zander, that's wonderful news. And Sophie is well?"

"Hale and hearty."

Phaeton nodded. "Well, done Mrs. Farrell. Oh, and her name?"

"Fiona Sophrinia Camille." A proud smile and shrug. "We've shortened it considerably—already calling her Fee."

"Let me buy you a pint, Zander. Celebrate." Phaeton doffed his hat and held open the door. "Join us, sir?"

Chilcott almost looked pleased at the invite. "Order me a bite of roast beef on toast. I'll be down shortly."

Outside the office, on their way to the Rising Sun, Phaeton couldn't shake a disconcerting thought. What if America was with child? He had used protection only—dear God. Once. Rather foolhardy of him.

"Hope you don't mind a tagalong?"

Phaeton shut the cab door behind them. "Nonsense, Dex. These immortals rarely appear in public. And in such splendid form."

A cordon of Metropolitan police blocked off Egyptian Avenue. Phaeton took the lead and ran them through the gauntlet of officers. Rounding a circular row of crypts, they found Dr. Exeter supervising the unloading of a large stone sarcophagus. Much of the mausoleum had been reduced to a pile of rubble.

"What the devil?" Phaeton grinned and shuddered simultaneously.

Exeter signed for the delivery. "Between feats of admirable

fornication, they also have episodes of ferocious disagreement. Arguments of the most disturbing, homicidal nature."

Phaeton surveyed the damage. Not much was left standing but the inner chamber. "Lightning bolts and such?"

Exeter nodded. "If they were human, they'd both be toes up by now."

Moore picked his way among the steaming rock. "I say, something nasty caused this jumble."

"Yes, nasty would describe it." Phaeton turned back to Exeter. "Is it safe for us to have a look?"

Exeter led the way. "As best as we can make out, three thousand years ago. Anubis was off having a dalliance when our young goddess was accosted by an angry mob of priests. He arrived home too late. Found her entombed—watch that rubble." Exeter jogged around a pile of smoking debris. "Racked with grief and guilt, one supposes, he submitted himself to the same ceremony and was returned to the earth. Made the religious zealots promise to bury him beside her. Apparently left a curse on every last man before they turned him to dust."

Phaeton mused over Exeter's story. "No doubt the priests didn't account for the restorative powers of the Thames."

Exeter chuckled. "Not likely. Both gods are resting rather peacefully at the moment. In fact, I'm glad you're here. Now that the sarcophagus has arrived, I might need your assistance in reminding Anubis of his obligation."

Exeter's face seemed drawn, lines deeper around the eyes and mouth. "Have you had any rest?"

"Not much. Nipped a few hours in a paddy wagon last night."

"I'll take it from here if you wish."

Exeter shook his head. "I've actually managed to become a kind of liaison of sorts, with the help of our translator."

"Stickles is still here?"

"Wouldn't miss this for the world, Mr. Black." The doddering old curator dipped his head to exit what still remained standing of the marble crypt.

"Right." Phaeton looked around and noted a curious but somewhat anxious look on Moore's face. "I've quite forgotten introductions. Inspector Moore, I'm pleased to introduce Mr. Stickles, British Library Curator, and Doctor Exeter, a civilian conscripted for duty to the Crown."

Exeter nodded to Moore and waved him forward. "Shall we have a look in at the gods?"

Pale green lights swirled through the murky mist of the inner chamber. On the stone slab in the center of the room, two indistinct shapes lay entwined as one. Exactly the spot where he had last seen Anubis wielding his flail upon a robust derriere. Inspiration, no doubt, for his own abduction and manhandling of Miss Jones.

"Watch your step," Stickles warned in a hush voice. A fog-like bank of storm clouds hugged the floor. "Our every movement disturbs the atmosphere." The heavy mist crackled with light and rumbled with thunder as they ventured inside the crypt.

Qadesh turned toward their whispered voices. Liquid ebony eyes blinked at the group of men. Her rather stunning breasts were exposed. Round and perfect, nipples raw from the jackal's love bites. Moore's jaw dropped sufficiently to please the vain little goddess and her gaze moved on.

"Fay-ton." She smiled. The sated sort of grin of a well-pleasured woman. "You have returned to me."

A deep grunt shook the room. Another flash of lightning and rumble of thunder swept through the clouds around their knees. Christ, a man could get electrocuted.

"Qadesh speaks far better English than her husband."

Anubis yawned, baring long, razor-sharp teeth. The ebony-headed god trained a suspicious eye on Phaeton. After a long, uncomfortable evaluation, the jackal turned to his mistress. A long pink tongue slipped out from between fangs and licked her ear. The gesture was clear. Mine.

Phaeton exhaled. "All right then. Had a good long re-union, I understand. Time to"—he backed away as Anubis stood up (Good God, he was half again the size of a normal man, and that phallus was ready for another go)—"pack it in. Jump in the roomy new sarcophagus for the trip home."

Qadesh propped herself up on an elbow. "Fay-ton, you promise to return us to Kemet?"

Stickles dipped closer. "The ancients referred to Egypt as the black land—Kemet. Scholars believe the name references the fertile dark soil deposited along the Nile."

"No time like the present for a history lesson." With a sudden clarity, Phaeton realized, much to his surprise, the two gods appeared ready to go. He bowed deeply to Qadesh. "You have my word, Your Grace."

Lighter than air, Qadesh slid off the top of the crypt and approached him. "You have returned my husband to me." The stunning, nude goddess pressed against him and spoke softly.

Phaeton took in ruby lips and kohl-black eyes. Yes. A man felt increasingly virile around such a fertile goddess. "I would not have hurt your woman."

He raised a brow. "Truly?"

Her eyes shifted away and back. The crafty minx evaded the question and smiled brightly. "I leave you a gift, Fay-ton. Entrust its power only to those who would never abuse it."

Odd request, coming from a goddess who had wrecked vicious havoc all over the row streets of London. Qadesh stepped back, and joined her husband. "We are ready."

"Right." Phaeton turned to Exeter. "Might we clear the commons of all unnecessary personnel?"

"I don't believe we need to worry about such details."

A glow of light surrounded the two gods and in a sudden burst of fire and light, they disappeared entirely.

"Shall we check the sarcophagus?" Exeter headed for the exit.

They marched out into the lane of crypts and peered into

the coffin. "There they are." Huddled together on a pocket of sand in the corner of the reliquary were two small, doll-like figures. He sighed. So the gods trembled as well.

Phaeton heard an orchestra in his head. Strains of *Aida* thrummed in his brain, loud enough that he was quite sure that everyone on Egyptian Avenue could hear the mournful notes of the aria.

Phaeton shared the far-off look in Exeter's eyes. Yes. He was quite sure the doctor heard the same refrains. The end of act four, Radames is sealed in a vault with Aida. *La fatal pietra sovra me si chiuse.* Phaeton whispered the familiar words, " 'The fatal stone now closes over me. *Morir! Si pura e bella.* ' "

The doctor moved to one end of the sarcophagus and positioned himself to slide the coffin lid in place. "Gentlemen?" Ceremoniously, they lifted the heavy cover and closed off the stone reliquary. He glanced around at the men surrounding the sarcophagus. Dear God, Stickles looked as though he might shed a tear. Phaeton brushed off his hands.

The aria spoke of death, he mused, but these gods were quite content to rest through the centuries. Perhaps they waited for a time to come, a world they could reign—with a people to worship them. "Mr. Stickles." Phaeton modified the aria's lyrics. "Shall we pray the gods '*rest*, so pure and simple?' " He smiled at the wizened old curator.

"Phaeton. You might have a look at this." Moore struggled over boulders of displaced stone and waved them over. Likely too stunned to move, the inspector hadn't left the crypt until now. Something must have prompted him to exit in a hurry.

Exeter and Stickles walked Phaeton back into the remains of the mausoleum. Until this moment he had not thought much about the poor chap that lay buried inside the stately family repository struck down by the gods.

A single shaft of light illuminated an object so unusual, it stopped all three men dead in their tracks. Something the size of a melon sat atop of the stone coffin in the middle of the room.

An orb as black as ebony, polished to a deep sheen. The surface appeared both opaque and transparent at once. There was some sort of glow from within—and heat. Phaeton leaned in for closer look, and felt the warmth on his cheek. Something shivered inside. A sparkling, fizzy sort of energy. The kind of essence Ping referred to as relic dust and champagne.

"Good God, it's an egg."

Chapter Thirty-three

"WHAT IS IT, PHAETON?" America stared at the dark orb with the strange inner glow on the pantry table.

He glowered at the mysterious ebony object and sighed. "Some sort of devil's spawn, Miss Jones."

She crept forward. "Is it dangerous?"

"I don't believe so." He lifted a good tumbler full of whiskey. "Not at the moment anyway." After a deep swallow he moved a lazy gaze over her. "One of your new gowns, is it? What color is that exactly?"

"Bleuet." She smiled. "Cornflower blue." But then, he didn't really care to know.

Another gulp of whiskey. "I understand you have accepted the British Museum's offer."

"Yes." She nodded, gauging his reaction, a flash of concern beneath hooded eyes. "I surmise Scotland Yard—"

"Wants the case closed and swept away. In this case as far as Cairo."

She nodded. "Alexandria, actually." Awkward small talk made her nervous.

He popped the cork on the bottle. "Care to join?"

She could use a drink right about now. "Yes, I believe I will." America sat down across the table.

"I've never seen you drink anything stronger than bitters, Miss Jones. Need a good jolt of whiskey to gather your courage?" Phaeton stepped into the pantry and opened a cabinet. He shooed the familiar grey gargoyle over and rummaged for a glass.

Edvar whimpered.

"Does . . . he need feeding or something?"

"He is not a pet; he's a demon. It is my greatest wish he might one day turn to stone and be mounted on an unoccupied parapet of Nôtre Dame."

"Don't listen to him, Edvar, he's quite fond of you. He just pretends not to care." She drilled into the back of his head with her stare. "Like anyone or anything that gets uncomfortably close. Isn't that right, Phaeton?"

He swung around. "Actually, he's rather distraught you are leaving us, Miss Jones."

She would miss the irascible, meddling little monster. Perhaps, both.

He set down a clean tumbler and poured her a drink. "Shall we have a toast?"

"We sail on the afternoon tide, tomorrow."

"Ah." Phaeton settled into his chair before meeting her gaze. "Then we need a seaworthy farewell." He lifted a brow and his glass. "To—?"

"To the wind that blows, the ship that goes, and the lass that loves a sailor." America clinked her glass against his. "Come with me, Phaeton."

"I'm no sailor." His eyes never left hers as he took a swallow. He slapped his empty glass on the table. "Stay."

She sighed. "I have been offered a lucrative cargo. And I suspect you were behind the offer. Convenient way to send me off."

"I only heard of it yesterday." Phaeton gasped out a laugh. "Besides, I thought you wished to captain the *Topaz*. Get the business flourishing once again."

She turned the near empty glass of whiskey in her hand. "No man will ever love me the way you do." She could not quite believe she had blurted out the words. Her cheeks flushed with heat.

Phaeton blinked. Gingerly, he picked up the bottle and poured them each another glass.

"Of course, you mean the moaning kind of love." Leaning back in his chair, he scratched his head. "You are a wanton strumpet, a women of great courage and loyalty. What more could any man ever ask for?" He tilted his chair back and threw up his hands. "Why do women not understand they hold all the power? You will find any man a quick study for a taste of heaven, my dove. That lovely sheath of yours is a temple, teach him how to worship."

She rolled her eyes and bit her lip. "What will become of us?"

"You will return to your shipping business and I will, doubtless, muddle on. Solve the occasional odd crime of an occult nature."

She shifted her gaze away. "So, you really don't love me."

"You and I don't believe in love."

"I don't understand." All her lip chewing did nothing to assuage her confusion. "There were so many proofs of love."

"Proofs? What proofs?" Brows raised, he appeared genuinely surprised.

"I hardly know where to begin." Nervously, she pressed lips together to moisten them. "From the very beginning, actually. That first night in the row, when you saved me from Yanky Willem's men."

"As I recall, the pleasure was all mine." She expected a grin to punctuate the remark. Yes, there it was, right on cue, but this time, something darker veiled his eyes.

"You found the night shelter and offered me work."

"A lapse in judgment."

"All right, let's call them small proofs, then." She twisted up a wry pout. "And what about that shopping trip and all those lovely clothes you purchased?"

"You owe me six hundred and seventy-five pounds."

"I owe you a great deal more than that, Phaeton."

He shrugged. "After a few profitable voyages you can look me up and repay the loan."

A scowl formed at the edges of her mouth. "You were nearly killed chasing after pirates on my behalf. Twice."

He ignored his empty glass and swigged directly from the bottle.

"Whether you care or not, you are a hero, Phaeton."

"I'm uncomfortable with the term, Miss Jones. It comes with expectations."

She picked up her glass and tossed the hot burning liquid down her throat. "There are more proofs—" She gasped, nearly choking on whiskey fumes.

"I had no idea you were counting."

"You rescued me from Qadesh."

He tilted his chair back. "I'd call us even on that score. You even donated blood to my cause. I'm afraid we cancel each other out."

America smiled. "And what about Mrs. Horsley?"

"The pompous boardinghouse matron?" His incredulous look was almost comical.

"You didn't have to torture her, Phaeton."

"She was a cunt."

She stabbed him with a look. "Nasty word."

"Nasty woman."

She sighed. "Yes, she was." A smile might have tipped the edges of her mouth. "You distracted the pirates so both Inspector Moore and I could get away."

"A fluke of luck."

"You walked the plank for it."

"Got keel hauled, as well." Phaeton leaned forward, returning all four legs of his chair to the floor. "We've been over this—"

"You taught me how to experience pleasure."

He took his time answering, his smile uneven. "Lust, Miss Jones. No proof of love." He corked the bottle and returned the whiskey to the pantry cabinet.

Her heart sank. She was so sure he cared. And her father was almost never wrong about these things regarding men's odd behaviors. Something had to have happened to change him into such a cool character. "Phaeton." She looked up. "All those monsters you confronted as a child."

"What about them, my dear?"

"It must have been quite horrifying, at such an impressionable age, to discover your night terrors were real . . ." She drifted off, hardly able to complete the thought.

"Quite beyond the pale, Miss Jones, to wake up with a succubus on my chest, attempting to suck the life from my body." He stood behind her chair and nuzzled her neck. "Checking under the bed for ogres and finding one."

A tingle of arousal and horror shivered down her spine. She closed her eyes and pictured a frightened young boy and a fragile, clairvoyant mother whose soul departed this world, leaving her small, defenseless son behind to fend for himself.

He spoke softly in her ear. "I think you should leave before I carry you to my bed and beg you to abuse me."

In the deepest reaches of her soul, she knew she was close to unlocking his heart. Why else was he asking her to leave? She lowered her eyes and shifted gently into a trance, reaching out to connect with his secrets. "You lost your *maman*, your only defender, but there was another female—" A flash of terror, as the devil's red eyes pierced the veil. A horned creature with the cloven hooves and the legs of a beast, strode toward a terrified girl. "There was a young woman—when you were in still in school."

He stepped away from her.

America stood up and whirled around. "I saw a young lady. She trembled with fear. What happened to her?"

She held her breath as he paced the floor. Rolling his head from shoulder to shoulder, he vigorously rubbed the back of his neck. He pivoted midstride and returned her gaze with a glower. "You don't really want to hear this."

"Yes, Phaeton. I do." She set her chin.

"Georgette Pfeiffer. Thought I was in love with a professor's daughter at Cambridge. One night on our way home from a social, we stopped off at a pub. I was attacked by something large and hulking, and we were both dragged into a back alley. Exeter rescued us from Beelzebub or whatever the hell it was."

She knitted her brows. "Doctor Exeter?"

Phaeton shrugged. "Destined to keep crossing paths with the man. I suppose he was there adding letters to his numerous degrees; I don't know."

"Does this happen often, Phaeton? Monsters popping out of bushes, bent on mayhem?"

"Often enough." The cocky grin was replaced by something more wistful. "Sometimes they carry knives and demand I mount them against a wall."

She ignored his reference to her behavior in the alley. "And Miss Pfeiffer?"

"Unhappily married to a linguistics instructor." His mouth settled into a grim line. "The night of the attack, Exeter managed to pull me away. She took the brunt of it. Torn clothes. Terrible claw marks on her flesh. Left her soaked in blood."

America's knees wavered.

"Occasionally I get a wire. 'Come quickly, Phaeton.' Georgette has become a presage. She has quite dazzling dreams and terrifying possessions. l am the only one who can talk her off the ceiling." He shrugged. "Could be worse, she could have ended up in Bedlam. Living in chains, taking the ice bath cure."

He rubbed his face, scratching day-old stubble. "Have you ever been submerged into ice water? Feels like a million tiny needles stabbing at your flesh." The set of his mouth was pained, rueful. "Calms the terrors."

She tried to focus on the enchanted young woman rather than the fear that trickled into her heart. Horrified and close to tears, she needed to either cry or scream. Perhaps both. "I take it you fight shy of women now. Other than the occasional doxy, to trim the sails."

"I stay away from attachments of any sort, male or female. Surely you can see what happens to people around me? I place all of you in jeopardy of your lives." He seemed to tower over her. "Do not push me any further on the subject."

Like an errant, uncoiled bedspring, her patience unraveled along with her temper. "You will die a wizened, lonely old man, Phaeton Black, without a single grandchild to bounce on your knee."

He took her by the shoulders and shook her until her teeth rattled. "Exactly right, Miss Jones. Why would I want to put my children through the same kinds of terrors I experienced? Imagine your worst nightmare come alive in the nursery."

Stunned, she blinked at him. "But this time, they might have two parents to watch over them."

"What are you saying?"

"Nothing."

His eyes narrowed, darkened. "You're sure?"

She sighed. "I just meant to imply—if, you and I, were to have children—"

"You just assured me we are not."

Her lower lip quivered. "We are not."

She had finally needled him straight over the edge. With his secrets shattered and his guard down, his temper was now free to rage. She braced herself for further assault, but he backed off, flexing fingers that had dug through jacket and dress to bruise the flesh of her shoulders. "For the last time, I beg you to leave, Miss Jones."

The silence, the stillness, finally became unbearable. "Good-bye, Phaeton."

She managed a shaky climb up the stairs and a dazed walk out of the house. Even with her vision somewhat impaired, she found Charing Cross Road and waited for a ride.

"Cab's empty, miss."

She hardly noticed the hansom stopped at the corner. "So it is."

The driver jumped down and opened the door. "Miss?" The man's face was a blur. "Is there something the matter, miss? You look like you've lost yer best friend in the world."

America sniffed and climbed in. "Hardly a friend."

Phaeton Black was so much more than that. But a person cannot be brought to love by force or other device. Even a strong heart like Phaeton's, darkened by years of terror, was likely damaged beyond repair. As the carriage lurched off, the jolt shook the first tear from her eyes.

Chapter Thirty-four

PHAETON SET THE EGGLIKE ODDITY INSIDE A RAGGED OLD PORTMANTEAU, and stuffed a number of soft rags around the orb. Gaseous trails of life, either seen or imagined, one could never be sure, swirled deep inside the object's mystifying depths.

A zephyr of whispers and snarls wafted across the pantry. "You're in a nasty mood." He snapped the worn leather bag shut.

A pair of disembodied golden eyes blinked. Edvar materialized on the edge of the counter. A swish of slithering tail curled a tight coil around the bony, sullen frame.

"Miss Jones is far better off without us." The gargoyle cocked his head and hissed at the moan and creak of stair treads

"You here, Phaeton?" Exeter paused for a glimpse at the flat below.

"Caught me on my way out." He glanced upward. "About to pay a visit to a certain back alley in Limehouse."

The doctor finished his descent. "Off for an afternoon with Julian Ping or the dream pipe? Perhaps, both?" Exeter eyed the bulging portmanteau. "I suggest your destination is Pennyfields Lane, and you're to about to meet with The Gentlemen Shades."

"Bloody schoolyard name for a band of Gothic mesmerists who fancy themselves warlocks." Phaeton didn't hold back an impatient sigh. He opened a cabinet and brought down a near empty bottle. "Enough for a dram each." He handed over a glass. "Who is your sponsor?"

"Gaspar." Exeter sniffed the whiskey. "Oak and orange peel with a nice bit of smoke."

"Talisker's finest." Phaeton studied Exeter. It was the first time either of them had formally acknowledged the occultist organization comprised of peculiar hominoids and the odd, remnant peer of the realm. "Gaspar Sinclair. The dissipated and delusional Viscount Stuart of Findhorn. Pipe never leaves the hand of that lotus-eater."

The doctor edged up a one-sided shrug. "I take it your sponsor is Ping."

"Rather drunk one night, skulking about Pennyfield's looking for a smoke, knocked on the wrong door." His mind drifted back to the alley lined with opium dens. "Ping or Jin answered. One can never be entirely sure."

True to form, the doctor raised a supercilious brow. "And how is that?"

He tossed back his whiskey and set the glass on the counter. "You will find out soon enough, when you are alone with him." He grinned. "Or her."

Exeter's gaze left the travel bag. "And you trust him—or her—with the orb?"

"What would you have me do, twiddle thumbs and wait 'round for this thing to hatch? Or worse—give it to Chilcott." Phaeton snorted.

The doctor seemed strident this afternoon, troubled. The imposing, stoic man strolled the perimeter of the table and sipped his whiskey. "I didn't expect to find you at home. Thought you'd be down at the docks, waving bon voyage. Perhaps even sailing off to Cairo with Miss Jones."

"Alexandria." Phaeton leaned back against the pantry counter, arms crossed over chest. "And why on earth would you think that?"

"Because, you two are—like spirits, are you not? Among all the beings of the earth and stars, you have crossed paths with the special one, Mr. Black." Exeter appeared genuinely concerned. "Do you not feel love?"

"I do not wish to fall in love."

"Ah, Phaeton. It's too late." Exeter had the nerve to grin. "You already have."

He shook his head, eyes darting about under the man's stare. "I'll get over it. It is infatuation."

Exeter frowned. "You could learn something from Anubis."

"Ha!" Phaeton snorted. "Who couldn't?"

The doctor was not amused. "Anubis, in his prime, was overseer of the weighing of souls. Is your heart lighter than a feather, Phaeton?"

He grimaced. "I'm damned to hell in this life, why not the next?" The last thing he wanted was to appear cornered—wild-eyed.

No answer, the doctor just stared.

He drained the last drops of whiskey and dropped the empty bottle in the dustbin. "This missing her will only hurt for a while. Pain can be tolerated."

"What if it doesn't hurt for a while. What if it hurts for a lifetime?"

Phaeton swung around. "Well, that's just it. You see what follows me about. What lurks in my pantry closets. She could be injured or killed."

"The rationale of a frightened little boy. Not a man."

Phaeton's eyes darkened, narrowed, even as his jaw clenched.

Exeter backed away. "Shall I remove my jacket?"

His gaze landed on his frock coat hanging on a wall hook. "No sense bruising knuckles. I've got a standard issue Webley Mk1 in my jacket pocket."

If this tête-à-tête was a chess game, Phaeton had just called check. "Miss Jones knows everything. All about Georgette. My obligation—"

"That demon was after Miss Pfeiffer." Exeter shook his

head. "The fact that you were with her, Phaeton, most likely saved her life. Both your energies, under tremendous psychic assault, attracted me to the scene."

How his jaw got from clamped together to hanging open was behind him. Phaeton clapped his mouth shut. "Left quite a bloody mess for an apparition."

"Our world, the universe, and everything in it—we all play a part in this very persistent illusion." Exeter stepped closer. "Georgette always had abilities. No doubt the attack triggered something more powerful. She is gradually learning to control the episodes of transference." He leaned against the pantry counter beside him. "You owe Miss Pfeiffer nothing more than your continued friendship, Phaeton."

He studied the man beside him. "You've been working with her?"

"Only on occasion, like yourself."

The doctor leaned a bit closer. "There is really nothing stopping you from accompanying Miss Jones on an ocean voyage. You're free to go, Phaeton."

He thought his brain might explode, either from relief or his disconcerting, rapidly rising disquiet. America was gone. "I cannot . . ." He hesitated, searching his words, thoughts. Since early this morning, he had existed in a state of utter turmoil, body and brain tied up in knots. She had walked up those stairs and out of his life, in all probability, forever.

"Yes, Phaeton?"

They both stared at each other for what seemed like an eon of time. "Christ, Jason, I miss her beyond words." Phaeton glanced away. "It's too late anyway, the *Topaz Star* sailed on the tide."

"I'm sure she did."

"Impossible to catch up at this point. Likely there's also a good breeze along the Thames to tack along with."

"Very likely, yes." Exeter sympathized. "Unless . . ."

Phaeton choked a bit on the knot in his throat. "Unless?"

"Unless one had at his disposal another ship." A flash of light sparked in those piercing green eyes. "Something fast and a good deal lighter than air."

Phaeton blinked. "The airship?"

Deep creases formed to each side of Exeter's grin. "I happen to be out for an afternoon of aeronautics. Last year, Esmeralda had a large archery target painted on the roof. Makes for convenient access—"

Phaeton stood upright. "That explains how you are able to slip in and out of here."

Exeter pressed further. "We could chase her down. Waylay her."

Something swelled inside his chest. "Doubt whether she's much past Greenwich."

"Worth a try, wouldn't you say?"

A million thoughts bombarded at once, but the picture of America, standing at the helm of her ship, wind in her hair, eyes trained on the sea, easily muted a battery of warning, internal voices. With her image locked fast in his heart, the last "no-you-don't" and "you-bloody-fool" faded away.

He met Exeter's maddening grin with one of his own. "Always wanted to see the pyramids."

"Pack a bag and meet me on the roof." Exeter climbed the stairs. "Quickly, Phaeton."

Jerked into action, he piled shirts and drawers, trousers and coats into a large traveling case. He slammed the lid shut.

On second thought, he reopened the bag. An irritating bit of snuffling and whining emanated from the bedpost. He gestured impatiently to his slithery companion perched upon a finial. "All right then, jump in."

An indentation formed among his clothes, a nest between hose and shirt collars.

"Phaeton, are you leaving us?" Lizzie stood at the entry to his room. "I overheard the doctor and Mrs. Parker in the salon."

Phaeton closed and latched the case. "You're looking well, Lizzie."

"Oh yes, sir. Much improved. No sign of fangs." She bared her teeth, but the smile soon faded. "Will we ever see you again?"

He slouched into his coat. "Not as a paying customer." He doffed his hat, gripped the suitcase in one hand and the smaller carpetbag in the other.

He slipped past, but not before he kissed her cheek and gave a wink. "Pass that along to the girls for me, Lizzie."

Phaeton made his way up two flights of stairs and found the narrow door to the attic. A cool, invigorating breeze greeted him as he clamored onto the roof.

"Detective Black. Lovely afternoon for a trip down the Thames." Mr. Tandi took care of both his suitcases.

Exeter's man Friday untied the moorings as Phaeton stepped onto the ladder and climbed aboard ship. Exeter stood behind the mysterious globe at the helm of the craft and checked his pocket watch. "No time to lose."

"And where is your lovely ward today?"

"Off to Oxford. Their latest curriculum for women. Still no degrees offered, as yet."

Phaeton's stomach lurched as the dirigible lifted into the air with surprising speed. Gliding over the dome of St. Paul's, Phaeton turned back for one last glimpse of his fair city. Slanted, golden rays backlit thousands of rooftop chimneys all chugging black soot up into the atmosphere.

Phaeton blinked. The sight brought tears to one's eyes, quite literally. Rather than linger too long on a city he had come to have great affection for, he changed the subject. "So, your young lady is grown up and off to college."

"Yes, I will greatly miss her company."

He could not hold back a grin. "I have no doubt it. Only—"

"Only what?" The doctor's eyes turned to knives, or something equally deadly.

"It's just that the casual observer might . . . observe, that Miss Chadwick is stunningly attractive, and a bright vivacious young lady. A man would have to be blind not to notice the attraction between you."

"Mia is not yet eighteen years of age. She is my ward. A responsibility I undertake with a great deal of seriousness." Exeter took his eyes off the globe and stared. "What are you implying, Phaeton?"

"Look, I believe that's Greenwich, is it not?" Phaeton clasped his hands behind his back, took a step toward the prow of the gondola, but swiveled back. "Simply put, she adores you."

A glimmer of something—hope, possibly, mixed with a cloud of confusion in Exeter's eyes. The doctor tried to protest, then clapped his mouth shut.

"Jason, it's not as though you're related by blood. There is a world of possibilities open to you both." Phaeton winked.

At the bow, he was confronted with a hodgepodge fleet of sailing ships and steamers all making their way toward the channel. He had no doubt he would find her among the tall ships in the broadening section of river.

Too large. Too—foreign. He remembered a jaunty red and white striped jib sail.

"Ho! The *Topaz!*" Phaeton leaned over the bow and squinted. Yes, he was sure of it. "Can we take her down lower?" He looked for Exeter.

No one was at the helm. "Mr. Tandi will steer the airship, while I attempt to guide you down." Exeter stood right behind him.

Phaeton's gaze shifted nervously from Tandi to Exeter. "What exactly do you have in mind?"

The doctor grinned. "Take her down low, Mr. Tandi." The airship made a gentle turn as graceful as a diving bird. "Up on the rails, Phaeton. We're going to be coming in very low and very fast. Prepare to jump when I say so."

Balanced on the edge of the bow, Phaeton glanced back at Exeter a bit wild-eyed. "Jump—?"

"You trust me, don't you?"

Far below he heard shouts from the crew onboard ship. Phaeton turned to see a number of hands scurrying to get a look at the dirigible plunging toward them. Was that America? Hand above her eyes, trying to make out who or what sailed the skies above them. Yes, it was her.

Something foreign, but rather warm and glowing seized his chest. He turned back to the doctor. "This is good-bye then."

"There is never good-bye for you and me. À la prochaine fois, till we meet again." The doctor's broad smile crinkled his eyes.

"How is it, all these years—" Phaeton stopped to catch his breath, savor the moment. "You've chased off devils and dragons, and now these last two bloody demigods . . ."

"Perhaps I just know where I am needed."

He nodded toward the ragged old carpetbag. "Deliver the orb to Pennyfields for me."

"Time to go, Phaeton."

An electrical charge shot through his body as a strange, yet familiar force carried him up into the air and flung him over the side of the gondola. He dangled for a moment, suspended in midair, before plunging downward.

Soaring through the airspace above the *Topaz*, he heard a scream. Quite sure it was America, he tucked in his arms and landed with a hard thwack on the billowing, unfurled sail of the mizzen mast. Sliding downward, he felt the raw burn of the canvas to his backside. The very ordinary force of gravity pulled him to earth. He cracked his skull on a yardarm and tumbled onto the deck. Rolling across slick mahogany planks, he came to a rather rude stop against the ship's rails.

He shook his head to alleviate the ringing in his ears.

A shapely shadow formed overhead. "What a ridiculous stunt."

The low-angle of the sun's rays caused him to blink. "Ah yes, I'd recognize those fists on hips anywhere. Hello, my love."

"Phaeton, you could have killed yourself with such dangerous acrobatics."

Another thwack from up above. "Watch yourself."

His traveling case hit the sail and landed with a wincing thunk on the deck beside them. The bag rattled.

"You brought Edvar?"

He smiled. "He missed you so. Begged me to chase after you. I didn't have the heart to throw him off the airship alone. Thought I'd come along." He experienced a most exhilarating sensation, a sudden lightness of being. "He'll make a jolly good figurehead."

"I shall put him to work—he'll be assigned crow's nest duty." How he loved that openmouthed, sly hint of a smile. She reached out a hand.

He struggled to his feet and felt for broken bones.

"What are you trying to prove, Phaeton?" Dazzling and spirited, she stood before him, a strong breeze whipped strands of curls across her face.

"You are so beautiful when you are cross. Come here." He pulled her against his body and turned her around within his arms. "Look." He pointed upward. High above the airship banked a graceful turn, heading back toward them. The tall, dark, silhouetted figure waved. Phaeton lifted an arm.

He nuzzled her hair and inhaled the salty scent of sea air and America Jones. She leaned back against him. He kissed her temple and that little place behind her ear.

She shivered.

Sunset cast a golden light across her cheek. Vaguely aware of a reverberation in his chest, the oddest sensation rumbled up and escaped his mouth.

"Phaeton, you're laughing."

"Yes. I suppose I am."

"You never laugh."

The doctor's voice drifted down from above. "Everything all right?" The airship hovered directly overhead, not ten feet above the mast.

"Good God, man. You could have waited to toss me into the wind."

"Sorry, Phaeton, slight error in judgment. Didn't expect you to fly over the side on the first try. I'd forgotten"—Exeter leaned over the rails as the airship lifted into the air—"those who claim they don't believe in love fall the hardest."

Phaeton Black and America Jones's adventures
continue in

THE MOONSTONE AND MISS JONES

A Brava trade paperback on sale in October 2012.

Turn the page for a special excerpt!

"What can one say about you, Mister Black? You are part devil and angel." The bold beauty stepped closer. Hair, a honeyed shade of brown, lovely aquiline nose, and those eyes sparkled like gemstones—green, he thought. No blue.

No green. The color of the seas off Crete.

Phaeton took another leisurely perusal of the young lady's wares. For the sparest of moments, he thought about warning off the intriguing girl. That was before his gaze lowered to her bosom. "I'd have to say largely devil."

Her pale hand swept over the buttons of his trousers. Brazen chit! Delicate fingers found what they searched for. "Largely, indeed." Her touch was light and fleeting, but the very notion she dared such public foreplay cheered him greatly. Apparently, it also amused the naughty little vixen. Those astonishing aquamarine eyes traced the bulge in his pants. "Rumor has it you are made of wicked wood and when you play the seducer you are so very, very . . ."

A clearing of his throat ended in a grin. "Shocking?"

Her faraway glance about the room returned to him. "Sublime."

He quirked a brow, gaze steady. "Are we discussing length and breadth or technique?"

"Not sure." The wily minx tossed a wink over her shoulder and flounced away. "But I mean to find out." He watched the bob and sway of her bustle as she wove her retreat between chattering passengers.

They were nearing the dinner hour. The ship's salon swelled with first-class passengers swilling aperitifs. Phaeton drew in a breath, and exhaled slowly. Miss Georgiana Ryder turned out to be a most charming ingénue with a saucy, hoyden-like quality about her. Quite irresistible. And her siblings Velvet and Flurey, a delightful sisterly trio—each one as lovely as the next. He scanned the salon and found Velvet standing among a cluster of oglers. Her gleaming dark eyes and sultry pout beckoned without words. He met her gaze and lingered for a brief flirtation before he caught a blur of Flurey. The fey, dancing wisp of a girl instantly distracted. Phaeton watched the youngest sibling flutter about the room, much like a hummingbird hovers and flits from daisy to delphinium.

"Are you enjoying the voyage, Mister Black?"

"My return trip to London grows more diverting by the hour." Phaeton tore his eyes off the pretty chit and nodded a polite bow to the young lady's mother. "Mrs. Ryder." He formed something he hoped resembled a pleasant expression. "Most especially since I have been fortunate enough make acquaintance with you and your family."

If truth be told, he found the cloying mother barely tolerable and Mr. Ryder, the stout man slurping sherry in the corner, to be a degenerate troll who conducted himself as more of a procurer than a father anxious to see his daughters well-spoken for. In point of fact, the entire family was odd. For one thing, they were inexplicably interested in him.

He had dressed early for dinner and entered the main salon in hopes of finding a tumbler full of whiskey. The Ryder clan, which included the mister, missus and assorted lovelies, had singled him out from a number of wealthy, titled gentleman aboard the RMS *Empress of Asia*. He considered the obvious question, why? And decided it could wait for later.

Yes, the voyage home was going to be interesting. The

ocean journey that had once been tedious and despairing, quite suddenly brimmed with intrigue. Phaeton nodded perfunctorily to the mother's ramblings, as the woman found it an unnecessary bother to either pause or think between sentences.

He perused the room looking for his evening's distraction, Georgiana. The young lady's mother might indeed be a harpy in disguise and the father no better than a common pimp, but the eldest daughter? The bewitching dream of a young woman stood between two heavily whiskered gents whose eyes never left her astonishing assets.

Phaeton took another look for himself. There was nothing overly voluptuous or buxom about any part of her. It's just that all parts of her were so very . . . luscious. Aware of his attention she turned and made eye contact across the crowded salon. Gazes locked, the little vixen opened her mouth ever so slightly. A pink tongue swept the underside of a prettily peaked upper lip. The room, for a second, collapsed in size around them. The gesture caused a number of his vital organs to rush a surge of blood to his favorite extremity.

Phaeton tipped his glass for a last swallow.

A white-gloved servant entered the salon and rang a melodious set of chimes. The dinner bell. Another man, liveried in a brass-buttoned jacket, opened a double set of doors. Georgiana turned to leave, but not in the direction of the dining room.

Somewhat absently, Phaeton took in the fancy laces and bright colored silks of the fashionably attired as they drifted into supper. He set his empty on a silver tray and wound his way past a blur of beau monde, in the opposite direction of sustenance. This evening his appetites lay elsewhere.

Phaeton stepped through the hatch onto the promenade deck. The night was clear and warm with a bit of moisture in the air. A sparkling carpet of stars spread across the sky above head. He strolled toward the front of the ship and thought about a cigar, and then thought better of it.

He found her standing near the starboard bow. Phaeton could have pressed close, but instead, kept some distance between them. She turned and struck a pretty pose with her back to the rail.

They were alone. He did know how he knew this, for he made no inspection of the deck. And frankly he did not care. Her gown rippled with the breeze.

"Lift your skirt."

She tilted her head and rolled her eyes in the prettiest fashion. Not a refusal, mind, more of a flirtation. Her hand caressed a curve of hip and lifted her skirt enough to expose a dainty turn of ankle. His arousal was prodigious, and still, he held back and trifled with her.

He used two fingers to gesture upward. Inch by inch, her skirt and petticoats rose. A delightful show of calf. A pretty knee. A silk-flowered garter. And above the top of her hose, a hint of peach-colored flesh.

With only a small measure of control left, Phaeton closed the distance between them. He pressed her against the ship's rail. Not too hard. Certainly not as hard as his burgeoning need. "Georgiana?"

"Mr. Black?" Droplets of perspiration, like tiny diamonds, sparkled across her nose and cheeks.

"Please, call me Phaeton." He kissed the bridge of her nose and tasted salt—and a whiff of something spicy. The stubble of his beard brushed her cheekbone as he worked his way toward an earlobe and reached under her skirts. A shudder ran through her body and her head rolled back. "Kiss me, Phaeton."

He lowered his gaze her mouth. "And if I kiss you, what is my reward?" He enjoyed the playful squint in her eyes and saucy turn to her cheek almost more than her words.

"What do you desire?"

He dropped his hands below her bustle and cupped her buttocks. "Your pantalettes off." He rubbed gently, as softly as a balmy breeze off the East China Sea. She wrapped a limber leg around him. Good girl.

The corners of her mouth lifted. "And I shall see your saber snuggly sheathed."

He found the ribbon on her lacey undergarment and pulled. Silk fabric slipped over a rounded cheek, exposing a lovely derriere. Firm with just the right amount of jiggle. He moved in between her thighs and slipped the tips of his fingers along the sensitive inside flesh of her limbs. She spread her legs wider.

Phaeton smiled. He didn't even have to ask.

He caught a tell-tale flash of scarlet in her eyes and caught his breath. Just a ripple of color but even a hint of suspicion was bad enough. He lifted silk pantalettes and retied the bow. "Arousing to see you again, Georgiana, or I should say Mademoiselle Gorgós?" He stepped away.

Something slightly reptilian materialized before him. Her flesh took on a pale and curiously ethereal form, as deep crimson swirled behind midnight blue eyes. Her dress unraveled to lay bare high-set breasts and rounded hips. A gossamer of silk snaked over her nude form, entwining itself around voluptuous curves.

"Ah, so there you are." Somewhat wistfully, one side of his lip curled upward.

Fully formed, she was feline and serpentine all at once. Her skin glistened with pearl-sized, translucent scales that rippled with every rise and fall of breath. A new, darker gaze traveled the length of his frame, admiring, exploring. She grabbed hold of his lapels and pressed him back against the ship's rails. Every fiber of this female entity appeared to quake with anticipation. Sweeping aside her meandering skirt she pressed his hand to her mound of Venus, but his fingers retreated. In fact, his arm jerked backward. Awkward, even for Phaeton.

Regretfully, he stepped away. "Not that my soul is worth

saving, but I make it a point never to lie with otherworldly creatures." His tsk was more of a sigh. "You might have saved this for later—crawled into my berth for a suffocating climax?"

A fierce wave of energy knocked him down and he slid along the polished wood deck. Before he could lift his head she swarmed over him, thrusting herself against his manly parts. He groaned. "Such a naughty succubus." Between caresses, this night creature would attempt to mount, then strangle him. There was nothing left to do but feign a struggle.

At some point he would need to be released from her sexual alchemy. But not . . . immediately. He rather enjoyed this part of the macabre dance. There would soon come a delightful, helpless paralysis, and he would chance a moment or two of pleasure before those invisible bonds began their choke hold.

Georgiana was becoming decidedly less attractive. Bulbous eyes, wide and unblinking, swiveled up and down his torso. Within the saucerlike orbs, irises contracted into vertical slits.

The buttons on his trousers loosed. "Dangerous play, love."

Phaeton looked down as his cock sprung to life. It couldn't hurt to ask. "Might the pretty succubus swallow the dragon?"

Her answer came in the form of a pink tongue covered in shimmering scales and a long hiss. Soon, she would genuflect on his chest. Bearing down, the she-devil would squeeze with all her considerable might and crush the air out of his lungs, the life from his body.

The scaled tongue lengthened and tickled his earlobe. Plump, moist lips nibbled at his neck as elongated fingers wrapped around his shaft. Good God, he ached for release.

The vixen's luscious mouth uttered a deep, throaty sigh and moved lower. "Cocks up, Mr. Black."

"Mm-m, the pleasure is mine—" Phaeton reached into thin air.

"Got nothing to do with your pleasure, sir. They're comin'

fer ye. Shake a leg now and be quick about it. We made Port o' London last night."

His eyelids flew open. The blurry visage of an old sea dog squinted down at him. Phaeton jerked awake at the sight of the grey-bearded geezer. "Crew sez they lost their share at cards last evening."

Phaeton rubbed his eyes.

His *tête-à-tête* with a night terror had been a stimulating hallucination—while it lasted. He blinked again, and brought a wild bristle of chin hairs into focus. "Good God. That you, Mr. Grubb?" He barely recognized the croak in his own voice.

Rummy old Joe Grubb flattened weathered lips into a thin line. "Claim ye cheated 'em."

Despite the blistering hangover, Phaeton vaguely remembered a card game as well as a good deal of grog guzzling. "Preposterous." Lifting his pounding head, he reached down to scratch his crotch. A rat chewed on a trouser button.

Phaeton hurled himself out of his hammock. "Bloody hell." He caught a swinging section of knotted rope, and managed to remain upright. The rodent skittered away into the deeper shadows of the crew's quarters. Listing to one side, he called after the creature. "Georgiana?"

He ventured a squint about his surroundings. "Where am I?" This was no luxury ocean liner but a rat hole in the bowels of a seagoing vessel. A number of men slept in the hammocks strung about the hold. He was aboard a cargo ship. But not the *Topaz*. And what had happened to America Jones?

He recalled making port in Shanghai, a few screeching arguments and a long pointed weapon tossed at him. On further consideration—he shook his head—he was quite certain, the altercation between he and America had not been the cause of their separation. Again, Phaeton tried to shake the whiskey fog from his brain.

The gruff old seabird poked him in the rib. "Crew sez ye could see through their cards." One good eye circled about. "As if by magic."

A blast of rotten breath sent Phaeton backward. "Possibly, but—"

Something surly and imposing stepped through the hatch, tossing a cutlass back and forth between clenched hands. Good God. The brute-sized sailor did seem familiar. Phaeton struggled to recall last evening through a cloud of smoke and amber spirits.

"Now see here—" He straightened up and backed away from the angry seaman. "Let me assure you, I have no peculiar ability at cards, luck of the draw—" A broad swipe of sword took out several hammocks, which fell onto a cold damp floor. He grimaced. "Stroke of bad luck, wot?"

Phaeton quickly assessed his situation. More sailors, rudely awakened, pockets lightened by grog and card play. His heart rate and blood flow elevated to the correct level of alarm. He feigned to his left and tilted sideways, avoiding the next slash of blade. A number of rousted sea dogs fell in behind the hovering thug with the menacing sword. Air buffeted his face from yet another swoosh of the cutlass.

He wiggled his nose and retreated. No time to lose.

Using a bit of potent lift, learned from a man full of such tricks, Phaeton flung himself into the air, banked off the ceiling and landed atop a sleeping sailor. Arms out to his sides for balance, Phaeton grabbed hold of a line overhead and pushed off the grunting body beneath his boots. He aimed straight for the seamen in pursuit, swinging across the barracks, head down, balls out, he struck the lead man and the rest of the crew toppled over like nine pins. Phaeton released the rope and landed near the main hatch. He grabbed his hat from a nearby hook and the loose cutlass sliding across floorboards.

Joe Grubb broadened a toothless grin. "Cut and run, Mr. Black."

He flicked the brim of his bowler. "Pricks to the wind, Chief."

Phaeton bolted into the cargo hold, removing belaying pins as he ran. A flurry of cargo net enveloped, then whisked him out of the hold and into the air. Several good swings of the blade loosed the knotted web of rope and he dropped onto the wooden deck. He did not look back until he was well across the gangplank.

Christ. The bloody lot of them were following on behind.

He made a mad dash along the narrow pier stacked with cargo and crowded with dockworkers. He vaulted over bales of cotton and dodged cart loads of whiskey. Sprinting over the footbridge, he turned away from the chaos of the docks and hoofed it into a covered alleyway.

Phaeton ducked into a dank passage off the lane and waited for his pursuers to pass by. Once the seamen were well ahead, he darted back into the lane and made his way toward the cab stand on Westferry Road. Trotting along behind a drayage cart he was steps away from the bustling thoroughfare, when one of the sea hounds gave a shout from behind.

Phaeton pivoted towards the surly bloke who came at him hoisting a belaying pin. He drew a pistol from his coat knowing full well the chamber held no bullets. The sailor lunged just as a fast moving carriage passed between them. The brief respite afforded him the opportunity to abandon all sense of propriety. He wrenched open the door of the passing vehicle and tossed himself inside.

From the floor of the carriage, amidst a flutter of pretty lace ruffles and petticoats, Phaeton perused shapely legs covered in pale stockings. "My word, things are looking up."